Books by the author

YOUNG MR. KEEFE

BARBARA GREER

Barbara Greer

STEPHEN BIRMINGHAM

Barbara Greer

LITTLE, BROWN AND COMPANY

boston • toronto

Published simultaneously in Canada
by Little, Brown & Company (Canada) Limited

PRINTED IN THE UNITED STATES OF AMERICA

For Carol Brandt

Barbara Greer

I

THEY WERE SITTING SIDE BY SIDE IN CANVAS CHAIRS ON THE little terrace behind the house. Between them, a glass-topped table held an ash tray crowded with lipsticked cigarette butts, their empty iced-tea glasses resting on moist paper napkins, a crumpled match folder, two heart-shaped gold earrings that Nancy Rafferty had removed because they pinched her ears, Barbara Greer's folded sunglasses — the relics of a summer afternoon. Barbara turned in her chair and began aimlessly arranging the objects on the table in a sort of pattern. Nancy had come to the end of her story a few minutes before and now there seemed to be nothing to say. Barbara sat silently wishing that Nancy had never begun it, or, better still, that there had never been any story to tell. Then Flora came out of the kitchen door, untying her apron as she came. "It's ten of five, Mrs. Greer," Flora said. "I'd better go now if I'm going to catch my bus."

"All right, Flora," Barbara said.

"Is there anything else, Mrs. Greer?"

"No thanks."

"The boys are in the kitchen having their supper. Well, good night, Mrs. Greer. See you tomorrow. Nice to see you, Miss Rafferty."

Barbara looked quickly at Nancy. "I hope Miss Rafferty will spend the night," she said. "Will you, Nance? Not drive all the way back —"

"Well —" Nancy said hesitantly.

Flora looked doubtful. "I haven't fixed the guest bedroom, Mrs. Greer," she said.

"I can do it," Barbara said.

"Oh, it's too much trouble," Nancy said.

3

"No, no, it's no trouble at all."

"Well — if you're sure you don't mind —"

"Don't be silly!" Barbara said.

"Well, then I'll see you both tomorrow," Flora said. "Good night."

"Good night, Flora."

They were alone again and Barbara lighted a cigarette. She put her head back and looked at the sky, blowing out a slow stream of cigarette smoke.

"I suppose you're terribly shocked, aren't you, Barb?" Nancy asked after a moment.

"No, not shocked," Barbara said. "I'm just so sorry, Nancy."

"I had to tell you," Nancy said quietly. "I just had to tell somebody. Needless to say, there isn't another person in the world I've told."

"You poor dear!"

"Look," Nancy said. She leaned forward, opening her pale blue eyes wide, and pointed with one finger to a thin line just above her cheekbone. "Can you see that?"

"What is it?"

Nancy's eyes seemed to grow wider and bluer. "My scar," she said. "She told me, 'If you scream, I'll hit you.' I screamed and she hit me. I had a black eye. I wore dark glasses for two weeks."

Barbara looked away with a little shudder. "Oh, Nancy!" she said.

Nancy sat back again and uttered a short little laugh. "I have other scars in other places of course," she said. "But that's the only one that shows! I guess I'm lucky. It was horrible, but I suppose it could have been worse."

"You poor dear," Barbara said again. She sat there then, holding her cigarette, saying nothing. It had been a hot day and the afternoon lay oppressively upon her. She felt above her eyes the beginning of a headache, and she gazed across the terrace toward the house, at the climbing blue clematis that reached, now, almost

4

to the low eaves across the wide pebbled roof to where, at the apex, the gilded rooster stood rigidly on the artificial weather vane, pointing arbitrarily east. The air was full of sounds that were both distant and close. From the kitchen she could hear the boys, Dobie and Michael, talking as they ate their supper; Dobie seemed to be having a conversation with himself as Michael banged his spoon on the tray of the high chair. From the window box in front of the kitchen window flies were buzzing in the red blooms of the geraniums. From next door she could hear Muriel Hodgson's voice talking on the telephone, saying, "Okay . . . okay . . . Sure, sweetie." Farther off, from the highway at the foot of the hill, she could hear traffic sounds. All these sounds were deeply familiar. But, hearing them, she felt suddenly mournful, and the shadowy, slanting afternoon sunlight seemed to transform the house and the terrace, to change them from solid areas of home to oddly disconnected places of singular loneliness. The terrace seemed unfamiliar, foreign, and she and Nancy Rafferty, her old friend from college, seemed like two strangers cast aimlessly adrift upon it. The chairs they sat in seemed to be floating apart. Something, perhaps the heat, made her feel dizzy; she wondered if a salt pill would help. She still could think of nothing to say. She wished that, by some magic, it were still four o'clock before Nancy had begun the story. She wished that when — a few minutes ago — she had asked Nancy to spend the night, Nancy had said flatly no. She started to raise her cigarette to her lips and then, not wanting it, she tossed it. It landed neatly in a flower bed. She stood up, straightened the waistband of her shorts and tucked in the bottom of her striped cotton shirt.

Barbara Greer was a tall girl, slim and dark. Her long legs, below her abbreviated shorts, were darkly and evenly tanned from being held, stretched out straight in front of her, for at least half an hour each day in the summer sun. She pushed her hands into the pockets of her shorts and stood slightly forward, almost on tiptoe, in the pose of a girl on a beach who might be looking for a sail on the

5

horizon. Then she turned to Nancy. "I think I'll run down and pick up Carson at the office," she said.

Nancy looked up at her. "Do you always do that?"

"After a day like today he'll be tired," Barbara said. "If I hurry, I'll catch him before he gets into that sweaty car-pool. And besides —" She left the sentence unfinished.

"Are you sure you meant what you said, Barb? That you wanted me to spend the night?"

"Of course," Barbara said. "You're like one of the family, Nance. Carson would hate to miss you."

"I could honestly go —"

"Oh, stay. You don't want to drive all the way back to Philadelphia tonight. Stay, and after the kids go to bed we'll have a cocktail and maybe eat out here on the terrace. You can start back in the morning *refreshed*."

"Well, you know I'd love to."

"Then do it!" Barbara said cheerfully. "I'll run down and pick up Carson. Be back in fifteen minutes." She pointed toward the house. "If the kids ask for something — you know, just give it to them. Anything within reason, that is." She started across the terrace.

"Barbara?" Nancy called.

She stopped and turned to her.

"You won't — you know — you won't mention any of this to him, will you? You won't tell him, will you?"

"Of course not."

"I don't want him to — to know about it. I mean, I think Carson still has a few shreds of respect for me!" She laughed a little wildly.

"Respect! He's got all *sorts* of respect for you, Nance! Don't be silly. Now, when he gets home, let's be cheerful. Let's not be gloomy. After all, this will be the poor guy's last night home for six weeks."

"Oh, I'm afraid I'm intruding!" Nancy said.

"Let's just not be gloomy!" Barbara said.

6

She walked quickly across the terrace and down the short flight of brick steps to the driveway where the car was parked.

In the car, she glanced briefly at her reflection in the rear-view mirror, pushed her dark hair tighter behind the red scarf that she had tied, bandeau-fashion, around her head, and ran a tentative finger along the thin ridge of her nose where she had burned slightly and was peeling. She looked, she decided, presentable. She was always pleased with her appearance when she had a tan. She started the car and backed out of the driveway.

It was five and three-tenths miles from their house on Bayberry Lane to the main office of the Locustville Chemical Company, and Barbara Greer could make it in almost as many minutes. She liked to drive fast, and at the foot of the hill where the lane met Locust-ville Pike, several clear, uncluttered miles of road stretched out straight in front of her. There was traffic, but, at this hour, most of it was coming the other way, away from the town. The road dipped and rose as it crossed the low, rolling Pennsylvania hills, but it was straight; she could see, in the distance directly ahead of her, the skyline — such as it was — of Locustville: water-storage towers, the new television tower of WLOC-TV, and Locustville's single skyscraper, the ten-story Conestoga Hotel. On her right she passed the sign that said:

TOWN OF
LOCUSTVILLE, PA.
SETTLED 1730

WE LOVE OUR CHILDREN
DRIVE SLOW

And Barbara Greer, who loved her children but hated Locustville, drove faster in defiance of the sign — knowing that there was not a stop light nor a stop sign for miles, that the road was straight and unpatrolled, that all the traffic would continue to be coming the other way.

7

Locustville, as Locustville residents were quick to point out, was not a little town, but a city of somewhat more than sixty thousand souls. It was one of the few American cities of its size to deserve an article a column and a half long in the *Encyclopedia Britannica.* It had been the birthplace of one U. S. President and the residence of two others; it was the center of one of the most highly cultivated agricultural districts in the country, producing tobacco, corn, wheat and dairy products; the Locustville stockyards were one of the largest east of Chicago, and the Locustville airport was served by four major airlines, with direct flights daily to New York, Boston, Pittsburgh and St. Louis. It was an important industrial center, too; principal manufactures were candy, toys, television tubes, industrial paints and finishes, and gunpowder. It was also a city that offered a rich cultural life. Such institutions as the Locustville Symphony Orchestra, the Locustville Community Theatre, the Locustville Art League, the Locustville Lecture Series (which had recently heard Sir Edmund Hillary), and the Locustville Community Concert Series all received enthusiastic public support. In addition, plays and musical shows occasionally had pre-Broadway try-outs in Locustville because, as the Locustville *Evening Herald* pointed out, "Producers know that cosmopolitan Locustvillians are typical of big-city theater-goers. If it's a hit in Locustville it will be a hit on the Great White Way, and vice versa." In summer, especially, the city received a generous influx of tourists. It was a quaint city, and thanks to the efforts of the Locustville Historical Society, much of its quaintness was being efficiently preserved. Downtown Locustville contained a number of quaint cobblestone streets and quaint red brick sidewalks; old brick houses in this section were carefully maintained, their brass door knockers polished, their ironwork painted, their window boxes filled with bright flowers. Along these streets, the old shade trees that rose from the sidewalks were regularly clipped and fed and sprayed. The population of Locustville also contained a quaint element — a number of Amish and Mennonites — who wore quaint, un-

8

adorned clothes, drove horse wagons rather than motor cars, and spoke a quaint language all their own. Gift Shoppes specializing in Pennsylvania Dutch crafts did a thriving business. Driving toward the town, Barbara passed one, then another, of these quaint shops now.

Driving along the Locustville Pike at sixty miles an hour in the early summer evening, with the top down and the wind blowing her hair forward about her face, with all the traffic rushing toward her instead of with her, she found herself losing, or leaving behind, the sad, dizzy feeling that had swept over her sitting on the terrace; she began, in the sheer enjoyment of breaking Locustville's speed limit, to forget about the story Nancy Rafferty had told her, and to look forward to the evening ahead. She slowed the car at the last rise and signaled, though no one was behind her, that she was about to turn into the circular drive that led to the new brick and glass office building of the Locustville Chemical Company, manufacturers of industrial paints and finishes.

She stopped the car at the foot of the wide granite steps and waited with the motor running, her arms stretched forward on the steering wheel. People were beginning to file out of the building now. She looked for Carson. Then she saw him, sounded the horn and waved. "Carson!" she called. He saw her, smiled, and started down the steps toward her. His jacket was off, slung over his shoulder, held hooked in a finger of his right hand. His shirt collar was unbuttoned, tie loosened. He looked young and tired and cheerful, and as he walked out of the building's shadow the sun caught his dark hair, momentarily bleaching it, and she had a sudden vision of how he would look as an older man, how he would look at fifty. And she thought at once: How distinguished he'll look with gray hair! The thought made her smile and she was still smiling when he came to the side of the car, bent and kissed her. "What's so funny?" he asked her.

"When you were right *there*," she pointed, "the sun made your

9

hair look white! Now I know what you'll look like twenty years from now — just like Spencer Tracy!"

"It feels white already," he said. "Want me to drive?"

"I'll drive."

He tossed his jacket across the back seat, went around the front of the car and climbed in beside her. He slumped in the seat. "Christ, it's hot," he said.

"Terrible!" she said.

She started the car forward, and as another car turned in front of her, she gave it two short, scolding blasts with the horn.

"Hey," Carson said, "that's Clyde Adams."

"Beep-beep, Clyde Adams!"

"You're in a good mood tonight."

"I'm in a silly mood," she said. "How was your day? Busy?"

"Yes. Hot as hell, mostly."

"Poor darling!"

At the end of the drive she turned right, toward the center of town. "Where are you going?" Carson asked.

"I've got to buy some French bread," she said. "I've got a surprise. At least I hope you'll think it's a surprise. I mean I hope you'll be pleased."

"What sort of surprise?"

She smiled. "You'll see."

"French bread means somebody for dinner. Who is it?"

"You'll see."

He sat back, stretching his long legs forward. He clasped his hands behind his head, fingers interlaced, yawned widely and closed his eyes. "Let's see," he murmured, "who could it be? The mayor of Locustville? The chief of police? Spencer Tracy, maybe? No — I'll bet it's good Old Nancy Rafferty."

"How did you guess?" she asked.

"Who else drops in for surprise visits?"

"Are you angry?"

"Why should I be angry?"

"Are you pleased then?"

"Yes. No. I don't care."

"Sometimes I think you don't like Nancy," she said.

"Oh, I like her. But —"

"But what?"

"Well, she's always dropping in at times like this. Doesn't she know I'm going away tomorrow?"

"Yes."

"You see? My God, this is my last night home for six weeks. Why do I have to spend it with Nancy Rafferty?"

"You *are* angry."

"No, no," he said. "It's just that — well, she always picks the damnedest times to drop in. I suppose she's spending the night."

"I asked her to, yes."

"Ah. I thought so."

"You wouldn't want her to drive all the way back to Philadelphia at night, would you? Besides, it's going to work out perfectly. Your plane's at eight tomorrow morning. Flora doesn't get get to the house till nine. Nancy can stay with the kids while I drive you to the airport."

"I thought we were going to take the kids to the airport?"

"Oh, but this is so much simpler," Barbara said.

He said nothing.

Barbara slowed the car now and pulled up against the curb in front of the delicatessen. "Will you run in and get a loaf of French bread, darling?" she asked him. "And, oh yes, a jar of olives."

He got out of the car and went into the store. She sat behind the wheel, shoulders back, tapping a little rhythm on the steering wheel with her fingertips. She turned her face to the sun which, though it was past five o'clock, was still warm and bright, and closed her eyes, letting the sunlight form swirling, reddish specks against her eyelids. Her skin felt pleasantly tight and warm, the way her whole body used to feel — at the farm — after a day of tennis or a day of lying, doing absolutely nothing, by the pool.

She thought: Here it is June twenty-something, twenty-fifth, the summer seems half over, and I haven't played tennis at all; there is no pool in Locustville and no time any more to do absolutely nothing. She felt, rather than saw, Carson come back to the car. He opened the door, slid across the seat beside her, and she continued to look at the fiery image of the sun through her closed eyes.

"Are you asleep?" he asked her.

"No, just thinking."

"What about?"

She opened her eyes and started the car. "About Nancy," she said. She swung the car in a wide U-turn and headed back along the Pike toward home. "I feel so sorry for her, Carson," she said.

"Sorry for Nancy? Why?"

"She's all alone, she has nobody to tell things to. No mother or father. Only us."

He said nothing, merely stared ahead at the road. They were moving slowly now, with the out-of-city traffic.

"All alone, in Philadelphia," she said.

"She always talks as though she had plenty of fun in Philadelphia."

"Yes, but — well, talk is one thing and the way she really lives is something else again."

"She's got boy friends all over the place. My God, to hear her talk every man in Philadelphia is trying to go to bed with her."

Barbara frowned. "Yes," she said, "but she isn't happy."

"Why doesn't she marry one of those guys?"

"Perhaps — perhaps they don't ask her. I don't know."

"Why doesn't she get a job?"

"She has a job."

"What kind of a job is that — going through nurse's training?"

"She wants to be a nurse."

"Well, she wanted to be a teacher once, too, remember? She went back to school and got an M.A. Then she decided that she wanted to be a lawyer. She went to law school for a year. All she's ever done is go to school."

"Well," she said, "I think nursing is it. I think that's what she really wants to do."

He yawned again. "Well, there've been a lot of things that Nancy has really wanted to do. She really wanted to be an interior decorator once, and another time she really wanted to run a ski lodge in Vermont, and —"

"Please!" Barbara said sharply, "Please don't criticize her. After all, Nancy is my dearest friend. I'm sorry you don't like her, but —"

"I do like her," he said. "But, my God, she's nearly thirty. What she ought to do is get married."

"Marriage," she said sarcastically, "is the solution to everything, isn't it?"

"Look," he said, "I'm not trying to pick a fight! I merely said —"

"You resent her, don't you? And your reasons are pretty transparent!"

"What are they? What are these transparent reasons?"

"You resent her simply because she's someone from the outside world. And she reminds me how much I hate this place!"

"I resent her because she's always barging in on us without an invitation, that's all," he said. "I resented it when she joined us on our wedding anniversary. And when I came home from four months in South America, I resented having Nancy on the welcoming committee with you. And tonight — Jesus Christ, Barbara —"

"No, no," she said. There were tears in her eyes and she brushed at them quickly with her wrist. "You resent her because she's my best friend!"

"Have you ever noticed that the minute she shows up you and I start fighting?"

"That's not true!"

"It is. She's an unhappy, mixed-up girl — not even a girl, a grown woman. And being around her makes you unhappy, too."

"Listen," Barbara said, "if you'd heard what she told me this afternoon —"

"What?"

"No. I can't tell you. I promised her."

"Something awful, I'm sure, that involved a man."

"Yes."

"You see? That's all I said. She ought to get married."

"It's not that easy," she said.

"She talks about all the men who are fighting over her —"

"Those men!"

"Ah," he said. "I thought so. She invented them."

"I didn't mean that. What are you doing, calling her a liar?"

"She's the only girl in the world who's always available for a last-minute blind date on New Year's Eve," he said.

She turned to him sharply. "How can you be so horrible!" she cried. "How can you?"

"Please, keep your eyes on the road . . ."

"Oh!" she sobbed. She pressed her foot on the brake pedal, slowing the car. "You'd better drive," she said. But she didn't stop the car. She continued, slowly, in the crowded lane of traffic.

"All right," he said. "I'll drive if you want."

She ignored him. "I thought it was going to be such a wonderful evening," she said. "I thought we'd have a little farewell party — for you. I thought we'd have such fun. Now you've ruined it."

"Why is it *me* who's ruined it? It seems to me that —"

"That *I've* ruined it, is that what you mean? Don't you know what ruins everything? *Locustville* ruins everything! And we're in Locustville because of you!"

He sat back in the seat. "All right, Barbara," he said quietly. "The rules. Remember the rules."

"The rules involve your being a little considerate of me, too."

"Very well. I'm sorry. I apologize. I'm sorry that I said anything to hurt your feelings. Nancy is a sweet, wonderful girl and I'm just dying to see her again."

"And the rules include not being sarcastic!"

"I'm sorry. And the rules include apologies from both of us."

She was silent for a moment. Then she said, "I'm sorry, Carson."

"There. Now it's all over."

"Yes. All over."

They drove on in silence.

A few minutes later, she said, "Darling, anyway, be *nice* to her tonight. Will you please? Because I do feel sorry for her. And try to *act* as though you're pleased that she came tonight — your last night before your trip and so forth. Will you?"

"Sure," he said. "Sure I will."

"Because she loves us so, she really does! In a way, she depends on us. I really think so. Because she has no mother or father — only a few crazy aunts and uncles that she can't stand — no brothers, no sisters! Don't forget, darling, that she and I were roommates at college. She used to come to the farm for vacations and week ends. Mother and Daddy sort of adopted her, really! And we spent that year in Hawaii together, and she was one of my bridesmaids. I feel — oh, I feel sort of responsible for her! I really do! So be nice to her tonight, will you, Carson?"

"Of course I will," he said.

"Even if she gets — you know, Nancy-ish. And talks the way she does sometimes. Be nice to her."

"I will."

"Promise?"

"I promise. Cross my heart and hope to die."

"And don't be sarcastic, Carson!"

Barbara took her left hand from the wheel and let it trail out the car window, getting ready to signal for her turn.

Their house was in a section of Locustville called Sunrise Heights. It was a name that had been given to it by the developer, since the subdivision was arranged across the side of an east-facing hill. Sunrise Heights itself was divided into three smaller sections — like Gaul, Barbara often said. In one of these, the streets were named for flowers — Arbutus Lane, Bluebell Lane, Columbine Lane, Daffodil Lane. In the second, where Barbara and Carson lived, the motif was trees — Appletree Lane, Bayberry Lane, Cherry Lane, Dogwood, Evergreen (the street names in each area followed an alphabetical pattern). And in the third, it was precious and semiprecious stones — Amethyst, Beryl, Coral, Diamond and so on, through Ruby. The three parts of Sunrise Heights were also separated architecturally. In the floral-streeted section, the houses were all Colonial; in Barbara and Carson's, they were Ranch; in the precious stones section, they were Modern.

All the houses in Sunrise Heights were "pre-built with custom details," which meant that Barbara and Carson, when they were buying their house on Bayberry Lane, had been given a choice of six Ranch-style floor plans and had been able to select their interior color scheme. Optional, at extra cost, were such features — which the Greers' house had — as a two-car semi-attached garage, a flagstone terrace, and such decorative touches as window boxes and the golden rooster weather vane. Sunrise Heights, though it was a development, fortunately had only a slight "development look." On the whole, the area had been well-used. The streets, which were winding and followed the contour of the hill, were planted with trees, the houses were well spaced and well land-scaped. If there was any similarity, or feeling of monotony, it came from the fact that the houses were all about the same size — three or four bedrooms — and had been built to cost about the same, between twenty-five and thirty-five thousand dollars, and all — even the Greers' Ranch-style three bedroom house — showed strong signs of southeastern Pennsylvania's regional preference for brick, as opposed to wood, construction. Carson and Barbara were not particularly fond of Sunrise Heights, or even of their house. It was not, as they often said, the sort of house they eventually wanted. They considered Locustville only temporary. Still, they had lived in Locustville, and in their house, for more than five years. Barbara Greer turned now into Bayberry Lane and drove up the gentle, winding hill. Bayberry Lane houses, by choice, were not numbered. Signs, with the owner's names pricked out in reflector lights, were used instead. Sage . . . Bryson . . . Bishop . . . Hodgson . . . Greer . . . the little signs read as she drove up the street and turned into the driveway.

Nancy Rafferty came around from the terrace. She had put on the heart-shaped earrings again, had brushed her reddish-brown hair and put on fresh lipstick. She was not a tall girl, several inches shorter than Barbara, and in her light linen dress, standing at the top of the brick steps, she looked very slim and pretty. Though she was thirty, she looked, as she raised her arm and waved gaily, smiling, much the way she had looked at nineteen.

The two little boys — Dobie, who was four, and Michael, who was two and a half — appeared behind her and came running down the steps, still wearing their bibs from supper. Dobie cried, "Daddy-Daddy-Daddy-Daddy!" holding out his arms to be picked up.

"Hi-de-ho!" Nancy called.

"Hi, kids. Hi, Nancy," Carson said cheerfully, and Barbara thought, yes, it's going to be a nice evening; I know it is.

2

BY THE TIME THE CHILDREN HAD BEEN PUT TO BED, IT WAS nearly eight o'clock. Carson mixed cocktails in a silver pitcher — his ushers' gift — and Barbara arranged a plate of cheese and crackers which she placed on the glass-topped table on the terrace. The three of them sat in a semicircle around the table in the lingering twilight, talking in low voices because, on other back-yard terraces all around them, voices of neighbors they could not see talked over other twilight cocktails.

Carson said, "See? Even in Locustville we've got gracious living."

Barbara gave him a grateful smile. "Cool," she said, pushing her dark hair back with her hands. "Isn't it wonderful to have it cool!"

"It's worse in Philadelphia," Nancy said. "You can't believe how hot it gets in Philadelphia."

Carson filled their glasses a second time with the pale, crystal liquid from the pitcher and Nancy sat holding her cocktail glass in front of her, with both hands, like a little chalice. Her eyes shone. "Remember Hawaii, Barb?" she asked, pronouncing it with four syllables — "Ha-wa-i-i."

"Oh, of course."

"Those two Navy lieutenants that used to take us out. Remember? What were their names? Lieutenant Boles and Lieutenant Harvey, wasn't it? Both named Charlie! Charlie and Charlie, the gold-dust twins we called them." She laughed.

"Yes," Barbara said.

"*My* Charlie always liked you best, though," Nancy said. "Of course your Charlie liked you, too. But you were always true to Carson." She flashed a smile at Carson. "She was, too, Carson," she said. "She used to write to you every day. I'll never forget. Every single, solitary day she sat down and wrote to you. I was horribly jealous. I used to think: here's Barbara, who has two Charlies absolutely mad about her — and Carson, too! And I had nobody. Remember all the coffee we used to drink in the morning, Barb? Cup after cup after cup! We measured out our life in coffee spoons!"

Barbara smiled, remembering their year in Hawaii. It had been her idea, going there, to have some sort of a career before settling down to marriage with Carson. And it had seemed a good way to spend the time while Carson did his two-year stint in the Army, after college. She had applied for a job in the Pan American Airlines office in Honolulu and persuaded Nancy to apply for a job, too. "It was a wonderful year, wasn't it?" Barbara said.

"Oh yes. Remember, Barb, I didn't want to go? I wanted to work in New York, live in Greenwich Village. Thank God you talked me into going to Hawaii instead. Remember Schuyler Osata?"

"Yes, yes . . ."

"What a wonderful boy. What a wonderful name — Schuyler Osata! He was —" she turned to Carson again. "He was part Japanese, part English, part Hawaiian and part something else. Beautiful, beautiful Polynesian eyes and he could swim like a fish. He used to swim out into the sea and ride on the backs of those big sea turtles. He did! He'd grab one of those enormous turtles by the flippers and let it carry him around. Oh, incredible! Schuyler was in love with Barbara, too — not me."

"Now, *that* isn't true," Barbara said.

"Oh yes, yes it was," Nancy said. She sighed, put her head back, looking up at the darkening sky. "I don't know why it was. They all liked you, Barb, better than they liked me. Yes, I do know why it was," she said and leaned forward again, taking a sip of her cocktail.

"What do you mean?" Barbara asked.

"It's true," Nancy said, her eyes widening, looking first at Carson, then at Barbara. "You see, my real trouble is — was — that I was an only child. I never had any sisters or brothers. Brothers, particularly. That was why, in college, I used to be known as a tease."

"Oh, you weren't!" Barbara said.

"Oh yes I was, I was," Nancy insisted. "I was a tease. That was what they called me, wasn't it, Carson?" She gave Carson a searching, affectionate look as if to say: Tell me, Carson, how dreadful my reputation was in college; tell me, I'll understand. But Carson shook his head soberly back and forth. "Honestly, I never heard anybody say that, Nance," he said.

19

"Well, I was. I got that reputation. It was because I didn't know. And my father, you know, died when I was five years old, so I never knew anything about boys. It was because I wanted to find out — you know, what boys were *like*. That was why I used to neck so much and play feely-feely . . ."

Carson made a muffled, throat-clearing sound.

"No, but seriously," Nancy said quickly. "I *did* play a lot of feely-feely and neck a lot. I didn't know how hard it was for a boy, how difficult. I didn't know then what I know now — that sometimes it's almost impossible for a boy."

"What's impossible for a boy?" Carson asked.

"Oh, *you* know, Carson! Heavens, you ought to know. How sometimes when a boy gets, you know, excited, it becomes almost impossible for him — not to. I mean it's really unfair of a girl to get a boy excited, to let him get himself so excited and then — then not let him. To draw the line and not let him go the limit. I mean, it's very painful — physically painful for a boy. Isn't it?"

Carson smiled. "That," he said, "is a rumor that the male sex has done a good job of circulating — for obvious reasons."

"You mean it isn't true?"

"How about another one of these?" Barbara said, offering Nancy the plate of cheese and crackers.

"No thank you," Nancy said quickly. And then, "No, but don't you see what I mean? I mean if I'd known then what I know now — about boys — I might not have made so many, well, mistakes. My God, I sometimes think that now I know too much about men! Working at the hospital and everything, I mean."

Neither Carson nor Barbara said anything. Carson lifted his cocktail glass and stared, smiling slightly, into the shallow bowl. Barbara reached for a cigarette and lighted it. It was growing quite dark. "I think there's going to be a moon," Barbara said.

After a moment Carson turned to Nancy. "Any prospects in Philadelphia?" he asked.

"You mean *marital* prospects? Oh, goodness, I don't know. I have lots of dates, if that's what you mean. Doctors at the hospital. But doctors are — you know — kind of funny, don't you think?"

"How do you mean?" Carson asked.

"Oh, I don't mean doctors as a *breed*. I don't mean practicing doctors. But young doctors, interns, that kind of doctor. They're always — well, none of them have any money, for one thing. They've all got a long time to go before they're practicing and making any money. That makes them all rather cautious — about getting involved with a girl. They don't want to think about getting married — they're not ready. So they want — you know — what they can get from a girl, without marrying her."

"I see."

"Oh, it's not that bad. There's this one, this Jewish doctor . . ."

"Who is he?"

"His name is Klein, Sidney Klein. He's Jewish. He's asked me to marry him. But I don't know. He's very nice, but do you think I should marry someone who is Jewish?"

Carson smiled. "If you have to ask that, you shouldn't," he said.

"No, no, that's not what Nancy means," Barbara said quickly. "She means —"

"No, Carson's right," Nancy said. "He's right. It's not the religious thing that bothers me. God knows I'm not religious! It's just that, well, I don't know if I want to be Mrs. Sidney Klein — married to a Jew. And he's not even a rich Jew!" She laughed. "He comes from the Bronx."

There was another, longer silence.

"How about another cocktail?" Carson asked.

"Oh, thanks," Nancy said. "These are delicious, Carson. Wonderful Martinis. What proportions do you use?"

"I think I'll put the peas on," Barbara said. She stood up and went into the kitchen.

In the kitchen she put water in a pan, turned up one of the

burners on the stove and unwrapped a package of frozen peas. The room was quite dark, lighted only by the flame from the stove; she turned on no lights. The screened door was open and from the terrace she could hear Nancy's voice, raised somewhat now in the exuberance of three Martinis. "You're right, Carson," Nancy was saying. "I shouldn't marry Sidney feeling the way I do. You're absolutely right. But the trouble is when I get up here — like tonight, with you and Barbara — and when I see how happy you two are, then I think goodness me, I'm thirty years old. What's going to happen to me? I think I must marry *somebody*. Only I mustn't rush into it. I mean, after all, you and Barbara didn't rush into it. You'd known each other for years. You came from the same background. That's why *you're* happy, because you didn't just rush into it. What I should do is marry somebody I grew up with, not somebody like Sidney *Klein!* But the trouble is, everybody I grew up with is already married! Oh, well . . ."

Barbara came out again and sat down. "Oh, there *is* a moon," she said.

"I love this house," Nancy said. "It's just beautiful. This terrace is just beautiful. This is the life. You're so lucky, Barb."

"Oh, Locustville is only temporary," Barbara said.

"But you love one house, don't you, Barb?"

"It's all right, I suppose. But some day we want a bigger house — and not ranch-style like this but colonial, with fireplaces, with a big dining room, and a big, sweeping staircase."

"I know just what you mean," Nancy said. "You mean a place like your father's farm, don't you?"

"Well, not *quite* as big as that," Barbara said.

Nancy turned to Carson. "Don't you adore that place?" she asked. "The Woodcocks' farm? I remember, before I ever went there, Barbara used to talk about the farm and I thought — oh, you know, barns and cows and chickens and things. I never dreamed what it would be like. Such a beautiful old house and

those beautiful gardens, and Mrs. Woodcock's beautiful things —
such perfect taste. And the pool, and the lake, and the little
guesthouse, and the boats on the lake —"

"Daddy sold the boats," Barbara said.

"Did he? Why?"

"No one used them any more."

"But the little guesthouse is still there, isn't it?"

"Oh, yes."

"Oh, that place! So isolated, miles from anything. Even *I* could
be happy on that farm!"

Barbara looked at Carson. It was hard now, in the dark, to see
the expression on his face. "I think you'd have a little trouble getting Carson to move back to the farm," she said.

"I like the farm," Carson said.

"Your sister and her husband are living there, aren't they?"
Nancy asked.

"Yes."

"Well, goodness knows, the place is big enough for all of you —
if you wanted to."

"If I wanted to work for the Woodcock Paper Company, you
mean," Carson said.

"Which you probably don't want to do," Nancy said.

"Not particularly," Carson said.

"Though your sister's husband does, doesn't he, Barb? Doesn't
Peggy's husband work for the paper company?"

"Yes," Barbara said.

"Well," Nancy said, *"chacun à son gout!"*

There was another short silence. Then Nancy spoke again.
"Speaking of the farm and the Woodcocks," she said, "there ought
to be some Woodcock male that would be good for me. Don't you
have any unmarried cousins or nephews or something, Barb? So
that *I* could live at the farm?"

Barbara laughed. "Well, let's see," she said, "There's my cousin
Jeff. He might be a little young for you, though. He's twenty-

two. He just graduated from Yale, and I think he's practically engaged already. Then there's Woody, of course —"

"Perfect!" Nancy said. "Ideal! Oh, I'd adore to be Mrs. Woody deWinter — so much better than Mrs. Sidney Klein! And Woody's just about the handsomest thing I ever laid eyes on," she smiled at Carson, "present company excepted! Woody's not engaged or anything, is he?"

"No."

Nancy leaned forward, holding her now empty cocktail glass, smiling. "You know, Barb, I'm only half-kidding about this. How can we arrange it — to get Woody for me. Why he'd be perfect. That's what I need for a husband — somebody who's exactly like Woody. Oh, I do think a girl ought to marry somebody who's got some money, too, don't you? And all the Woodcocks are rich as Croesus, aren't they? What is Woody — your first or second cousin?"

"Second," Barbara said. "His mother is Daddy's first cousin."

"No, but seriously," Nancy said, "I mean it. Can you get me a date with Woody, Barb?"

Carson put down his glass on the table. "Is dinner nearly ready, Barb?" he asked.

"Yes — almost. I've just got to —"

"Well, I'm going to be a piggy and have another one of these," Nancy said. "Is there a drop more in that extremely handsome pitcher?" She held out her glass.

Carson filled her glass. "Taste it," he said without a hint of sarcasm. "And see if it's strong enough for you. It may have gotten diluted —"

Nancy took a sip. "Perfect," she said. "One hundred per cent. Are you afraid I'm having tee many Martoonies, Carson?" She laughed gaily, swinging her glass so that some of the contents spilled and trickled down the stem, across her fingers. "Now I'd like a cigarette," she said, looking around for one.

Carson offered her a pack and she extracted a cigarette. She

24

held it in her hand for a moment, contemplating it, her lips frozen in a smile. "No, but seriously," she said. "Woody would be perfect."

Carson struck a match and held it out toward her. She placed the cigarette between her lips.

"You're going to light the wrong end," Carson said.

Quickly, and in some confusion, Nancy Rafferty reversed the cigarette, placing the filter end in her mouth. She reached out, cupping her hand around the lighted match that Carson offered, shielding the flame from the wind. Her hand began to tremble. "Thank you, Carson," she breathed, when she had the cigarette going. She sat back. "Oh!" she said. "Perhaps I have had too many."

"I'll put dinner on," Barbara said. She stood up and went into the kitchen.

They had dinner on the terrace.

Later, as they sipped their coffee, the night grew even cooler and Barbara and Nancy threw sweaters over their shoulders; still, it was pleasanter on the terrace than in the house. The candles in the hurricane lamps on the table where they had eaten sputtered out and they went back to their original semi-circle of chairs with the full moon behind them, casting shadows in front of them, talking about Locustville. "Let's keep our voices down," Barbara cautioned. "It's amazing the way sounds travel across these back yards at night."

"But you can't really mean that you *hate* Locustville," Nancy whispered.

"Well, hate may be a little strong," Barbara said. "But really, it's such a stuffy town. And everybody's terribly *old*. Do you know what I mean? I don't mean that there are no young people — there are. But even the young people have this funny, old attitude. And it's terrible to have to live in the same town with the main office of Carson's company. That's really the worst thing. We have to have all these *company* friends. And if we entertain

25

one person from the Locustville Chemical Company, we always have to have about three others. It's all organized."

"Well, it's really not that bad," Carson said.

"Oh, it is!" Barbara insisted. "Now you've got two supervisors. We can't invite one supervisor to dinner without inviting the other one, can we? That's what I mean."

"Well, there's a reason for all that," Carson said.

"What reason?" Barbara said. "I can't see any reason for it except — oh, I know what you mean. The company comes first. First, last and always. You don't think of yourself. You think of yourself in relation to the company." She smiled. "But it will be different as soon as we're transferred."

"Where will you go?" Nancy said.

"Well, the company has seven sales offices," Barbara said. "New York, Boston, Detroit, Chicago, Milwaukee, San Francisco and Los Angeles."

"Which would you pick if you had your choice?"

"New York, Boston, Detroit, Chicago, Milwaukee, San Francisco or Los Angeles," Barbara said. "Any place but Locustville. Isn't that right, darling?" she smiled at Carson.

Carson looked at her steadily. Then he said, "That's right. Any place but Locustville, darling."

"Of course I meant — eventually," Barbara said quickly.

"How simple!" Nancy laughed. "How simple to have only seven cities to choose from! You don't even have to *consider* Paris . . . London . . . Rome . . . Madrid . . . Istanbul! That's why I envy you two. My problem is so much more complex." She laughed, her shoulders shaking; she put down her coffee cup noisily in the saucer, bent forward, still laughing, clutching her sides. "Oh! Oh! Oh!" she sobbed, "Oh, isn't it funny! Isn't it!"

"Nancy, dear!" Barbara said. "The neighbors."

"Oh, I can't, I can't!" Nancy said. But, gradually, her laughter subsided. She sat forward in her chair, her hands over her eyes, rocking backward and forward. "Oh, I'm sorry. I'm sorry," she said. "I get — I guess I get sort of hysterical sometimes. I guess — oh, God!" she said, removing her hands from her face. Her eyes shone with tears. "Carson, fix me a little drink, will you? Scotch?"

"Nance, do you really think you should?" Barbara asked.

"Please. I — I guess I'm tired. I'm sorry. What I need is a drink. May I?"

Carson stood up and went into the house.

Nancy suddenly reached for Barbara's hand and gripped it tightly in her own. "I'm sorry, Barb," she said. "You understand, don't you? Oh, Barb, you're the only friend I've got in the world! *The only one!* Oh, Barbara! It's just that all of a sudden I'm thirty! I'm thirty!"

"So am I, Nance," Barbara said softly.

"It's no fun, is it? It's *not* a fun age, is it! It's a terrible age to be, Barbara, isn't it?"

"I know, I know," Barbara said.

Carson returned with a drink in his hand.

"Oh, Carson, thank you!" Nancy cried. "You're an absolute angel, Carson, you really are!"

A little later, Carson yawned. "I've really got to turn in," he said. "I've got to be up pretty early — I'm catching an eight o'clock plane."

"Oh, poor Carson," Nancy said, "I'm afraid I've intruded tonight. I *told* Barb I didn't want to intrude. I knew it would be your last night home. Where is it you're going?"

"London first," Carson said. "Then a week in Paris, a week in Zurich, a week in Brussels, back to London and home again."

"Oh, how I envy you. Just going to any *one* of those places."

"Well, it's pretty much all business. Calling on distributors. It's not as glamorous as it sounds."

"And Locustville salesmen do *not* take their wives on trips," Barbara said. "That's one of the rules."

Carson stood up. "So," he said a little lamely, "I've got to get to bed."

"Poor Carson!" Nancy said again. "I shouldn't have stayed. I've kept you up too late, haven't I?"

"Oh no," he said. "Not at all. It's been wonderful seeing you, Nance."

"Would you mind terribly, Carson, if I kept your wife up a wee bit longer?" Nancy asked. "So we can have a bit more of a girly-girly visit? We see each other so seldomly any more. Seldomly? Is that a word?" she laughed.

Carson looked briefly at Barbara.

"I'll be in in just a minute," Barbara said.

"All right. Good night then," Carson said.

"Good night, Carson!" Nancy said. She raised her hand to her lips and blew him a kiss. "Good night!"

After Carson left, the two women sat alone on the terrace, smoking cigarettes. Finally, Barbara said, "Do you think it's getting a little chilly?"

"It is, yes," Nancy said. "Why don't we sit in the living room?" She picked up her empty glass.

They went into the house, through the kitchen, through the dining alcove, into the living room that was quite large and had a tall glass window that faced east. Barbara turned on lights as she went.

Nancy went to the window and looked out. In the distance the lights of Locustville glittered. "What a fabulous room," Nancy said. "I absolutely adore this room."

"The view is prettier at night than it is in the daytime," Barbara said. "In fact, at night, I sometimes find myself liking Locustville. It seems so quiet and peaceful."

Nancy turned to her. "Where does he keep his stuff?" she asked. "What stuff?"

"His liquor, naturally! Don't you think we ought to have a little nightcap?"

Barbara frowned at her. "Haven't you had enough already, dear?" she asked.

"Oh, Barbara!" Nancy said. "What's the matter with you? Why have you suddenly gotten so — so moralistic? I've only had one drink since dinner, for goodness sake!"

"Give me your glass, I'll fix it," Barbara said.

"I'll come with you. Where is it?"

"In the kitchen."

Nancy followed Barbara into the kitchen. The whiskey was in the cupboard beneath the sink; Barbara removed the Scotch bottle and went to the refrigerator for ice cubes.

"Aren't you going to have one?" Nancy asked.

"Oh, I don't think so," Barbara said.

"Well, you've certainly gotten very — very Locustville-ish. So proper!"

"All right, I'll have one," Barbara said.

"Are you afraid I'm becoming an alcoholic?" Nancy asked. She had taken over the drink-mixing and was pouring a generous amount of Scotch over the ice cubes in her glass and Barbara's. "Well, don't be, honestly. Weeks, months go by without me having a single drink. It's just —" She handed one glass to Barbara with a little nervous laugh. "— It's just that I guess I'm a little upset tonight. Telling you what I told you this afternoon — that upset me," she said.

"I understand," Barbara said.

They walked back into the living room.

"I'm sorry I got so — sort of hysterical a while ago," Nancy said. "But that was part of it, too. Barbara," she said, "do you think I ought to see someone? An analyst or something?"

"I don't know," Barbara said quietly. "Why?"

"I get so — so darned *depressed* sometimes!" She laughed. "But not now. Not tonight. I don't feel depressed. I feel — terrific!" She lifted her glass. "Here's mud in your eye!" she said. "Remember, Barb, in Hawaii, when you and I always used to toast each other that way? It was what one of the lieutenants — one of the gold-dust twins — always used to say: 'Here's mud in your eye!' "

"Yes, I remember that."

"You and I were both rather naughty little girls, weren't we, back in Hawaii? Not that I'd tell Carson of course, but we were, weren't we? Remember that funny little apartment we had, and how we used to take turns —"

"Oh, let's not go into all that!" Barbara said. "Do you realize how long ago that was? That was almost seven years ago, Nance. We've both grown up a little bit since then."

"Yes, but I only mentioned it because, well, you are suddenly being so moralistic about having a little nightcap," she said. She took a sip of her drink, and then sat down at one end of the long green sofa, tucking one foot underneath her. "I didn't mean to bring back unpleasant memories, Barb," she said.

"But it was so long ago," Barbara said.

"And you did write Carson every day, you really did."

"Of course I did."

"You aren't sore at me, are you, Barb?" Nancy asked, and her face, all at once, was crossed with anxiety. "Are you?"

"No, of course not. You're like my own sister, Nancy."

"I think Carson was a little sore at me tonight," she said. "When I was talking about Woody. I don't think he liked that."

"Why should he mind that?"

"No, but actually," Nancy said, "why don't you — oh, you know, sort of remind Woody of me the next time you go up to the farm? Couldn't you do that? I don't mean make a specific date for me or anything like that, but sort of remind him of me. Tell him that I am — well, unattached at the moment, and that I could always come up to New York or something, if he could come down."

"I'll mention it," Barbara said, "but I'm really afraid Woody is a confirmed bachelor. He's got that apartment of his now, you

30

know — everything just so, the way he wants it. The family's sort of given up on Woody getting married."

"I don't mean imply to him that I'm — well, that I'm round-heeled or whatever the expression is! Because that's the trouble. That's the reputation I've got. That's the trouble with this Sidney Klein. He seems to think that if he's asked a girl to marry him, then she ought to be willing to go to bed with him."

"And you haven't done this, I take it."

Nancy was silent for several moments. "Well, to be perfectly frank," she said, then she took another swallow of her drink. "But what can I do, Barbara?" she asked suddenly. "What can I do? Is there any other way? How can I keep a man if I say no! There isn't any other way, no other way! I've had to — to submit. Even with Sidney! Oh, God!" All at once tears were streaming down her face. She raised her hand and wiped them away. "Oh, I don't know, I don't know," Nancy said. "That's why sometimes I think I need an analyst. Only the trouble is I'm afraid an analyst will tell me what's wrong with me — and I don't want to know. What I told you this afternoon — that's only part of the trouble."

Barbara came and sat down beside her on the sofa. She put her hand on Nancy's shoulder. "Perhaps you ought to go to bed, Nance," she said.

Nancy straightened up. "You're so darned motherly!" she said, and laughed. "Don't forget Hawaii, Barb. Don't ever forget Hawaii. You weren't always so pure."

"I know, I know," Barbara said.

Nancy reached for her glass and took a swallow of her drink that seemed endless. When she put it down the glass was empty. "There!" she said triumphantly, "There! Now I feel better." She lay back heavily across the sofa cushions and closed her eyes.

Barbara stood up and walked across the room. She didn't know, precisely, where she was going or what she was going to do. She went to the coffee table and arranged the two silver ash trays, shaped like maple leaves — wedding presents — on either side of the glass bowl in which she had placed, just that morning, a bunch of scarlet zinnias. She turned and looked at the room. It seemed empty, cool, antiseptic. Even the zinnias on the coffee table, even the other vase, the taller vase, of red climbing roses on the desk against the wall, seemed rigid and artificial. The arrangement of the furniture in the room, chairs set at angles, facing this way and that, seemed arbitrary — as arbitrary as the rooster weather vane, she thought, that even in a northern gale pointed resolutely east. It was like a hospital. And the girl in the linen dress who lay across the green sofa, stockings twisted, her body at a slanting angle, looking as though any minute she might slide to the floor in a heap, did not look like Nancy Rafferty any more, or anyone she had ever known, but looked instead like a patient in a hospital. A memory of hospital smells assailed her, overpowering the other fragrances — perfume, furniture polish, roses, cigarette smoke, that the room contained. And the irony of it was that Nancy was studying to be a nurse. Now she was being required to nurse Nancy. She felt angry and confused. What was she expected to do? She wondered if she should wake Carson, tell him to come. She felt as if she, like Nancy's outstretched body, were perched uncertainly over some abyss. It was like the feeling she had had earlier on the terrace, when she had suddenly wished that Nancy Rafferty was thousands of miles away. It was an unkind wish, certainly, because Nancy was one of the very few old friends whom she saw with any frequency any more. She crossed the room to where Nancy lay. "Nancy!" she said loudly, "Nancy!"

"Hm?" Nancy said, opening her eyes.

"Please, let's go to bed. I've got to take Carson to the airport at seven o'clock. It's half past one now."

"Yes, yes," Nancy said. "Must get to bed. Did you think I'd passed out? I hadn't. I was just thinking."

"What were you thinking?"

Nancy smiled. "About Woody. Does he still have that wonderful blond, wavy hair?"

"Yes. Now, please — let's get to bed."

"Not getting bald or anything?"

"No, not getting bald or anything."

Nancy sat up now. "I promise, cross my heart, not to have an affair with him, Barbara. I promise, cross my heart."

"All right. Now let's —"

"Let's have another little drink, shall we?"

"Oh, *please*, Nancy!"

Nancy tossed her head back and laughed. "Oh, Miss Sobersides! Miss Solomon J. Sobersides! Scold, scold, scold! Just like old Miss Whosis, what's-her-name, at college, the one with the enormous buzzooms! 'Girls, girls, *girls!* Watch your language, *please*, girls!' What was that old fart's name? You know, the one with the enormous —"

"Miss Abernathy," Barbara said. "Now let's go to bed."

"Do you know who gave me my very first drink, Barb? Do you? It was your father — your own father! Oh, I love your father, Barb. How is he? I'll never forget. Do you know how I remember? You and I were both sixteen. I'd come down to the farm with you for the week end. We were going to a dance, remember? And all at once, the night of the dance, it was something I ate or other, and I broke out in absolutely enormous hives! Remember? I was miserable. I was so miserable. I couldn't go to the dance. You went. I stayed behind. And your father — your wonderful father — came into the room where I was lying in absolute agony and said to me: 'Nancy, what you need is a nice, stiff drink.' And he fixed me the nicest, stiffest drink I ever had. It was my very first." She smiled and picked up her empty glass. "I'll always remember that first one. He was always a bit of a lush, your father — even then. A very, very *nice* lush. Oh, of course I've had many, many drinks since then. Like affairs. I've had many, many affairs, too. I've lost count. All I have is affairs. I wonder why I have so many affairs." She stared darkly and intently at the side of the glass, bringing her face close to it, stroking the side of it hard with her thumbnail. "Mirror, mirror on the wall . . ."

"I don't know, Nancy, but honestly we must get to bed. Come on. In the morning we can talk some more."

"Of course you've had affairs, too," Nancy said, still gazing at the glass. "Perhaps it's normal. I don't know. I remember you in Hawaii, and then, even later, after you married Carson I remember you telling me about affairs —"

"I'm sorry, but I haven't had any affairs — as you call it — since I married Carson. So come to bed."

Nancy Rafferty looked up, startled. "Oh, but that's not true! What about that time you told me? You know — about you and Barney, your sister's husband."

Barbara laughed shortly. "I never had an affair with Barney!"

"But you told me! Or you told me that you considered it anyway!"

"I didn't even consider it."

"But you *told* me! I know you told me!"

"I didn't tell you anything of the sort," Barbara said. "What I told you was — well, I'm sorry I even told you if you're going to attach that sort of meaning to it!" Her voice was rising angrily. "There was nothing like that between me and Barney. It was just — just nothing. For God's sake, now, come to bed!"

"Sorry, sorry, sorry!" Nancy said. "Sorry I brought it up. But I remembered you told me something. Oh, I know why it is. You're pretty. You always were. Pretty — prettier than me." She picked up the glass again. "Mirror, mirror on the wall? Who is the fairest of us all? Barbara Woodcock! Fairest — of — us — all!" She pounded her feet in rhythm to the words.

There was a sound. Barbara turned. Carson was standing in the doorway in his pajamas and yellow terry bathrobe; on the breast pocket of the robe were his initials in black — C.V.G. His hair was tousled and his face was clouded with sleep and anger. "Jesus Christ," he said. "Aren't you two ever coming to bed? Do you know what time it is? Do you know I've got to get up in the morning?"

"Car-son!" Nancy cried gaily. "Come join us! Fix us all a drink!"

"Don't you know it's late? Don't you know it's damned near two?" He thrust his fists deep into the pockets of the terry robe. This caused the robe to fall open at the middle and Barbara suddenly saw that the front of his pajamas, also, was open.

Nancy saw it too. "One o'clock in the pajama factory!" she cried.

"Jesus Christ!" Carson said in disgust, turned on his heel and stalked out of the room.

"Carson!" Barbara called.

"He forgets I work in a hospital," Nancy said. "I've seen worse things than that —"

"I'm going to bed," Barbara said.

"All right, all right!" Nancy stood up, somewhat unsteadily. She performed, then, a few little tap-dance steps in front of the sofa. "Put your little foot, put your little foot, put your little foot right down!" she sang in a wavery voice. Then she said, "Good night, Barb." She turned and started toward the hall.

"You're in the guest room," Barbara said.

"I can find it. Nitey-night!"

Nancy walked slowly down the hall. Barbara heard the guest room door open, then close with a bang.

One of the boys — Michael? — cried out softly in his sleep.

"Damn her!" Barbara said, and her eyes filled with hot tears.

She started around the room, rapidly emptying ash trays into the silent butler, picking up the glasses, turning off the lamps. She carried the two glasses into the kitchen and placed them in the sink. She put the Scotch bottle back in the cupboard. Then she turned off the kitchen lights.

The house was dark now, except for the hall light.

She went down the hall and softly pushed open the door of the boys' room. Using only the light from the hall, she tiptoed across the room. Michael was out of his covers. Gently she lifted the blanket. She hesitated, then reached down, under his sleepers, checking his diaper. He was dry. She covered him then, tucking the blanket tightly around his shoulders. She went to Dobie's bed and looked down at him. He was covered, asleep.

She went out into the hall, closed the door, and turned off the light.

In the dark she went on to her own room, let herself in, and closed the door behind her. In the darkened room she heard Carson's steady breathing.

She found the small light beside her dressing table and turned it on. With a piece of tissue paper, she blotted her lipstick. Then she sat down at the dressing table in front of her dim reflection in the mirror and began to brush her hair. She lifted her hair, a bit at a time, and rolled each strand into a flat curl with her fingers. She spread bobby pins with her teeth (she had been taught never to do this, but was there any other way?) and secured each curl tight against her head.

Behind her, Carson said, "She gets nuttier by the day, doesn't she?"

"Yes," Barbara said.

"Why do you put up with her?"

"She's an old friend," she said simply.

"I've got old friends. They don't act like that."

"I know."

She finished putting up her hair and turned off the light. She undressed in the dark, placing her clothes across the chair. Then she got into bed beside him.

"I'm sorry," she said.

"Gracious living!" he said.

"Please. I feel sorry for her."

"So you said."

"She told me the most dreadful thing this afternoon. Do you want to know what she told me?"

"Not very much."

"She's had this — this affair with a doctor. Not the Jewish one she mentioned, but another one. She got pregnant by him."

"Of course," he said.

"She wanted an abortion. He said he could do it himself — knew how, that is — but he wouldn't. He said he'd help pay for it. Not pay for it — just *help* pay! He sent her to someone he knew — not even a doctor but some old horrible nurse who'd been in jail once. Nancy went to her. The nurse did it in her kitchen. How horrible! The nurse's old mother was right in the room, smoking a cigarette and playing solitaire! Then the old mother had to come — to hold Nancy down. The nurse said, 'If you scream I'll hit you.' And Nancy did scream and the nurse hit her and blacked her eye. Oh, Carson! I don't think I've ever heard anything so horrible ever, in my whole life!"

"Well," Carson said, "yes. It is horrible. But typical."

"Oh, darling, don't say that!"

"It is, though."

"Afterward, something — an infection — developed. She went to the hospital. They cut her all up, Carson. It ended up being a hysterectomy!"

For a while they lay silently in the darkness.

Then Barbara said, "Carson?"

"What?"

"How temporary is this place? Locustville."

"What do you mean?"

"How temporary? How many more years?"

"Two or three."

"Oh, God! That's not temporary. That's forever!"

There was another silence. Then: "Are you crying?"

"No."

37

And then there was another, longer silence.

Then Barbara said, "Carson? We're not like that, are we? We're not horrible or sordid or anything like that, are we? We have two beautiful children, don't we, and there's really nothing unhappy about our lives, is there? There's nothing mean or selfish or cruel . . ."

"Of course not," he said.

"Of course not," she repeated. Then, "Oh, I wish you weren't going away tomorrow!"

"So do I. But I've got to."

"You were right," she said, "this afternoon in the car. I was wrong, Carson. I shouldn't have let her stay. I see that now, Carson. She ruined our last evening together. I'm sorry."

"That's all right."

"It isn't. I'm sorry. And I'm sorry I complained about Locustville tonight. I know we'll leave eventually, and as you always say, when we're here we should try to be happy . . ."

"Yes," he said.

"And we are happy, aren't we? Most of the time?"

"Yes."

"And you were right to remember the rules," she said.

A little later she put her arms around him. "Are you awake?" she asked.

But he was asleep.

Her eyes were growing accustomed to the darkness.

The nights in Locustville, Pennsylvania were certainly the most beautiful time. They had, in summer at least, much of the quality of Italian nights that she remembered from trips to Europe, summer trips, with her mother and father when she was a girl. Italian — in that the darkness had a color to it, a prismatic, purplish color. From the bedroom which faced a corner of the patio and which took in a view, from the wide windows, of the town below, the sky held an aurora of light from the town and it was possible, very possible, from the dark bedroom through the

38

silent window, to dream that the city was not Locustville, Pennsylvania — not Locustville, but —

Naples!

Naples, and she was a girl on a hill above it. And those swirling deeps below which were actually long yellow fields of farms and darkened houses, they were crests and waves and combers of the sea! Holding this impossible image in her mind she closed her eyes, trapping it there, pressing it like a flower between the pages of a book.

She thought about the farm.

Once, when she was a little girl, she had been helping her mother transplant clumps of violets from behind the house, moving them into the garden. Her mother had suddenly sat back upon her heels, dropped her trowel, and looked at the fingers of her outstretched hand. The diamond from her engagement ring, the center diamond, had fallen from the prongs that held it.

They had stayed there all afternoon, looking for it, going back and forth over every inch of earth, looking under every leaf, patting the earth, crumbling it in their fingers, and, when they were tired, stopping for a minute to wipe their hands on their clothes. Her mother kept closing her eyes, trying to imagine where it might be. When it was nearly dark, her mother's face had been streaked and dirty. Then suddenly she cried, "I see it!" and plunged her hand into the grass. "No, it's only a drop of dew!" she said. She sat there on her knees and began to cry, and Barbara, who always started to cry when her mother did, cried too. And her mother had pulled her into her arms and said, "There, there. There, there," over and over again. "It's lost, that's all there is to it. That's all there is to it."

For weeks afterward, whenever she went out of the house alone, she searched for her mother's diamond, careful not to let a drop of dew fool her. Finally, after she had spent most of one summer that way, looking only in that one spot behind the house where they had been digging up violets, she began looking farther afield in places where her mother *might* have been. And the next summer, the place had nothing to do with it. She looked for the diamond wherever she might be, whenever she happened to think of it. She let her cousin Woody deWinter in on the secret and when they played together one of them would suddenly say, "Let's look for the diamond!" Immediately they would separate, running in different directions, shouting that they had just thought of a place where they had not looked. And when they returned, one of them might pretend that he had found it, or that they had found another diamond, a different one, and after a while they lost interest in the game and forgot about the diamond altogether. Years later, Barbara had been sitting with her mother on the terrace behind the house and suddenly thought of it again. "Remember the day you lost your diamond?" she asked her. "Did you ever find it?" "No," her mother said, smiling, holding up her ring finger, "but it was insured; I got a new one that I really think I like better."

Woody had been practically her only playmate at the farm. Woody lived several miles away but his mother brought him over frequently, especially during the summer. The farm had a swimming pool and Woody's house, which was closer to town, did not. Barbara and Woody had been taught to swim together by a Yale boy named Danny, who was also a lifeguard and who came to the Woodcocks' pool two afternoons a week to earn extra summer money. "Keep your faces down . . . keep your shoulders even with the water . . ." she could remember clearly Danny's somewhat flat voice saying. She had carried on, over the course of several summers, a fantasy love affair with Danny in which he courted her elaborately with flowers and boxes of candy. Woody, too, had worshiped Danny and they planned, together once, to adopt Danny and take him with them wherever they went for the rest of their lives. He would be very happy with them, they were sure, because they would treat him only with the utmost deference and respect, always. Once, when he had not seemed to return their admiration for him, Barbara and Woody had even attempted to kidnap him.

Barbara and Woody had systematically excluded Peggy, Barbara's sister, who was five years younger, from all their play and secrets. The girls had had a governess then, Fraulein Ungewitter, and try as the Fraulein might, there was no way that she could get all three children to play together. That was how it happened that Barbara and Woody had been alone in the nursery with Fraulein Ungewitter the day Fraulein Ungewitter suddenly died, and Peggy had been in another part of the house. Fraulein Ungewitter was very tall and thin, with a face that always looked bright and polished and oiled; her hair was a clear, metallic gray and she kept it always in a black hair net. That afternoon Barbara and Woody had been playing in the nursery and Fraulein Ungewitter had come in from the bathroom, holding the black hair net in her hand, her long gray hair loose around her shoulders. "My hair!" she had said, and her face had been pale. "What's happened to it? It's turned gray!" It was apparently the first time she had noticed the change, though it had been gray for longer than Barbara could remember, and Fraulein held up the black hair net wordlessly as if to show that the fibers no longer matched. Then — whether from the shock of the discovery or not they never knew — she pitched forward on her hands, cried out, and was dead. Barbara and Woody stood silently looking at her fallen body for several minutes; then they both began to scream.

They were hurried out of the house. At first they were only awed and frightened. Then, convinced that what they had seen was real, they began to feel somewhat joyous — mischievous and evil, lucky to have witnessed some spectacular human event. The new mood crept over them and seized them completely. (How many twelve-year-old children have had a person go through the swift steps of dying right before their eyes?) Excited, feeling wise, knowing now all there was to know about death, having seen it happen, they discussed it in whispers behind the house. Woody had seen a cat, once, going through some sort of mouth-foaming fit, then dying, which he told about.

They wandered away from the house that was by this time too busy and distraught to wonder where the children were, and walked across the wide back lawn to where the bridle path began, down the hill, under the slim ironwood and maple branches, past the skeletons of the two tall, blighted chestnut trees, and into the woods, where immediately a swarm of mosquitoes rose to meet them. They raced from the mosquitoes, clambered across the rocks and trunks of fallen trees, under the rusted tangle of barbed wire that had enclosed some long-ago pasture, to the brook that held, clasped between two slim arms, a tiny island. It was their secret island. On it, in beds made of leaves and grass, they kept their collection of dolls, sheltered from the weather by a piece of old canvas. They raised the canvas and looked at the sleeping dolls; then they made their selection. Among the muddy green of cowslips, adder's-tongue and wild arbutus that grew on the island, they dug a grave in which they placed with solemn ceremony, an imaginary Fraulein. Woody spoke a few words . . . Ashes to ashes.

Far, then, from her native Bavaria — farther still than Bavaria in distances measured by the wandering heart — Barbara Woodcock and Woody deWinter laid Fraulein Ungewitter's effigy to rest. Here, where black snakes sometimes slithered and, in early spring, where tiny polliwogs no bigger than Fraulein's shoebuttons darted on the sandy brook bottom; where once the children had set free the goldfish to find their way to the sea and where innumerable toy boats had been christened and launched; where they had grown luxurious and fanciful gardens, created citadels and fortresses of mud and pebbled, lofty palladia that lifted their spires to the tallest reaches of the mind — here, in this wild and bosky place, they said farewell to Fraulein Ungewitter. And then in a transport, apparently, of excitement — with a kind of furious longing that seemed to spring directly from the ritual they had just performed — they became more hushed and conspiratorial. They looked at each other. And in the quiet leaves, they undressed and lay down, kissing each other with — perhaps — a passion and a violence and (if it could be called that) a love which, for its unsuccess, was deeper and more meaningful than anything they would ever experience again.

Years afterward, it had become a private joke between them. "Remember," one of them would ask, "the day we buried Fraulein Ungewitter?" And they would exchange a little secret smile, knowing that it is always the most vivid things in childhood that become the funniest jokes when you grow up.

The farm.

She had been married at the farm, a summer wedding in her mother's garden. ("Two Prominent Eastern Families Unite," the Burketown *Eagle* had said.) She had been at the farm, too, several years later when she had first met Barney Callahan.

It had been one of her lonely summers. Carson had been away on his sales trip to South America. She had persuaded Flora, who ordinarily worked for her five days a week, to stay for a week end with Dobie and Michael. She had arrived at the farm in the early twilight, and after changing her clothes, she had come downstairs and joined her mother on the terrace. She remembered John, her mother's houseman, bringing them mint juleps in silver cups with silver straws. It had been exactly two summers ago. She remembered the terrace candles, lighted, and beyond their glow, fireflies performing hesitantly in the dusk.

Her mother held her julep cup in her hand and smiled quietly at Barbara for a moment. Then she lifted the cup to her lips, sipped from the straw, and looked away. "There's some news, darling," she said. "Peggy's brought a young man down with her." She paused. "From Boston. She wants to marry him, or so she says. They're down at the pool now, having a swim before dinner. His name is Barney Callahan. He seems perfectly nice. The auspices of course are absolutely wrong. They could not be worse. For one thing, he's a Catholic, or *was* one until recently. Of course, with a name like Callahan! I know nothing about his family except that they're poor Boston Irish. His father, Peggy says, runs a candy store or grocery store or some such thing. I'm fairly distressed about the whole thing, but what can I do? I discussed it at some length with your father this morning and we both agree that there is nothing to do except say absolutely nothing. You know how Peggy is. Anything we say will make her only more determined. She told me his history and expected me to be shocked. I was shocked, of course, but wise enough not to show it and that, of course, disappointed Peggy! She wanted a scene, a screaming scene. I refused to give her one. So now she's being merely sullen. I'm hoping it will blow over. Let's all hope it will blow over! So, Barbara, just don't say anything to her — please. Just act perfectly, normally pleased about it and pray that it blows over. On the plus side, he has some education. He worked his way through Boston University peddling — I think Peggy said it was — milk." Mrs. Woodcock suddenly laughed. "Imagine," she said, "my daughter marrying a milkman! However. Be that as it may. He was in the Army, in Korea, and now he's finishing up at Harvard Business School on that G.I. Bill or whatever it is. I thought I ought to fill you in quickly on all this, Barbara, because you'll be meeting him very soon, at dinner. In fact, here he comes now."

The young man came up the series of wide flagstone steps that led, between rhododendron bushes, from the pool, which was at the farthest end of the garden, to the terrace. He was very tall, very dark and slender. He wore swimming trunks and a white bathtowel hung around his neck. He came toward them.

"Barney," Edith Woodcock said, "this is my other daughter, Peggy's sister, Barbara Greer. Barbara, this is Barney Callahan."

He shook hands with her; his hand was wet and water dripped from his hair. "How do you do?" he said.

44

"Hello, Barney," Barbara said.

Mrs. Woodcock stood up, smoothing the front of her gray dress. "Excuse me a moment," she said. "I'm going to run in and get a sweater. It's getting a little chilly this evening, but thank goodness the bugs seem to have left us." She turned and walked toward the house.

Barney sat down in the iron chair Mrs. Woodcock had just left. He sat back, stretching his bare legs out in front of him. He put his elbows on the arms on the chair and brought his hands together, making a steeple of his fingers. "You live in Locustville, Pennsylvania, don't you?" he asked.

"Yes," she said.

It was growing dark and it was hard to see his features distinctly. He was not looking at her, but straight ahead, through the steepled fingers, and his eyes seemed very dark and deeply set. They seemed, also, heavy-lidded, with a quality of sleepiness, of gazing dreamily at something in the middle distance, not the shadow of the horizon where the sun had set, nor at his hands, but at something somewhere in between. His chin was dark and there was something curious and surprising in the sight of those dreaming eyes above the heavy beard.

"Did you have a nice swim?" she asked him.

"Do you want to know a secret?" he asked her.

"What?" she asked.

He looked at her and smiled; a rather shy and nervous smile. "I can't swim a stroke. I pretended, though, just now. I doused myself in the shallow end and splashed around."

"Really?" she said.

"Not a stroke."

"Well," she said, "we'll have to teach you! That's all there is to it. Everybody in this family swims."

He looked at her for a moment. "Good," he said. "Fine, I'll be waiting for my first lesson."

Abruptly he stood up, turned and walked away from her,

45

leaving her alone on the terrace. Puzzled, she watched him, walking somewhat gingerly on his bare feet across the hard stones of the terrace. He started back down the stone steps toward the pool. Little by little, as he went slowly down, the shadows and the heavy branches of the bordering shrubbery cut him off; the flash of white towel about his shoulders disappeared and he was gone as though the darkness and rhododendrons had swallowed him, enveloped him, shrouded him in layers of blackness like soft veils, one upon another, of sleep.

3

I T WAS FIFTEEN MILES TO THE LOCUSTVILLE AIRPORT. THEY drove in the chilly early morning light, Carson behind the wheel, Barbara beside him. His suitcase was on the back seat. After five years in the International Sales Division, which involved frequent trips like this one, Carson had got packing down to an exact science; even on the longest journeys he was never encumbered with more than one piece of luggage. As they drove, he went over a little list of last-minute instructions for her.

"If a letter comes from Ted Sloane, from South America, open it and see what he says," he said. "It may be he's planning to come up. I forgot to tell him I'd be away. Of course if he writes to the office, they'll take care of it there, but if he writes to the house — and he may — call Clyde Adams and tell him whatever the letter says. Clyde will take care of entertaining him when he gets here. Oh, and Barb, you'd better call what's-his-name, DeLuca, and have him come and clean out the oil burner. It should have been done last month, actually. Ask him if he thinks the chimney should be cleaned. My God, Harry Walsh had a fire in his chimney the other day and his house is the same age as ours! Don't forget to send my mother some flowers or something on her birthday, July nineteenth. I'll pick her up something wherever I am, but if the old girl doesn't get something right *on* her birthday she'll be on the phone saying nobody loves her any more. Let's see, what else?"

"I think I'll have the rug cleaners come," Barbara said. "It's only forty dollars and the rugs could use it, don't you think?"

"Sure," he said. "Fine. Go ahead." He frowned. "I keep thinking there's something I've forgotten to tell you," he said.

She moved closer to him and rested her head on his shoulder. "You haven't asked me if I'm going to miss you?" she asked.

"Are you?"

"Terribly of course."

"I'm sorry I blew up last night," he said, "at Nancy. But — ye gods! I do think sometimes she's on the verge of going off her rocker. But I didn't know about — you know — the abortion thing. That is too bad. So I understand why you asked her to spend the night."

"No," she said, "I shouldn't have. It ruined our evening."

"You couldn't help it. It wasn't your fault."

"Yes," she insisted. "It was my fault."

"Well, let's not argue about whose fault it was."

"You're right. I'm sorry."

"It's over and done with. Let's forget it."

"Yes," she said. "Let's forget it and always remember the rules."

"I'll try to be more tolerant of Nancy in the future," he said.

"I had to keep reminding myself to be — well, tolerant of her last night," she said. "I know she was saying some pretty silly things."

"One o'clock in the pajama factory, for God's sake."

Barbara laughed softly. "Well, at least that was accurate," she said.

They drove on in silence.

Barbara said, "I keep remembering what a nice, bright girl she used to be."

"Yes," he said.

"I was thinking — while you're away I might call Mother and ask her if I could bring Nancy up to the farm for a week end. Who knows? Woody just may be the answer."

"I don't think so," Carson said. "Not Woody."

"Why not?"

"I just don't think that Woody's her type. Or that she's his."

"It's funny, I always keep forgetting," Barbara said. "That you knew Woody before you knew me."

"Uh-huh," he said.

"You don't think it might be worthwhile? Just to bring them together?"

"Why get her hopes all up, and then — ?"

"And then what?"

"And then not have it work out I mean," he said.

"You think Woody's a confirmed bachelor then," she said.

"I'm afraid so," he said.

After a moment she said, "Well, I might go up to the farm for a few days anyway. For a week end, perhaps. You wouldn't mind if I did that, would you?"

"And take the kids?"

"Either that or see whether Flora can stay . . ."

"You really love that old place, don't you?" he asked.

"What? The farm?"

"Yes."

"Of course I love it . . . it's home," she said. And then, "It gets so lonesome here when you're away. I don't know whether you realize."

"I know," he said. "I get lonesome, too. Being away."

They were approaching the airport now.

"That must be your plane," Barbara said.

"Yes," he said.

He parked the car in the parking lot, removed the keys and handed them to her. He lifted his suitcase from the back seat, tossed his raincoat over his arm. They walked together toward the terminal, to the door that was marked DEPARTING PASSENGERS.

For five years now she had seen Carson as a departing, or an arriving, passenger. And yet it was comforting to know, when he was away and his very existence seemed tenuous and uncertain, that somewhere, on some plane or train, he was a passenger. His travels were controlled, and safeguarded, by little slips of paper — tickets, baggage checks, itineraries, confirmations of reservations, passports, visas and memoranda. Because a passenger, whether arriving or departing, was at least an entity, a being. Carson's ticket was checked now; his baggage weighed and tagged and they stood together in the terminal, in that suddenly embarrassed and uncertain pre-departure mood, talking, each not really listening to what the other was saying but waiting for the voice from the loudspeaker to signal that the passage was beginning.

"I wish — and I always say this — that I was going with you!" she said.

"So do I. Some time."

"Yes. Some time."

"Give my love to the farm if you go. To your Mother, your Dad. Peggy, Barney, the whole family."

"Yes, yes, I will," she said.

"Well, then —"

"Yes."

"I think I've thought of everything. I'll cable when I arrive."

"Yes."

"Well, then —"

And then the loudspeaker announcement came. Now loading at Gate Two. And they were hurrying, side by side, to the gate. At the gate he hurriedly kissed her and she said, "I love you! Write as often as you can!"

"I will," he said, "I will!"

And other hurrying passengers pushed behind him and he released her and started across the stretch of asphalt toward the plane. He turned to wave and she waved to him and blew him a kiss from her fingertips. He went up the steps and was gone. She waited a while at the gate with a few other people until the ramp was rolled away, the door closed, the propellers started, and the plane began slowly to move away. Then she turned and walked back out of the terminal to where he had parked the car.

When she got back to the house she found Nancy sitting, tailor-fashion on the green living room sofa, still wearing a borrowed pair of Barbara's white pajamas. She had a cigarette going, and in her hands she held a steaming cup of coffee from which she took little sips. "I wasn't a very good baby-sitter, I'm afraid," she said. "I let Dobie and Michael climb all over me in bed, and when they got tired of doing that I gave them my purse to play with. They had a marvelous time painting each other with my lipstick."

Barbara sat down wearily in the chair opposite her.

"Fortunately, your Flora showed up and took over, Nancy said.

"I'm exhausted," Barbara said. "I couldn't seem to get to sleep last night."

Nancy put her coffee cup in its saucer. "It's all my fault," she said. "I kept you up. I'm sorry."

"Oh, that's all right," Barbara said.

"Did Carson get his plane?"

"Yes."

"I'm sorry I got him mad at me last night. Honestly, I didn't mean to! I'm afraid I was a naughty little girl," she said, "but I'm paying for my sins this morning. I'm feeling — how did we use to say it? — a little leftover?"

"That's too bad."

"I'm sorry, I really am."

"Don't worry about it, Nance."

"Poor Carson, I —"

"He understood," Barbara said.

Flora came into the room with an envelope in her hand.

"I found this on the garbage can, Mrs. Greer," she said. "When I went out to empty the trash." She handed the envelope to Barbara.

"On the garbage can?" Barbara said.

"Stuck there with a little piece of Scotch tape."

Barbara looked at the envelope. On the front, printed in pencil, were the words, "Mrs. C. Greer." She tore it open.

The letter said:

> Mrs. Greer:
> All of us live in this neighborhood and we should all be as good neighbors as possible. From where your garbage can is placed it is in full view of five houses. It is a disgrace. It is always overflowing and very untidily kept. Let us be better neighbors and keep neatness in mind for the sake of other property owners.

The letter was unsigned. Barbara read it through again.

"Well, what *is* it?" Nancy asked.

She handed the letter to Nancy.

"Why, for heaven's sake!" Nancy exclaimed, reading it.

Barbara turned to Flora. "Somebody doesn't think we've been keeping our garbage can neat enough," she said. "How was it this morning?"

"Well, there was a couple of tin cans around," Flora said.

Barbara sighed. "Let's try to keep it neater," she said. And then, "I'm not blaming you, Flora. It's probably Mr. Greer's fault and mine as much as anybody's."

Flora went back toward the kitchen and Nancy returned the letter to Barbara. "Is that typical around here?" Nancy asked. "Anonymous notes and things?"

"This is the first anonymous note," Barbara said.

"Who could it be from? Do you have any idea?"

"As it says, it could be from any one of five people. What difference does it make?" She glanced at the letter again. Suddenly she was angry. She stood up. "How idiotic!" she said. She seized the letter and tore it down the center, then into smaller and smaller strips. She walked to the fireplace and tossed the bits of paper over the dead ashes. "Do you see why I hate this town?" she asked. "Imagine! An anonymous letter — *printed*, to disguise the handwriting!"

"It's incredible!" Nancy said.

"About a year ago, the Brysons, down the street, had a huge, horrible Collie named Lady. Everybody hated that dog — not only me. It used to come and yank Flora's sheets off the line and do its businesses all over our lawn. You couldn't go out the door without stepping into a pile of — well, anyway, somebody poisoned Lady. Helen Bryson *claimed* Lady was poisoned, anyway. Lady died, and Helen Bryson had the nerve to come over here and ask me if I'd done it! She said, 'I won't be able to sleep nights until I know whether it was you who killed my Lady!' "

"Incredible!" Nancy said again.

"Oh, we have a lovely, lovely group of neighbors!"

"How do you stand it, Barb?"

Barbara said nothing. She stood by the fireplace for a moment, gazing at the scraps of paper among the ashes. Then she returned to her chair. Dobie came running into the room. He was wearing a cowboy hat and a brace of pistols swung from his belt. "Can I go over to Jimmy's house?" he asked. "Can I, can I, can I?"

"Did Jimmy's mommy say you could?" Barbara asked.

"Yes," he said, nodding solemnly. He turned suddenly and pointed at Nancy. "Aunt Nancy let us put her lipstick all over our faces, like Indians!" he said. "Flora made us wash it all off. It hurt."

"It's naughty to play with lipstick," Barbara said.

"Aunt Nancy let us!"

"Well, run along to Jimmy's house," she said.

He raced out of the room.

"He's such a sweet little guy," Nancy said. "I couldn't resist letting them play with the lipstick. I'm sorry."

"Wait till you have children of your own," Barbara said. Then she bit her lip, remembering that Nancy could not have children of her own. "I mean —" she began.

Nancy laughed. "Well," she said. She picked up her coffee cup, took a sip, and set it down again. She stood up. "Well, I've got to be going," she said. "I've got a career to get back to — a wonderful, exciting career." She walked toward the door. She stopped. "You know," she said, "sometimes I don't think I want to be a nurse at all. Sometimes I think — I wonder what in the world I'm doing!" She went down the hall toward the guest room.

When she came out she was dressed as she had been the night before, her purse in her hand. "I made the bed," she said.

Barbara stood up. "Thank you, Nance."

"Thank *you*. Oh, Barb, it was a wonderful evening. Thank you for letting me stay. I hope I wasn't too — you know, idiotic. You're so wonderful for my morale."

They walked toward the front door. "Good-by, Flora!" Nancy called toward the kitchen door. "And thank you."

"Good-by, Miss Rafferty."

"She's a jewel," she whispered to Barbara. "You're lucky to have her."

At the front stairs they said good-by.

"Come up again soon," Barbara said. "You can boost *my* morale."

"I will," Nancy said. "And if you should happen to — to see or talk to Woody . . . well, there would be nothing to lose, would there?"

Barbara smiled. "I'll see what I can do," she said.

Nancy went down the steps to the driveway where her car was parked. Barbara waved good-by to her again and watched as Nancy started the car, backed out of the driveway, turned into Bayberry Lane and drove away.

Barbara went back into the house. Flora said, "Imagine that woman letting the boys paint themselves with her lipstick! What's she thinking of?"

"She has no children of her own," Barbara said.

"I'm going to take Michael with me to the market, in the stroller," Flora said. "We need a few things — butter, eggs, something for the boys' lunch . . ."

"Do you want me to take you in the car?" Barbara asked.

"Oh, it's a lovely day. Michael and me, we'll enjoy the walk," Flora said. "Walking's good exercise. The best you can do. My father walked two miles every day and lived to be eighty-eight."

"My grandfather lived to be eighty-eight, too," Barbara said.

"Quite a walker, was he?"

"I don't think so," Barbara said. "At least not that I can remember."

After Flora left, she was all alone. In the kitchen, she poured herself a cup of coffee and carried it into the living room. She sat down on the sofa. Sun streamed through the window, lighting dust motes that swirled in the air. From the kitchen the dishwasher groaned and entered the final phase of its automatic cycle. Then the house was silent. Barbara kicked off her shoes and brought her feet up beneath her on the sofa. She sat nestled comfortably against the pillows, sipping her coffee. When she had finished, she put the cup down and reached for a cigarette from the glass box on the coffee table. The silver lighter, after several tries, appeared to be out of fluid and she fished for matches in the pocket of her skirt. She found a pack and lighted her cigarette. On the coffee table there was a copy of *House & Garden*; she picked it up.

She smoked and read, and for a long time there was no sound at all in the room except the slow turning of her pages; no movement except for the smoke that rose, floated, and hung in the air. She read an article on how to turn an old foundation into a sunken garden, and then an article called "Color Magic," during which she imagined her own bedroom in a deep Chinese red with pure white raw silk drapes and flounces about the bed, more Chinese red in a slipper chair and a tufted toss pillow. It would look, she concluded, hideous; when they moved, when they had the kind of house she ultimately wanted, there would be nothing like this in it, nothing that looked phony or decorator-ish. She would select each color, each fabric, each piece of furniture with great care, but there would be no swags of raw silk, no lacquered chests, no Chinese red chairs or walls or pillows. Everything, she decided, would be very simple, very comfortable, very homey and warm. The square of sunlight from the window advanced across the room and a warm patch fell precisely where she would have asked it to — upon her stockinged feet. She moved into it until sunlight lay all along her leg. She heard, in the distance, a succession of automobile horns — a wedding, she decided. She let her magazine drop and closed her eyes. She dozed off.

She was wakened by the sound of the postman dropping letters into the slot beside the front door. She rubbed her eyes and stood up. She walked to the door without bothering to put on her shoes, picked up the letters that lay on the floor inside the door, and carried them back into the living room. She always looked forward to the morning mail, but today she could see at a glance that there was nothing of importance — nothing that was even worth opening: a letter from an insurance company, a seed catalogue, three bills from department stores, a free trial offer from a publisher of children's encyclopedias, a few business letters addressed to Carson. And looking through the letters she was reminded again of the letter Flora had found on the garbage can. How had it been put there? She pictured one of her neighbors — a woman, probably — tiptoeing stealthily across the back yards at night, ducking like a thief around the shadows of the low hedges that separated the houses. She went to the back window and looked out across the terrace. There were indeed five rooftops visible;

55

she counted them. She felt angry and ashamed. She turned away from the window and went to the desk, the letters still in her hand. She placed the bills in the cubbyhole where they belonged and tossed the rest of the mail in a drawer. She thought: I've got to get away from here for a few days! I simply do. She picked up the telephone and dialed.

"Operator?" she said. "I want to call Burketown, Connecticut, Buccaneer 3-7090." She gave the operator her own number and waited.

After a minute or two, she heard a man's voice answer, "Woodcock residence."

"Hello? John?"

"No," the voice said, "who is this?"

"This is Barbara. Who's this? Is this — ?"

"Oh, hi," he said, "this is Barney."

She began to laugh. "Do you *always* answer the phone that way? Woodcock residence?"

"Well, I happened to be standing beside it when it rang and I thought —"

"I'm sorry. It sounded funny, that's all. How are you? How's Peggy?"

"Fine, fine," he said. "Everybody's fine."

"Good. Is Mother there?"

"She and Peggy went to New Haven. Shopping."

"Oh," she said, "Well, I —"

"Your Dad's still in bed. Want me to call him?"

"No, no, don't bother him. I was just calling to — well, to see how everybody was. Carson left today, this morning, for England, and I was just wondering how everybody was."

"We're all fine," he said. "When are you coming up?"

"Well —" she said.

"Are you going to?"

"Well, I was thinking that perhaps —"

"Am I ever going to get those swimming lessons?" he asked her.

She laughed again. "Am I the only one who can give them to you?"

"You're the one I want to give them to me," he said.

"Well —"

"Seriously," his soft voice said, "will you come? There are a lot of things I want to tell you."

She hesitated. Then she said, "Please, Barney, don't talk like that. I thought we agreed —"

"Please come, Barbara," he said quietly. "Please come."

She stood, a little stiffly, holding the telephone against her ear. "I'll have to see if Flora can stay with the boys . . ."

"That's right," he said. "See if Flora can stay with the boys."

"All right. I'll call back when I've talked to her."

"Come tonight," he said.

"I'll call back. Good-by."

She replaced the receiver in its cradle and for a while stood looking absently out the window, across the five rooftops.

A little later when Flora returned with Michael, Barbara went into the kitchen and perched on the high stool. "Flora?" she asked. "I've been thinking that I might run up to Connecticut for a few days — to the farm, my family's place. Do you think you could come and stay for a few days?"

Flora gazed at the linoleum for a moment. "I've raised my rates for overnight, Mrs. Greer," she said at last. "I'm sorry, but I had to. I'm fourteen dollars now instead of twelve. It's what my sister gets. It's what they all get, Mrs. Greer."

"Well, I think that will be all right, Flora," Barbara said.

"When were you planning on going, Mrs. Greer?"

"If you can stay, I'll go this afternoon."

Flora considered this. "Yes," she said finally. "Sure. I'll stay, Mrs. Greer if you'll drive me home first so I can pick up some things."

"Oh, that's wonderful, Flora."

"How long do you plan to be gone, Mrs. Greer?"

"Just for the week end, I think."

"You get up there, you'll want to stay longer. You know that."

"I'll be back Monday. I'll be back Monday — or else I'll call you."

"You love that farm, don't you, Mrs. Greer? You love it because it's home. I know how you feel because my home is in Ohio. But I *live* in Pennsylvania. Your home is in Connecticut, but you live in Pennsylvania! Funny, isn't it? But did you know — here's an interesting thing: Pennsylvania and Connecticut have the same state flower! Did you know that? Did you?" Flora asked. "I'm a student of the state flowers," she said.

4

WE LIVE, AS WE ALL KNOW, IN A CIVILIZATION WHERE CERtain Christian names of women enjoy certain periods of vogue, then fall into disuse. Barbara Woodcock had been born in the age of Barbaras, Sandras, Patricias, Nancys and Lucys. There were — she had once counted them — twenty-three other Barbaras in her class at Vassar. Somewhat later came the age of Dianas and Carolyns and Susans, Lindas and Bettys and now, when a girl child is born, she is apt to be named Pamela or Deborah or Amanda or Rebecca. Who, nowadays, names a child Shirley or Ruth or Helen — or Barbara, or even Mary? Barbara's mother, on the other hand — Edith Woodcock — was born with other Ediths, Ruths, Marys, Loises and Louises. Who names a child Edith any more, or Gertrude or Mildred or Charlotte or Marian? Everything passes, including mastoid operations, of which Barbara had had three when she was a little girl, from which she still bore thin scars behind her ears. Who dresses their little girls as Barbara had been dressed, in white starched dresses imported from France, petticoats with Swiss embroidery, Mary Jane shoes? Who is taught to ride a horse the way Barbara had been, by first learning the precarious Italian seat? Who nowadays gives their child tennis lessons every summer, swimming lessons and French lessons? How many families gather on their lawns on summer evenings for croquet? Who has a room that is truly a "nursery," or has a governess to dress the little girls in their white frilly dresses, brush their hair and bring them downstairs to join their mother and her friends for tea? Even Edith Woodcock, perhaps, was an anachronism. Born in 1904 in a brick house on a hill in Providence, Rhode Island, the daughter of a college professor, she carried with her to Burketown, Connecticut, relics of the Victorianism which she had inherited from her own mother. In the nineteen twenties when other girls her age had been talking boldly of Freud and sex, experimenting with lipstick, cigarettes and whiskey, Edith had continued in a world of Thursday afternoons and calling cards in little envelopes placed on silver salvers. When she married Preston Woodcock, in 1925, she brought to him her excellent manners, her cultured speaking voice, her ability to handle servants, and a grand piano that had belonged to her mother, who had studied abroad under Paderewski. She brought with her other traits that her husband loved, such as her ability, always, to carry a fragrance about her, a smell of powders, colognes and sachets that established itself forever in her closets, her bathroom, and in her dresser drawers, where she kept such vestiges of an older time as rose petals tied in a linen handkerchief and an orange pomander pierced with hundreds of cloves.

It was in this — possibly old-fashioned, certainly mannered — atmosphere that Barbara Woodcock had grown up. She had been educated, as little girls in Providence had been, first by a private tutor and later at a girls' boarding school in Massachusetts. She made her debut, as little girls in Providence had done, at a tea dance under a marquee set up in the garden. She had broken with tradition somewhat by going to college (her mother saw no need for it), but when she married Carson Greer she had worn her mother's wedding dress with a train that ran exactly twenty feet behind her and she had carried a nosegay of pink rosebuds. To prepare her for marriage, Edith had given Barbara the same little book printed by the Episcopalian Church that her own mother had given to her. In it the responsibilities of a married woman were sketched in quaintly unspecific language. But this, to Barbara, did not present a problem because, while her parents remained somewhat fortressed within the past, she herself — away at school and college — had been able to observe the twentieth century as it matured around her.

Still, Barbara liked to think that she contained within herself fragments of each world. She could enjoy the brashness and noisiness of the "modern" life in which she moved, and yet she could respect the somewhat stately, ordered existence that her mother's world imposed. It was certainly not typical, she knew, of girls her age to harbor the feelings for her childhood home which she did; the farm, to her, evoked a true nostalgia — memories of ease and happiness and comfort. In this day and age, what girl longed as Barbara so often did, to go home again and let the waves of the past lap gently all about her? What other girl her age still grew moist-eyed reading *Black Beauty* or *Sentimental Tommy*? In an age of synthetics, she still loved silk velvets and brocades; in an age when elaboration was in disrepute, she still loved the carved plaster ceilings of the farm and the crystal prisms that hung from the chandeliers. Her tastes were unfashionable, she knew, but she was proud of them. To her, it seemed important that these loves be kept intact. They were a heritage which, one day, she would pass to her children. She thought about these things as she sped northward on the New Jersey Turnpike in the open car that afternoon — a pretty girl in a convertible speeding along a superhighway, heading from one of her two worlds toward the other.

Burketown, Connecticut was twenty-seven miles northwest of New Haven. Its Chamber of Commerce had named it "The City of Village Charm." It was a town that was smaller, actually, than

Locustville. Its population was just under twenty-five thousand and it was a town that, until recent years, had been supported by a single industry — paper manufacturing. There were three paper mills — Valley Paper, owned by the Harcourt family, Woodcock Paper, owned by the Woodcocks, and a third, smaller company called Burketown Paper Products Company. Burketown, as the name indicated, had been founded by a family named Burke. And though there were no longer any Burkes in Burketown, both the Woodcock and Harcourt family trees were liberally sprinkled with them. Although the Woodcocks were somewhat later comers to Burketown than the Harcourts (the first Preston Woodcock had migrated from Scotland as recently as 1830), they had managed to make their presence there more deeply felt; in the paper business the Woodcocks, it was generally agreed, had been more successful. Monuments to the family were in evidence everywhere. There was a street called Woodcock Avenue, and on Main Street the largest office building, where all the doctors' and dentists' offices were, was called the Woodcock Building. There was the Dobie C. Woodcock Memorial Library, named after Barbara's great-grandfather, and the Elizabeth Burke Woodcock Memorial High School, named after Barbara's great-aunt, Mrs. William Dobie Woodcock.

On a hill on the west side of the town, overlooking the valley of the Wampanauck River that originally had powered the mills, was a wide street called Prospect Avenue. Once it had been a street of lawns, canopied by elms — a street of gateways, flanked by rhododendrons and laurels, that opened to manicured driveways that led to porte-cocheres of houses with sharply peaked gables, turrets, tall chimneys and stained-glass windows. It was here, in the old days, that the best families of Burketown had lived, and it was in one of these gaunt old houses, at 700 Prospect Avenue, that Barbara Woodcock had been born. Even then, however, Burketown had begun its relentless commercial march westward; just two blocks to the east, a movie theater went up, then

61

next to it a drugstore, and next to that a dry-cleaning company. Now 700 Prospect Avenue was the Halcyon Rest Home and the house, one block north, that had belonged to Barbara's Great-Uncle William, had been razed to make room for an apartment building. Only one Woodcock remained on the street now, Barbara's grandmother, who still lived at the corner of Prospect Avenue and High Street, once the most fashionable corner in town, in the house to which her husband had brought her as a bride in 1890. She was ninety-three now, nearly blind, pushed to the high parlor windows in a wheel chair by her nurse or housekeeper once a day to get the sun. From these windows now there was a view of a Wayside Furniture store; at night, from the parlor windows that had once looked across most of the valley past the smoking chimneys of the Woodcock mills to the distant church steeple of Hanscomb Corners nine miles away, the old lady had a view that was, in its own way, cruelly ironic — a rocking chair drawn in neon tubing that rocked, mechanically, back and forth above a legend that read, YOU CAN'T BEAT WAYSIDE PRICES. It was a blessing, the family often said, that Grandfather Woodcock had not lived to see it, and that, for his widow, whose clouded eyes dreamed from her wheel chair by the window, the neon sign took on other, more comforting shapes — summer lightning, perhaps, or northern lights.

Earlier than most Prospect Avenue residents, Barbara's father had seen the inexorable coming of change. When Barbara was seven years old and Peggy was two, he had heard about a farm that was for sale in the country, ten miles outside Burketown. He bought it — it had been vacant for several years and was being sold for taxes — and moved the family there.

Barbara could hardly remember living on Prospect Avenue. If she happened to drive by the Halcyon Rest on her way to see her grandmother, it was hard for her to believe that this curiously shabby house had once been her home. Still, she had driven Barney there — that summer two years ago, a few days after she had first met him on the terrace, that summer during Carson's South American trip when she had come to the farm for a week end and stayed somewhat longer. She had slowed the car in front of the Halcyon Rest, "That's the house where Peggy and I were born," she said.

"Stop the car," he said.

"Why?"

"I want to walk around, I want to see it," he said.

"What on earth for?" she asked.

"Let's get out and walk," he said.

"There's no place to walk. We can't go in. All we can do is walk up and down the sidewalk."

"That's all right," he said, "that's all I want to do."

So she made a U-turn in Prospect Avenue and started back toward the Halcyon Rest. She stopped in front of it and they got out. They walked slowly along the sidewalk, looking at the house.

"I don't see why you want to look at this old place," she said. "It's depressing, actually. Let's go."

"No," he said, "it's interesting. Interesting. Wherever we live is part of our lives. This is part of yours and your family's. Do you blame me for wanting to understand it?"

"But it's depressing, Barney!" she said. "Please, let's go."

"Not yet, not yet," he said. He stood, arms folded, gazing at the old house with a shingled turret that rose above the crowded shrubbery. It was a long time before she could persuade him to get into the car again and drive back to the farm.

The main house at the farm had been built in the early nineteen twenties by a millionaire from New Haven as a summer place. He had evidently been a man of whims, for part of the house was built of stone, in a style that was close to, if not exactly, Tudor. Another part of it was built of white frame, in a Georgian style. The house had a complex of chimneys, most of which were not functional but ornamental, although the house did have seven

working fireplaces. All the windows were large and many-mul-
lioned and several of these, too, were false — imposed upon certain sections of exterior wall for decorative effect. The house
had been written up once in an architectural magazine that had
called it, "A conversation-piece house, sprawling and capricious,
full of surprises — còrners, cubbyholes, passageways and nooks."
The description was accurate. Rooms appeared unexpectedly off
narrow galleries; doors opened upon flights of steps that led to odd
little rooms that, because of their whimsical sizes and shapes, were
of no use to anyone except to children playing hide-and-seek. It
was a house that seemed to ask to be explored, that was built for
rainy afternoons.

The house had four living rooms strung together in a row. A
vase of flowers, placed before the mirror in the farthest room,
could be seen through a series of four identical archways from the
front hall. In one of these rooms, according to one story, the New
Haven millionaire had shot himself after the Crash in '29; a long,
jagged crack in the black marble mantel marked, supposedly, the
spot where his first bullet had gone astray. But there were at least
three other theories that were equally well supported. One, that
he had shot himself in his office in New Haven; another, that he
had done it in the garden behind the house and had been discovered by a faithful servant (the others had run off, like slaves
after Emancipation, when their wages were suddenly stopped)
lying in the basin of the fountain with the stone frog spewing
water over him; and a third — the one that the Woodcocks sub-
scribed to — that he had killed himself in the room of a cheap
hotel in New York. After his death, a rumor had sprung up that
the house was haunted. Ghostly lights were reported, seen on
winter nights, moving through the empty rooms. But the restless
shade of Mr. Harlow P. Lerner had never been glimpsed by the
Woodcocks — not even in the spot he frequented oftenest during
his days there, the greenhouse, where he had grown prize-winning
tuberous begonias.

It was Preston Woodcock's idea to turn the place into an operating farm. He had begun by tearing down one wing of the house and building a new wing in its place. With Edith's help on matters of interior decoration, he had modernized the whole house, added bathrooms, a gas furnace and insulation. Preston had built the other buildings, the barn, the stable and quarters above it, the playhouse for Barbara and Peggy, and the swimming pool. The property included a lake, and on one shore, Preston had built a dock and a boathouse. On the opposite side, he had built another dock and a three-room guest cottage. It had been Preston Woodcock's idea that for large houseparties some of his guests could have the fun of crossing the lake to their rooms by boat. For this purpose he had bought two small motorboats. But when the war came and the girls were away at school, and houseparties, large or small, were few, he had sold the boats. There remained, bottom-up on the shore, only an old canoe that had been Barbara's. "What are those words painted on it?" Barney had asked that summer, two years ago, when she had taken him down the hill to show him the lake.

"It's named the *Bobby-Boo*, I'm afraid," she had laughed.

"Bobby-Boo?" he had asked very seriously. "What does that mean?"

"When I was a little girl and used to sail boats in the bathtub, I called them Bobby-Boos — for Barbara's boats. Daddy remembered it and had it painted on the canoe. It's one of the troubles with having adoring parents."

"The *Bobby-Boo*," he repeated. "Shall we take her out?"

"I'm afraid she isn't seaworthy any more," Barbara said. "Her bottom's full of holes."

With his blue-sneakered toe he kicked, very gently, the side of the canoe; the canoe's side yielded even to this slight pressure for her boards were soft with rot and her green canvas covering was as brittle as old paper.

The trip from Locustville to Burketown took six hours by car;

she had left shortly after one o'clock, and considering that it was a summer Saturday afternoon, she made good time. As she turned the car into the road that led to the farm, she glanced at the clock on the dashboard. It was ten minutes of seven. The twisting road that led to the house was rutted and unpaved, kept that way to discourage sightseers. It had been six months since she had been to the farm last, and tonight — perhaps because she was driving fast, in a hurry to get home — the road seemed rougher than usual. But as it neared the house, rounded the last turn that brought the house into view, the road improved. It turned, at the end, into a wide, paved circle in front of the front door. She stopped the car, removed her sunglasses, and looked at her reflection in the rear-view mirror. She reached in her purse for lipstick and painted her lips. Then she pulled the scarf from her hair, letting it fall loose, and with her purse comb, she arranged it. She opened the door and stepped out of the car; carrying her overnight case, she went up the white marble steps to the front door. She did not ring the bell, but tried the handle; the door was unlocked. She opened it and let herself in, setting her suitcase down in the hall. To her eyes, blinded from driving the last twenty miles westward toward the declining sun, the hall seemed dim and shadowy.

From the library came the sound of music and she walked toward it, her heels clicking on the bare, polished oak floor. At the door to the library she stopped, looking into its deep, carpeted depths. It was a long room, its walls lined with bookcases. The furniture was dark, heavy and comfortable. Shafts of pale sunlight spread from the high windows, and in one corner of the room, a lamp was lighted, sending out its own soft yellow pool of light. In the opposite corner a bright pinprick of red light glowed from the control panel of the phonograph, where a record was playing. At first the room seemed empty, filled only with Vivaldi; then, from behind the curved back of the brown velvet sofa that faced into the room, away from her, concealing its occupant, a stream of blue cigarette smoke floated up. She walked to the sofa,

66

looked down, and the young man who lay on his back stretched full length upon it, smiled up at her. Then he slowly raised his arm in a high, stiffly exaggerated gesture of welcome. "Hail!" he said. "Behold! My beloved comes. Leaping upon the mountains, skipping upon the hills!" His voice was deep and theatrical.

"Hello, Woody," she said. She leaned across the sofa's back. He raised himself slightly on his elbows and she kissed him lightly on the cheek.

"Behold, thou art fair, my love. Thou hast dove's eyes," he said. He let himself back into the cushions, then suddenly raised a finger to his lips. "Sssh!" he said tensely. "Listen to this!" Violins, from the phonograph, came forward plaintively. "That passage undoes me," he said in a whisper, then he went limp, letting one arm trail to the floor.

She went around the sofa and sat down in one of the two armchairs, facing him. "How've you been, Woody?" she asked.

"Fine," he said, "can't complain." With his trailing hand he groped about the floor beside him, picked up an object that lay there. It was attached to a black wire that led somewhere under the sofa out of sight. "Take a look at this," he said. "Remote volume control." He turned a small dial and, immediately, the music diminished in the background. "Pretty tricky, eh?"

"It is," she said.

"I'm a sucker for gadgets," he said, dangling the control device by its wire and lowering it slowly to the floor again. "And how have you been?"

"Fine," she said, "just wonderful. Where is everybody?"

He looked at her with an expression of shocked surprise. "Where do you think?" he asked. "Preparing for your arrival, of course! My dear, you have no idea the commotion you have caused in this house today! Eleven o'clock — first bulletin: Barbara *may* come. Frantic excitement! Will she or won't she be able to get Flora to stay with her children! Tension! Wild speculation!

Eleven-fifteen — second bulletin: Barbara *is* coming! This afternoon! Bring on the minnesingers! Fill the house with flowers! Butcher the fatted calf! The prodigal daughter is returning!"

Barbara laughed weakly. "Oh, Woody!" she said. "You are a nut!"

He raised one eyebrow, pushed it upward, actually, with the tip of his finger. "I notice," he said, "that dear old Carson barely gets a chance to get off the ground and on his way somewhere before you take it on the lam yourself."

"Now you're being mean," she said.

"Well, anyway," he said, "you've caused untold chaos in this house. Do you realize —" he shook his finger at her "that the cocktail hour which always begins at six o'clock on the nose has been postponed a whole *hour* — just because of you?" He smiled at her.

"Good!" she said. "It will do you good to wait."

"Believe me, it hasn't been easy," he said. Moving only with his elbows he adjusted his position on the sofa.

It was true, as Nancy Rafferty had said, that — of the younger generation of Woodcock males — Woodcock deWinter was easily the handsomest. Though he was thirty, he looked younger, with smooth, fair skin and very blond, very curly hair.

Woody and his mother — Barbara's cousin Mary-Adams — did not get along. They were too much alike, people said. When he had reached his majority, after college, Woody had moved out of his parents' house and taken a bachelor apartment in town, which he had decorated in serene, pale colors and furnished with low, modern furniture. Periodically, Woody showed up at the farm, driving out in his small Italian sports car that was the color of black-raspberry sherbert — dressed rather extravagantly, as he was now, in a heavy hand-knit orange sweater and a pair of very slim, very tapered black trousers, black silk socks and black loafers — bringing with him when he came a stack of his favorite records. Preston and Edith Woodcock were fond of

68

Woody; he was one of the few Woodcocks, Preston often said, who didn't take himself too seriously, and Edith, who admitted that she would have liked to have had a son, often said Woody was exactly the sort of young man she would have wanted that son to be. When Woody dropped in, he didn't have to be entertained. He brought his own entertainment — his records. And if there happened to be some little chore to be done around the house, Woody was always cheerfully willing to do it. Five days a week, from nine to five, Woody worked for the Woodcock Paper Company; he worked hard and had been given the title of Advertising Director. Although he was not an artist, he had good taste and occasionally worked with the art department on designs for letter-papers. He was courteous and observant, quick to notice and remark upon any new, small detail of food, service or décor at the farm — to compliment Edith on a flower arrangement or a dress or choice of jewelry. "You're looking singularly gorgeous tonight, Mrs. W.," he would say. "You've done something different with your hair." And Edith, pleased, would exclaim, "Why, Woody, aren't you clever! I don't believe even Preston noticed it!"

He turned now to Barbara and said, "You look singularly gorgeous tonight, Mrs. Greer."

Barbara laughed. "Ah, Woody," she said, "are you still using that same old line?"

"I mean it," he said. "You look very pretty in this soft light."

"Because it hides the wrinkles," she said.

He rolled over on his side. "Tell me," he said, "where is dear old Carson off to this time?"

"London first," she said. "Then Paris, Zurich, Brussels and back to London. He'll be gone six weeks."

Woody sighed. "Lucky guy!" he said.

"Well," Barbara said, "I don't think Carson looks at it quite that way . . ."

"He'd rather stay in *Locustville,* you mean?"

"No, no, not that. But it's just part of his job. And he's pretty sick of traveling."

"Well, I wouldn't be," he said. "Never."

"Well, you're not Carson," she said.

"No, I'm not Carson. Carson is solid! Respectable!" He raised one orange-sweatered arm and shook his fist. "Carson is solid as — as the Prudential Life Insurance Company. Dear old Carson." He let his arm fall to his side.

"Please stop calling him dear old Carson," she said. "He's done very well and you know it."

"I know, I know," he said absently. He frowned and began to pluck invisible bits of lint from the front of his orange sweater.

"Woody," she said, "where *do* you get your clothes?"

He continued picking lint. "From here, from there," he said. "From the Spice Islands and Samoa, from lands that lie by torpid seas, where lovely ladies weave their lazy looms."

She smiled. "What is that a quote from?"

"A poem by Woodcock deWinter," he said. "The only poet who's been able to capture the rhythm and mystery of his age." He looked at her again. "Do you know what I did yesterday?" he asked her.

"What?"

"I *did* write a poem."

"Really?"

"Yes. Want to hear it?"

"Yes."

He lowered his voice. "My only love, my heart's design, I long to hold your hand in mine; my love is true, if true is thine, then won't you be my valentine?"

"What in the world — ?"

"Coming next spring — a new line of valentines by the Woodcock Paper Company. Very beautiful. They're going to be printed on scented paper, and do you know what they're going to be called? Can you guess? 'Sweet *Scent*iments' by Woodcock. Get it?"

"Oh, Woody, that's priceless!" she said.

"What's wrong with it?" he asked in mock anger. "Oh, God!" he said, striking his forehead with the heel of his palm. "You critics! Strangling a poet in the middle of his art!"

"Woody, you're wonderful," she said. "And speaking of sentiments — I've got a T.L. for you, as we used to say."

"What is it?"

"Do you remember Nancy Rafferty? Who was with me at Vassar?"

"Sure," he said. "Short, skinny —"

"Well," she said, interrupting him, "Nancy's living in Philadelphia now, going to nursing school —"

"Ye gods," he said. "Nursing school?"

"Yes, she wants to be a nurse. Anyway, she drove down last night. I'm slightly sore at her, by the way — she kept me up half the night — but anyway, she's a very dear, sweet person and she's always found you terribly attractive."

"Stop," he said. "I know what's coming next."

"What?"

"So — why don't I call her up the next time I'm in Philadelphia? Well, the answer to that's very simple — I'm never in Philadelphia."

"But she comes to New York from time to time, and —"

"Look," he said. Abruptly he sat up and swung his trousered legs over the side of the sofa. "Please, now, don't try to pair off your poor old cousin Woody with some female. Please don't be like Peggy."

"Why? What's Peggy done?"

"She's tried it. She brought some creature over here the other day. 'She'd be perfect for you, Woody,' she said. The creature's name was Betty Lou or Bonnie Mae, I can't remember. Dear little Peggy had the whole thing worked out. I think she'd even picked out the organist for the wedding. My God, little Peggy's gotten militant!"

"What do you mean?"

"I forget," he said. "You haven't been around here lately. Marriage is certainly changing our little Peggy. She marches around like a major general. Hup, two, three, four! Now, hear this! She's turned into a regular little organizer. She's got plans for everybody."

Barbara was puzzled. "What sort of plans?" she asked.

He sat back in the sofa and gazed upward at the ceiling. "Elaborate plans," he said. "Plans and schemes. But I think I've got it figured out. She plans to take over the company."

"Now, Woody!" Barbara said.

He leaned forward, suddenly serious. "I'm not kidding," he said. "I really, actually think that's what she wants to do. Not herself, of course, but Barney. She's got it figured out that Barney is going to be president of the paper company some day, and she's going to be the power behind the throne."

"Really?"

"I mean it. She's taken a sudden interest in the company. Quizzing your dad — quizzing Cousin Billy — quizzing me. Wanting to know this and that about the set-up of the company. Cousin Billy came into my office the other day and said, 'Woody, the funniest thing just happened. Peggy dropped into my office and wanted to look at some of our balance sheets.' Balance sheets! Ye gods, what's she want with balance sheets — unless —" He spread his hands in a wide, somewhat despairing gesture. "Well," he said, "maybe it's not a bad idea. Maybe Peggy and Barney ought to run the company. Under the circumstances."

"What do you mean, under the circumstances."

"Well, it's no secret, is it?" he asked. "All of us know it. Sales have been falling. Not fast, but bit by bit. A little bit each year. For some time now."

"I didn't know that," Barbara said quietly. It was strange. She had never thought, really, of the company, in terms of sales going either up or down. The company, in her mind, had always been *there*; permanent, steady, a feature of all their lives, nothing that was in any way subject to change — a family company, the place where most of the family worked. Even she, the summer of her freshman year at college, had worked at the company as a clerk in the accounting department.

"You watch Peggy while you're here," Woody said. "Listen to her. Notice the way she talks — the way when she says anything she turns to Barney, to get him to agree. Watch her. See if you don't think I'm right."

"Why, I think that's the strangest thing," she said.

"Why is it so strange? She's got a good candidate there, in Barney. Harvard Business School and everything. Remember before they were married, when they were still engaged?"

"Yes," she said.

"He didn't plan to work for the company then. He had another job all lined up, with General Mills or something. All of a sudden he changed his mind. Or Peggy changed it for him."

"I'm sure it was Barney's decision," she said.

"It's hard to say," he said. "Who knows? It's hard to say too much about Barney. Hard for me, anyway. He's — well, I see him every day and have almost since the day they were married. And I still don't know him very well. He imitates. Lord knows what I mean by that, but he does — he imitates. Of course," he said, "you probably know him better."

"What do you mean?" she asked. "Why should I — ?"

"Oh," he said, "you know — when he first came here, when they were engaged. You and he hit it off pretty well, didn't you?"

"Well — I always liked Barney. He always seemed — well, very nice. Perfect for Peggy."

"Yes," he said. "Perfect for Peggy." He stared absently at the backs of his hands.

73

"And what about Daddy?" she asked. "Does Daddy know anything about this?"

"I don't know that either. If he knows — if he knows he's in some funny kind of power battle with Peggy — he's reacting in a funny way." He laughed almost inaudibly.

"How?" she asked.

"He's writing a book."

"Oh, no!"

"Oh, yes!" He smiled at her. "He's writing a book about your grandfather."

"I can't believe it."

"Well, he is. And he doesn't know I know about it, so don't mention it to him. The other day we were in the board room and he asked me to step back into his office and get something out of his briefcase. I went back, opened the briefcase, and there was a wad of papers. A manuscript. I looked at the title page. It said, 'Preston Littell Woodcock the Second, The Biography of a Connecticut Industrialist.'"

After a moment, she said, "Now why in the world would he want to do that?"

"Again — who knows?" Suddenly, he clapped his hands together. "Hey," he said. "My God but we've gotten serious! This is supposed to be a night of levity and celebration!" He raised himself slightly on the sofa and from the pocket of his black trousers pulled out a heavy gold watch and flipped it open. "It's way after seven. Cocktails were specifically promised us at seven o'clock. So let's you and I have ours anyway. Shall we? He stood up and stretched his arms high above his head, yawning widely. "Shall we?"

"All right," she said.

"And don't look so worried!" he said. "Maybe your father just wants to write a book? What's wrong with that?" He started across the room. He had a graceful walk, forward, on the balls of his feet; he was an excellent dancer. He reached out as he passed and snapped off the phonograph completely. Just off the library, in one of the small, unexplained rooms that the house contained, Barbara's father had built a small bar with shelves for bottles and glasses, a built-in sink and refrigerator. Woody disappeared through this door and presently she heard him cracking open ice trays. "What'll it be?" he called.

"Anything," she said. "Whatever you're having."

"Scotch and water?"

"Yes, fine."

He came back, carrying a drink in each hand. He gave her one. "Now please?" he asked. "Can we forget mundane things like problems of the paper business?"

"All right," she said.

"Promise? Cross your heart?"

She smiled up at him. "Cross my heart."

"Good!" He touched his glass to hers. "To you!" he said. "Now — come with me to the piano, love, and I will play a song."

She rose and followed him to the piano bench, took a swallow of her drink, and put it down. He placed his fingers on the keys and began to play a series of soft, ruminative chords. "What shall it be?" he asked her, his long fingers musing on the keys. "Something, I think, infinitely sad! Something bittersweet, in keeping with our mood. Do you remember —" He played random chords, searching for a tune among them, his hands crossing and recrossing. He smiled broadly up at her, showing his astonishingly white and even teeth. "Remember the day we buried Fraulein Ungewitter?"

Though he was not an expert pianist — he played entirely by ear — he had an extravagant style, tinkly and sentimental, with elaborate use of the pedals. Then he started to play a tune that she knew. "Sing!" he commanded.

She took another sip of her drink, then leaned forward, resting her elbows on the closed top of the piano, and sang:

75

"I love you as I've never loved before —
Since first I met you on the village green.
Come to me e'er my dream of love is o'er;
I'll love you as I loved you
When you were sweet — when you were sweet sixteen!"

"And now once more —" he said.

She laughed and came around the piano behind him. She placed her hands on his orange-sweatered shoulders and began the song again.

She was really very fond of Woody. She had known him all her life. As children, in their games of pretending, they had always been a pair — mother and father, husband and wife, brother and sister, twins. He was even closer than a brother, and in some ways, closer than a husband or a father, closer than a twin. In an odd way, he reflected her, captured her image in himself somehow, and returned the image to her in his swift smiles. His shoulders rolled beneath her hands as he played, lifted his wrists, spread his fingers for the chords. She finished the song and he immediately began to play something else, something she did not know, but she continued to stand behind him, reluctant to do anything that would break the mood, disturb the reflection. Once they had had a miniature circus tent; painted on its inside walls were gaudy cages of lions, tigers, zebras, giraffes and little smiling monkeys. She remembered distinctly the hot and musty canvas smell on summer afternoons. In the tent he had solemnly told her, "I'm going to Africa some day." He had never gone to Africa, but perhaps there were places more bizarre than Africa where he had observed stranger curiosities, had more meaningful adventures — adventures she herself might have had if she had possessed his particular, flashy courage — the courage it took to wear an orange sweater.

Suddenly she remembered that, a few years ago, Woody had, indeed, had come close to death; the memory surprised her because she had trained herself to forget it, and the training, the effort, had been almost successful. Out of habit now, and training, she pushed the memory back where unhappy memories belonged.

A sound at the library door interrupted her thoughts. She turned and saw her mother standing, looking straight and slim in a pale blue cotton dress, her pure white hair piled high on her head, framed in the doorway. Her mother held out her arms. "My darling!" she said.

Barbara quickly crossed the room and took the outstretched hands her mother offered and kissed her on the cheek. She was surrounded, once more, with that familiar perfume of sachets, colognes and powders that her mother always wore about her.

"Darling!" Edith Woodcock said, "I'm so happy —"

"It's wonderful to be here, Mother!"

"How are my two little angels? Dobie and Michael?"

"Just fine, both wonderful."

"But it's good to get away from the children, isn't it? No matter how much you love them!"

They crossed the room, arms entwined, to the piano where Woody sat, still playing arpeggios. "Woody, dear," Edith said, "Don't *pound* so! I remember what my mother used to say. Treat the piano as though she were a beautiful lady — a beautiful lady who wants to sing! Play something pretty."

But Woody stopped altogether, dropped his hands in his lap. "Is it finally the cocktail hour?" he asked.

Edith Woodcock laughed a soft little laugh. "You seem to have begun it already, dear," she said. "But that's all right. Preston will be down in a minute and so will Peggy and Barney."

Woody stood up. "Are you going to let me come dressed like this?" he asked. He gestured toward his clothes.

"Of *course!*" Edith said. "It's just going to be the six of us. Very informal. I think we'll have our drinks in the garden and then come back into the house for our little dinner."

"Oh, I can't stay for dinner, Aunt Edith," he said.

"Why not, dear?"

"Well —" he began.

"You must," she said. "I want you to. I'm planning on it. I want all my little family together tonight — and you're one of them, Woody, you know that."

Barbara said, "Well, I must change. Or at least wash. I've been on the highway all afternoon."

"Well, hurry then, dear," her mother said. "Run upstairs. John has brought your bag up. We'll wait for you in the garden."

Cocktails were an evening ritual at the farm. When she came back downstairs a few minutes later and walked through the archways of the front rooms to the wide glass doors that opened into the garden, she could see that the ritual was beginning.

Her father was there now, with Woody and her mother. They sat on green-cushioned garden chairs. Though it was not yet dark, the garden candles had been lighted. A small, low table was placed beside her father's chair and John, the Negro houseman, wearing his white serving coat, had placed the heavy silver tray, holding decanters, glasses and a bowl of ice, on the little table.

Preston Woodcock measured and mixed each drink precisely, according to formulas based on individual preferences which he had long known. As he finished each drink he presented it to John, who waited at his side with a smaller silver tray. John then placed a linen cocktail napkin, folded, on the tray next to the glass and bore the tray, offering it with a barely perceptible, polite bow, to the person for whom Preston had concocted the drink. John served Edith first, then Woody. Then he placed within Preston Woodcock's easy reach the small silver pitcher that contained — prepared ahead of time and already chilled — Preston's special mixture of Martinis. Then he withdrew to a corner

78

of the garden, perhaps twenty feet away, and stood, waiting for his next order.

As Barbara paused just inside the door watching this faultless ceremony, watching it momentarily end, she saw her father now fill his own glass. He lifted it and she could see his mouth forming the customary words of salute — a toast that took in memories of identical cocktail hours in the past, and hopes for a continuance of cocktail hours in the future: "Here's to another pleasant evening for all of us." He smiled and the two others also smiled and lifted their glasses. Her father then sat back in his chair, crossing one pale trousered knee upon the other.

She thought suddenly, watching him, that her father looked a little tired. His face seemed somewhat haggard — older, perhaps, than when she had last seen him. He was four years older than her mother; he was fifty-seven. But ordinarily he managed to create about himself an atmosphere of youthfulness. His frame, his carriage and his step were still remarkably athletic. He had been captain of the track team at Yale and was a firm believer in regular exercise. In winter he played squash three times a week without fail and in summer played golf every Thursday and Saturday afternoon, and took a morning and an evening swim every day. As a result he concealed his age somewhat with a trim waistline and a healthy tan. He had the tan tonight but still there seemed to be a certain grayness and weariness in his face as she watched him reach for the silver pitcher and fill his glass. She opened the glass door and went down the steps. Seeing her, her father rose. "Hello, Daddy," she said, and when he kissed her and squeezed her shoulders tightly, his smile was so warm and cheerful that the illusion she had had a moment before, of old age, vanished completely.

"Baby!" he said. "It's great to see you. How're those two little boys? And Carson?"

"Just wonderful, Daddy."

"Off on one of his trips, I understand."

"Yes. Off on one of his trips."

"Well, if it gets you back home, I don't mind these trips," he said. "A light Scotch and water for you?"

"Yes, please, Daddy." She sat down in one of the chairs.

John greeted her when he brought her drink to her. "Good evening, Miss Barbara," he said softly.

"Hello, John. How have you been?"

He murmured a reply that she understood to be in the affirmative. John, whether by nature or as a result of eleven years of her mother's training, spoke in a voice that rarely rose above a whisper.

Her father smiled and raised his glass to her. "Welcome home, Barbara," he said.

Her mother turned to her and said, "Barbara, one of the first things I want you to do tomorrow is go and see your grandmother. Will you promise to do that, dear? It won't be an easy visit — I know that. The poor dear is so confused these days. I went to see her yesterday and she kept asking me where your grandfather was. He hadn't been home for *days,* she said. I didn't know what to say. I couldn't say he'd been dead for five years, so I said he was at the mill and would be home in a little while — thinking that would get her mind off it. Then she turned to me and said, 'No, he's dead.' What could I say then? I just sat there!"

"She telephoned the mill last week and asked to speak to him," Woody said. "Poor Betty at the switchboard didn't know what to do, so she gave the call to me."

"Really?" Preston asked. "You didn't tell me that, Woody."

"Didn't I, Uncle Pres? I guess I forgot. I meant to."

"Poor thing," Barbara said.

"She was ninety-three in April," Edith said. "Heaven spare me from living that long." She turned to her husband. "I know she's your mother, dear, and you love her, and I love her too! But ninety-three is too old — it's just too long for a person to live. I hate to say it. It sounds cruel, but it's true, don't you think?"

80

"Oh, I know you're right, Edith," he said. "The only thing I hope is — well, you know she sometimes tries to get out of her chair by herself. And I hope — all I hope is that Mother dies peacefully some night in her sleep — not in a fall or an accident."

"Well, let's not talk about that," Edith said quickly. And, to Barbara, she said, "I told her on the phone this afternoon that you were coming and she sounded delighted. She seemed perfectly clear about it. Sometimes she's perfectly clear! But if you get there and find that she doesn't know who you are, don't let it upset you, dear. Just say, 'I'm your granddaughter, Barbara,' very gently, and keep reminding her, filling her in on details."

"Oh, I know how to handle her, Mother," Barbara said.

"I'm sure you do."

Preston Woodcock reached for the little pitcher and slowly refilled his glass. Barbara, watching him, remembered what Nancy Rafferty had said the night before, about her father being a lush; but a nice lush. The remark had startled her at the time because she had never, that she could remember, seen her father drunk, or seen him show any of the outward signs of drunkenness. He drank, she had always thought, as much as other men drank. And of the couples she knew it was usually the men who seemed to drink, and enjoy drinking, more than the women. The informal rule at the farm had always been two, or at the most three, cocktails before dinner. Still, she realized now that her father, with his customary little pitcher and his habit of refilling his glass when it was only half empty, possibly drank more than three. But, she assured herself, even that did not make him a lush. He looked at her now and smiled. "Well," he said, "how's everything down in Locustville, baby?"

"Just the same," she said. "Nothing very exciting has happened. Busy with the children, of course, and —"

"Have you done any entertaining recently?" her mother asked.

"Nancy Rafferty stopped by yesterday," Barbara said. "I asked her to stay for dinner and spend the night."

"Oh, that's nice," Edith said. "I always liked Nancy. Such a sweet girl. Isn't it a pity she hasn't found a husband?" She lifted her wrist and turned the small gold watch that dangled among her bracelets. "It's getting late!" she said. "What on earth is keeping Peggy and Barney?"

"I heard them talking in their room as I went by," Preston said. "They'll probably be down in a minute."

Edith turned to John who stood politely waiting. "John?" she said. "Will you run up, please, and just tap on Peggy's door? Tell her we're waiting for them in the garden."

John started toward the house. Then Edith said, "Oh, here they come now."

Barbara looked up. Barney Callahan stood in the open doorway, the light at his back. John, who was halfway up the steps, stopped, and Barney came down the steps to meet him. They stood together for a brief moment — John saying something, Barney listening, nodding. Though she could not hear what John was saying, she imagined him whispering, "Mrs. Woodcock sent me to call you," because Barney now bowed slightly, acknowledging the message, and John also bowed. Barney's face was grave and, seeing this odd, rather courtly, little double bow — one man white-skinned and dark-suited, the other man dark-skinned and white-coated — the movement seemed like part of a cotillion figure, or a sharp, small vignette from a ballet. Barney turned, came down the steps, and as she sat forward, smiling, forming her lips to say hello, she saw that there was Peggy, whom she had not even noticed, right behind him.

5

ON A BRILLIANT AFTERNOON IN AUGUST OF THAT SUMMER two years ago, when Edith and Peggy Woodcock were in New York for a fitting of Peggy's wedding dress, Barbara and Barney Callahan sat together on the edge of the dock, looking across the motionless surface of the lake, and Barney said to her —

There are a lot of romantic stories about the poor little boy from the house in the village who falls in love with the beautiful girl who lives in the house on the hill. I suppose that's what you think about me wanting to marry Peggy. I'm sure it's what your mother thinks. Perhaps even Peggy thinks this, too. But my case is a little different. I wasn't born in Boston. I was born in Hancock, Massachusetts, which is a good distance away. If you don't know where Hancock is, it doesn't make any difference; it's a very small town and I hardly remember it. We moved from Hancock to Boston in 1936, when I was seven years old. I don't remember anything about the trip except that the car was a DeSoto and I got carsick about every twenty miles.

There were five of us then, including my mother and father. Later on, there were six. I have one brother and two sisters. I am the oldest. Not quite enough children, I suppose, to qualify us as a good Catholic family. But it was a good-sized family just the same. My father owns a drugstore which he inherited from an uncle — this was why we left Hancock, dreaming of an inheritance and a life of ease! But my father is not a pharmacist, which is probably why the drugstore has never made as much money for him as it made for his uncle. There's nothing my father can do with the store but rent it to a druggist. Most of the time, my father stays home. He's never been well. What it is, I'm sure, is just hypochondria.

He's one of those men who's had twenty-seven doctors give up on him. They can't find anything wrong with him, but that doesn't make his ailments any less real — to him. He's done a lot of different things. He has made money at some of them. He had an oil burner service, once, that made money. He owned a restaurant once, too, and made money. But during the depression he didn't make much money at anything he tried, and he tried a lot of things. Something has always gone wrong with every job he's ever had. If he was working for someone else, he'd get mad at his boss and quit, or if he was working for himself, he'd get discouraged and lose interest, or else get sick and not be able to carry on.

He made a significant remark to me once. He said, "It's funny, whenever I start making good money at a job, I get scared." This is why it's probably just as well that he doesn't do anything any more but stay at home and collect a monthly rent check — most of which must go to pay doctors' bills. Doctors have charged him thousands of dollars for telling him that he's perfectly healthy. From all this you may gather that I don't have much use for my father, and you're right. I don't. But anyway, my father is not the interesting one. The interesting one is my mother.

My mother is an artist, a painter. She has painted hundreds and hundreds of pictures. Her canvases are all over the house, either hanging or stacked away in closets. I don't know much about art myself, but some of her pictures seem very good to me. I once asked her why she didn't show them, or try to sell them, but she said no, she didn't think they were good enough and — besides — she didn't paint pictures to sell; she painted them for her own personal enjoyment, for the sense of fulfillment that a finished picture gave her.

But there is something essentially wrong with the pictures my mother paints. It is probably because they reflect her personal point of view too strongly, and her personal point of view is a curious one. She is an extremely religious woman, but it is an odd, old-fashioned and rather stubborn religiosity. She is a Catholic because she was born a Catholic and she has never seen any reason to question her faith beyond this point. She is not at all an intellectual Catholic, as many Catholics are. Her Catholicism is completely mindless and emotional. She has never tried to understand — I truly think — Catholicism at all. She accepts its teachings at face value. The Church says so, therefore that is the way it is. There is nothing more to it. This has always struck me as a strange point of view for an artist to have. But then, everything about my mother is contradictory.

In a church, I think, she might as well be in a jungle. What goes on there affects her deeply and emotionally, stirs her the way kneeling in the center of a jungle full of wild, terrifying noises would stir a person. The Church affects her heart, not her mind. She will kneel for hours in a church with her beads, transfixed, with angel choirs singing to her and saints smiling down upon her, with tears streaming down her face, beseeching the Blessed Virgin for something. For what? She would not be able to tell you in exact words. Beauty. Happiness. Purpose. Saintliness! She is a very romantic person, a sentimental Catholic. She talks a great deal about the Eternal Verities and her paintings reflect her search for these. A wistful picture of rain falling on a flower garden, which she calls "Benediction." She paints cathedrals she recalls from childhood, the Shrine at Lourdes — which she has never seen, scenes of mountains, pastures, forests, saints' faces with tearful smiles that look much like her own. She paints birds building nests, little children kneeling in shafts of sunlight, and also symbolic pictures — Truth, glittering like a sword in the shadows, Honor bursting like a flower from the rubble of the world, Virtue lifting her lovely head from a wallow of seaminess, souls rising at the sound of the Last Trump, the human spirit winding its arduous way toward God, Daybreak at Eden — a

85

confusion of styles and thoughts and images. Nothing so prosaic as the Stations of the Cross! But everything she does reflects her own personal, human, sentimental and nostalgic view of herself, life, and the after-life. To hear her talk, you would think that Good and Evil exist in strict terms of black and white to her — virtue and sin. But oddly enough, as she has lived her life, they have become all mixed up. Anyway, she brought me up that way. Like a beacon in the night, so shone my mother in a naughty world.

Of the three other children besides myself, only my younger brother, Jerry, I think, has any promise. He is three years younger than I am and we have always been quite close. Jerry has a lot of grit, by which I mean he has determination and courage. I've never once seen Jerry cry. He's a little guy, almost a head shorter than I am, and when he was a kid playing baseball in a back lot or playing football, the bigger kids used to trample all over him, but he never cried. He's a knobby little guy and he used to want to be a ballplayer. His dream was to play for the Red Sox. But his size was always against him and now he's working his way through Law School, working very hard. I think he'll be a great lawyer someday, but the only thing is, he's got to break away from home sometime, from my father and mother, as I've done. Sooner or later, he must do this.

There is only one other person who affects my family and who is important to know about. That is Father Timmons, my mother's priest. I say my mother's priest because I suppose it is common for someone like my mother to have her own, special priest. If I were picking priests for my mother, I would not have picked Father Timmons. I have known many priests in my life who impressed me as sincere, decent, intelligent men — even godly men. But Father Timmons is not this sort. He is a fat little man who smokes cigars — huge cigars. And I think I could even forgive him being ignorant and bigoted — stupid, really, is what he is — if he were not pompous. He struts. He pontificates. He lectures.

86

He thinks of himself as being very kind and beatific — my mother was forever reminding all of us how kind Father Timmons was to us — but his kindness always emerged seeming rather oily and patronizing. He was always patting us on the head, linking arms with us, as he lectured to us. But somewhere along the line he came to fill a gap in my mother's life, to mean more, perhaps, to her than any one else in the family. It began, I think, with her pictures. Though I'm sure he didn't understand them, he praised them — and encouraged her to paint more. She began to have — and perhaps she had it before she met him; I don't know — an idea for a picture. It would be her great, her final work. And it would be her interpretation of the ecstasy of Saint Theresa. She told Father Timmons about it, and he approved. The two of them would sit on the sofa, evening after evening, discussing it, sipping sherry which Father Timmons sometimes brought, while they listened to the radio or to records on the wind-up Victrola. It was queer, listening to them talk about Saint Theresa with "Oh, Susannah" playing in the background. She had not attempted to begin the picture. "I'm still not quite ready for it, Father," she would say. "But I feel that I'm constantly getting closer to it." It was her conscience, she said, that troubled her the most. After all, who was she to think that she could express on a square of canvas something that the poets and mystics of the Church had been trying to get clear in their minds for centuries? And Father Timmons, of course, told her not to begin the picture until she was sure, absolutely sure, until the idea was clear as crystal, like a vision before her. Then she would bring out one of her other paintings and show it to him, and they would discuss it. He would congratulate her on her use of color, on an effect of sunlight that she managed to get across the waves, or glinting on a barn roof. "I just dabbed a bit of white *there,* and there it was," she would say. "A complete accident." And Father Timmons would carefully explain to her that it was not an accident. He convinced her, I am sure, that at her easel a divine hand was guiding her own.

He began to convince her that she, too, might be a mystic.

Then, on these evenings, with my father sick in bed, they'd talk about her children and she would call for us. We would all troop in and sit around, listening to Father Timmons's wisdom. If there were bad marks at school, he would have heard about them from the Sisters, and he would lecture to us about the virtues of studiousness and endeavor and, eventually, we would all kneel and listen while Father Timmons thanked the angels and all the saints and the Blessed Virgin for such bounties as life bestowed, and for life's suffering, too. At the end of these prayers, Mother would stand up and — with a wide gesture of her arms that included all her children — say, "Children, the Holy Mother and Father Timmons are more of a mother and father to you than your earthly parents!" And she believed this.

One summer when I was sixteen we rented a house at the shore, at Marblehead, for two weeks. Perhaps it was Father Timmons himself who rented the house. I don't know, but anyway we all drove down with him in his new car, except for my father, who stayed behind in Boston. It was a big old ramshackle house with a damp stone cellar with stone steps leading down, and a garden full of rambler roses in the back yard. Father Timmons left us there, but then he came back to visit. I thought I was very sophisticated in those days; I was sixteen. But it was my brother Jerry who first noticed that something was wrong, that something was different, that my mother's relationship with Father Timmons was no longer that of parishioner with priest. He mentioned it to me. It was nothing that he had actually seen. It was just a feeling, an uneasiness, something in their behavior that confused him and worried him. Perhaps the idea came to him in a vision! Anyway, he told me and at first I was only terribly frightened. I can remember only being suddenly almost sick with fear. I saw all of us struck instantly by a lightning bolt from heaven, then wandering forever through purgatory. Then I told him that it couldn't be true, to forget about it. But of course I couldn't forget about it and neither could he. Because we were watching, now, we began to notice things — the looks he gave her, the way, on the porch glider as they sat together, he would squeeze her hand — the ashes from his cigar in parts of the house where they had no business being. But Mother seemed so blissful and happy it was hard for us to believe that she was engaged in committing a mortal sin. Adultery — and with a priest.

It was Jerry, then, who wrote to my father. He told me, after he had sent the letter so there was nothing I could do. My father came and there was a terrible scene — terrible to me because everybody was weeping. My mother, my father, Father Timmons — everyone wept. Even I wept, though Jerry did not, because he never cried. I went out alone to the beach and thought. I thought: What if there has been a terrible injustice done? What if none of it is true? So I went back to the house, determined to ask my mother. The house seemed empty. I hunted upstairs and downstairs for her, everywhere, and then I found her. She was sitting on a little stool in the cellar, painting. Her face was clear. She was even smiling and in the light from the cellar window she did appear to be bathed in some sort of holy radiance. She seemed to be in a trance and I thought at once of Saint Theresa. In some mad way, my mother *was* Saint Theresa, and she had had her ecstasy. I looked at the picture she was painting. It was all sunshine with yellows and reds and big, golden jonquils, and in every corner of the canvas, strewn all over that sunlike design, were human forms, people scattered about like flowers in a park after May Day. There was no saint there. I made her put down the brushes and come with me upstairs and out into the garden where the sun was so hot it was visibly blistering and flaking the paint off the Adirondack chairs, and the heat haze was so thick and bright that we had to shield our eyes to see each others' faces clearly. I sat her down. I looked at her and asked her, "Is it true?" And she looked straight up at me, her eyes enormous, and answered, "Yes."

After that, I left home. I got a job and lived in a series of crazy rooming houses. I went back, from time to time, but only to see Jerry and I never stayed long. I lived like that for a year, then I decided to finish high school — I still had one more year — so I got a different job, working at nights, and went back to school. I decided I wanted to go to college, and so I did. I entered B.U., still living the same way, working nights at whatever job I could get, studying whenever I could. And then I went into the Army and went to Korea. I didn't even find God again in Korea, the way I have heard one is supposed to do. Perhaps it was because I had lost Him too thoroughly. Or perhaps I was more frightened of finding God again than of being killed.

When I got out of the Army I decided that the thing I needed to learn was how to make money, and it seemed to me that Business School was the place to do it. So I went to Harvard. Last year I met Peggy with a group of other Wellesley girls, at a party at the Business School. We started going out together. She was different from the other girls I'd known — not pretty, really, not as pretty as you are — but different. Bright and attractive and sensible. We discussed our different backgrounds. She told me that she came from a prominent, well-to-do family in Connecticut, that she would be a wealthy woman some day. We talked and I told her everything — what I've just told you — and we agreed, together, to get married. It wouldn't be true to say that I'm marrying her *for* her money. But it is true to say that Peggy's money is going to be very important to us. You cannot serve God and Mammon, I understand. Well, since I can't serve God, I'm going to serve Mammon. If Peggy has money, then I intend to serve it, and serve it as well as I can. I'll devote myself to it the way another man might devote himself to God. I asked Peggy if this made sense. She told me yes it did.

After he finished they sat quietly for a long time at the edge of the dock, on the little wooden pier. Then Barbara said, "You're very honest. Thank you for being honest."

He laughed bitterly. "Honest!" he said. "Yes, perhaps that's one thing you can say for me — that I'm honest."

"No," she insisted, "I admire honest people!"

And he stared across the still water of the lake for a long time. Then he said, "But there are other things — almost as important."

"What things?" she asked.

"There's a certain manner," he said.

"What?"

"There's a certain manner, a way of doing things, that I want to learn."

"I don't understand."

"It's hard to explain," he said. "But there's something, a manner, that I was never taught and I need to learn it now. It's something you know already, because you were taught it. You grew up with it and got it that way. I didn't, that's all."

"I think you have lovely manners," she said, laughing.

"I'm not talking about *manners*," he said and his voice was cross. "I'm talking about — well, about things like this." He leaned his head toward her. "Smell my hair," he said.

"Why?"

"Just go ahead, smell my hair . . ."

She sniffed his dark head; it smelled warmly of pine and, possibly, lemon. "Very nice," she said. She smiled at him, puzzled and amused.

But his face was serious. "Cologne," he said. "I poured it on my head without thinking — by mistake. Do you see what I mean? I used to think that it was — you know, very correct — in very good taste — to pour cologne on my head! So I bought this cologne — bay rum, in a fancy bottle. But just the other day I found out that it *isn't* good taste — it's something only fops do! But this morning I did it again, out of habit. You see — I've got so many crazy and wrong ideas to get out of my head. And there are so many things I've got to learn."

"Are things like that really so important to you?" she asked him.

"Of course they are. They're important to anyone who doesn't have them. The word for what I'm talking about is *poise*."

"But I think you have a great deal of poise."

"I don't, not really. I'm trying to learn it by watching people."

"What people?"

"People like your mother and father," he said. He looked at her. "Why am I telling you all this?" he asked.

"I'm rather glad you are," she said.

"Well, it's important to me — very important now. I want, you see, to be inconspicuous among people like — well, like your family. I want to be unobtrusive, not to be noticed. I don't want to stand out. That's what poise is."

"You're a funny boy," she said. "That's not what I would say poise was. Not at all."

"I know," he said, "it's not the same thing for you. I know that. But to me — well, to me it's like a Persian cat. Have you ever noticed the way a Persian cat goes from room to room? He goes so quietly no one really sees him come and go, but every move is made with dignity. And grace. That's the way I want to be. . . ."

Then he said, "You see — at Harvard — I met boys who knew exactly what they wanted to be like — they wanted to be like their fathers. In fact, things were so certain for them that they didn't even have to worry about what they *wanted* to be like! They *would* be like their fathers, that's all. But I'm different, because I don't want to be like my father. I'd rather be like yours."

They sat silently for a while. A breeze ruffled the lake and the hot sun beat down upon them. Finally Barney said, "I suppose Peggy and your mother will be getting home soon."

"Yes."

They stood up. Suddenly, almost impulsively, he reached for her hands. "You know," he said, "you're very nice. I like you very much. You're very nice." And then he kissed her. It was a strange kiss, a quick touch of her cheek with his mouth, but it startled her because of its swiftness and strength.

Immediately he said, "I'm sorry I did that. Forgive me."

So she laughed lightly and said, "Of course."

6

DRIVING FAST UNDER THE TREES, WOODY ASKED HER, "WHAT are you thinking about?"

Though she was not, she said, "I'm thinking about what will happen if there's another war, how awful it will be."

"Ah . . ." he said. "Why are you thinking about that on a beautiful summer night?"

Because the answer to his first question had been a lie, this one was more difficult. She dodged it. "I'm thinking about a lot of things," she said. She felt him look at her briefly, then fix his eyes on the road again. They sped along, in Woody's raspberry-colored car, toward Burketown. The night had grown cold and she hugged her elbows against her sides. The wind whipped around her, over the low windshield. Woody had turned up the turtle collar of his orange sweater and had put on a jaunty, black suède snap-brim cap. She was very tired. She had not actually wanted to come with him. But after dinner he had started telling her about his apartment. He had redecorated it since she had seen it last, he told her, and it looked its best at night. He begged her to let him show it to her. Her opinion of it, he insisted, was essential, so she had said yes, though it was nearly midnight.

"Cold?" he asked her.

"No, no," she lied again.

"Tell me," he said, "What are you really thinking about?" She hesitated. "Do you suppose they're happy?" she asked him.

"Who?"

"Peggy and Barney."

"Oh, I suppose so," he said.

"Why do you suppose so?"

"Because it seems to me that if Peggy happened to think that being happy was a necessary part of being married, she'd insist on it. She's that kind of girl."

"You're rather down on Peggy these days, aren't you, Woody?" she asked. "Don't you like her?"

She looked at him and he was smiling slightly. "I never cared for militant women," he said. "Besides, of the Woodcock girls, you were always my favorite."

They drove on in silence. She thought of Peggy's small, brown, intense face — a round, snub face, framed in a circle of short, smooth, dark brown hair. Her eyes were wide and dark and earnest. They had been sitting at opposite ends of Peggy's big bed one night that summer when Peggy had first told her that she was determined to marry Barney. "Of course they disapprove!" Peggy had said. "Of course. I was prepared for it. But I'm twenty-three years old. I'm a free agent. They can disapprove all they want, but they can't stop me! I'll listen to all their arguments — let them lecture me on how *unwise* it is, how oil and water won't mix! I'll listen to them — but it won't make any difference. I'll go along with them — up to a point. Beyond that point, I draw the line." And, with her lacquered fingernail, she drew a swift, sharp line across the surface of the bedspread in demonstration. "Barney is a leader," she said, "a leader! A champion — that kind of leader. Everything he's done, he's done for himself. He can do anything he sets out to do. Whatever he begins, he'll finish — and

94

right at the top! Because that's the kind of person Barney is. A *leader*."

They were coming into Burketown now and Woody slowed the car.

Woody's apartment was on Main Street, over the Burketown First National Bank. Woody loved to make jokes about his address. "I'm thinking of cutting a trap door through my floor down to the bank," he said once. "In fact, I told old Mr. Willard, the treasurer, about it and he was quite startled. Startled is hardly the word. For a minute I thought he was going to give up the ghost then and there, right at his desk. Then he cleared his throat and said, 'I don't think we could permit that, Woodcock!' So I told him that my plan didn't involve asking permission — that if I did it I'd do it in the dead of night with a trusted accomplice. The poor old soul got even more startled. Then he explained, very carefully, that my plan was 'not feasible.' It would set off, he told me, all sorts of burglar alarms. I told him I'd taken all that into consideration — I'd figured out a way to cut the wires. Poor Mr. Willard — he still gives me funny looks whenever I come into the bank."

He drew the car up, now, in front of the bank and stopped. "Good old Burketown First National," he said. "It gives me a cozy feeling, going to sleep at night, thinking of all George P. Willard's money down there, right underneath me."

They got out of the car and entered the building by a side door that led up a flight of stairs. She followed him. At the top, he produced a key and unlocked his door. She waited while he groped for the light switch.

Originally, the apartment had contained four small rooms. When he moved in, Woody had gotten permission to knock down the partitions and now the apartment consisted of one enormous room. He turned on the lights — two lamps that hung, suspended from the ceiling by thin wires, in plastic bubble shades, and two small spotlights, concealed in two corners of the room, that were arranged so that their beams merged, precisely, upon a Jackson Pollock print that hung against one wall. She immediately saw that, with the exception of the picture and the arrangement of lights, he had, indeed, changed everything. When she had last seen the apartment, its walls had been stark, flat white. Now they were covered in pale, golden burlap. Between the two tall windows at the end of the room hung an assortment of primitive African masks; in the mouth of one of these, Woody had whimsically placed an antique meerschaum pipe, that dangled from the mask's lips at a rakish angle. Even much of the furniture was new. Gone were the low, delicate modern pieces on slender brass legs. Instead, in the center of the room, set in a square, was an arrangement of three wide sofas covered in a heavy Harris tweed. In the center of this square, facing her, its mouth opened wide in a savage snarl, was an immense polar bear rug.

"Well, what do you think of it?" Woody asked her.

"Fantastic!" she said.

He moved around the room, showing her the cabinets that opened with sliding doors, revealing bookcases, the components of his high-fidelity phonograph, and his collection of records. Closets, too, were concealed behind sliding doors and he opened these, showing her where his suits were neatly hung, row upon row, and the racks that held his shoes, the narrow drawers that contained his neatly folded shirts, arranged according to color.

"You're a wonderful housekeeper, Woody," she said.

"But do you *like* it?" he asked, closing the doors and turning to the room again.

"Oh, I do, I do!"

"It's a new me," he said half-seriously. "I expect a whole new personality to emerge. I'm through with all that effete, modern stuff. This is to be my explorer personality. See the shrunken head?" He pointed to the shriveled head that hung, from a knot of black hair, on a wooden peg.

"Where in the world did you get that?"

"Same taxidermist that sold me the polar bear. He *assured* me, however, that it was not his own handiwork."

She shivered. "It's ghastly," she said.

"Do you think so? I think it's rather charming."

"Oh, Woody!" she said. "I approve of everything else. But not that head."

"Let me fix you a nightcap," he said cheerfully.

"Oh, I really must get back. It's terribly late."

"Just a short one."

"All right," she said. "Very short."

He went to the corner of the room where his kitchen was, and removed an ice tray from the wall refrigerator. Barbara sat down in one of the deep, tweed sofas, burying her shoes in the polar bear's white fur. "It's a little like a movie set," she said.

"Is that an insult or a compliment?" he asked her. He crossed the room carrying two drinks in short glasses. He gave her one and sank down beside her on the sofa.

"No, I like it very much," she said. "Except for that one detail."

"The head? Well, do you remember when your grandmother went through that spiritualism business and was all mixed up with communicating with the other world?"

"Yes," she said, "years ago."

"Well, she used to have what she called a control. The guy she got her messages *through*, or something. And the control was some old Indian — he had a name, too, but I've forgotten what it was. Anyway, I've got a theory —" he pointed, "that your grandmother's Indian and my Indian are one and the same guy!"

She laughed. "Of *course!*" she said.

He touched his glass to hers. "Cheers!" he said. "And may fair fortune continue to smile upon your lovely face." He took a swallow of his drink and then sat back, pushing his shoulders deep into the sofa cushions. He sighed.

"It was a nice evening tonight, didn't you think?" Barbara asked.

He stared straight ahead. "Yes," he said. And then, suddenly, "Do you think he's a conniver?"

"Who?"

"Barney."

"Why do you ask that?"

"I don't understand it. I don't quite know what's going on. Did you watch them tonight?"

"They seemed perfectly normal to me."

"Did you hear Peggy after dinner — talking to your father?"

She said, "I saw Peggy talking to Daddy, yes. I didn't hear what they talked about."

He laughed, then frowned quickly and stared into his glass. "Stock," he said. "They were talking about paper company stock. From the way she talked, I got the idea she wants to buy some more."

Barbara hesitated. "Well," she said slowly, "of course Peggy and I both own a little stock. And, I suppose, if Peggy wants some more — well, why shouldn't she buy some more?"

He turned and looked at her intently. "But why?" he asked. "*Why* does she want more stock? Unless it's for the reason I mentioned before. And whose idea is it — hers or Barney's? Do you think he's put her up to it — because the stock isn't available to him? Who is running that little ménage, I wonder?"

"Well," she said, "it really doesn't sound so — mysterious or sinister to me. Perhaps they're planning on having a baby or something and they're sort of trying to set things up."

"I don't know," he said. "I just don't know. She's certainly been different since she married him. And he — well, he's a complete enigma. At the mill everybody loves him. He's very polite, co-operative — works hard. And yet there's something about him — I don't know. It's as though, when you talk to him, he pulls a little curtain down between you — like a scrim. You can see

98

part of him through the scrim, but not all. Have you noticed that?"

She glanced quickly at her wrist watch. It was twenty minutes of one. "Not really, no," she said.

He was still looking at her. "Of course," he said, "I wouldn't be surprised if you knew Barney better than anybody else in the family. With the exception of Peggy. He always liked you. He still does."

She smiled at him. "Woody," she said, "I think you're making mountains of molehills, I really do. I'm sure there's nothing —"

"But you did, didn't you? Get to know him quite well, I mean? That summer you were both here — before he and Peggy got married?"

"Well, we talked, of course and —"

"And he does like you. I can tell. Tonight, for instance, I noticed that whenever he had anything to say — even if he was saying it to somebody else — he seemed to be saying it to you."

"It's just my fatal charm," she said.

"I'm quite serious. I think — I thought tonight — that probably if you hadn't been married already, he would have wanted to marry you — not Peggy."

"Really, Woody," she said, "that's pretty silly." She put down her glass. "It's getting terribly late. I really must get home."

He didn't move. "You know," he said, "we've never met any of his family? There's a brother he talks about sometimes — but he's never shown up around here. His father and mother didn't come to the wedding. They've never come down. Don't you think that's a little strange?"

She remembered, once, asking him whether his mother and father would be at the wedding. He had said no, and when she asked him why not, he had answered, simply, "Because I'm ashamed of them." But now, to Woody, she said, "Don't forget, Woody, that Barney made a very big decision once — to leave the Church. There was undoubtedly family feeling there — there probably still is. I don't think there's anything particularly *wrong* with a young man who wants to build his own life, break away from his parents. I understand his childhood wasn't particularly happy — and I frankly admire that quality in Barney. He wants to carve his own niche. I think he's a very honest, straightforward and sincere person. I don't think he has any ulterior motives — or guile — or whatever you want to call it. I think he's — well, just what he seems to be. A nice, normal, sensible person. And as far as Peggy goes — perhaps she is ambitious for him. It's natural for a wife to be ambitious for her husband."

He took a swallow of his drink, then slowly began to smile at her. "Then why," he asked, "a few minutes ago, in the car, did you ask me if I thought they were happy?"

Suddenly she was a little angry. "Peggy happens to be my sister," she said, "and I don't think it's strange for me to hope that my sister's happy!"

"Hope. Yes, hope, you *hope* so. You're not sure."

"Woody, it's very late and we're talking in circles. Please take me home. I'm very tired."

"I'm sorry, Cousin," he said softly. I didn't mean to make you mad. It's just that I think you and I are both worried about them. Perhaps we ought to both admit that we're worried."

She stood up. "I'm worried about getting some sleep," she said.

He still sat, looking up at her from the sofa. "I'm sorry, Barb. I really am. Let's not squabble. You and I don't like it when we squabble."

She smiled. "All right," she said. "I'm sorry, too." She held out her hand to him. "Come. Drive me back to the farm like a good boy."

He took her outstretched hand and held it. "Beautiful Barbara Woodcock," he said. He gazed at her admiringly for a moment, then let her pull him slowly to his feet. "I always thought," he said, standing in front of her, "that it was shame that a beautiful girl like you should have a name like Barbara Woodcock — all those hard vowels and consonants! It should be something like — what was that name we used to pretend when we were little? Do you remember? I was Count Alfredo Francisco, remember? And you were —"

"Oh yes!" she said. "Yes, I remember! You were Count Alfredo and I was Lilias de Falange!"

"Ah!" he said. "Lilias! Yes, Lilias de Falange. We did a play, once, remember? We wrote it ourselves. My favorite line was, 'Lilias, come with me and brighten my gloomy castle with your shining eyes!' Do you remember that, Barb? Do you?"

"Yes, yes."

He held both her hands in his. "I used to think," he said, "I used to wonder: can cousins marry cousins? We both used to wonder that, didn't we? Do you remember when we used to talk like that?"

She had, suddenly, a soft and inward curiosity, wondering: is he going to kiss me? But he released her hands. "Your eyes still shine," he said a little sadly, "but not for me." He turned and slowly started toward the door. "You do like it, then? The apartment?"

"Oh yes," she said. Her voice was almost a whisper. "Yes, I do, Woody."

"My explorer personality. You know," he said, "the trouble with me is — the trouble with me is, I don't have any personality at all. But you're right. The shrunken head must go."

She followed him across the room. He opened the door, then stood back and bowed from the waist. "Thank you, madame, for brightening my gloomy castle for a little time."

She stepped out into the hall, and when he closed the door behind them, she turned to him in the darkened hallway and kissed his cheek. "Thank you, Count Alfredo," she said. And then, "One of the nicest things about coming home, Woody, is you."

"Just for that," he said, "I'll put the top up for the drive back."

They went down the stairs and out onto the street where he had parked the car. In the car, she put her head against his shoulder, the rough texture of his orange sweater, and closed her eyes.

When she woke they were at the farm. Woody climbed out of the car, crossed in front of the headlights, and opened the door for her. She slid across the leather seat. "Good night, Woody," she said sleepily. "Thank you. I'll see you soon."

"Good night, Barb."

She went up the steps and unlocked the front door with her key. Behind her, the little car started up, roared around the circle and sped away, down the road.

She stepped into the hall and closed the door behind her. The house was very quiet. A few lamps had been left lighted for her in the hall and on the stairs.

She did not immediately go up. For some reason — perhaps it was the little nap she had had in the car — she no longer felt as sleepy as she had. She turned and started walking slowly through the half-lit, empty rooms, under the four identical archways of the four strung-together living rooms, noticing the way the receding light from the hall managed to travel with her, catching certain gleaming surfaces — polished tops of tables, mirrors, bowls of lamps, silver ash trays, candlesticks — reflecting them, lighting her way. Moving across the soft, hushed carpets, trailing her finger across the backs of chairs, guided by these little glimmers as well as by a sense of deep familiarity, of knowing, really, that she could traverse most of the house in total darkness and feel, instinctively, the doorways and the places where chairs and tables had always been, guided by the tickings of familiar clocks, she went like a sleepwalker, with her hands raised slightly, reluctant to turn on any lights. She realized that she was also guided by scents, that the fruitwood chest had an odor of its own, as did the silk drapes in the second room, a dusty perfume, and the Oriental rugs in the third — and, all at once, smelling the unmistakable perfume of roses, she saw, from the gleam of a silver bowl, that there was, indeed, a vase of roses on her mother's writing desk. At night, she thought, when everyone else is asleep, is the best time to get to know a house again.

In the doorway just ahead of her, shining from her father's study, she saw a new source of light. Wondering if her father could be still awake, she walked toward it. But the little study, when she entered it, was empty. One lamp was lighted on his desk, apparently left by accident. She crossed the room to turn it off.

As she reached for the switch, she saw several sheets of yellow foolscap, secured with a paper clip, lying on the desk. At the head of the top sheet, written in her father's small, precise hand, were the words,

PRESTON LITTELL WOODCOCK, II

The Biography of a Connecticut Industrialist
by his son
Preston Littell Woodcock, III

It was the manuscript Woody had told her about. He had evidently been working on it tonight, for his black fountain pen lay across it.

Her first impulse was to turn off the light and leave it there. Then she hesitated, hovering between reading it and not reading it. Then she sat down in her father's chair, picked up the sheaf of papers and read:

My father, Preston Littell Woodcock, II, was born November 21, 1865 in Burketown, Connecticut, the son of Dobie Woodcock and the former Miss Barbara Louise Dalton. Father was born in the family home in which he died, an imposing residence at 1045 Prospect Avenue, built of local stone, a house that for many years has been a landmark in this community.

Father himself, in many ways, was built of local stone. Privately educated until he was seventeen, when he entered Yale University, he was a member of Zeta Psi fraternity and Skull & Bones. He was graduated from Yale in the class of 1887 with a B.A. degree and special Honors in History.

Upon graduation, Father embarked upon a year's tour of Europe. From the letters he wrote to his parents at the time, it is clear that he found the world on the other side of the Atlantic not to his liking. An acute observer of social mores, as well as economics, he found Europe degenerate, morally impoverished, and "behind the times" economically. In a letter to a Yale classmate, Father described Europe as "a continent that has seen its better days." (In view of current events in Europe at this writing, Father's remark of seventy years ago indicates that he was able to size up trends and even to prophesy them; this ability was to serve him well in his business career which was then yet to come.) He was never happier than at the moment when he set foot once more on his native soil and during his long lifetime he was never tempted to venture abroad again.

In 1889, he entered the employ of the Woodcock Paper Company, a paper-products manufacturing concern in Burketown. This company was founded by his grandfather (my great-grandfather), who bore the same name, in 1838. At the time of my father's entrance into the company, my grandfather was president, the company's founder having died in 1870. But in 1900, my father was handed the managerial reins, and he is most to be credited for having built the company to its present prominence as one of the largest in this section of the state. In this, he was aided for a time by his brother, the late William Dobie Woodcock.

Father's philosophy, often stated, was "Waste Not, Want Not," and it is to this stanch philosophy that is credited the fact that, during the 1930's, a period which saw the failure of many similar companies in the area, the Woodcock Paper Company was able to keep its flag aloft and its doors open. During the hostilities of World War II, the company turned its efforts, patriotically, to the Nation's defense, filling major government paper contracts. In 1943, the company was awarded the Government "E" for Efficiency.

In 1890, Father married Miss Mary Owens of Burketown who bore him one son (myself), although this did not occur until eleven years after their union, when Father was approaching middle life.

Father was a public-spirited man. He was a Republican and was active throughout his lifetime in civic affairs in Burketown, twice a candidate for Councilman. A stalwart opponent of Withholding, he strongly supported Mrs. Vivian Kellems, another Connecticut manufacturer, in her refusal to deduct federal taxes from the wages of her employees. While his health permitted, he enjoyed golf and was a member of the Burketown Country Club. He was a Mason and a member of various clubs and societies, including the University Club of New York City. He was at one time a nominee for Alumni Trustee of Yale and once served as President of the Yale Alumni Association of Burketown. Throughout his life he served his alma mater well as a benefactor and was among the "regulars" who returned to Yale for class reunions. In 1924, he set aside funds for the establishment of a public library in Burketown, which was named in memory of his father.

Father died July 14, 1953, in the summer of his eighty-eighth year, "in the autumn of life." His end was swift and peaceful.

I have heard it said that Father placed an indelible imprint upon all with whom he associated, in business as well as in private life. It is beyond the shadow of a doubt that my father placed an indelible imprint upon myself, his son.

The above is intended to sketch in, roughly, the chronology of his life. It shall not be necessary, as a result, in the pages to follow, to refer to this chronology again. For the story that follows will concern itself mainly with those years during which I knew Father best, the years during which I was associated with him in business, or the last twenty-nine years of his long life.

I went to work for the Woodcock Paper Company in the late spring of 1923, following the footsteps of my forebears.

On this note, which sounded curiously like an ending as well as a beginning, the manuscript stopped.

Feeling sad, Barbara put the pages down. She reassembled them carefully and fastened them with the paper clip. She placed the fountain pen across the top page, as she had found it.

There was a fading photograph of her grandfather on her father's desk. It showed a man she had never known, a stiff, stern-faced and formal little man who stood on the front doorsteps of his house holding a gold-tipped walking stick in which, Woody had once told her, her grandfather was rumored to have kept a sword. She had known a later man than that — a gaunt old man whose eyes were as pale as ice and whose face, when she reached up to kiss it, had felt cold and whiskery, smelling of pipe smoke and cough syrup; and, later, she had known the invalid whose dark silences had been even more terrible to hear than his gasping spells of coughing.

She remembered, clearly, the July afternoon five years ago when Grandfather Woodcock had died. She had been in New York with her mother. The two of them had met for a few days' shopping together; her mother was to help pick out things for the new house in Locustville. They had returned to the St. Regis after spending an afternoon sitting with bolts of fabrics rolled out in front of them, and there had been a message advising Edith to call the farm.

Edith talked to her husband quietly for a few minutes. Then she hung up and told Barbara the news.

That night, Barbara and her mother had dinner at a small Italian restaurant in East Fiftieth Street. "I need a drink," her mother had said when they were seated, which was, for Edith Woodcock, an untypical remark. She ordered a double Scotch.

The drink had seemed to release her. She did not become mournful. She did not cry. Her speech, if anything, became clearer. She became quite animated, quite gay. She laughed. "Oh, my God, Barbara!" she had said, her eyes shining brightly. "Do you know what this means? Do you *know!* I've had twenty-six years of him. He hated us. Ruled our lives. Oh, thank God he's dead! Oh, if there's a Hell, he'll go there! Do you see what this means for your father and me? It means we're free! We're free!" The next day they had taken the train to Burketown together.

Barbara stood up now and turned off the light. She started back slowly through the darkened house, moving cautiously since her eyes were now unaccustomed to the dark, walking on tiptoe. Then, through the archways, standing in the lighted hallway, she saw a figure. She stopped, almost screamed. Then she saw that it was Barney. He wore a light raincoat and evidently he had seen her, or heard her, for he stood, facing her, his hands deep in his coat pockets. "Who is it?" he said quietly.

"Barbara," she said. She came toward him. "What are you doing up?" she asked.

"I couldn't sleep," he said. "I went for a walk. A few minutes ago I thought I heard a car drive in."

"Woody drove me downtown to see his apartment," she said. "He just drove me back."

"Oh, I see," he said.

"Well," she said, with a nervous laugh, "it's awfully late. We'd both better get some sleep."

"Yes," he said.

"It was a nice evening tonight, wasn't it?"

"Yes, very nice," he said.

"Well," she said, "Good night, Barney."

"Good night."

He stood, courteously waiting, and when she realized what he was waiting for she said "Good night" again, turned and started up the stairs. She went down the upstairs hall to her room, let herself in, and closed the door. Then she heard him slowly mount the stairs, walk down the hall to his own room, open the door and close it. Then the house was still again. She turned on the light.

There was a note on her pillow. She unfolded it. On a piece of her mother's pale blue monogrammed stationery, she read:

Darling—

While you were out, your Flora telephoned to say that a cablegram had arrived at your house from Carson. He says simply, "Arrived safely London. Smooth flight. Love to you and the boys. Carson."

Sleep well, darling. It is so lovely to have you home again.

Mother

7

How do we know when first thoughts occur? And how do we know, with any degree of truth, why? In that summer, perhaps, there were countless beginnings of thoughts, wonderings that began — fanciful and idle at first — like thoughts just before sleep when the human body is at its most self-indulgent state, when thoughts of others are most easily excluded, when the warm figure in the bedclothes has only itself to care for, only itself to comfort and make happy. Perhaps that was the true beginning, on a night like this, suddenly between sleep and wakefulness, thinking: I *wonder*. Or perhaps it had come at a more conscious point, when thought followed thought with strict sequence and order, when little suggestions, curiosities, questions arose, pleasantly nagging, and, one question answered, it was possible to go on to the second question, and then the third. When the first question — *Does he like me?* — was answered with a yes, is it ever possible to avoid the second question, the second simple, childish, playful question: *How much?* And there had been other people, too, involved in it, with their own suggestions. Her mother, for example, who came swiftly into the room one day and said, "Sit down, darling. I want to talk to you." And when she sat down, smiling, saying, "Yes. What is it?" her mother had said, "It's about Barney, dear. You've been simply wonderful — entertaining him while Peggy and I have been so busy with so many preparations. We've *both* appreciated it, Peggy and I. But I'd like to mention one tiny thing. It's clear that he likes you. Of course. Everyone likes you. But remember, dear, that you are an unusually attractive girl and men are — well, *men*. I'd hate to think that you'd let your attractiveness — well, that you'd let it take another person to such a point that it might do irreparable harm to a third person, if you see what I mean. I mean, Barbara, that Peggy is obviously head over heels in love with Barney. I personally wish it were otherwise — that it were someone else — but since it's not, I'm trying to be a good mother and think first of my daughter's happiness. I personally wish she had found someone like — well, someone like you have found, like Carson. But since she hasn't, and it's to be Barney — well, then Barney it is! I do like him. One can't help but like him. He's gentlemanly and courteous and seems very kind. No money and no family is — well, just no money and no family! That's all! But the point is, dear, I keep remembering when you were both little girls. You were always the prettier one, everyone said so, and as a result — try as we all might — you did, dear, get away with murder! With murder, dearest, you know you did. We spoiled you, I suppose, but perhaps it's not too wrong to spoil a child. Anyway, little Peggy always had the harder row to hoe. Always the harder row. You got things, *received* things, that really ought to have been Peggy's. I don't need to enumerate, cite examples. You know what they were. And being our dear little spoiled girl whom we loved so much, you sometimes — oh, only sometimes — enjoyed, or rather *seemed* to enjoy, taking things away from your sister. To show that you could, I mean. Of course you outgrew it. We all outgrow things. But the point is, I've been watching you — not snooping, darling, but I have seen you — with Barney. He's charming and you like him and there is no doubt that he likes you. But he is Peggy's, Barbara. That's all I want to remind you of, my dear. You have a dear, wonderful husband whom you love and two adorable little children. And this one — this other"— Edith's voice grew firmer — "is for Peggy. This is Peggy's. Do remember it."

Perhaps that, or the moments following that conversation, had given her the first thought, or at least had been what had brought the first thought to consciousness, given it words. Because after that the words, the idea, began to hover all around her, flutter around her, wherever she went.

She had not had two men in love with her at once for a long time, and when she stopped to think about it, except for reasons that were so clearly obvious that she dismissed them, was there any reason why she should not now? That was the third, and final, question of that summer.

Then, in September, Carson had come back from South America. She had gone back to Locustville to meet him and, a few days later, they had had a quarrel. And perhaps the quarrel had had something to do with pushing those thoughts further forward in her mind; it was hard to say. No motive is ever simple, but an intricate arrangement of smaller motives. Only when mixed to an essential consistency do little motives became a compelling one. Perhaps one of those little motives had been revenge.

They had given a party. It was their turn. They had been entertained by the Hodgsons, the Sages, the Williamsons, the Brysons and the Bishops — the neighbors and company friends — and, Carson reminded her, the time had come to repay the party debts. So Barbara had telephoned Muriel Hodgson, Betty Lou Sage, Prudie Williamson, Kate Bryson and Sue Bishop and invited them for cocktails on Saturday night.

She had worked on the party all day. She had made hot hors d'oeuvres and a lobster casserole which she planned to serve, buffet-style, at eight o'clock. In addition to Flora, she had hired another girl to help in the kitchen. She filled vases with tall gladioli from the garden and placed fresh pink tapers in the dining room candelabrum, thinking that she would serve the supper by candlelight.

The party began all right and it was difficult to tell, exactly, at just what point it had begun to go wrong. Looking back on it later, she could see it had begun when Muriel Hodgson had mentioned a restaurant in Locustville called Pete's.

Barbara had been sitting beside her on the sofa. "Pete's?" she asked. "I don't believe I've heard of that one. Is it good?"

"Oh, it's divine!" Muriel said, shaking her bright yellow curls enthusiastically. "You should *try* it. Pete's Pizzeria. It's simply divine."

"Pete's what?"

"Pizzeria. Pete's Pizzeria. Isn't that a cute name?"

Barbara said, "Oh, I see — they make pizzas there?"

Muriel looked at Barbara suspiciously. "What's the matter?" she asked. "Don't you like pizzas?"

"Oh, I do!" Barbara said.

"Well, try Pete's. They're terrific."

"They sure are," Bert Hodgson said. "They have about, oh, maybe a dozen different flavors, but the kind to order is their special de luxe combination. They make it with anchovies, ripe olives, mozzarella cheese, Italian sausage — the works." He turned to Carson. "Do you like pizzas?" he asked.

"Sure," Carson said.

"Anybody who doesn't like pizzas should have his head examined," Bert said.

"And Bert's right about their special de luxe combination. It's simply divine," Muriel said.

"I must try it," Barbara said.

More cocktails were poured and voices rose to a new pitch and intensity. Barbara thought: At least they're enjoying themselves. Then Flora beckoned her into the kitchen. Was the casserole ready? Barbara looked at it; it was cooking more slowly than she had expected. The strips of lobster meat were still translucent. "Give it another few minutes, Flora," she said.

In the living room Bert Hodgson was doing his imitation of Pocahontas; Muriel was playing Captain John Smith. The room swayed with laughter, and from the phonograph, Marlene Dietrich spoke bittersweet German songs. Carson moved dutifully among the guests with his silver cocktail pitcher. Barbara listened as Kate Bryson confessed that she had always wanted to be a comedy actress. Then, suddenly, Muriel Hodgson was standing in front of her, saying something. "What?" Barbara asked.

"*Pete's!*" Muriel shouted. "That's the name of it." Voices in the room swiftly fell and Muriel said, more quietly, "Pete's."

"Yes, what about it?" Barbara asked.

"I could have been, too," Kate Bryson said. "I had this teacher in this drama course they gave. She said so. She said I had born acting talent."

"Pete's Pizzeria," Muriel said to Barbara. "The place I was telling you about."

Muriel turned to the others. "So what do we all say?" she cried. "All in favor?"

"Favor?" Barbara asked. "In favor of what?"

"I think we could eat three large ones, don't you? Or no. No, we'd better make it four," Muriel said. "Large, four large. Bert can eat a whole one by himself!"

"Sure can!" Bert said.

"Would anyone like another cocktail?" Carson asked.

"No. We're going to send out for pizzas," Muriel said. She turned to the others in the room. "Oh, that's a wonderful idea, isn't it, gals? Then none of us will have to bother fixing dinner! Get on the phone, Bert."

"Well —" Carson began.

"What's the number?" Bert asked.

"Lambert 9-0790," Muriel said.

Barbara said, "I don't think we'll need pizzas. I've got —"

"Of course we do. What's the matter with you? Don't you like pizzas?" Muriel turned, suddenly to Sue Bishop and said, "By the way. You can eat pizzas, can't you?" Her voice was full of solicitude for Sue, who, before she had married Ed Bishop, had been Sue Goldman, and was Jewish. "I mean — it's all *right* for you, isn't it?"

"Oh, yes," Sue replied.

"Good. I didn't know."

"I love pizzas," Prudie Williamson, who had not said much, said. "Do you know what I do, Muriel?"

"What do you do?"

"I buy them by the dozen and keep them in the deep-freeze. They're wonderful that way. Just run them under the broiler for a few minutes to thaw them out. You can keep them that way for months. They don't get soggy at *all*."

"I'll have to try that," Muriel said. "Bert — make that call!"

"I save a lot of money shopping in quantity," Prudie Williamson said.

"Oh, so do I," Muriel said. "Bert, what's the matter with you? Why don't you call Pete's? I'm getting hungry just sitting here *thinking* about pizzas!" She rubbed her stomach.

"I'm waiting for a little quiet," Bert said. "Hey! Everybody! Keep it down, will ya? Keep it down to a dull roar. I'm trying to make a phone call."

"Bert," Barbara began, "I've actually got a —"

"As long as Hank and I *both* eat them, I don't mind," Prudie Williamson said. "If he eats them by himself, I can't stand to have him get close to me with his breath." She laughed and then blushed violently, as she realized that she might have said something vulgar.

"Oh, hurry, Bert!" Muriel said. "*Hurry!* All you have to say is four large special de luxe combination pizzas and tell them you'll be down in fifteen minutes to pick them up." She turned to Barbara. "The nice thing about Pete's is they're very prompt. If Bert phones now, they'll be ready by the time he gets there." She turned to Bert, looking at him levelly. "*If Bert phones now*," she said.

"Quiet!" Bert said. He had begun to dial.

"Have them make one without onions," Betty Lou Sage said.

"No, Bert," said Muriel. "Just tell them to leave the onions off *half* of one. That's all. The rest of us want onions for goodness' sake!" She looked at Betty Lou. "Don't worry," she said. "They'll leave the onions off half of one."

Barbara stood in the center of the room, holding her cocktail glass.

"Hello?" Bert said. "Is this Pete's? Look. This is Bert Hodgson. Out on Bayberry Lane. That's right. Look — can we have four large special de luxe combinations? That's right . . ."

"Bert —" Barbara said.

Carson turned to Muriel Hodgson. "Barbara's got something fixed already," he said. "She's got a —"

"Oh, we don't want you to go to any trouble!" Muriel said, turning to Barbara. "No kidding, honey. That's the wonderful thing about pizzas. They're so simple! No dirty dishes. We can eat them right out of the box."

"I've got a lobster dish in the kitchen," Barbara said. "And I —"

"Oh, don't bother with that," Prudie Williamson said. "I'm allergic to seafood anyway."

"Four . . . large . . . special de luxe combinations," Bert was saying. "And look. Leave off the —"

Barbara turned to Carson, who shrugged his shoulders, gave her a brief despairing look. She turned to Bert. "Bert!" she said.

"What? Wait a minute." He covered the telephone mouthpiece with his hand.

Suddenly everyone in the room was silent, looking at Barbara.

"Bert, don't order pizzas," she said quietly.

"Why not, for Christ's sake?"

"Because I don't want them."

"What the —"

"You heard me!" she said. And though she hadn't meant it to, her voice rose shrilly. "I don't want pizzas! If I'd wanted pizzas I'd have ordered them myself! It's my party, isn't it? Isn't it?" She sobbed, suddenly, turned and ran out of the room, her cocktail splashing from her glass as she ran.

Behind her, Muriel Hodgson said, "Well! What's eating her for God's sake?"

Later, Carson came into the bedroom.

"Oh, I don't know, I don't know!" she sobbed. "I don't know what happened! Suddenly I couldn't stand them — any of them! I couldn't stand looking at their stupid faces and listening to their stupid voices! I couldn't stand them."

"Muriel was just trying to be helpful," he said.

"Helpful!" she said angrily. "Who is she! Just who is she! She's nothing but a stupid, stupid, mediocre little tramp. And he — he's even worse. All of them! I hate them all. I can't stand this town. I can't stand this street, I simply can't stand it any more."

"Where would you like to go?"

She buried her face in the pillow, sobbing. "That's the trouble! I don't know what I want. I don't know where I want to go. Oh, I'm so unhappy — so unhappy —"

He said nothing.

"I've got to go somewhere! I've got to get away!"

After a while, he said, "Would you like me to fix you a little nightcap?"

She sat up, fumbled under the pillow for her wadded handkerchief, found it and blew her nose. "All right," she said. "I'd love that."

He went into the kitchen. She heard the sound of him mixing drinks. She sat on the bed, pushing the damp hair out of her eyes.

He returned with the two drinks, handed her one, and sat down on the bed beside her. He seemed singularly quiet. Then he said, "Of course Bert's one of my supervisors. But of course you knew that."

"I don't care!" she said. "I don't care who he is. He's still a stupid, boorish little man."

"Well, I hope you'll apologize anyway. For my sake, at least."

116

"I won't!" she said.

"And apologize to Muriel, too, in the morning."

"I certainly won't!"

"You've never tried," he said. "You've never tried to get to know any of these people, that's the only trouble. They're all perfectly decent people. But you've never tried to get to know them, or understand them, at all."

"I have tried," she said. "I've tried very hard. You certainly can't say that I haven't tried."

He was silent for a moment. Then he said, "I wish I could see how you've tried. This past summer, for example — as far as I can see you spent most of it up in Burketown at the farm."

And then the quarrel began in earnest.

It ended, in sobbing hysteria, early in the morning.

But it was not ended, in the sense that anything had been settled, or even — as would have been best — forgotten, though she had done as he had asked, telephoned the Hodgsons the next day and apologized. It was still remembered two weeks later when, early on a Friday morning, they started off for Burketown in the car for Peggy's wedding, which was to be at three o'clock that Sunday afternoon.

An autumn wedding, in the afternoon, under bright blue late September skies was what Edith Woodcock wanted. But when Barbara and Carson arrived on Friday, it did not appear that Edith's wish would be granted; the day was cold and windy and the sky was gray and overcast, not blue. Leaves from the elms and maples blue against the windowpanes and the wind tossed and bent the heads of chrysanthemums and the remaining roses. But Edith, as she said, was being philosophical about the weather; plans had to proceed anyway; one could only pray that Sunday would dawn with sunshine. Four hundred guests were coming. Wisely, considering the weather's unpredictability, Edith had decided against erecting a marquee in the garden. Instead, the reception was to be held at Grandmother Woodcock's house on Prospect Avenue, which, because it was an old house built in the grand manner of the late nineteenth century, had a ballroom. It was here, then, and not at the farm, that the most feverish preparations were taking place. It was at the old house opposite the Wayside Furniture store — the house that passing motorists often mistook to be either a convent or nursing home or a school for girls — that precious services of Limoges were being washed, French crystal and heavy English silver were being polished, satin draperies, freshly cleaned, were being rehung, floors were being waxed and buffed. Here in the garden, which, before Maple Street had been cut through behind it, had extended for four hundred feet beyond two identical iron gazebos, the bronze and verdigrised fountain that had been carried around the Horn from China was being put in working order. Delivery trucks arrived with wedding presents; florists' trucks arrived with tubs of flowers; caterers' trucks arrived with food and champagne. And, in the middle of it all, praying silently for a fair dawn on Sunday — and also that Grandmother Woodcock would not die from the excitement of the activity in her house — was Edith Woodcock, her white hair in disarray, in an apron and comfortable shoes, working with the servants.

Barbara saw Barney only once during that Friday afternoon. She came upon him unexpectedly in her grandmother's library; he was standing at the window, watching the workmen in the windy garden. She sat down with him and they lighted cigarettes together.

Because she had thought that it might amuse him, she told him about Muriel Hodgson and the pizzas — though not, of course, about the quarrel that had followed. "Did you ever hear of such an impolite thing?" she had asked him.

But he had seemed preoccupied, nervous, his mind on other things. His eyes kept wandering away from her, around the room, to the window, to the workmen in the garden beyond. He took sharp, rapid puffs of his cigarette and murmured, "Yes . . . yes. Uh-huh. . . ."

Then he told her what she had not known before — that, after he and Peggy came back from their wedding trip to Bermuda, he was going to work for the Woodcock Paper Company. He looked at Barbara intently, as if eager to get her reaction to this.

"But why?" she had asked him. "I thought you had so many other offers?"

"I did," he said. "I had several. A couple of them were quite interesting. But this — to me — this is really exciting, Barbara."

"I don't think anyone's ever called our little company *exciting* before," she said.

He jumped up and walked to the window. He stood, tensely looking out with his hands pushed deep in his trousers pockets. "Well, it is," he said in a tone that was almost belligerent. "When your father and your cousin Billy made me the offer, I didn't hesitate a minute."

"And you'd spend your life in the paper business?"

He turned to her sharply. "What's wrong with paper? Look," he said. "At Harvard I was trained for management, and when you're trained for management you can manage anything. The product doesn't matter. Paper or soap, it's all the same, and besides —" he stopped.

"Yes? What?"

"Well," he said slowly, "I am marrying into the Woodcock family. It's going to be my family too, you see. So shouldn't I do everything I can for the family? Your father never had a son. Maybe I can be — well, *like* a son."

She smiled at him. He looked away, his face flushed, as though, by accident he had suddenly allowed one of his heart's preserves to open, and had let her peer inside. He faced the window again.

"I love this family," he said simply. "I love everything about it. The farm, the people — all of you. I'm going to be very happy here."

"So you'll be living in Burketown," she said.

"Yes. At the farm."

"At the *farm?*" she asked, surprised.

"Yes," he said. "Temporarily."

And then, later that afternoon, back at the farm, because her mother had asked her to do it, Barbara went into Peggy's room to talk to her. Peggy seemed remarkably composed, although her bedroom was in a disorder of packing, with open suitcases on the chairs and piles of dresses lying across the bed. They sat on the floor; it was the only place to sit. Peggy pulled the bottoms of her gray slacks up above her calves, crossed her legs and rested her chin upon her folded hands when Barbara asked her whether there was anything — any questions — about marriage, anything Peggy didn't understand. "Don't forget, I'm a veteran of nearly four years of it," Barbara had said.

But Peggy knew all about sex. She knew enough, anyway. When she had been — what? About nine or ten? — there had been Charlie Muir, who cared for the horses and went riding with the girls. "Remember Charlie Muir?" she asked Barbara. Once, riding through the woods behind the house, Charlie had offered to show Peggy something. There was no need to dismount, Charlie said. And when she said yes, she would like to see it, he had unbuttoned himself and shown it to her. Then he suggested that she hold this object in her hand as they rode, side by side, quietly under the trees. Afterward, she had told Barbara about it. Barbara had been shocked. "Don't ever, ever do a thing like that with a man!" she had said, and with the wisdom five added years gave her, had added, "If you do, he'll want to do something else — much worse." Nevertheless, Peggy had done it again.

And, to be sure, one day Charlie Muir had suggested a more ambitious experiment and this had frightened her. This time she had told her mother. Her mother had listened quietly, asked her one or two questions, but had not seemed to be alarmed. That afternoon, however, her father had returned from the office early, with two other men. They had gone to the stable where Charlie lived, and after that, Charlie Muir had never been seen or mentioned at the farm again.

Then, when Peggy was a little older and understood things more fully, she had had another, and possibly ruder, shock. Peggy was fourteen, Barbara was in college, and Peggy had developed the habit — whenever Barbara was not at home — of sneaking into her sister's room to read the letters that were tucked into the bottom of Barbara's dresser drawer, and — whenever its little flap was left unlocked — to read Barbara's diary. She liked the letters better than the diary, though. And one day — it was after Barbara had started going with Carson Greer and had invited him to the farm a few times — Peggy discovered a new letter in the drawer from Carson, which, when she read it — and she read it and reread it several times — made it quite clear that Barbara and Carson, in the expression Peggy and her friends used, had "gone the limit." It had happened in the little guesthouse across the lake, but at precisely what time the incident or incidents had occurred was not clear from the letter. What was clear — and what startled Peggy the most — was that neither Carson nor Barbara, apparently, were the least bit remorseful for what they had done. In Carson's view, it was something beautiful, secret, and holy that they had shared. And Carson's language of thanks, to Barbara, for her part in this sharing was oddly flowery, even prayerful, quite unlike any language she had ever heard before from a man, and different from what she had always supposed would be used to describe an act of illicit love. In her mind, at fourteen, she had sometimes imagined such letters; in them, the guilty man — for it was the man always who was guilty — accused himself of veniality, lack of courage, compared himself to a rough-booted soldier who had marched through and muddied a beautiful garden. Yet in Carson's letter, the details were quite explicit. And it appeared not to have been Carson alone who was guilty, who was the aggressor.

Peggy's first reaction had been horror and fury with her sister. How could she! How could she have subjected herself to such a thing? Every shred of respect she had once had for Barbara vanished instantly, as though one of the soft and comforting lights that bathed her existence had been suddenly switched off. She went to her own room. On her dressing table, a photograph of Barbara stood in a pink leather frame. She picked up the picture, spat at the face, and threw the picture to the floor, smashing the glass. She bent, and from the sharp splinters she ripped the photograph into tiny shreds. Then she threw herself across her bed and cried for a long time, pounding the bedclothes with her angry fists. Never, never, never, she promised herself, would she speak to or look at Barbara again.

But this presented a problem. She could not stop speaking to or looking at Barbara without telling Barbara why. And she could not tell Barbara why without admitting her own guilt. Reading another person's mail was, as Barbara had often grimly reminded her, a federal offense, punishable by fine or imprisonment, or both. So, though Peggy continued to be disturbed by her knowledge for several weeks afterward, she had never mentioned it to Barbara. And, gradually, she began to forgive her. But since the revelation of that afternoon, her attitude toward Barbara was never again precisely the same. The golden face she had worshiped as a child was tarnished.

All this she told Barbara now as she sat cross-legged on the floor in her gray slacks, a little smile on her round, snub face.

Then it was time for the ritual of cocktails — somewhat earlier that evening because there was a busy night ahead — and dinner. Then, at eight-thirty, it was time for the men to leave for the bachelor party Cousin Billy was giving for Barney. Carson, Barney, Preston Woodcock and Woody — who had come for dinner that Friday night — departed in various cars for Cousin Billy's house on Hillside Road. Edith and Peggy, along with Edith's servants, were to take the station wagon back to Grandmother Woodcock's house on Prospect Avenue to finish the decorations, begun that afternoon, so that everything would be in order for the photographers who, most of Saturday morning, would be taking pictures there. Barbara was welcome to come along, they said — they could use as many hands as they could get — but Barbara, who was tired and who had developed a throbbing headache during the day, asked to be excused, and suddenly, at nine o'clock, she found herself absolutely alone in the house.

She had gone to her room, undressed, and put on her blue quilted robe. She propped pillows against the headboard of her bed, swallowed an aspirin tablet, and lay down against the pillows with a book. She alternately read and dozed, experiencing the curious sensation of having — when her eyelids closed — the book that she was reading continue with an improbable new plot, new characters, in her dreams. At last she put the book aside, sat up straighter, and began, idly, chipping the lacquer from her fingernails. When she had created a tiny crimson snowstorm of chips about her on the sheet, she decided to do the job properly. She got out of bed, went to her dressing table, and, with a bottle of remover, cotton balls, nail file, orange stick and polish, began seriously to do her nails. Her door into the hall was open and suddenly, in the middle of her concentration, she heard a sound and turned and saw Barney standing there. He looked weary, leaning with one hand against the doorjamb.

Startled, she asked, "Is the party over?"

"No," he said. "It's still going on."

"What happened? Why did you leave?"

"I couldn't take it any longer," he said.

"What was wrong with it?"

He sighed. "Nothing, I guess. During the movie, I decided

to take a walk. Nobody seemed to notice when I left, so I decided to come home. Is Peggy back yet?"

"Not yet," she said. "What do you mean — during the movie?"

"The dirty movie," he said. "Doesn't every bachelor party have a dirty movie? This one was different, though. There were four — four that I saw, anyway. Maybe there are more."

"Really?" she asked. "That doesn't sound like Cousin Billy!"

He laughed shortly. "Doesn't it? I gathered it was typical —" Then he broke off. "I'm sorry," he said. "I don't know, really. Mind if I sit down?"

"No," she said. "No — please do."

He came into the room and sat on the upholstered bench at the foot of her bed.

Then, it seemed, a deep and terrifying silence fell between them. She raised her hand, still damp with nail polish and waved it absently in the air. Then she lowered it.

Finally she said, "What's the matter?"

"Something very simple," he said.

"What?" Her voice was barely above a whisper.

"I'm marrying the wrong Woodcock girl," he said.

It was difficult to remember what she had felt — what, exactly, her emotions were then. They had seemed to change with breathless speed. The thought, the idea, the idle, dreaming, half-conscious thought — put into words just that one time by her mother — had been only an aimless and impractical wondering. It had not been a specific thought; it had not involved any specific plan of action. It had been only a daydream up to then and the realization, so swift, that she had walked to the end of the daydream into a specific place where specific words and specific actions were required stunned her, blurred her thoughts, dizzied her. Up to then, the fanciful thought that had begun that summer had involved the word "affair." Her friends, married and unmarried — Nancy Rafferty, all the rest — talked of affairs they had had or would like to have. In this vernacular, there was nothing — other than the one obvious thing — wrong with having an affair. It was modern, everyone did it — or seemed to do it. As long as an affair was all that it was — because *affair* meant something brief, handled sensibly. It meant something temporary, quickly over, quickly forgotten and forgiven.

But now, with him sitting there, his deep eyes looking inexpressibly sad, having just said what he had said with the meaning that could not be misunderstood, it was too late to think of it in terms of the word *affair*. He, or perhaps she herself, had somehow pushed everything far beyond the word affair into an area that was complicated, treacherous, deep — not temporary, but forever. And so everything changed; the old thoughts, quaintly mixed with self-flattery, idle curiosity, a perfectly selfish longing for excitement, a smug feeling of I'll-go-into-it-with-my-eyes-open — all that vanished. She was sitting face to face, soberly, with the victory her dreaming mind had been devising, but the victory had betrayed her because she was looking now at the face of a man with whom an affair was no longer possible. Since what he had just said had meant that he was in love with her, how else could she answer him except by saying that she loved him, too? Methodically, now, appeared in her mind, the steps ahead: Divorcing Carson, taking the children, leaving — at last — Locustville, waiting for a little while, then marrying Barney. Peggy would be heartbroken, of course, but after all these were the cruel demands of love. She could no longer have two men in love with her at once.

She did not remember, exactly, what she had said to him. She remembered asking him to repeat what he had just said, and when he had, saying that he must not say such a thing unless he meant it truly and always and when he had said yes, he had, that it had been growing with him all through the summer, she remembered that she had begun to cry — not sob, but to sit, swaying slightly, with unexpected tears streaming down her face. At some point then he had stood up, come to her and brushed the tears from

her face with his fingertips and out of all the jumble and confusion of thoughts running wild in her head, old thoughts racing
with new, she had one overwhelming thought: the house was
empty, they were all alone there. She remembered asking him if
the things she herself had felt all summer long — the curious
wish, desire, longing and the little furtive thoughts — had, could
have been, love? Could they? She herself did not know. She
hardly remembered what his answer was because suddenly from
the turmoil of feelings there came a great, smooth calm and she
thought: *All is well; it is as it should be.* She felt blissful and
serene, as if she were about to perform some ancient and noble
rite, moving toward the bed; he knelt, she remembered, on the
rug beside the bed and she reached for him to lift him to her. He
kissed her. He said — she remembered the jarring sound of his
words — "I was taught that adultery is a mortal sin. If it is, we'll
both be punished for it," and she remembered her own equally
jarring words — "I don't care."

Then, from the floor below, was the sound of the front door
opening and her mother's clear voice saying to Peggy, "Darling,
I'm exhausted, aren't you?" and the sound of the door being
closed again and their high heels moving across the polished
floor. Instantly, Barney was gone. She was left alone staring
blindly at the white ceiling of the room, at the rippled crimson
border above the pretty flowered wallpaper.

On Sunday, the *Burketown Evening Eagle* said:

> The sun made a surprise appearance today to
> brighten the wedding of Miss Margaret McPartland
> Woodcock of Burketown to Mr. Bernard Joseph Cal-
> lahan of Boston, Massachusetts. St. John's Episcopal
> Church, decorated for the occasion with autumn
> flowers and colorful fall foliage, was the scene of the
> three o'clock solemnization. The Reverend Hartley L.
> Waterman officiated.

The bride, a member of a prominent Burketown family, wore an heirloom gown of ecru silk brocade, created for her paternal grandmother by Worth of Paris. Her shoulder-length veil, also an heirloom, was fashioned of Chantilly lace. She carried a prayerbook marked with miniature white orchids and Bouvardia.

The former Miss Woodcock is the daughter of Mr. and Mrs. Preston Littell Woodcock, III, of "Orchard Farm," Valley Road, and the granddaughter of Mrs. Preston L. Woodcock, II, of 1045 Prospect Avenue, this city, and the late Mr. Woodcock. Her maternal grandparents were the late Professor and Mrs. Andrew B. McPartland of Providence, R. I. Prof. McPartland was formerly Chairman of the History Department of Brown University.

The bride was graduated from the Westover School, Middlebury, and Wellesley College. She was presented to society in 1952 at a dance given by her parents in their home and also at the Junior League Ball in New Haven. She is a member (Provisional) of the New Haven Junior League.

Serving as matron of honor was the bride's sister, Mrs. Carson V. Greer of Locustville, Pa. Mr. Greer served as best man. Miss Susan Robinson Woodcock, age six, the daughter of Mr. and Mrs. William D. Woodcock, III, and a cousin of the bride, was flower girl. Following the ceremony a reception was held at the Prospect Avenue residence of Mrs. Preston Woodcock, II.

The groom, the son of Mr. and Mrs. James Gerald Callahan of Boston, was graduated in the class of 1950 from Boston University and from Harvard Business School. After a honeymoon in Bermuda, the couple will reside in Burketown.

"It was a nice wedding," Carson said.

"Yes," she said.

They were driving back to Locustville late Sunday night. He had to be at the office Monday morning.

"The reception was nice, too," he said.

"Yes," she said. "It's too bad we couldn't have stayed longer."

"Were you enjoying it that much?"

She put her head back across the smooth leather seat of the car. "No," she said, "but anything seems like more fun than going back to Locustville."

He glanced at her, then looked back at the road ahead. "Barbara," he said, "I've been thinking. I'm afraid it's pretty hopeless with you and me. I think we should go our separate ways for a while. As far as I'm concerned, Locustville is where I work and it's where I live. It has certain disadvantages, perhaps, but I'm willing to put up with them. There are people there that I like, and I like the job pretty well. You, on the other hand, can never be happy there. I see that now. You've never tried to be, but then it's possible you don't know how to try. So, this week, I'd like to have you get your things together, and next Saturday morning I'll drive you, Dobie and Michael back up to Burketown and leave you there. You can have the car. I'll take the train back. And whatever arrangements you want to work out after that — well, we'll work them out, that's all."

In the dark front seat she had sat back, pressed hard against the leather, unable to speak, feeling only a kind of total terror. For a long time she sat motionless as Carson drove on, southward, on the New Jersey Turnpike.

Then she said softly, "Oh, please, Carson! Please give me another chance, please! I'll try, darling. I'll try so hard! I promise you."

She continued to sit, with the reflected lights of cars flashing past her closed eyes, waiting for him to speak, thinking only that she had just lost one of the two men who loved her; she could not lose the other now, the one, indeed, that she loved the most.

"I love you!" she said.

And she still sat, waiting for him to answer her.

That had been the end of that summer.

Monday came, then Tuesday. And then the rules were established — the first few anyway; others came as they were needed. They were rules of consideration, politeness, tact. Quarrels were to be extinguished by the quickest means. Complaints were to be silenced. Locustville was to be tolerated.

It had seemed a shame that they needed to have rules for how to get along together. But it had seemed to them then that the rules would help, and, of course, the rules had helped. They helped even when they were broken because — as they reminded each other — each act of breaking the rules reaffirmed the fact that the rules were there. The rules were only for the time they lived in Locustville. But, of course, if one lives by rules one can live anywhere, and for any time.

On Wednesday she had Muriel Hodgson over for tea. On Thursday she bought two tickets for the Locustville Symphony Orchestra's first concert of the fall season. And, on Friday night, she and Carson went to it. "I'm trying," she said to him.

"I know you are," he said.

"It's fun to try."

It was fun to try, but not easy. It made the days and weeks and months that followed seem to form ranks, then battalions, that arrayed themselves in front of her and marched slowly forward, toward her, over her. They came — October, November, December, January — and they obliterated, with their steady pace, all the careless summer scenes behind.

Now, alone in her room, the lighted face of her little clock said half past two.

She was alone, in the darkness, with its electric purring. On the table beside her bed, her mother's note containing Carson's cabled message lay folded.

She remembered him this morning. "If a letter comes from Ted Sloane, open it and see what he says . . . Call Clyde Adams and tell him . . . And you'd better call what's-his-name, DeLuca, and have him come and clean out the oil burner. It should have been done last month, actually. Ask him if the chimney needs to be cleaned. Don't forget to send my mother something on her birthday. . . ."

She remembered the instructions he had given her, this departing passenger. And it was queer that she should remember them so clearly now. This morning, after he had left, she had forgotten them. She had forgotten to call DeLuca. If a letter had come from Ted Sloane, she had not noticed it in her careless glance at the mail. She had forgotten the date of Carson's mother's birthday.

She tried to console herself by thinking that none of the things she had forgotten were important. They could wait until she got back. Still, in the dark bedroom, forgotten duties, broken promises, rose and haunted her, swarmed like wasps in the attic of her mind. She saw vital letters buried in her desk. Oil burners exploded and she saw chimney fires ("Harry Walsh had a fire in his chimney the other day, and his house is the same age as ours.") Though she knew that these infernos were all created out of darkness and sleeplessness and loneliness, it was no use trying to extinguish them. So, when the clock said three, she gave up the struggle. She got up, went into the bathroom, swallowed one of her yellow sleeping pills and crept humbly back to bed.

Barney had said he could not sleep either.

The darkness was blue. She closed her eyes and wondered sadly if she had been lying awake, waiting for him.

And then, in a brief and vivid dream, she was a child again and struggling in the grass somewhere with him, in the dark and steaming grass near the secret island where the doll's grave was. She awoke with tears in her eyes and tried to sleep again.

8

IN LONDON IT WAS NINE O'CLOCK, A CLEAR AND COOL SUNDAY morning. And thank goodness it was quiet. He was at the back of the hotel, away from the street, and his window overlooked a narrow passageway that ran between two buildings. He was up and half dressed, in his socks, shorts and shirt, and he had stopped dressing midway, after fastening his garters, when he had remembered a request made the night before, that had not been attended to. He decided to wait, to make a little test, and so he got back into bed, pulled the bedspread up over his bare knees, lighted a cigarette and waited for the phone to ring. Ten minutes later, gauged by the time it took to smoke the cigarette, he picked up the phone. When the clerk at the desk answered, he asked, "What time is it, please?"

There was a pause. Then, "Nine-thirteen, sir."

"I thought I asked to be called at nine," Carson said.

"Sorry, sir."

Carson hung up the phone, letting it drop with a bang. He was in that sort of mood. It was not that he expected de luxe service — far from it; certainly not in a hotel like this one. But even at the incredibly low rate of a guinea a day he expected a few minimal things, like being called in the morning when he had asked to be called. He raised his knees, making two mountains under the bedspread, lifted the ashtray from the night stand, floated it in the valley between the mountains, and lighted another cigarette. The sunshine and the quiet of the room did little to rid him of his disgruntlement; the faded yellow wallpaper and chipped and bubbled plaster ceiling were the features that annoyed him most, that canceled out any cheeriness the day itself offered. He smoked, enjoying feeling martyred and enjoying the thought that he had got out on the wrong side of the bed, a singularly lumpy bed.

What he was doing was playing the system. His official hotel for the trip, the one stated on his itinerary, was the Dorchester. This hotel — and this morning he couldn't even remember the name of it — had been one he'd found last night running through the list of hotels in the telephone directory at the airport. It was in Paddington, near the station, some distance from the Dorchester. This morning, after breakfast, he would wander over to the Dorchester, leave his name at the desk, ask that messages and mail be held for him, tip the message clerk ten shillings and that would be that. That was the way the system worked. The difference between the Dorchester and the place where he was staying was four pounds, or about eleven dollars, a day. This was the difference between what the company paid him for a hotel room, and what he paid. It was differences like this that had bought Clyde Adams his Rolleiflex camera, his slide projector and screen. It was what had paid for Muriel Hodgson's Schiaparelli cocktail dress from Paris and it bought countless leather handbags, bottles of perfume, French gloves, English shoes for other salesmen and their wives. In the fraternity of salesmen for the Locustville Chemical Company there was no secret made of it. It was the system.

It was a little too simple to say that he disapproved of it; it was too late for disapproval. He had been participating in it for too long. He knew it was dishonest, and looking back, perhaps, if he had wanted to be a crusader, he might have made an issue of it. At one time, he could have. But not now. He had let himself be pulled into it by the others and by now the system had worked to his advantage too many times. It would be even more dishonest if now he should suddenly, indignantly, protest the system, and expose it. If he wanted an excuse for playing the system, one had been given him, plainly enough, by Jesse Talbot, head of the Export Division.

It had come as a result of something that happened during his first foreign trip.

Carson had arrived in Paris, where he had been scheduled to meet Bert Hodgson, who was flying in from Geneva. Both men were to be staying at the Georges Cinq, and when Carson got to the hotel, he asked whether Bert had arrived. Bert had not. Carson registered, went to his room, and unpacked his suitcase. A little later, after phoning several times to see whether Bert had checked in, Carson decided to go down to the bar for a drink.

He was crossing the lobby when he saw Bert Hodgson come through the door from the street, wearing his hat and coat but carrying no briefcase, accompanied by no luggage. Bert greeted him warmly.

"Hey," Bert said, "I got a real swell place — over near the University. It works out to about a buck-eighty a day."

"Aren't you staying here?" Carson asked.

"Hell, no," Bert said. "Are you?"

"Yes."

"What the hell for?"

"It's on the itinerary," Carson said. And then he said, "Besides, it's one of the nicest hotels in Paris."

Bert's eyes had clouded. "Is that so?" he asked. "Well. Pretty fancy, aren't you, Greer?"

When he got back to Locustville, Jesse Talbot had said, "By the way, Bert Hodgson says you two did fine in Paris."

"It went pretty well."

"You like to treat yourself in style, Bert says. You like the finer things of life."

"I don't know what Bert means by that."

"Says you were staying at the Georges Cinq."

"That's right."

"What were you doing there?" Talbot asked.

"That was my hotel," Carson said. "On my itinerary."

Jesse Talbot paused and scrutinized him for a moment. "Are you kidding?" he asked finally. "You really stayed at the Georges Cinq?" Then, cheerfully, he had said, "Well, you're new here. You've got a lot to learn. Yes, you've really got a lot to learn."

Jesse Talbot was a division head, and a vice-president. So, if he wanted, Carson could rationalize that the company actually expected him to cheat it. Looking around the room of his third-class hotel now, he thought: yes, they're giving me the glorious opportunity to cheat them out of eleven dollars a day, and I, by accepting it, am expected to give them my labor and devotion, some of my youth and, I suppose, part of my pride. He snuffed out his cigarette in the ash tray and, doing so, tipped over the ash tray, scattering black ashes across the top of the bedspread. He brushed at them angrily with his hand.

He had never told Barbara about the system. It wasn't just because he was ashamed of it, though that was part of it. It was mostly because he knew that the system would give her just one more reason to resent Locustville. And so, as far as even Barbara knew, he was always at the Dorchester in London . . . the Georges Cinq in Paris . . . the Excelsior in Rome.

But the thing was, of course, that Barbara was right. At least partly. The trouble — most of it — came from working in, and out of, the town where the company's main office was. It was the town, more than the company, that had put them in the peculiar situation they were in. Everyone knew, apparently, that Carson and Barbara — as the Locustville friends would put it — "had money from somewhere else." And they did — inheritances, a couple of small trusts, stock that brought them a small income. They did not have as large a private income as Locustville probably thought they had, but they had some; enough to make Locustville suspicious. God knew he had heard a few remarks made — not pointed ones, but little, casual, half-smiling, half-resentful remarks about them, about money, about things the Greers could afford that the others couldn't. A small mistake, an oversight, like staying at the Georges Cinq that first time, was enough to confirm the suspicions. After all, everybody connected with the company knew pretty much — or could guess — what he earned. Asked to estimate the size of Carson's semimonthly paycheck, any one of their friends could have come within ten dollars of the exact figure. And his semimonthly paycheck was not large.

Locustville permitted the Greers to have their private income. But it did not permit them to show it. Barbara had managed to collect, on birthdays and anniversaries, three good fur coats, a diamond cocktail ring, an emerald bracelet, two pairs of diamond earrings. None of these could be worn in Locustville. An exception was having Flora, their maid. Barbara had insisted on that, even though the other salesmen's wives did not have maids. Still, she had lied about it — telling the others that she paid Flora much less than she actually did. In fact, both Carson and Barbara had become accomplished poseurs, skillful liars; they nodded sympathetically when their friends complained about the size of their monthly car payments. "Yes, of course, we know," they said, as they sat at cocktail parties discussing mortgages, pay-as-you-go plans, interest rates on personal notes, freezer-plans and endowment policies that would one day assure their children of a college education. Actually, Barbara had never worried about paying a bill and foresaw no time in the future when she ever would worry. At least there was no need to worry as long as they lived in Locustville, where they were forced to live on less money than they had. Carson smiled. Life in Locustville might be inhibitive, but it was economical.

He kicked the bedspread to the foot of the bed and swung his legs over the side. This put him in view of a crazed and yellowed door mirror and he examined himself, dispassionately, in its reflection. Hair receding perhaps, but neatly, in two even arrows above his temples, but not on top. And there was, he knew, an invisible roll of stomach under his shirt that appeared when he sat down, but otherwise he was in good shape. He decided to get up, finish dressing, and get some breakfast. He did not like to lie around in bed too much, even on a Sunday. But the trouble was, after breakfast what could he do? This was one reason he hated to start a trip on a Sunday. Sundays, in the selling business, were solitary days, especially the very first, the arrival Sunday. Later on, if you were lucky, you met someone who asked you to Sunday dinner, or one of the distributors asked you out to his house for the afternoon. But today, this Sunday, loomed blankly ahead of him with nothing to do but walk around, looking in the windows of closed stores, walk in the park, walk to the Thames embankment and look at the excursion boats. Or else sit in his room and look at the walls. Barbara had packed a couple of books, but he didn't feel like reading. Still, he thought, perhaps that was what he would do — carry a book out to breakfast with him and, afterward, take it to Hyde Park or to the Thames embankment, find a bench and read it. He stood up beside the bed, feeling at loose ends, thinking: where do I go from here?

He walked to the window and stood in his shirt, shorts and socks, looking out. Opposite him was a blank brick wall. Below, the passageway — a street, really, but too narrow for traffic — ran a short cobblestoned distance, then turned the corner of the building and went out of sight. It was empty and he rested the heels of his palms against the window sill and looked down at the emptiness. A boy — tall, golden and oddly flowery — appeared from around the corner and suddenly, unexpectedly looked up and saw him there. Surprised, Carson noticed that the boy looked remarkably like Woody deWinter. And the boy stopped, tilted his head and smiled at him. Blushing, Carson stepped quickly back into the room. (Christ, a fairy! he thought.) He went back to the bed and sat down upon it, staring at his stockinged feet.

The trip was beginning all wrong. All the auspices were wrong. It had started wrong as long ago as Friday night with Nancy

136

Rafferty arriving, getting tight, acting like an ass. He tried to be tolerant of Nancy; after all, she was an old friend of Barbara's. Barbara felt sorry for Nancy and so, he supposed, did he, but somehow — to him — feeling sorry for someone was a pretty fruitless occupation. You could spend your whole life, he supposed, feeling sorrier and sorrier for someone. He could feel sorry for that boy in the alleyway just now, for instance, the boy who had looked like Woody. Or he could feel sorry for Woody. In fact, at one time, he had felt sorry for Woody.

He thought: Ah, poor Woody.

It was through Woody that he had first met Barbara. He and Woody had been in the same class at Princeton. And for the first semester of their freshman year, they had been roommates — not through choice, but as the result of one of those arbitrary room assignments made by the dean's office. They could not have had less in common.

They had tried, of course, to be friends during the first few weeks of college. They had tried because all roommates were supposed to be friends. But it soon became clear to both of them, in one of those subtle understandings that only two young men can reach with one another — understandings that evolve wordlessly, without rancor, that call for no explanation or apology — that friendship was not destined for them. They planned to join different clubs. They allied themselves with different groups of friends. Carson, who that summer before going off to college had been fattening himself and muscling himself with exercise, eight hours of sleep every night, and three quarts of milk every day because he wanted to make the football team, got on the freshman squad. When he and Woody met on campus, they smiled pleasantly and called "Hi!" to each other. Studying together, in their room, they exchanged a few pleasant, casual remarks, then lapsed into silence, each retreating carefully into his own book. If they spoke at all during these quiet, studious evenings, it was with elaborate politeness.

"Mind if I open the window, Woody? It's getting a little smoky in here."

"Sure, Carson. Go ahead."

"There. How's that? Too much air for you, old man?"

"No, no, that's fine, Carson. That's perfect."

"Are you sure?"

"Sure."

And then, a little later: "Carson, would you mind if I lowered that window about an inch? It's getting a little chilly in here."

"No, I don't mind, Woody. Go right ahead, please."

"There. How's that? Is that all right for you . . . ?"

And like any two young men who must live together and yet acknowledge, mutely, that some design, biological or celestial, has set them forever at variance to one another, they were fiercely loyal to each other in the company of others. "You know what I think?" one of Carson's friends had said. "I think your roommate deWinter is a queer." And of course there were jokes made about Woodcock deWinter's somewhat dandified name.

"It's a damned dirty lie," Carson had said. "Woody's a great guy."

Woody was an inch or two shorter than Carson, blond and slightly built. Someone had told Woody once that his face resembled one of the faces of the Sistine ceiling — the face of the young Adam stretching out his fingertips to God: it was not an ascetic face, but it was pale, soft and brooding. At seventeen, Woody liked to fancy himself both intellectual and musical, although, for some reason, he was poor at his studies and only mediocre at music. He dreamed, too, in those days of becoming an actor. "I want to contribute," he told Carson earnestly. He had come to Princeton with a phonograph and a large collection of records. He studied better, he said, while listening to music. Often, at night, he would turn to where Carson sat — they had desks at opposite sides of the room and sat back to back — and ask, politely, "Mind if I play my Vic, Carson?"

138

Without turning, keeping his eyes focused on the page of the book in front of him, Carson would reply, "No, I don't mind. Go right ahead, Woody."

"I'll keep the volume low," Woody would say.

Listening to his records, however, Woody would not appear to be studying. He would sit, tailor-fashion, on the floor in front of the record-player, staring into space with a rapt expression, his hands moving to the rhythm of the music, as though he were conducting the orchestra. Carson continued to study. Sometimes one or two of Woody's friends dropped in and together they would listen to the music, whispering occasional words of conversation until Woody said, "Ssh! Carson's studying." Then it would be quiet in the room except for the strains of — almost always in those days — Ravel.

They were days, as Carson looked back on them, that passed like an odd, unhappy dream. With music hovering behind them, he and Woody moved within the framework of the suite on tiptoe, as though each boy was treading cautiously, taking care not to brush against a raw edge of feeling or step upon an exposed and tender nerve. Nerves and feelings and little tendrils of pain stretched like cobwebs all about them, and when they were alone in the suite together, Carson began to notice a strange heaviness and thickness around his heart. The suite had two rooms, a common study and a common bedroom. One night Carson took a deep breath and said, "You know, Woody, I've been thinking. You like to listen to your music so much and — no kidding — I enjoy it, too. I really do, but — well — sometimes when I'm studying, with the music going and all — well, sometimes it's a little hard to *concentrate*. Do you know what I mean? Honestly, I don't want you to stop playing your Vic, — hell, Woody, I enjoy it as much as you do — but, well, I've been thinking. After all, we've got the two rooms here. I could move my desk into the bedroom and you could move your bed out here, where your desk and Vic are. Then we could close the doors between . . ."

Woody was silent, his face grave. Woody had a nervous mannerism of reaching up, with the two forefingers of his right hand and tugging at the forelock of his blond hair, his two fingers working like scissors. He began to do this now. Finally, he said, "Sure, Carson. Sure. That's a good idea." And then he said, "I hope —"

"What?"

"Nothing."

They moved the furniture that night.

The door that closed between them, separating them more than physically, might have severed them completely from each other. They might have stopped speaking. They almost stopped speaking, but not quite.

That was how it happened that, one afternoon about a week before the Triangle Club dance, Carson returned from a lab and found Woody with his dinner jacket out across the bed, brushing lint from its midnight blue lapels. Carson said a polite "Hi," and then, just before going into the other room and shutting himself off, he paused and said, "Who're you bringing down for the week end, Woody?"

Woody shrugged. "My cousin Barbara," he said.

"Are you kidding? Your *cousin?*"

"Yes," Woody said. "She's my second cousin." And he added, "I'll probably end up marrying her some day."

Carson laughed. "You don't sound too pleased with that idea, old man," he said.

"Oh, she's all right," Woody said. "She's not so bad." He pulled his wallet out of his back pocket. "I've got a picture of her. Want to see it?" he asked.

Looking at the picture, which showed Barbara in tennis shorts, her dark hair pulled back in a scarf, Carson agreed that she was not bad, not bad at all.

And so, at the dance, when Carson caught sight of Woody across the crowded floor of the Dillon Gymnasium, dancing with his cousin Barbara, he made his way through the moving couples and cut in on them. There were cheerful introductions and, for a moment, Carson and Woody were laughing, best-friend room-mates. "Watch out for him, Barb!" Woody said. "He's a notorious masher. That's why he came stag."

"Oh, I doubt that," Barbara Woodcock said, smiling. And a few minutes later when they were alone on the dance floor, she looked at Carson directly and smiled again. Her smile was the carefully developed, practiced smile of a pretty girl, wide and lipsticked, and she knew how to make her eyes sparkle, but still it was a wonderful smile and she swept him with it. "You're exactly the way Woody described you in his letters," she said. "Exactly!"

Carson laughed. "That's a loyal roommate for you!" he said. "How did he describe me?"

She looked at him very seriously. "You're very good for Woody," she said. "Did you know that? He hasn't been too happy at Princeton. But you've been one of the saving factors. He admires you so."

They danced, and then — too soon for Carson — Ed Hill cut in on them.

Perhaps two hours later, going down the steps to the men's room, Carson met Woody, alone, coming up. Woody's hand gripped the stair rail. "Carson!" Woody said, reaching out with his free hand to stop him. "Carson — wait a minute." His voice sounded strange and choked and his blue eyes were clouded. Woody held his face close and Carson could smell the faint, sweet odor of whiskey.

"What have you done with Barbara, old man?" Carson asked easily.

"She's all right. Listen, Carson," Woody said. "I want to talk to you. Can I talk to you?"

"Sure," Carson said. "What's on your mind?"

"Listen," Woody said. "Listen, I mean it. I've got to talk to you.

141

Can we —" He gestured around him loosely. "Can we talk somewhere where it's not so public?"

"Sure. Where?" Carson said, and he added, "Are you sure Barbara's okay?"

"She's fine. Fine. Don't worry about Barbara. Look," he pointed. "Let's go down there — those other stairs."

"To the basement you mean?"

"No — just over there. Behind that door. Where it's not so public."

Carson followed Woody slowly down the steps to the door that led to the basement stairs. Woody pushed open the heavy door and the two of them stepped inside, on the darkened landing.

"What's on your mind?" Carson asked again.

"Don't worry about Barbara," Woody repeated. "Don't *ever* worry about Barbara, Carson, she's always fine. Always." He giggled. "I'm drunk, Carson," he said.

"Why don't you get a cup of coffee?"

"No, no," Woody said. "I *want* to be drunk, that's why I'm drunk. Listen, Carson."

"What?"

"Listen — I'm telling you," Woody said. There was only a faint light shining from a street light through an upper window; in it, Carson could not see the expression on Woody's face. "Carson —" Woody began.

"Yes. What's the matter?"

"She told you."

"What are you talking about?"

"She told you. She told me she told you."

"Who told me what?"

"Barbara. She told you. She told you how much I admire you."

"Well —" he began.

"No. Stop interrupting," Woody said. "Let me finish." His hands twitched as if tugged by invisible wires. "I know she told you because she said she did. She told you that I thought you were one of the few things — the few *admirable* things in the Class of 1950. In the Classes of 1947, 1948, 1949 and 1950. In this whole damn, snotty, phony, middle-class white shoe college! And it's true, Carson, because all the rest of them, *all* the rest, are nothing but shits. Shits."

"Okay," Carson said pleasantly. "Now look, let's go up and —"

"No, I haven't finished. Listen. You're my roommate, Carson. Sometimes I just don't think. I forget. With the music, I mean. I didn't want to disturb you. You used to say you enjoyed it!"

"Sure," Carson said. "Sure, Woody. I did. I did enjoy it. It was very nice."

"Do you mean that?" he asked. He was speaking faster now. "Do you mean that? Because — that day — that night — that time you said — you, know that time you moved out? It hurt me. It did. It hurt me terribly. It was like — it was as if you had put a knife right through my stomach, through *here*. Do you know what I mean, do you know how much I wanted — do you under- stand, Danny, do you?"

"Danny?" he said. "Who's Danny?"

"I mean Carson. Danny's someone you remind me of — some- one who used to give me swimming lessons. You remind me of him. But what I'm saying is, do you understand?"

"Sure," Carson said kindly. "Sure I do. So let's —"

"Listen!" Woody commanded. "Listen! I'm telling you every- thing. I've got to. Everything. The one thing, the important thing. What two people — like the Greeks used to say. Because — be- cause I *do* admire you Carson. Worship you because you *are* fine. You're *fine*. And decent. And true, and if you loved the music, if you say you really, truly loved the music, then . . ." His voice seemed to vanish, to become a whisper. "Then . . . then . . . are you listening to me? Do you understand?"

A warning, then, swift and sudden came like a short cold gasp in his chest and stomach; Carson felt it, wondered why he hadn't felt it there before. He thought: oh, Christ! A fairy. But immediately innocence, or perhaps loyalty, made him dismiss the thought, ignore it, try to save the moment. "I understand," he said quickly. "Let's go back to the dance."

But Woody had refused to have the moment saved. "No," he said in a distant, whispery voice. "No," he said despairingly. "You don't understand. You don't see, you don't understand that I love you, Carson. I love you," and Woody's hand groped toward him palely in the dark.

Carson drew back, hard, against the door, almost falling upon it. He turned and pulled it open, shouldered through it, and let it slam closed behind him. He ran up the stairs.

He hadn't been sure, exactly, where he was going. Then he saw Barbara Woodcock standing alone. His first impulse was to avoid her, but she had seen him and started toward him.

"Where in the world is Woody?" she asked him, her eyes worried.

He forced himself to smile. "Let's dance," he said, and then, as he led her toward the floor, he said, "I guess Woody had — you know — I guess he must have had a little too much to drink. I guess he's gone somewhere to sleep it off."

"Oh *dear*," she said. "Do you think we should try to find him?"

"No. Let's just let him sleep it off. That's the best thing."

They danced. Woody did not appear again that evening.

They danced and danced. Carson talked a good deal. Whether he was compensating for his experience on the stairs or not, he did not know, but he became quite animated. He told Barbara funny stories about his days at Lawrenceville, all the hare-brained things he and his friends had done, about what characters some of the teachers were. Barbara seemed to enjoy the stories enormously. "You're one of the wittiest people I've ever met!" she said once. She laughed until the tears came to her eyes. Then she told him about her own times at school, and about Burketown, where she and Woody both lived, about her father's farm where they kept saddle horses and had a lake for boating, and about her little sister, Peggy, and about her mother, father, grandmother and grandfather, and what seemed like innumerable aunts, uncles and cousins — all of whom lived in this same middle-sized Connecticut city. "They ought to call it Woodcockville," Carson said once, and she laughed as if he had said the funniest thing in the world. "Don't let anybody cut in on us," she said. And later, "I never had so much fun with anyone in my life!" And still later, "Do you think we ought to see where Woody is?" "Don't worry," he told her.

Walking her slowly back to her room at the Inn, along the dark, shadowy sidewalks, under the lighted Gothic windows of the dormitories from which flowed music and laughter and, inevitably, the sound of showers running, Carson decided that he was in love with her and walked more slowly, swinging her hand in his. They talked, and their talk was both intense and trivial.

"The trouble is, I'm not smart," Barbara said. "I'm wasting Daddy's money going to college. I wanted to go to college, but now I'm afraid I'm wasting his money. I keep wondering if it wouldn't be better if I got a job somewhere and *did* something."

"Of course you're smart," he told her. "What do you mean you're not smart?"

"I'm not, I'm not," she insisted soberly. "I cram furiously for tests and pass them — just barely — and three days later I've forgotten everything I learned. My friend Nancy Rafferty is just the opposite. She's brilliant, really — gets nothing but A's. She's the sort of person who deserves to go to college."

"Oh, I'm no great brain either," Carson said. "Don't get the idea that I'm a great brain."

"Oh, yes you are," she said. "I can tell. You're very intelligent and Woody's told me what good marks you get."

"Ah, what difference do marks make? Do marks make any difference?"

"Yes," she said, "they do. They make a great deal of difference.

That's why I know you're quite smart and I'm not. I daydream too much . . ."

"Yes, that's my trouble, too."

"Daydreaming?"

"Yes."

"You don't seem to be like a daydreamer, Carson. Not really. No, you don't strike me as that type at all."

"I do, though. Daydream a lot."

"What do you daydream about?"

"Lots of things. Life, going into the Army, the future. What life means, things like that. The trouble with me is, I'm an idealist."

"Are you, Carson?"

"Yes."

"Isn't that funny! Because I'm an idealist, too!"

Remembering that evening now, so many years later, made him smile. Having confessed that they were both idealists, their relationship for the next few months continued on a quaintly cerebral level. Maintaining it was difficult, but eventually they had decided that hedonists were what they really were.

He had never mentioned the incident with Woody to anyone. How could he have? Whom could he have told? Born in Maryland, birthplace of gentlemen, Carson had taken the gentleman's code to live by. Born to a world that called its father "sir," and clicked its heels perceptibly when spoken to by its elders, trained to look another man square in the eye and give him a firm handshake, instructed to believe that strenuous exercise was the best way to rid the mind of impure thoughts, that a man should start each day with a bath, a clean shirt and two clean handkerchiefs, that the only scent a man should have about him was the scent of soap, that suspenders were more healthful than belts for the male abdomen, that socks should be of dark, solid colors and neckties should never be red, he had also been taught never to intrude upon the sorrows of the less fortunate, nor speak of them to others.

146

Besides, it was not the sort of thing one could tell another person. Even years later, after he and Barbara were married, after they had become accustomed to talking of such things between themselves with freedom and candor, without embarrassment, he never told her. Part of it was because he lived by the gentleman's code. But part of it, too, was because, somewhere in his head, he had always had a vision of constancy and loyalty, an old-fashioned sort of honor and this picture, when he chose to glance at it, reassured him and bolstered him.

During their engagement and after they were married, Carson and Barbara saw Woody deWinter from time to time. It was inevitable. After all, he was Barbara's cousin and lived in the same town her parents did. He and Woody, whenever they met, spoke to each other pleasantly and politely. But Carson knew. And Woody knew he knew. That was all, and enough. No one else would ever know it, and each man knew this. In fact, their mutual silence may have, after a number of years had passed, given each man a small, tough kernel of respect for the other — a respect that they would otherwise not have shared.

But, at the time, Carson only felt sorry for Woody.

Woody went home to Burketown for Christmas vacation that year and, Carson heard later, tried to hang himself with the twisted silk cord of his bathrobe from the high clothes-bar in his bedroom closet. He had been found, half alive, by his mother's maid, and had been revived. A note — the contents of which were never revealed — was in the roll of his portable typewriter.

When Carson had heard about this, back at Princeton, he felt very sorry indeed for Woody. Sorrier than he had ever felt for any person. But by that time, of course, they were no longer roommates.

He sat, now, on the edge of his bed in the London hotel, thinking of home. He did not encourage thoughts of home on his trips, since he found them saddening and considered them unbusiness-like. Yet, without wanting them to, his thoughts wandered fondly across the Atlantic to the house in Locustville, to Dobie's and Michael's faces, to Barbara's face, to the thought of how slim and pretty she looked in some of the dresses he liked the best. Suddenly, for no clear reason, he remembered her on Friday night, walking across the terrace to put the peas on for dinner — her high, slim-hipped walk. He missed her terribly. He was sorry they had quarreled the night before he left; it was too bad because it had been their first quarrel in quite a long time. Of course, being away from home made the picture of home more poignant and more dear. He smiled, knowing that perfection exists mostly in retrospect and at a distance, that, if he were home now, he'd probably be paddling Dobie for smearing all the bathroom combs with shaving cream or some such four-year-old indiscretion, and he might yell at Barbara, "Why can't you make these kids behave?" Or something else that would cause them to remind each other to remember the rules.

But that wasn't the point, really. The point was that he loved them, and the far-away idyllic dream of them all, living in a never-never land of perfect peace and happiness, only made the truth that much more apparent to him — that he loved them. If he let himself, he could ache with homesickness. But he wasn't going to let himself. So he stood up, pulled on his trousers, tossed a necktie around his neck and knotted it, in front of the cracked and yellowed mirror, firmly. He washed his face with chilly water and combed his hair. He put on his shoes then, buffing their toes just slightly with the soles of his socks, put on his jacket, took two handkerchiefs from his open suitcase, folded one in his breast pocket — remembering the little lesson, "One for blow and one for show" — and squared his cuffs. He surveyed his finished self once more in the mirror and decided that he looked like an American.

First, he would have some breakfast. Then he would go over to the Dorchester and settle the arrangements for his mail.

He had been brooding for several days — perhaps it was weeks

148

or months — about where he was going. It was not that there was anything wrong, actually, with where he was. He had progressed, with the company, at a normal rate of speed. He was thirty years old; by the time he was forty, perhaps, he would be a vice-president. Forty sounded old, but so, in fact, did thirty. Time disturbed him, the advance of it, joined with the increasing wonder: where am I going? In a company with the size and structure of Locustville Chemical, one thing was clear: he would never be president. But that was not what bothered him. He did not want, really, to be president of Locustville Chemical. That had not been his ambition when he joined the company.

He couldn't remember, really, what his precise ambition had been then. He supposed he had had one, but it must have been one that was vague and ill-defined. To get ahead was probably what it had been. But now that he had gotten, so to speak, ahead, it seemed as though he ought to have some more specific goal. And yet he really had none. And the thought of being thirty years old and goal-less was not a pleasant one. Barbara hated Locustville; she had said so often enough. He had tried to cheer her with general promises, telling her that the answer to the future lay in one of those seven cities where the company had sales offices. But he had not told her the truth about how he felt. Somehow, with the rules they tried to live by, a thing like telling her the truth about how he felt was hard to do; it seemed impolite to do. And it was a hard thing, besides, to put into words. But perhaps he should try.

With a start, he realized that he had been staring blindly at his image in the mirror, as though hypnotized with the view of Carson Vickers Greer. He straightened the knot of his tie, turned away, picked up his room key, and went to the door. He opened the door and stepped out into the narrow hall, closing the door behind him.

His room was on the third floor. Next to the single, wire-caged elevator shaft, a flight of stairs descended. He knew that in a hotel like this one the lift, as its name implied, was for upward trips, not downward. And yet, with a slight feeling of vindictiveness because he had not been wakened at nine o'clock as he had asked, he decided not to use the stairs, but to make the lift come up and get him. He pushed the call button hard and heard its bell ring out below.

Yes, he thought, perhaps he ought to talk to Barbara about the future, and himself, and his restlessness. Perhaps when he got home he would.

He waited.

But when a young man has come to that point in life where he does not know where he is going, where he is not sure who he is or whom he once wanted to be — when he is no longer sure why he first set out upon the course he has traveled or why he has continued for the distance that he has — at that point, much as he may love his wife, there are things that he cannot tell her. It is not only because there are rules of courtesy and kindness. It is because the admission of his uncertainty and unknowing might become, in a way, an admission of his lack of manhood. And there is only a shred of consolation in thinking that the questions, which he eventually must answer alone, are questions that a woman might not even understand.

So he waited for the lift to begin its creaking journey upward, feeling lost, though comforted again by knowing that Sunday is always a lost day in selling, but knowing that he was more lost, perhaps, this Sunday than other salesmen were.

Cables, visible behind the grillwork, began to tremble; the lift was coming up. At least he wasn't at the Dorchester. At least he was playing the game. At least he had found, stumbled upon, what was probably the cheapest hotel in London. When he ran into one of the other salesmen he would have something to talk about.

9

THE BAY WINDOW WHERE HER GRANDMOTHER SAT FACED THE garden; it was actually a five-windowed turret, and inside, below its sill, ran a narrow window seat covered with five green velvet cushions. The turret was on the sunny, southeast side, but the upper sash of each window was of stained glass — a random mosaic of amber, green, lavender and ruby pieces — so that the sunlight that came through seemed shifting and uncertain, a gaudy rainbow of oily colors. It was not a religious light even though in the center window, in letters of twisting lead, the glazier had inscribed the motto:

> *The kiss of the sun for pardon*
> *The song of the birds for mirth;*
> *One is nearer God's heart in a garden*
> *Than anywhere else on earth.*

Tall weeds and sunflowers overbore the garden now. God, or whatever mortal had tended it, had long since given up the chore. Lambs'-quarter and mustard-plant, wild morning glory and low, fluffy clumps of chickweed hid a place where, once, even borders of perennials had run, where delphinium and peonies and lupins had bloomed, and where still could be seen a few abandoned clumps of purple iris. In this ruin there was a kind of rank, billowy beauty now — like a once-lovely woman who has lazily let herself go in middle age. There was visible a shape, or memory, of what had been an intricate design of paths, measuring the garden into a series of triangles and hexagons. But now the luxurious summer weeds, their leaves hanging wilted in the brilliant morning sunshine, blurred the original geometry and turned the formal garden into a tropical rain forest topped with huge, improbable sunflower faces. In the exact center, almost hidden by tall grass, a silver gazing globe on a stone pedestal glittered in the sun. The sun moved now, slowly into the window where Barbara stood, fell upon the heavy twisted fringe of the velvet curtain. Her grandmother, as she often did these days, had dozed, her small head fallen forward on her bosom, gently breathing. Mrs. Zaretsky, the nurse, looked up from her knitting. "We get tired very easily," she said to Barbara. "But we'll wake up before we know it."

"Do you think I should leave?" Barbara asked.

"Oh, we love having visitors!" Mrs. Zaretsky said cheerfully.

"I hope I'm not tiring her."

Mrs. Zaretsky smiled a knowing nurse's smile behind her steel-rimmed glasses. "It's just as well," she said. "After one of these little snoozes we'll just forget to wake up, and that will be that."

"Yes," Barbara said quietly.

"It's simply remarkable," Mrs. Zaretsky said. "Doctor McDonald says that what she really is is sort of a freak. Her heart is fine, her hearing's perfect, she has all her own teeth! Imagine! Of course her eyesight's failed and — upstairs —" she tapped her head significantly with her finger, "she's gotten terribly fuzzy. But still and all, it's just remarkable. She's a remarkable old lady, she really is."

Barbara nodded silently. She turned to the window again.

"The blood doesn't get up to the brain fast enough," Mrs. Zaretsky said, dropping her voice to a loud whisper. "That's why she can't think straight. But sometimes she's just as clear as a bell! It's remarkable! Why, just the other day she all of a sudden started telling me about Burketown — the old Burketown she knew as a girl, and how it's changed and all. And believe it or not, I thought: Why she's really a very remarkable person! She remembered when they had trolley cars on High Street — everything. Now what I wish is that when she gets that way, you know, lucid, that somebody could come with one of those whatchamacallits, those things they take things down on, a recording machine. I thought that to have those remarks of hers down on a recording machine would be worth something, as a historical document, I really did. I mentioned it to Mr. deWinter when he was here on Wednesday and he said he thought it was a very good idea."

To change the subject, Barbara said, "Does she have someone to take care of the garden?"

"The garden? Oh, you mean *that* garden? Well, old Joe Martino comes to cut the grass, but goodness me, there isn't much point in trying to fix up that old garden, is there? I mean when she's gone they'll probably tear this house down, won't they? Or sell it to someone who could really use it for something?"

Barbara turned to her grandmother again, and with a little start, the old lady lifted her head and opened her eyes. "Oh!" she said.

Loudly, Mrs. Zaretsky said, "Your granddaughter's here to see you, Mrs. Woodcock. Remember?"

"Did you have a nice nap, Nana?" Barbara asked.

"Yes, dear. Thank you. I'm sorry. What time is it, dear?"

"Ten-thirty, Nana."

Mrs. Zaretsky consulted the heavy chronograph on her wrist. "Just ten thirty-four, Mrs. Woodcock," she said. "Would you like a nice, hot cup of broth?"

"No, thank you, not yet," Mrs. Woodcock said. "It's a lovely day, isn't it."

"It certainly is," Barbara said. She sat down on the little footstool by the chair and patted her grandmother's hand. "But it's going to be hot I'm afraid."

"This house is always cool, even on the hottest days," her grandmother said.

"It's wonderful to see you again, Nana," Barbara said. "You look so well."

"Thank you, dear."

If there had been any change, Barbara thought, in her grandmother's appearance since she had seen her last, it was only that she seemed to have grown, imperceptibly, smaller. She had always been a tiny, doll-like woman, barely five feet tall, with a pale and fragile face. She had always been proud of her size, of her small feet which wore a size-four shoe. A difficulty, in her old age, had been finding dresses that looked mature enough for a very old lady and yet were small enough to fit her delicate frame. Her dress size was seven, a size that in most department stores was reserved for teen-age girls. But she sat now in a black silk dress that had been made especially for her, and became her, turned her into a simple composition of black and white. Her eyes were so pale they seemed to have no color to them, her carefully curled hair was pure white, and the flesh of her face and tiny hands seemed to be composed of soft, chalky powder. About her neck she wore a silver and onyx lavaliere. Her only other jewelry was the wide gold wedding band that she had never removed. She sat, hands folded, in the wheel chair and across her knees was a white knitted afghan. She had been a picture-book child — posed, in a daguerreotype, holding a fluffy white kitten to her cheek; she had been a picture-book young woman, much admired for her graceful performance of cotillion figures, and, in a later photograph, a white lace fan had replaced the kitten at her cheek. And now, at ninety-three, sitting in her paneled library, beginning her day, which consisted of a series of little journeys between sunny windows, she still had much of the artificiality and perfection of a cameo, the picture of a little old lady that might have been used to decorate a box of candy.

She was a woman, Barbara had often heard, who had not been built for child-bearing, and yet she had managed to have two children — though the first, a baby girl, had lived only nineteen hours and a tiny headstone in the Burketown cemetery marked the grave of Cecilia Mary Woodcock, born January 7, 1894, died January 8, 1894. Beneath the dates the inscription read, "Suffer the little children to come unto me." Seven years later she had her second child, Preston, and the ordeal, it was understood, had nearly killed her. Though she had never been an invalid, she had, when she recovered, been given an invalid's care and attention. "Your grandmother," Barbara could remember her grandfather saying proudly, "is a woman who needs a man's arm to take her wherever she goes." And Barbara could remember her grandmother being guided and steered, helped and directed, through the rooms and passageways of life. She remembered that whenever a guide was not immediately there to offer Grandmother his arm she got lost; there had been many fond and indulgent searches for a little white-haired lady who, stepping from a hotel elevator, had turned as if by instinct the wrong way, or who had stepped out onto the sidewalk in front of Penrose's store after an afternoon of shopping and — not seeing her car — had decided to walk home along Maple Street which led, of course, toward Hanscomb Corners. Unwilling to ask directions, she would forge on resolutely away from her destination as if determined to escape her goal. Even in her own house, Barbara could remember her grandmother moving from the living room into the hall, then hesitating, uncertain as to where she was bound. "Preston?" she would call to her husband and he would answer "Just a minute, Mary," and when he appeared he would offer her his arm and set her on her course again. The wheel chair, then, possibly answered more than a physical need after her most trusted guide had gone; in its arms she felt confident, sure that whoever was pushing her would know better than she did where she wanted to go. It was curious that, just lately, she had made several attempts to get out of the chair.

Barbara sat silently, letting time pass; in the background, Mrs. Zaretsky's knitting needles clicked efficiently. Making conversation with the aged is always difficult but it was especially difficult with her grandmother. Nothing much had ever interested Mary Owens Woodcock, even as a young woman, outside of shoes and hats and dresses. These interests now had long vanished from her mind. She had never seemed, despite what Mrs. Zaretsky had said, to be concerned with changes or events in the world. To observe that there had once been trolley cars on High Street did not seem to Barbara to be a significant revelation. She had, at one time in her life, dipped her toe daintily into several fashionable religious cults — Couéism, Moral Rearmament, Christian Science, Spiritualism — but none of her experiences here seemed to have left any profound effect upon her soul. Mrs. Zaretsky sometimes read to her, but her enjoyment in this had never seemed to go beyond the lulling pleasure of hearing another human voice. So it was hard, as Barbara sat there, allowing a decent interval to elapse before leaving, to think of anything to say. At last she said, "Would you like me to read to you, Nana?"

"No, thank you, dear. Not right now," her grandmother said.

Mrs. Zaretsky glanced at her oversized wristwatch. "Quarter of eleven," she said. "Almost time for our medicine."

"Which medicine is it?" Mrs. Woodcock asked.

"The kind you like," Mrs. Zaretsky said.

Mrs. Woodcock turned suddenly to Barbara. "Did you find the papers you wanted, dear?"

"What papers, Nana?"

Mrs. Zaretsky looked quickly at Barbara and gave her a humorous wink. "That was your *other* granddaughter, Mrs. Woodcock," Mrs. Zaretsky said. "That was Peggy. This is Barbara."

"Oh of course," her grandmother said. "Of course, Barbara. Well, ask Peggy if she still wants those papers, if she's found them. I haven't had a chance to look for them. I don't know quite where to lay my hands on them."

"What papers, Nana?" Barbara asked again.

"Something your sister wanted," Mrs. Zaretsky said. "I'm sure she's found them, whatever they were." And she shook her head slowly back and forth, advising Barbara to pursue the subject no further.

"Ask Peggy to come to see me," her grandmother said.

"I will," Barbara said.

"She was just here on Friday," Mrs. Zaretsky said. "She comes to see you nearly twice a week."

Barbara opened her purse. "I have some pictures of my little boys here, Nana," she said. "Would you like to see them?"

"Oh, I'd love to, dear," her grandmother said.

Barbara held two snapshots up. "See? Haven't they gotten big?"

"She can't see them," Mrs. Zaretsky said.

"I can see them perfectly," her grandmother said. "They're beautiful children."

"They're your great-grandchildren," Mrs. Zaretsky said.

"Beautiful children," Mrs. Woodcock said. Barbara put the pictures back in her purse.

Mrs. Zaretsky put down her knitting. "Time for our medicine now," she said briskly, and then, "Oooh! I'm so stiff from sitting." Bending forward, her large hands pressing her thighs, she walked slowly out of the room.

Barbara sat quietly on the footstool and her grandmother nodded her head, up and down, "Beautiful children," she said again.

"Dobie and Michael," Barbara said.

"Yes. My husband's father was named Dobie. Such a handsome man."

Mrs. Zaretsky returned with a small tray that held a bottle, a spoon and a glass of water.

"What is this now?" Mrs. Woodcock asked.

"This is the kind we like," Mrs. Zaretsky said. She filled the spoon and held it toward the old lady. "Open wide," she said. "Atta girl!" She popped the spoon inside. "Now here's a nice glass of water to take away the taste."

Mrs. Woodcock took a swallow from the water glass, then smiled. "Why do you say it's the kind I like, Binky, when you know it's the kind I *don't* like?"

Mrs. Zaretsky, called Binky since the days before she was married and had worked in the hospital as Loretta Binks, drew back, pretending shock. "What do you *mean?*" she asked. "We like everything that's good for us, don't we?"

"Not necessarily," the old lady said.

Barbara stood up. "I really must go, Nana," she said, giving her grandmother's powdery hand a gentle squeeze. "I've got to get back to the farm. But I'll drop by to see you again before I go."

"Thank you, dear," her grandmother said. "It's always so nice to see you." She lifted her face to be kissed and Barbara bent to kiss her.

"Good-by," she said.

"Bye-bye. Come again," Mrs. Zaretsky said. "We're always home."

"Good-by. I will." She blew her grandmother a kiss, turned and walked out into the hall to the front door.

She went down the front steps into the harsh sunlight that glittered on the concrete driveway. She opened the door of her car, got in, and reached in her purse for the keys. Then, in the rearview mirror, she saw another car turn into the driveway behind her. She turned and saw that it was Barney.

He got out of his car and walked up the driveway toward her. "Hello," he said.

"Hello, Barney," she smiled. "What are you doing here?" He was dressed in a dark business suit, white shirt and tie.

"I had to pick up a couple of things at the office," he said. "I thought I'd drop by here on the way back — just to say hello to your grandmother."

"I've just spent about half an hour with her," Barbara said.

"How is she?"

"Oh, just about the same. A little muddled. She got me mixed up with Peggy once, but otherwise she doesn't seem much different."

Barney looked toward the house. "I come by to see her from time to time," he said. "It's funny — I've always rather liked old people. Talking to her is very calming."

Barbara laughed. "Calming? With old Binky Zaretsky inter-rupting all the time?"

"Oh, I don't mind her."

"She's such a ghoul!"

He rested the palms of his hands on the side of her car and stared down at the driveway beneath his feet. "Well —" he said.

"Are you going in to see her?" she asked.

"I don't know. She may be tired now. Having just had a visitor."

"Yes — she may," Barbara said and suddenly the strip of sun-light between them seemed oddly crowded, the air thick. He raised his eyes and looked at her, frowning; she looked at him, then away, toward the corner of the drive.

"Did you — ?" he began.

"What?"

He cleared his throat. "Were you finally able to get to sleep last night?"

"Oh, yes," she said brightly. "Yes — I was asleep the minute my head touched the pillow!" She laughed, a little wildly. "Did you — get to sleep?"

"Yes," he said. "Finally."

"You scared me half to death," she said. "Seeing you — like that — in the hall."

"I thought you were a ghost," he said. "I thought you were the ghost of Harlow J. Lerner, come back to haunt us."

She laughed.

"What were you doing? Walking through the house with no lights on?"

"Yes," she said. "I was. I don't know why I was."

He continued to stand, his hands on the door of her car, and she resisted looking at him, though she could feel his eyes on her. She looked straight ahead, her hands resting on the steering wheel. "Well," she said finally, "I must get back."

He stepped away from the car. "Yes," he said. "I suppose you have to."

"Yes," she said.

He seemed to hesitate. "Do you have to get back right away?"

"I think I should," she said. "Why?"

"I wondered — would you like to go for a drive?"

"A drive?"

"Yes."

"Well — what time is it?"

"Around eleven," he said. "Lunch isn't until one."

"Well —" she said.

"It's a nice day."

"Yes, it is a nice day," she said. And then, "All right."

"You will go?"

"All right."

"My car's blocking yours," he said. "Let's take mine."

"I guess I can leave mine here for a minute," she said.

"Sure," he said.

She got out of the car and walked slowly ahead of him along the driveway to where his car was. She opened the door and got inside. He walked around the car and opened the other door and slid into the seat beside her.

"I'm glad you don't have a car like Woody's," she said. "That little thing of his is just too rakish for me!"

"There's something to be said," he said, "for a conservative model of the lower-priced three."

She laughed.

He started the car and backed it out of the driveway.

"Where shall we go?" she asked.

He didn't answer her, but at the corner of Prospect Avenue and High Street he turned left.

"Do you remember when you first drove me around this town?" he asked her after a moment.

"Oh yes," she said.

"That was a pleasant summer, wasn't it?"

"It was," she said.

They were driving through the West Hill section of Burketown now, a section of small, identical, boxlike houses that had been built immediately after the second World War. It was not Barbara's favorite part of town. Because it was a development, it reminded her of Sunrise Heights in Locustville. Along its winding streets, West Hill presented a panorama of brightly colored rooftops — red, blue, white and green; its backyards were aflutter with clotheslines decked with brightly colored wash; its front yards were a dotted pattern of sidewalks edged with round yews, square boxwoods, pyramidal spruces — foundation planting. Presently they were past West Hill, in the open country, heading toward the hilly woods that ringed the valley. Stone fences lined the road; here and there appeared a pasture, a farm house or barn. The road was narrower, and in the heat, the tarred surface seemed to swim ahead of the car in a shining haze. "Where are we going?" she asked.

"I don't really know," he said. "Just driving. Do you care?"

"I guess not." She put her head back on the seat. "Poor Nana," she said.

"Why?"

"I don't know. I think one of the things that upset me the most was seeing her garden all gone to weeds. It used to be such a beautiful garden. Now somebody's planted sunflowers all over the place. Everything else is dead."

"Sometimes," he said, "when things start dying it's just as well to let them die."

She looked at him. "That's cheerful!" she said. "You sound like Mrs. Zaretsky. She's ready for Nana to die at any minute."

"Well," he said, "it's true, isn't it? If she's going to die, she's going to die."

"What a gloomy mood you're in!"

"Ah —" he said.

He slowed the car now, pulled it to one side of the road and stopped. "Have you ever been here before?"

She looked around. A short path led between two boulders at the road's edge to a ravine where, between large rocks, a brook ran down.

"Why, yes!" she said. "I remember this place. We used to go swimming here! It was quite illegal, though. How did you discover it?"

"Just driving around one day. It's still illegal." He pointed to a NO TRESPASSING sign.

"It was a very daring place to go when I was in school," she said. "We used to come here at night."

"Let's look at the brook," he said. "I don't think they'd mind if we trespassed just a little."

"All right."

They got out of the car. They went down the path to a wide, flat rock that jutted out above the water. "We used to jump from here," Barbara said. "That brook's terribly cold. It comes out of a spring somewhere."

"Yes, I know."

"Have you been swimming here?"

"Just once."

"When?"

"At night one time," he said.

"How are your swimming lessons coming?"

He laughed shortly. "I haven't had any," he said. "I didn't come here to swim. I just rolled up my trousers and went wading — just as far up as the spring."

"At *night?*"

"It's very pretty here at night." He sat down on the flat rock, made a pillow of his hands behind his head and lay back, crossing his feet. She stood above him. He looked oddly out of place, in a dark business suit and tie, stretched out there, squinting up at her against the sun. She sat down beside him.

162

He lifted one arm now and with one finger he delicately touched the thin ridge of her nose. "You've got a little sunburn," he said. "You're peeling — right there."

"Yes."

"Your face always has a gleam," he said. "A kind of brown gleam, a shimmer. You look — always very fresh."

She turned her head away from him to discourage any further appraisal of it.

"It was one of the first things I noticed about you — your gleam. The way a very little girl's face gleams. Those first few days, when I first came to the farm, everything seemed to have a gleam like that." He smiled distantly. "Then I got to know it," he said.

"Barney," she said, "tell me what's the matter."

"You know what's the matter."

"No. Tell me."

"Why do you think I brought you here?" he asked.

She smiled. "Do you realize, it's been at least fourteen years since I've been to this place? It makes me realize I'm not a little girl any more. So — so, I think we ought both to try to be more mature, more sensible." She looked at him; he was staring straight up at the sky. "Do you have a cigarette?" she asked.

He reached in his pocket for cigarettes, found them, and offered the pack to her. He rolled over on his side and gave her a light. He tossed the match toward the water. "Yes," he said finally, "you're absolutely right."

"So let's forget about that other — that crazy summer," she said. "In fact, I —"

"In fact what?"

"Nothing."

"In fact you've forgotten?"

She said nothing.

"Have you, Barbara?"

When she still did not answer, he turned on his stomach and

lay with his face buried in his folded arms. He said something that she couldn't hear.

"What?" she asked.

"I said, so we'll just go on and let everything die around us."

"Let what die?"

"Your marriage and mine."

She laughed. "Nothing's dying. I'm very happy, really. And so are you. Or you ought to be."

"Everything is dying," he said, his voice coming from far away in the cavern between his folded arms.

"Oh, Barney!" she said gaily. "Don't be silly!"

"Listen," he said intensely, turning his head to look at her again, "Everyone used to shine — your mother, your father, Peggy — everybody — when I first came here, just as though they'd been freshly painted. In two years, the paint's chipped off."

"What are you talking about?"

"When I say things are dying, I mean it — literally. It's not just your grandmother and her flower garden, and it's not just Peggy and me. I was only half kidding about old Mr. Lerner's ghost. There is some kind of ghost haunting this whole family! The paper company is dying — did you know that? At best, I give it ten more years unless something radical is done. Your father's dying — committing suicide with drink! It's not that I understand it — I don't. And I don't know what to do about it, to stop it. Perhaps it can't be stopped. The only thing I know is that I was alive — or thought I was — when I first came here. But I don't seem to be any more. And you seemed alive, too, at first. Are you still? Or have we both caught the disease — ?"

"There's no disease," she said. "How could there be? Please don't talk this way —"

"Listen, listen to me!" he repeated. "Want to hear my symptoms? Want to know what's happened to me? I'll tell you what I did today. I lied to you. I didn't have anything to pick up at the office this morning. I went to church. To Saint Mary's. I went to Mass

— but I didn't. I couldn't. I couldn't go in. I got up the steps, to the door, but I couldn't go in. I saw that that wasn't the answer. It was no good trying to *pray* my way out of whatever I'm in. I couldn't. I stood on the steps of the church and heard the Mass begin and knew I was a hypocrite. Then I remembered your mother said this morning that you'd gone to your grandmother's house. So I went there, looking for you."

Her hand trembled as she lifted her cigarette to her lips. "Is it true what you said about Daddy?" she asked.

"What? That he's drinking himself to death? He drinks a quart of gin a day — sometimes more. How can you help seeing that it's true?"

She held her hand across her eyes, shielding them from the sun, and wondered if she was going to cry. "Please, Barney —" she said.

"Listen," he said. "Perhaps I am crazy. I think Peggy thinks so sometimes. But I've seen it — your family, here, this company, and everything — they're all hopeless. They're walking, happily, hand in hand, swinging along toward the grave. And Peggy is —"

"What's the matter with Peggy?"

"Never mind," he said. "Never mind Peggy. The only thing I know is that you and I — perhaps — can get away from it. Because we love each other."

She stood up abruptly. "No," she said. "It doesn't make any sense. It's not true. Let's go back."

"Because we love each other," he repeated.

"Please take me back."

He stood up now and faced her. She closed her eyes, pressing back tears. "Please," she said again.

"I love you," he said.

They stood there and she thought he seemed remarkably resolute, standing very still, his hands thrust deep in his pockets. She could feel, again, the thickness of air between them, thick as glass, thick because the distance between them was too wide to cross. She thought: I must say something, not stand here like a schoolgirl on a rock, where he has taken me because it has a pretty, romantic view. It was an innocent place for him to have brought her, full of memories of summer vacation nights, boys boldly changing into their trunks behind the shadows of bushes, girls, daringly wriggling into their suits in the car — a place of flashlights, damp hair and towels, slips and screams in the icy water. It was hard to translate this place into the present, to the two of them, this summer Sunday morning. She said quietly, "All right, Barney. Suppose you do. Suppose we love each other. What are we going to do next?"

"Go somewhere," he said.

"Where? Where will we go?"

His eyes wavered, just slightly. "We'll get our divorces first. Then get married."

"And live where?"

"Anywhere."

"Just anywhere?"

"Yes."

"We could never come back here, to this town."

"We wouldn't want to live here."

"You wanted to once."

"I was wrong," he said.

"No," she said. "You see? You haven't thought it out at all! You're the one who's impractical! You're the one who's the dreamer. It's impossible. And you'll be happier when you admit it. There's nothing you or I can do about it — ever. Now, take me back to Nana's house." She turned quickly and her heel slipped on the rock's smooth surface. He reached out and gripped her arm, steadying her.

"Barbara," he said.

"No," she said, pulling free.

"All right," he said, releasing her.

She started up the path toward the car and he followed her.

At 1045 Prospect Avenue the telephone rang. Mrs. Zaretsky got out of her chair and went into the hall to answer it.

"Oh, hello there, Mrs. Woodcock!" she said cheerfully. "Yes, she *was* here. Oh, we had a nice long visit and she left — oh, I'd say about half an hour ago. Her car's still here, though. What happened was, just as she was about to drive out, your son-in-law, Mr. Callahan, drove in. They talked a minute in the driveway, I happened to see, and then they got into his car and went somewhere. But I suppose she'll be back pretty quick, to pick up her car and all. If I see her when she comes back, want me to ask her to call you? All right, Mrs. Woodcock, then I won't try to be on the lookout for her. I know she'll be back soon because she said she had to get back out to the farm. That's all right, Mrs. Woodcock. Yes, we're all fine. 'Bye now."

"No, it wasn't for you," Mrs. Zaretsky said as she came back into the room.

Sundays at the farm were relaxed affairs. Because none of the Woodcocks were regular church-goers, Sunday breakfasts were served most of the morning, whenever people got up. And, by twelve o'clock — in summer especially — the cocktail hour started, because it was Sunday. And, because it was Sunday, there was none of the ritual of the weekday evening cocktail hours. It was informal, easy, as the day progressed slowly toward lunchtime.

Everyone was at the pool. Barbara sat with her mother on a folding canvas chair, holding a gin-and-tonic that someone had given her; they watched the crowd in the water. Barbara's cousin Jeffrey, just out of Yale, was there with his pretty fiancée, Marcia Symington. Jeffrey's older brother, Talcott, and his wife, Monique, were also there. Sally deWinter Pratt, who was Woody's older sister, had dropped by for a swim with a bearded man who, much to the family's displeasure, seemed to be Sally's present choice for a second husband. Peggy and Barney were both in the pool, too. Barney stood at the shallow end and Barbara watched as Peggy nimbly climbed the ladder to the high board, stepped forward, and performed a neat jacknife into the water.

Her mother was telling her about her morning. She had gone, after breakfast, to see her "family" on the hill, the Millers. Mrs. Miller, a widow, had seven children. They lived in great poverty, and caring for the Millers, supplying the smaller ones in winter with warm coats and boots, bringing them baskets of food, and generally seeing to their well-being, was Edith Woodcock's particular personal charity in Burketown. She grieved for the Miller children as she might for her own.

"I brought them six little roasting chickens this morning," Edith said. "I had Mr. Kaplan pack them in dry ice for me. Poor Mrs. Miller! I don't know what she's going to do, poor thing. Lottie, the oldest daughter's, pregnant! She's fifteen. What could I say? Mrs. Miller's upset enough about it. Always afraid, she said, that Lottie'd 'turn out bad.' Turn out bad! If she was afraid she'd turn out bad, why didn't she *do* something at the time? *Talk* to Lottie. Or *something!* Now it's a little too late. And Lottie! Barbara, you should see her. Fifteen years old, four months pregnant, and pleased as punch about it! Just delighted! She told me she hopes it'll be a little girl. Honestly, those people. I think I shall have to call the state social worker and have her talk to Lottie. I can't think of anything else to do. It makes me so sad, though, to think how poor Mrs. Miller's tried — so hard — to bring those children up. And now, to have this, which will set an example for all the younger ones, you can be sure of that. Mrs. Miller asked me what I thought she should have done, when she first suspected Lottie was misbehaving, as she put it, with this man. Who's married, by the way — of course! I was tempted to tell her — though of course I didn't — that her family's *moral* welfare was really not up to me."

Barbara sipped her drink. She nodded sympathetically. She had heard so many of the Millers' problems before. "Where's Daddy?" she asked.

"Resting. He'll be out in a minute."

The crowd in the pool was very gay. There was laughter, splashing. The blue water foamed and glittered in the sun about dark shoulders, white bathing caps. Sally's beau was showing himself to be something of a diver; he walked on his hands toward the end of the diving board, his feet pointing straight up in the air and his black beard pointing straight at the water. He waited, poised, then gave a powerful spring with his arms, arched in the air, curled into a miraculous high somersault, then dived straight as an arrow. There were cheers and applause.

She looked at Barney. It hurt her to see him there, standing at the shallow end of the pool, leaning back, resting his elbows on the coping, the line of water just below the top of his trunks. He looked so proud and defiant, as though anyone who touched him or made him move either forward or backward would set off an angry trigger instantly within him. He stood, tall, slim and arrogant, creating inadvertently an illusion of hauteur while actually, she thought, the illusion he was trying to create was something quite different. She wanted to get up, to go to him and speak to him, but it was too painful. She couldn't move. From the chair, holding the drink in her hand, she could only watch him helplessly.

Then Edith said quietly, "Barbara, you were with him this morning, weren't you. You went for a drive. Barbara, I've warned you before and I'll warn you again. *Don't*. Don't do this. If you must have someone, pick someone else — not him." Then Edith stood up. "I'm going to get my suit," she said. "It's just too hot a day to watch other people cooling off."

A little later, Barbara watched Barney come up the steps out of the pool and start toward the house. He went slowly, stepping gingerly in his bare feet across the hard, hot stones.

Presently Peggy came out of the pool dripping wet and sat down beside her.

10

Peggy said, "There's been so much going on this week
end, we've hardly had a chance to talk at all!" She tugged at
the strap of her bathing cap, pulled the cap off and fluffed her
damp hair with her fingers. She smiled, reached for a towel that
lay folded beside her chair and began blotting the water from her
face and arms.

Peggy was an extremely neat girl. She was meticulous and
efficient and an excellent housekeeper, which Barbara was not.
Unlike Barbara, who had a habit of stepping out of her clothes
and leaving them where they fell, Peggy's closets and dresser
drawers were always immaculate and perfectly organized. She cat-
alogued things. The quilted boxes in her closet bore little tags on
which were lettered their contents in Peggy's neat, round handwriting: "Sweater: periwinkle blue pullover; Sweater: lavender
cardigan; Sweater: white cardigan with appliqué floral front . . .
Shoes: beige silk pumps, medium heel; Sandals: black velvet. . . ."
and so on. She was efficient in her gestures, too. Every motion of
her hands was gracious and controlled. In one of her gracious and
controlled movements now, she refolded her towel, placed it beside the chair, then reached for a cigarette and tapped it slowly
and deliberately on the back of her now-dry wrist. Then she
placed the cigarette between her lips and lighted it, blowing out
the match with a stream of smoke. "Isn't it a shame that Carson
had to go on this trip," she said. "When he gets back, summer will
be over."

"Yes," Barbara said.

"He must get tired of it. Damned tired. Will he *always* have to
travel like this, do you think?"

"Oh, not always," Barbara said. "What he hopes to be, eventually, is a regional manager in one of their sales offices."

"I'm just crazy about Carson," Peggy said. "He really is a wonderful guy. But — ye gods — we never see him! He hasn't been up here in ages."

"I know."

Peggy held her cigarette between her thumb and forefinger, her hand cupped around it. "Of course I've always wondered," she said, "whether Carson enjoys coming up here or not."

"Oh, he likes it. It's just that —"

"I know, he's never home! Poor guy. But what I mean is, I don't think he has the feeling for this place that you and I have. But then, after all, why should he? It's not *his* home!"

"Yes, that's true."

"And how about you? I've been wondering — do you ever wish you didn't have to come up here? That it's a *duty* now, and not a pleasure any more? I mean, your children are in Locustville and you've got the house there. Do you ever think: oh, damn it, I suppose I've got to go up to the farm for a visit? I'm just curious, wondering if you'd ever get that sort of feeling."

Barbara laughed. "No," she said. "I love the children, yes. But Locustville is hardly home. It's strictly temporary. If anything, I sometimes feel the opposite — guilty for wanting to come up here so much!"

Peggy nodded. "Yes, I know what you mean. It's the farm, isn't it. The place. It's the house, here, and the family. It's funny that both of us should love it so. Young people nowadays aren't supposed to, you know. They're supposed to be — well, more like Barney, who's *rejected* everything, his past, his parents, everything. But in your case, it's more the farm, isn't it? These acres, how many ever there are. Not the town of Burketown or the company — but right *here* that you want to come back to."

"Yes, I suppose it is."

"And the company probably hardly ever enters your mind at all."

"What do you mean? What company?"

Peggy smiled. "The Woodcock Paper Company, dear. Ever hear of it? It's what's been giving us our bread and butter — and pretty damn nice bread and butter — for all these years!" She hesitated. "No," she said. "I'm not trying to be mean — forgive the sarcasm, Barb. It's just that I've more or less *had* to get involved, to get interested in the company these last few years, with Barney working there. Ye gods, half a dozen years ago, I didn't even know what the damn company made! Oh, paper of course, but paper is paper. I didn't know whether it made carbon paper or toilet paper and I bet you don't either, right this minute."

"Well, I know a little more about it than that," Barbara said.

"But seriously," Peggy said, "why should you? You're not involved in it the way I am. You get your dividend once a year and that's the end of it for you. But with me, having my mate in it, it's become one hell of an important thing." She smiled at Barbara again. "You think I'm driving at something, and I am. Quite frankly."

"What is it?" Barbara asked.

"Look. How much, exactly, do you know about what's going on there right now?"

"Well," Barbara said, "quite honestly, from a couple of things Woody said, I got the impression that things aren't going too well."

"Too well! No, dear, they're not going too well. Oh, it's no crisis, or at least I don't think so. But things aren't too good, either. Some of it's not our fault. This is a depressed area right now, this section of the state. Everybody's feeling it. Our sales are off this year. But they've also been off for the last five years. That's the big difference. And the funny thing is, they really haven't been *off*. What's happened is more that *other* plants — competing companies — have been going up, bit by bit. Old Woodcock Paper's just standing still, holding its own, but not moving. And I

172

don't know how much you know about business, dear, but from a business standpoint that ain't so good!"

Barbara studied her sister's face. "Peggy," she said, "you really surprise me sometimes. How did you get to know so much about business?"

"As I said, I've more or less *had* to, dear," Peggy said. "Living here, I've been involved in it — through Barney." She hesitated. "Barbara — how much do you miss Carson?"

"What do you mean?"

"I mean how much do you miss him when he's away?"

"That's a funny question. Can the amount someone misses someone else be measured? I don't know. I —"

"No," Peggy said. "I mean, do you miss him a great deal when he's gone, or do you miss him just a little? Or do you feel a little relieved? Do you think — *whew!* Now I can relax and live my own life for a few weeks!"

"No, I don't think that," Barbara said. "I certainly don't feel relieved! No, I miss him — a great deal, of course. I miss him terribly."

"I was just curious," Peggy said. "Just wondering. You've been married longer than I have. And of course in my case, Barney's right here — all the time. Built-in, so to speak! So I never have an opportunity to miss him. I was wondering how I would feel if he went away, on trips."

"You'd miss him, you can be sure of that."

"Would I? I suppose so." She tapped her cigarette, carefully shaping the ash against the side of the ash tray. "Barney is a very unusual person," she said. "He has an extremely acute business sense. He's a *sensitive* businessman, if you see what I mean. He's sensitive to trends, situations — a kind of intuition, which is very good in business and very rare. What he needs isn't guidance — which is what some of the people at the company seem to think he needs — he needs support. He needs all the support he can get. With the right kind of support he can — I'm convinced — turn

173

this company into a damned good thing. The kind of company it was in 1926 and 1927. You and I should give him all the support we can."

"What do you mean?"

Peggy's eyes gazed across the pool, toward the rising banks of rhododendron and laurel that filled the distance between the pool and the house and terrace beyond. "I mean," she said, "that you, yourself — just as much as I — ought to support him. For a purely practical reason. Because it's your company, too. You own stock in it. It could make us both rich some day — or it could leave us both poor as church mice, if the company goes bust. Look," she said, turning to Barbara now and looking at her intently. "Let's not be hypocrites. I've been thinking about this for a good long time and I've got a plan. You say you hate Locustville, you miss Carson when he takes these damn trips — all that. Well, frankly, I can guess what Carson makes at that job — not a hell of a lot, I imagine. Well, if you had some money — I'm talking now of quite a bit of money — why couldn't you get him to quit his job and move somewhere else. While he's finding a job you like better, and he likes better, you could have a nice little cushion of money to carry you along. You could be free agents, write your own ticket. I'm talking now of seventy-three thousand dollars."

"Where will seventy-three thousand dollars come from?" Barbara asked quietly.

"From your stock. Selling it to me. That's the book value of the stock you own. Since you wouldn't be selling at a profit, you'd have no gain — no taxes to pay on it. All you'd do is turn over your stock to me, and I'll give you a check for seventy-three thousand dollars."

"Do you have seventy-three thousand dollars?" Barbara asked.

"I have some of it. Not all of it, but the rest I can get. From the bank. I've talked to George Willard about it, and he's prepared to finance me. You have no *sentimental* attachment to the stock

174

you own, do you? You admitted you scarcely care what goes on here at the company, that you're really pretty out of touch —"

"But I don't see how my stock is going to make me a rich woman some day if I sell it all to you," Barbara said.

"Now, wait a minute," Peggy said. "Let me finish. I haven't finished telling you what my plan is. True, you'd be selling it to me. But, if you want, we could consider it temporary. After a few years, if you wanted to, you could buy back into the company. I'd agree to that — after a few years' time."

"Well then," Barbara said slowly, "suppose you tell me why you want my stock now."

"It's very simple," Peggy said. "I want it first to get Barney elected president. I need every damn share of stock I can get my hands on. And I need it, second, to give Barney a free rein for the next five — maybe ten — years, to do whatever he wants to pull this company back into shape."

"Well," Barbara said. "That's very ambitious."

"Of course it is. It will take somebody ambitious to do what I want done."

Barbara looked at the heads in the pool, representing cousins, shareholders, participants in the Woodcock Paper Company, members of her family — all of which, she supposed, were, in one way or another, involved in Peggy's plan. She wondered how many of them knew it. In the summer sunlight, playing together, laughing, tossing a bright striped beach ball in a half-serious water polo game, they seemed certainly unconcerned. Their inheritance, from common ancestors, from fathers who had been cousins, grandfathers who had been brothers, seemed to be serving them well enough. The most important member of the family, William Woodcock, was not there. Barbara asked Peggy quietly, "What about Cousin Billy? Does he know anything about this yet?"

Peggy smiled. "Cousin Billy will find out when I'm ready to have him find out. You're right — he won't like it." She laughed.

"After all, he's president now! When I have enough stock to out-vote him, that's when he'll find out!"

"And what about Daddy?"

"Daddy I'm handling in my own way," Peggy said. "What I'm interested in now is you. What do you think? Will you go along with me?"

Barbara considered this. "Well," she said finally, "this is all pretty sudden. And what you said about — about taking the money and moving to another town — I really don't think we could do that, or that Carson would want to. I mean, I don't think Carson is unhappy. And besides, I don't really see why you'd need to buy my stock. If I gave you my proxy for whatever you wanted to do, wouldn't that be enough? Would you have to own the stock outright?"

"Ah!" Peggy said, tapping out her cigarette with a series of hard, confident taps. "I was wrong. You *do* have a little business sense, don't you? I'm sorry. No, you're quite right. I don't have to buy your stock. But then I do need your proxy — no strings attached. And I'd need it for a good long time. Rome wasn't built in a day! This thing won't be easy, and I'm really just beginning. If you'll promise me your proxy for the next ten years, to let me vote your stock in any way I want, then — fine! Then it's a deal! Will you do it?"

"Let me think about it, will you, Peg? I don't have to decide this afternoon, do I?"

"I'd like a decision as soon as possible."

"I'd like to discuss it with Carson," Barbara said. "Let me write him and ask him what he thinks."

"What does Carson have to do with it? It's not his stock. It's yours. Why do you need to mention it to Carson at all?"

"Well, I'd like to. I'd just like to."

"I really can't see why it's any of Carson's business."

"Well, give me a little time, anyway, Peg. Truly don't make me say yes or no right now. Let me think about it."

176

Peggy shrugged. "All right. If you want to. But I'm telling you right now, it's the one thing that can save us — in the long run. This company needs something — something dramatic, dynamic! Not people like Cousin Billy. It's *because* of people like Cousin Billy — yes, and Daddy, too — that the company's in the shape it's in. The management has been too *fat* — too satisfied, willing to let things just coast along. Well, they've been coasting now for quite a while and the sled's been picking up speed. One of these mornings we'll all wake up at the bottom of the hill in a banged-up toboggan!" With her hand, she performed a nose-dive, in demonstration. "So think it over, dear. But don't take too long."

"I really didn't know things were that bad."

"Well, they are. That bad. And as far as what I said about getting Carson to quit and moving out of Locustville — well, it was only because I know how you hate that place. And sometimes, I think the woman *should* take the initiative, don't you? I mean, no matter what a man's capabilities are it sometimes takes a woman to bring them out, don't you think? And if you really miss him as much as you say you do — if you really resent these trips of his — well, hell, Barb, why be wishy-washy about it? Get him to quit for God's sake! Get him to take you some place else! Why not?"

Peggy looked hard at her, and Barbara shifted in her chair and looked away. She was beginning to feel uncomfortable with Peggy. "Some men are — well, different," she said lamely. And she added, "Besides, we'll work things out."

Suddenly Peggy put her head back and laughed. "God!" she said. "You are the devoted, all-American wife, aren't you?"

"Well," Barbara said, "perhaps I am."

"Don't get mad," Peggy said. "I think it's wonderful — I really do. I think it's very, very nice. As I say, I don't know whether I'd miss Barney if he had to go off on trips or not. Would I? I just don't know." She laughed again. "I think maybe I'd just say thank

God, I've got the bed to myself for a change. When they're gone — men, I mean — what is it that a woman misses? Is it their boyish charm, or their snoring, or that thing they've got in their pants?" She put her hand on Barbara's arm. "Remember Charlie Muir, Barb? Remember Charlie?"

Emily, her mother's maid, was coming down the path from the house, her white uniform brilliant in the sun.

"Which reminds me," Peggy said, still laughing, "have you heard the one about the boys who had this contest? And this one little colored boy — Rastus — came home to his mammy and said he'd won, and his mammy said, 'Rastus — ' "

"Shh!" Barbara said. "Emily's coming. Lunch must be ready —"

Emily approached along the pool's edge and said, "Mrs. Greer, a long distance call for you."

Barbara said, "Who in the world could this be?" She stood up and followed Emily toward the house. Halfway up the walk, she suddenly remembered the thoughts she had been having last night before going to sleep. Oil burners exploding. Chimney fires. And she thought, oh, dear God! The children! And she began to run. When she reached the telephone, she was out of breath. "Hello?" she gasped.

Then she was relieved to hear Nancy Rafferty's voice on the other end of the wire, "Oh, thank God it's you!" she said.

"Why?" Nancy asked. "What's the matter, Barb?"

"Nothing. But I thought — long distance. Perhaps it was Flora and there was something wrong —"

"I just talked to Flora," Nancy said. "Everything's fine. She told me you were at the farm. I was amazed! When did you go up there?"

"Yesterday," Barbara said.

"Right after I left? Goodness, you wasted no time, did you? What made you decide to go? I didn't think you'd fly the coop so quickly!"

"I — I just decided —"

178

"And what have you been doing? Weaving your fatal spell around Barney?" Nancy's laugh tinkled distantly.

"I don't think that's very funny."

"It isn't. I'm sorry! But what I really called about was — I've been in the depths. The absolute depths, Barb. And I need cheering."

"Why?"

"Can you cheer up an ex-nursing student?"

"What happened?"

"Me," Nancy said, "that's what happened. *I* happened! Oh Barb," her voice moaned, "I've been a very, very naughty girl. I've quit, resigned. Thrown in the proverbial towel. Or no, let's be frank. I didn't quit, I was *asked* to quit. I was thrown out on my proverbial ear, darling, and I've been mourning and so repentant! I've been in sackcloth and ashes, but no — I really haven't! I've been celebrating, actually. I've been saying, Hey! Whoopee! I wasn't cut out to be a nurse anyway! Oh, Barbara, you'll never, never in the wide world guess what awful things I've done!"

"What? What have you done?"

"Yesterday, after I left your house. I was feeling, how shall we say, a little bit leftover? Oh, God, but it was more than a little bit and I was really, truly praying that death would come on the highway, to take me out of my misery. I had a hangover," she laughed, "that should have been written up by the American Medical Association! Anyway, I had no luck — death didn't come on the highway and I got back to Philadelphia, unfortunately, intact, still living, and I found that I'd been called to go into a case in surgery, at the hospital. Well, like a good girl, I went — feeling worse than horrible. Got on my little uniform and went. It was some horrible old bum who'd had his head halfway cut off in a razor fight. Oh, God! I stood there, trying to hold your breakfast down while they tried to sew his damn head back on. And I could feel it coming. I thought: No, no, I can't, it's no use. I said to myself: Give up, kid, this is not your life, you've missed the call, so I turned on my heel and walked right out of the operating room — with some instruments still in my hand — and slammed the door. Oh, God! I don't know if you know much about the nursing profession, dear, but that is *not* one of the things one is supposed to do in nursing. In fact, it's just about the cardinal sin. So here I am, free as a bird!" She laughed gaily. "And I'm not drunk, either, much as you may suspect. Drunk with excitement, maybe. But I was going to ask you if I could buzz back down to Locustville and cry on your shoulder, but now that you're at the farm, would you mind if I buzzed up there? There's a train that will get me there by suppertime. Would you mind, terribly, Barb, having an old ex-roommate and ex-nursing student buzz in on you for comfort and consolation? Would you mind? Of course I really think it's your bounden duty to have me because, after all, it was your Martinis that did it Friday night — and your *excellent* Scotch somewhat later in the evening! Oh, I'm only kidding, Barb, but could I come? Could I please? And if you could just rally your cousin Woody for the occasion this evening, I'd love you forever! If you could manage to put Woody about — oh, about two feet away from me at the supper table I'd do my best to weave my fatal spell about him in my most alluring manner, and not disgrace you, really! I'll do it with perfume, not words. I'll invest in — what? Ah, yes! Tabu! I'll invest in a bottle of Tabu!"

I I

SOFT SUNLIGHT FILTERED THROUGH UPTURNED VENETIAN blinds into the small, dark-paneled study at the back of the house. Both windows were raised behind the blinds and a warm breeze blew in, stirring very slightly the heavy curtains. From the desk where he sat, Preston Woodcock could hear, distantly but identifiably, sounds of voices and laughter from the swimming pool, the clatter of the diving board as it pounded against its fulcrum, the noisy splashes into the water. But his attention was fixed on the sheets of paper before him. He wrote slowly, carefully, pausing frequently to reread what he had written, his lips moving deliberately, forming the words, almost whispering them aloud to himself. Now and then he would lift his pen and draw a thin line through a word or phrase that displeased him, editing, changing bits of punctuation, substituting one word for another, rearranging sentences, circling them, repositioning them with tiny arrows. His expression was thoughtful, frowning, his eyes intent behind the shell-rimmed glasses. At last he put his pen down, scooped up the pages in front of him, squared them with his hands, and stood up. He carried the manuscript to a leather chair, sat down heavily, placed one white-flanneled knee upon the other, and read it through once more.

As a biographer I should no doubt state now that I am not a writer. When I was a boy my father imposed upon me the stint of reading certain volumes which he felt were worthy: The Complete Works of Mark Twain, the works of Dickens, James Fenimore Cooper and Mr. Stoddard's *Lectures*. He also exhorted me to read with regularity the weekly editorials in the *Saturday Evening Post*. I regret to say that I was not faithful to any of these tasks; had I been, no doubt, my writing "style" would have been improved considerably, and I would have developed a facility with words. For my considerable shortcomings, therefore, I beg the reader's kind indulgence with the hope that the story of my father's life will prove absorbing enough to hold the reader's interest, though it be written without art.

Men who knew my father in his business life

considered him to be an austere person, difficult to know, a man who seldom showed his feelings and who often exhibited a kind of heartlessness or even cruelty. I am reminded of such instances as his firing of Joe Mount, a man well liked in this community, respected, a church-goer and family man, the father of five children. The firing of Joe Mount stirred up considerable resentment in this town against my father. It happened like this: Joe Mount had worked for my father for nine years in the office as a bookkeeper and accountant. Father truly liked Joe, praised his work, and intended (I think) one day to give Joe Mount a position of some importance with the company. Joe Mount, however, was a loyal Scot and devout Presbyterian, and these strains caused Joe to feel a certain kinship with Governor Woodrow Wilson of New Jersey, a man in whom the Scotch and Presbyterian strains also ran strong. Thus, in the summer of 1912, Joe Mount embarked upon a series of public speeches in Burketown endorsing Wilson's candidacy for President of the United States. My father was a man who insisted upon loyalty among every member of his organization. My father warned Joe Mount, politely at first, then more strongly. But Joe's zeal remained unslackened. And so it happened that one morning Joe found the door to his office locked, his final paycheck waiting for him at the cashier's desk.

It seemed at the time, and possibly still does, that Father performed an arbitrary and cruel act. And yet when one goes deeper into Father's reasons for insisting upon strict political loyalty among his employees, the firing of Joe Mount appears in a somewhat different light. My father demanded loyalty of his men because, to him, each disloyal act, each public

demonstration of a belief counter to his own, consti-
tuted a threat to his position, his power, and the private picture of himself which he kept in his mind's
eye. It is my theory, therefore, that Joe Mount was
fired not out of revenge or cruelty, but out of fear and
shame. My father was at heart a timid man and lived
most of his life in terror of other men. My father was
a coward, afraid of the dark. In his later years he developed the habit of keeping a revolver within his
reach at all times because of his baseless fear of assas-
sination. At night he would awake screaming from
terrible nightmares. This was a side of him no one
knew but my mother and myself. He was a very unusual man.

He had a private dream of himself that amounted
to an obsession, and it was a dream that involved all
of us. It involved me, my cousins Billy and Mary-
Adams, my daughters Barbara and Peggy, Mary-
Adams' children, Woody and Sally, Billy's children —
all of us. He wanted us, I am sure, to be a family,
a family of the Great Tradition, a Great American
Family. It is curious, because in the general scheme
of things the Woodcocks are pretty small potatoes.
But Father dreamed of us as growing, becoming
world-builders, of having our name grouped with
names like Huntington, Crocker in the West, Biddles,
Dorrances, Wideners in Philadelphia, DuPonts,
Adamses, Rockefellers, Cabots, Lodges, and all the
rest. How we were to accomplish this, Father did not
know. Perhaps that was his greatest failing, ignorance.
Stupidity. Father was a stupid man, too small for his
dream, too spiteful and petty, too easily beguiled by
things that didn't matter, too quick to resent and take
personally matters that could not be helped, such as

183

the fact that I had no sons. My father told me once that it is the male seed which carries the sex determinant. Whether this is true or not, I am not a student of biology enough to know. And yet he told me that because my seed had produced two daughters and no sons, my own physical make-up was out of balance, that I myself was womanish! He was bitterly disappointed in the sex of my two children and said so many times, saying that I had failed him in this respect.

I've heard it said that the children of the rich lack initiative and are apt to turn out badly. I do not think that I have turned out badly, though it is probably true that I lack initiative. Yet I lack it because Father took it away from me the year before he died. In fact, he began taking it away long before that. He began taking it, a little at a time, shortly after I joined the company. He did it because I made a mistake, a terrible mistake in Father's eyes, a mistake that ruined me.

Preston Woodcock put down the manuscript and rubbed his eyes. He sat there, cradling the manuscript in his lap, thinking that possibly this was a good place to start a new chapter. Presently there was a sound and he looked up. Edith was standing in the doorway. She wore sandals and a terry robe. Her hair was damp.

"I went for a swim," she said.

"Did you? Good," he said.

"It's *so* hot in the sun," she said. She stepped into the room. "Have you been here all along?" she asked. "Why didn't you come out?"

"I was working," he said.

"You've missed our nice cocktails. Everybody wondered where you were. Can you come now? Lunch is nearly ready."

"Yes, I'm finished for the moment."

She looked at the papers in his lap. "Preston, what *are* you doing?" she asked.

He smiled up at her. "Just a little project I'm working on," he said.

"Preston," she said, "there's something I want to discuss. It involves Barbara —"

He still smiled at her.

"Preston? Did you hear me?"

"Barbara's all right," he said.

She came closer to him.

"Are you feeling well, dear?" she asked him, studying him with concern. And he saw her eyes travel briefly to the corner of the study where, on a little table, quietly and shining, beaded and faceted, catching the light in carved crystal decanters, his treasures were. And roughly, angrily, he pulled himself away from her and marched toward them.

"Yes," he said, his voice louder than he had expected. "Yes, and don't you see? This is why! This is why! It's because of you!" He poured a drink and turned to her again, but she had left the room. He was alone, staring at the side of the glass which portrayed a hunting scene — a setter flushing a partridge — his eyes feeling watery and singularly heavy.

Peggy went to her room to change and when she opened the door she found Barney. He lay naked across the top of one of the twin beds and at the sound of the door opening he lifted one arm and pulled a corner of the sheet across him. "Christ, it's hot," he said.

"Then why do you stay up here in this stuffy room?" she asked him. "Why didn't you stay at the pool where it's cool?" She walked to her closet, opened the door, and took down the shoulder straps of her wet suit. She pulled the suit off, placed it across a dry towel on the back of a chair, and began to dress. She looked over at him. "You'd better get dressed, Barn-Barn," she said. "Lunch is nearly ready." She put on white shorts and a white cotton shirt embroidered, at the pocket, with a small blue alligator. She sat down at her dressing table and began brushing her short hair. "Well," she said, "I spoke to her."

"To Barbara?"

"Yes."

"What did she say?"

"I don't think she's going to give us any trouble," she said. "I think she saw the sense of what I said. She said she wants a little time to think about it."

"Ah," he said.

She continued brushing her hair. "Did you talk to Nana this morning?" she asked after a moment.

"No," he said. "When I got there, Barbara was there. I figured that after one visitor, she'd be tired. I thought I'd wait till later. Tomorrow perhaps."

"Oh, that's right," Peggy said. "I'd forgotten that Barbara was going to see her this morning." She put down her hair brush. "As a matter of fact," she said, "don't go to see her tomorrow. I think I've got a better idea."

"What's that?" he asked.

She turned to him. "You have keys to the office, don't you?"

"Yes."

She stood up. "Give them to me," she said. "I'm going to take a little trip down there this afternoon."

"What for?"

She smiled. "To look for something," she said.

"Bill Adkins, the watchman, will be there," he said.

"Bill knows me," she said. "He'll let me go in."

"You won't tell me what you're looking for?"

"I'll tell you *if* and *when* I find it," she said.

"I don't think you ought to be snooping around there, Peg, when the office is closed."

"Ha! Who'll know besides you and Bill Adkins?" She laughed and walked to the end of the bed.

"I'd better go with you," he said.

"No, no," she said. "I've another job for you, Barn-Barn."

"What's that?"

"Barbara. Devote your time to her this afternoon. Give her lots of attention. Show her what a nice fellow you are and convince her of what an excellent president you'd make."

He said nothing.

She reached for the bottom of the bed sheet and yanked it off him. "Come on, lazybones!" she laughed. "It's time for lunch!"

"Oh, Christ!" he said, sitting up sharply and putting his bare feet down hard on the floor.

As they moved toward the terrace where the luncheon table had been set, Barbara said to Edith, "Mother, Nancy Rafferty just called me from Philadelphia. She's terribly upset. She made some sort of mistake at nursing school, and they dismissed her."

"Oh, poor Nancy!" her mother said.

"She asked me if she could come up here tonight. I sort of had to tell her yes. I hope you don't mind."

"Of course I don't mind. I've always been very fond of Nancy."

"She's coming on the train. It will mean I'll have some one to drive back with tomorrow."

"*Tomorrow?* Are you going tomorrow, Barbara? Oh, I thought you were going to give us a *real* visit this time!"

"No, I really must get back," Barbara said. "Flora expects me back tomorrow."

And when the family was seated at the table, Emily came out of the house in her white uniform and crossed the terrace to where Barbara sat. "Mr. William Woodcock is on the phone, ma'am," Emily said. "He wonders can he see you?"

"Cousin Billy?" Peggy asked quickly. "He must want me, Emily."

"He said Mrs. Greer, ma'am."

Peggy shrugged. Barbara looked across the table at her sister and Peggy stared back at her.

Emily said, "He said, could he see you for a few minutes if he dropped by about two-thirty, quarter of three?"

"Of course," Barbara said. "Tell him I'd love to see him."

John moved toward the table with a silver serving dish, then stopped abruptly, for Preston Woodcock had lowered his head and begun to say grace. "We thank Thee, Lord, for these Thy gifts which we are about to receive . . ." And the others at the table waited quietly, surprised, until he had finished.

"Well, that was very nice, dear!" Edith Woodcock said.

Then lunch began.

12

WILLIAM DOBIE WOODCOCK THE THIRD STOOD IN FRONT OF the library window, holding a copy of the *Atlantic* that he had picked up from the coffee table, and absently turned the pages. When Barbara came into the room, he turned and smiled. He put down the magazine. "Hello, there, Barbara!" he said, holding out his hand. "How are you?"

"Hello, Billy," Barbara said.

"You're looking fine, just fine," he said.

"And so are you, Billy."

"Well, I can't complain!" he laughed.

He was a short, heavy-set young man, just six years older than Barbara. He had started losing his hair in college and was now completely bald; only a thin fringe of sandy-colored hair above his ears was left to explain the nickname he had hated in his youth — "Carrot Top" — and now his round, pink and shiny face gave him more the appearance of a wax cherub than a vegetable.

Still, his soft fleshiness and comfortable roundness (Cousin Billy often boasted then he was both a gourmet *and* a gourmand) gave him a singularly edible look. Unlike most plump men, he was extremely fastidious about his clothes. Today, though his face and forehead were aglow with perspiration, he wore an immaculately pressed seersucker suit, a crisp, small-figured bow tie, and white buckskin shoes that were unmarred by even the slightest smudge of dirt. He squeezed Barbara's hand between his soft, moist palms. "I was glad to hear you'd come up this week end," he said. "Sit down, Barbara."

They sat on the brown sofa and Billy Woodcock crossed his legs carefully, hitching up his trouser knees to preserve their crease. "How does the old place seem?" he asked her.

"Just the same as ever," she said.

"Well, good, good. That's good, Barbara. Yes indeedy," he said and rubbed his hands together. "It's a grand old place, this farm."

Barbara smiled. She had grown used, over the last few years, to Cousin Billy's jolly paternalism and his occasional pomposity. After all, he was president now of the paper company, and as a young man who had been given vast responsibilities in the family, he took these responsibilities with great seriousness.

"Well, Barbara," he said, "I suppose you're wondering why I wanted to have this little talk with you. Why I wanted to see you alone this afternoon."

"Well, frankly, I am," Barbara said.

"Don't blame you, by golly!" he said. "Don't blame you a bit. By the way," he said, looking around, "where is Peggy?"

"She's out," Barbara said. "She went somewhere in the car. I don't think she said where she was going —"

"Well," he said, "that's just as well. Just as well. I want this little talk to be strictly *entre nous*, Barbara. After all, you're the older of you two girls and on business matters, I'm counting on you to assume responsibility."

"Yes," she said.

189

"You know," he said, "I've always felt kind of sorry that you and I were — well, that we were never closer. And well, I guess I'm to blame for that. You know how it is with this company, Barbara. I eat, sleep and drink the paper business — not much time for socializing with the family. But it's too bad. We've never gotten to know each other the way we should because I've just been too busy with the company."

"Yes, I know," she said, and remembering that Cousin Billy responded quickly to simple flattery, she said, "Everyone's so grateful, Billy, for all you've done."

He smiled modestly. "Well," he said, "I've done my best. That's all I can do — my best."

"You've certainly done that, Billy."

His face grew serious again. "Well," he said, "this little matter I want to talk to you about today concerns your sister, concerns Peggy. Now, you know that nobody has a higher regard for your sister than I do. I'm very fond of Peggy, extremely fond. And I like her husband, too, Barney. Much to my surprise he's worked out pretty well down at the office, and I'm real pleased, all things considered. I think he's fitted in pretty fairly well, and that's a pleasure. Of course he's still got a lot to learn. This is a family company, always has been and always will be, and some of our — well, our methods — probably seem a little funny and strange to him. But what he's got to learn is that our methods, the way we do things, are based on experience and know-how, over a hundred years of experience and know-how. They've been time-tested you might say. However —" and he hesitated, holding up his hand, "that doesn't mean we're not receptive to new ideas when they come along, either. If the ideas are good ones, that is. Now, Barbara," he said, "how much do you know about human nature?"

"What do you mean?" she asked him.

"Well, let me put it this way. I'm quite a student of human nature. In this business, I've had to be. And human nature is a funny thing, a very funny thing. And yet if you size it up correctly you can pretty much predict what it will do. Now take this Barney character. I've been studying him and I think I've got him sized up pretty fairly well. What he is, is a misfit. Now, Barbara, don't interrupt. You may like him and so do I, we all do. Liking is one thing, but human nature is something else again. He's a misfit, he's a dissenter and he's a very unhappy and mixed-up fellow. Why? It's easy enough to see why. He walked into this family — off the street as it were — and found something pretty big. We've been big in this town for over a hundred years and he didn't expect that kind of bigness, didn't understand it. It's outside his realm of understanding, what we are and the way we do things. Still, he's no dope. He's come out of that Harvard Business School with a lot of smart-aleck ideas. 'Decentralization' he said to me the other day, or some other fool thing. Because he's no dope he tries — rather than to fit in — to make his presence felt by trying to switch things around, overturn the apple cart. That's what I mean by a misfit. He's a trouble-maker and if he doesn't decide to shape up pretty soon, I'm — no kidding — going to have to take a few steps. But anyway, the interesting thing about these misfit types, if you understand human nature, is that they're misfits wherever they go. What I mean is that if he's a misfit in this company, chances are he'll be a misfit in the next one — and the next one after that. It's too bad, really, but that's what it amounts to. It's according to the laws of human nature. Now the only unique thing about this company is that it's a family company, our family. In other words, the family is the company and vice versa. So what I say about him not fitting into the company applies to the family, too, don't you see? Which is what makes it too bad. Now I'm telling you all this because I think you're mature enough to understand it. Peggy isn't. She doesn't understand it — not yet. So she's pushing him along in his smart-aleck schemes and what she's doing is riding for a great, big fall. Barbara, has Peggy asked you anything about the stock you own?"

Barbara said, "Well, Billy, I can't lie to you. She has. She mentioned it this morning."

He smiled, satisfied. "I thought she would. She's been hounding all the stockholders — except me, of course. She's smart enough not to try to hound me! What did you tell her?"

"It came as quite a surprise to me," Barbara said. "I didn't know what to say, really. I asked her to let me think about it."

"Did she ask to buy it?"

"Either that or to let her have my proxy for a while."

He nodded. "Well, Barbara, what you do with your stock is up to you. Entirely. It's yours, you own it, and far be it from me to try to tell you one way or the other what to do. But I can tell you this: Whatever Peggy wants to do, she's not being very smart about it. In fact, she's being pretty stupid. Want to know why?"

"Yes," Barbara said, "why?"

"Well, let's start out by assuming she can get her hands on a majority of the stock. What could she do with it? Vote herself head of the company, or Barney? That's pretty ridiculous. We've got a couple hundred employees down there. Good, loyal and honest employees. Some of them like Sam Pike have been with us for over forty years. Do you know what the average length of service of our employees is? Well, the average length of service is a little over ten years, and that's a lot. It's one of the things we're proud of. Do you think any one of these men would sit back and let a woman tell them what to do? Not likely! Do you think they'd sit back and let a holy Roman Catholic tell them what to do, a guy who gets his orders straight from Rome? Never!"

"But Barney isn't a Catholic," Barbara said. "Not any more."

"Once a Catholic always a Catholic, that's what the Church itself says, isn't it? That's what my employees think, anyway. They don't care whether he still goes to church or not. I know these men, Barbara. I know them inside and out. But anyway, that's only reason A why she's being foolish. Want to hear reason B?"

"Yes," Barbara said. "What is reason B?"

"Reason A is assuming she *could* get her hands on enough stock to have controlling interest. Reason B is that she can't do it, anyway."

"Why not?"

"Where would she get it? She has stock of her own, true — about a hundred and thirty shares as I recall. Then you have stock — roughly the same amount. It was left to both you girls by your grandfather. Now your father also has some stock, but most of his is held in trust — he can't sell it, all he gets is the income from it. I'm one of the trustees and Mary-Adams is another. Your father owns a few shares outright — about twenty-five I think. If she could get your hundred and thirty, plus your father's twenty-five, along with her own hundred and thirty — that would still add up to only two hundred and eighty-five shares, or not enough. And I'd frankly be surprised if your father let her have those twenty-five shares of his. He wouldn't do it, not even in one of his most befuddled moments."

"What do you mean by that?" she asked quietly.

"I mean — I'm sorry, that wasn't a very nice thing to say," he said. "But you know as well as I, don't you, that your father these days sometimes gets a little — well, confused."

"You mean he drinks too much?"

"I didn't say that! I didn't say that, Barbara. But, well, he has been warned about the drinking. A couple of doctors I know have warned him, and I've warned him. But, far be it from me to tell him how he should live his life. How he lives his life is his business and nobody else's."

"If he's killing himself, it's our business, isn't it?" she asked. "It certainly is my business. Is it that serious?"

"Nobody says it's that serious," Billy said. "Nobody says that. I'm sorry we got on this subject, on this chain of thought, because it has nothing to do with what we're talking about." He removed a handkerchief from his pocket and swabbed his damp brow. "Well, anyway," he said, "to get back to cases. Peggy can't get enough stock anyway, to do what she wants. Mary-Adams and I each have over five hundred shares and needless to say we're not going to turn anything over to Peggy, nossirree! But anyway, there's a third reason which we can call reason C."

"What is reason C?" she asked him.

"Reason C is —" he paused significantly, "reason C is that any arrangement such as Peggy and her husband want, or any *attempt* to make an arrangement like that, would be out of keeping with the terms of your grandfather's will. Don't forget that it was your own grandfather, not even mine, but my grandfather's brother, who set things up the way they are. He's the one who established the status quo. And it was his express desire, expressed in his will and even long before he died, that control of his mills should rest in *my* side of the family, not your father's. But you've heard all about that before. You know that story, and why things are set up the way they are. There's no need to go into all that story again."

She did, indeed, know that story. She had not thought about it for some time, but it came back to her now with the realization that it was the story, undoubtedly, that her father was planning to tell in the book he was writing. She had heard it — not all at once, but in fragments. Most of it she had heard from her mother, but some of it had come from Woody and some from her other cousins, Jeffrey and Talcott. She remembered it all. She remembered, too, her grandfather's old office at the mill, where most of it had happened.

For the president of a company whose net worth was then estimated to be in the neighborhood of two and a half million dollars, Grandfather Woodcock's office had been austere. It was small, barely twelve feet square, and its furnishings were Spartan. In addition to his desk and tip-back chair, there were only two other pieces of furniture — a gaudily decorated Mosler safe of ancient vintage and a large, leather-cushioned chair with flat wooden arms, facing the desk, for visitors. Beside the chair stood a brass spittoon. The floor was uncarpeted and the single window was undraped. The amount of sunlight in the office could be regulated by raising or lowering the brown paper shade. No decorative touches had been supplied except, resting against the wall on top of the safe, Grandfather Woodcock's framed diploma from Yale on which the year 1887, in Roman numerals, was barely distinguishable, and on his desk, facing him, an autographed portrait of President Herbert Hoover. In one corner of the office, a high pile of shoeboxes contained samples of various Woodcock Paper products. One wall of the office was glass, permitting Grandfather Woodcock a clear view across the main floor of the mill; the other three walls were painted a muddy shade of brown. The office had no door so that his secretary, Mrs. McGraw, could hear every word spoken in the office from her desk, just outside. Though the office was gone now, replaced by more modern quarters, it was to this dusty and frowsty place that her father had gone that morning in the early 1930's, shortly after he had been given the title of executive vice-president, with his idea. She imagined her father, a young, handsome man, sitting opposite her grandfather in that cracked and sagging leather chair.

A parkway was being planned, a modern super-highway that would extend from the Connecticut-New York border at Greenwich to the outskirts of New Haven, across Fairfield and New Haven Counties. There had been rumors from the State Legislature in Hartford, and the rumors were rapidly becoming fact. Preston had studied the map of the area. It was clear to him that the parkway would pass through Burketown.

As he saw it, there were two possibilities. One, that the parkway would pass through the west side of town, through the section known as West Hill. Two, that the parkway would pass to the east. Preston asked his father to consider the general terrain of these two areas. West Hill was a gentle, sloping, uncleared rise with no physical obstructions; to build a parkway across West Hill would require little more than cutting a clearing in the woods.

On the east side, however, was the river and the hilly, rocky river bed. To direct a highway through this section would require, Preston was sure, building at least one and possibly two bridges across the winding little river; bridge-building, as everyone knew, added enormously to the cost of constructing a highway. Did it not — he asked his father — seem clearly logical that the parkway would thread its way across West Hill?

Grandfather Woodcock considered this for several minutes. Yes, he had finally agreed, perhaps it did, but what of it? He saw what Preston was driving at, but how could Preston predict the precise path of the parkway in the hundreds of acres on West Hill? Preston had a simple answer to this. It was not necessary to predict the exact route. If the parkway were to go through West Hill the entire surrounding area would quickly increase in value. A parkway meant roadside restaurants, gasoline stations, new sites for industry and housing developments. It was not, in other words, a ribbon of land that Barbara's father proposed to buy, but the entire area that the coming parkway would affect. It was roughly fourteen hundred acres and the average price of West Hill acreage was temptingly low.

Preston's plan, of course, involved a considerable sum of money. As Barbara remembered, it was around fifty thousand dollars. Connecticut had been harder-hit than most states by the depression, and the Woodcock Paper Company had fared only a little better than others. Though they had been able to keep their doors open, production had been cut and the mill was operating on only a fraction of its normal labor force. Fifty thousand dollars, at a time like this, was a lot. And yet Grandfather Woodcock had never turned down anything that promised to bring him a profitable return. He had studied the map for several days, tracing and retracing the two alternate routes that his son had mentioned. At last he called Preston into his office again and told him to go ahead with the plan.

The property was purchased in the name of the Woodcock

Paper Company. Preston handled all the details. When the purchase was completed, some months later, Preston had said to his father, "You won't regret it. Wait and see what happens to West Hill when the parkway goes through." He had been confident; it had been one of the most supremely confident moments in his life.

But, several months later, when the engineers' plans for the Merritt Parkway were published, the route chosen through Burketown was to the east, across the river. East-side property owners made tidy sums of money.

Afterward, Grandfather Woodcock said nothing. He refused to discuss it. He withdrew into a silence that, through the years, shadowed their whole relationship. He never trusted Preston's judgment again. To be sure, the West Hill property eventually became valuable. As the town grew during the war and after it, streets were built across its slopes and the little look-alike houses that Barbara had passed again this morning had been scattered along them. Soon the section was shorn of its covering trees and contained a shopping center, a drive-in movie theater and a roller-skating rink. But this, to Grandfather Woodcock, did not help exonerate his son. This had come too late, and it had come as an accident. His son had promised him a parkway. And he had faulted on the promise.

Grandfather Woodcock mentioned the West Hill incident to Preston only once, many years later. Barbara remembered it clearly. It was a few weeks before her grandfather had died and she and Carson had been at the farm and had heard her father tell her mother about it. Preston had visited his father in the Prospect Avenue house with another business proposition. Grandfather Woodcock was eighty-eight years old, and the proposition was not actually Preston's idea but was the result of urgings from the law firm that represented the company. Preston had tried, as tactfully as he could, to remind his father that eighty-eight was not exactly young and to explain to him the tax benefits that would be realized if his father would begin, now, to disburse his estate to younger members of the family. Grandfather Woodcock had stared at him coldly for a long time. At last, he had asked, "What time is it?"

Preston looked at his watch. "It's half past three, Father," he had said.

Then Grandfather Woodcock pulled out his own watch from his pocket and looked at it. "Your watch is wrong," he had said. "Just as everything about you has been always wrong. You have always been a little off. A little fast, or a little slow. Now get out of here."

Preston had taken his scolding humbly. Edith, when they discussed it that evening, told him that he was right not to get angry. That was the only way to be. Humble, subservient, take the old man's punishment, cater to his wishes, do what he said, take the tongue-lashings he administered with a grain of salt. That was wisest now, at this point. After all, the old man was very old. He was eighty-eight. He could not refuse to retire much longer. Look at him! He hadn't been outside his house for over six months. He had even been mistreating Preston's poor old mother, accusing her of trying to steal from him! He was impossible, but after all he was old, so old. One did not wish him dead, of course, but he was old; he had had a rich, full life. His mind, much as Edith hated to admit it, was often blurred. He faded in and out like an image on a television screen, one minute clear as a bell, the next minute far away in another century! Edith and Preston nodded sympathetically over their cocktails as they talked about him. The poor old man.

Best to humor him now, Edith counseled. Let him have his little tempers. Let him scold. After all, one day Preston would be president of the company and make his own rules. There was no doubt about that, no doubt at all.

But, as it happened, it did not work out that way. Two days later, at 1045 Prospect Avenue, Grandfather Woodcock rose from his chair and ordered his car brought around. He put on his hat and overcoat though the day was warm and ordered Roger, his chauffeur, to drive him to the mill. The arrival there of the old Chrysler with its incongruously dressed passenger, after so many months' absence, caused quite a little stir. What was the old man up to? In his office, Grandfather Woodcock picked up the telephone and personally called each of the nine company directors and ordered a board meeting for two o'clock that afternoon. At the farm, Edith took the message. She relayed it to Preston and her daughters, saying, "The poor old dear. I'm afraid his mind is really failing now."

By two o'clock, all nine were there. In addition to Grandfather Woodcock and Preston, the others were Cousin Billy, his mother, Victoria Woodcock — whose husband, William Woodcock, Junior had been killed with the 36th Division in Italy in 1943; Billy's younger brother, Talcott, fresh from his desk as vicepresident in charge of marketing; his aunt, Mary-Adams Woodcock deWinter, annoyed at having to leave a hair appointment early, before her hair was dry; her son, Woody deWinter; and Barbara and Peggy. Although the two girls owned, at the time, only token amounts of stock that had been given to them on birthdays and Christmases, they were board members automatically since, by tradition, all stockholders were considered directors.

Grandfather Woodcock had an announcement to make. He was retiring, he advised the board, after sixty-four years with the company. The fact had evidently been overlooked, he told them, that today, July second, 1953, marked his sixty-fourth anniversary with the company. The rest of the board looked uncomfortable; a few members protested that they had, indeed, remembered, but had not thought that their president would be feeling up to a celebration. In connection with his retirement, he announced, it would be necessary to hold an election for a new president.

It was a family company, with its shareholder-directors all members of the family. The election of officers was done by ballot, on the basis of shares held, each share representing one vote. The distribution of shares of stock was unequal; Grandfather Woodcock personally owned seventy-two per cent of the shares outstanding. This inequality had existed since 1907 when his brother William had needed cash in connection with a Mrs. Sylvia McCarthy, a housekeeper, whose threat of a lawsuit had been only a genteel form of blackmail. Grandfather Woodcock had supplied his brother with the money by purchasing roughly half of his brother's stock in the company; (the McCarthy woman, it was understood, was still alive, an old lady living comfortably in Hamden, though old William Woodcock, her benefactor, had been dead for many years).

As the voting began, pencils and sheets of yellow paper were passed around the room. Preston, as executive vice-president and secretary, quickly read off the list of shareholders, advising each member of the exact number of shares each owned. Then they voted.

The results were surprising. The position of president was given to William Dobie Woodcock the Third. Preston — to whom the job fell of counting the ballots — read off the results in a queer voice. Grandfather Woodcock merely nodded, satisfied. Then he turned to Cousin Billy, shook his hand, and said, "Congratulations." Billy, who looked pale and a little glassy-eyed, jumped slightly in his chair, taking his great-uncle's hand, and mumbling, "Thank you, sir."

The mood of the little group as they stood up and started out of the room had been a curious one. There were no exclamations of surprise, no congratulations. Cousin Billy fixed his eyes upon the floor. There were no admonishments, no expressions of regret or sympathy. In fact, there had been nothing at all, only silence. Outside a few faces broke. There were a few nervous smiles. Mary-Adams deWinter lighted a cigarette, patted the damp curlers in her hair. Then, briefly, she squeezed Barbara's and Peggy's hands, but said nothing. What had happened, of course, they all understood. Grandfather Woodcock had simply lifted control of the company from his side of the family, from his son, and placed it firmly with the other side — with his brother's son's child, the grandson of the brother who had been the ne'er-do-well, the black sheep, the fornicator and disgracer. Preston, who stood among them looking astonishingly composed, had been passed by. At fifty-two, he had been placed second in command of a company whose president was his second cousin, Billy, only thirty-one years old. And the same thought instantly occurred to all of them: it was all right for the old man to do this now, perhaps, awful though it was; but what would happen at his death? Where would his stock go then?

In the little anteroom, a few more cigarettes were lighted. There began to be quiet murmurs of conversation. "Are you driving into New Haven tonight, Talcott?" "Woody, is your car in the parking lot?" "Yes, Mother." "Mind if I take it, dear? I came by taxi and it's so *hard* to find one going back . . ."

Grandfather Woodcock, standing in the center of the group and yet, at the same time, apart from it, turned to the person next to him who happened to be his grandnephew, Woody. His chin was cocked and his bright old eyes flashed. He said, "Well, Woodcock? What do you think?"

It was the words, "Well, Woodcock?" that hushed everyone. It was a salutation that might have been addressed to all of them.

And Woody — Woody, the rebellious, the unpredictable one, the off-horse — turned his head sharply away, saying nothing. Then the others, conscious of this, increased the tempo of their talk just slightly to cover his silence. The weather: how odd these early-morning fogs had been, all week, drifting up the river valley from the Sound, chilling the mornings and then burning off by noon in the sun's heat! Such weather! Had there ever, in anyone's memory, been anything quite like it?

They all knew. They all understood. They were all family.

They had always been and they would always be, in some way, bound together by ties of love and pride, bright old ribbons the color of loyalty and courage. Ties that were truly stronger than either love or pride, for they could be so much more painful ties. They had been through so much together. Through William, Junior at Salerno. (Too old for the Army they had told him; they had been right, he had been killed.) They had been through births, deaths, one divorce (Sally), a failure at Yale (Talcott), a curious marriage (Talcott), an attempted suicide (Woody), that awful thing that no one would ever completely understand, nor would anyone but the family appreciate the struggle that had followed, the heartache, the trying times. They had been through the uncertain war years that had been profitable financially but which had taken their toll in a darker and more tragic battleground. Through all this they had been family and they would always be. Through all this they had suffered as they were suffering now and would surely suffer again, beginning their suffering with silence, polite silence, for what else but silence could so surely comfort the bereaved and so swiftly heal the wounded? They would follow silence with a little polite talk, and then, in a few weeks' time, it would all be forgotten; time for family parties again, little dinners, jokes and laughter. But forgetting was only an illusion of forgetting, they knew. Nothing was ever forgotten. Still, silence would bolster the illusion. Silence, politeness, and time.

Barbara sat, very quietly now, with Cousin Billy in the library, remembering it all. There seemed to be nothing left to say. At last she said softly, "Poor Daddy."

"Now, don't say that, Barbara," he said. "That isn't realistic. Don't forget, your father's been taken care of pretty fairly well all these years. Pretty fairly well."

"Yes, yes, I know . . ." she said.

On the terrace now, outside, she could hear voices. The swimmers had left the pool and were gathering for talk in the cool shadows of the garden shrubbery, on the green-cushioned chairs, away from the sun. She could hear them, the family, and their bright Sunday afternoon laughter.

Two and a half weeks after the board of directors had met, at 1045 Prospect Avenue Grandfather Woodcock spilled his milk. He had refused, somewhat testily, the curved glass sipping straw that Binky Zaretsky had offered him, and when he lifted the glass of vitamin-fortified milk to his lips, it fell from his fingers onto the floor. Tiger, his yellow cat, leaped from his lap for the milk. His wife, sitting next to him, said, "Binky will mop it up, dear," but old Mr. Woodcock bent, reaching apparently to pull Tiger back to his accustomed place on his lap, ("He wasn't the kind to care about milk spilled on the rug," Mrs. Zaretsky explained as she told the story later), and bending in his chair, his fingers clutching for the cat's fur, his heart stopped. A rich, full life was ended.

The night before the funeral, Edith and Preston talked.

"There's one thing you can be sure of," Preston had told her. "I won't stay here. I'm not going to stay here and work for Billy. We'll take whatever money comes and move away. We'll go to Florida. Or California. Would you like that, Edith? I'll either retire completely or — well, maybe just try retirement for a while and see how I like it. If I don't, there are dozens of companies that would be glad to take me on. The thing is, we won't have to worry any more! We can do exactly as we please, go where we want. Oh, I know how you love the farm. I love it, too. I love everything we've done here, all the work we've both put in on it. But now that he's gone, we won't have to worry, we'll be secure. When that stock of his comes to me, sure, I could elect myself president! But I won't do that! I won't stoop to that. Let Billy take it. If he wants the stock I get, I'll sell it to him. I just don't give a damn about the company any more. You and I will be secure, that's the big thing. We won't have to wait for those paychecks of his! We can go anywhere we want, Edith. We're not going to stay here."

She went to him, put her arms around him. Through tears, now, of joy, she saw him unchanged, youthful, the man she had married. "Oh, my darling!" she had said. "Is it any wonder I love you? Is it any wonder? Of course! I'll go wherever you want, to the ends of the earth!"

But, of course, they did not go anywhere.

The terms of his father's will, when they were revealed, precluded it. It was a beautiful will, the lawyers said. They had to admit, begrudgingly, that he had made a beautiful will, which was surprising, since he had not consulted them at all but composed it himself. It went to show, they said, that old Mr. Woodcock had been a remarkable man with a brilliant, remarkable mind, a kind of genius, right up until the very end.

There were the usual charitable bequests, including a sizable gift to Yale University, gifts to servants, nurses, a gift to the hospital in the name of his brother, a gift to the Dobie C. Woodcock Memorial Library, which he had founded in his father's memory, to be used to purchase books for a new reference section. Of his stock in the paper company, a third went to his widow. The remaining two thirds were divided four ways. There was a bequest of stock to Barbara and an equal bequest to Peggy. There was a sizable bequest to Cousin Billy, to give him ownership that befitted his title. To Preston, also, there was a stock bequest but it was directed to be held in trust. And the income from the trust, which gave Preston no voting privileges, was to be paid to Preston contingent upon his continued association with the company. Should Preston at any time leave the company, the will directed, the trust would pass directly to Cousin Billy. Upon Preston's death, the trust was to pass to Preston's two daughters, Barbara and Peggy, who would share it equally.

"It's quite an ingenious arrangement, Pres," one of the lawyers had told him. "And quite a compliment to you. Obviously the old man didn't like to think of what would happen to the company if you weren't on hand to help guide things along."

Cousin Billy stood up now and walked to the library window, puffing on his pipe. "So you see," he said, "there's nothing Peggy can do. And the sooner she realizes that, the better it will be for all of us. She's wasting her time, and so is Barney. So what I thought was, Barbara — that if you could tell her, just sort of explain to her the way things stand, remind her, it would be a help to her and a help to me. That's why I wanted to talk to you. It's better if it comes from you than if it comes from me. Your sister Peggy's never cared too much for my advice, I don't think. But if you remind her of all this, she ought to have sense enough to understand. What I want to avoid, what I want to forestall, is a big family ruckus, you know what I mean. If there's one thing I'd hate to have, it's a big family ruckus. It's like the old maxim says — a house divided against itself cannot stand! So talk to her, Barbara. That's really all I have to say."

The sky outside had grown suddenly darker and a heavy stillness had fallen upon the air. Then a wind came up, turning the leaves at the window so that they showed their white undersides. "Looks like a storm," Cousin Billy said. "I'd better run. Didn't bring an umbrella —" He turned to Barbara, and Barbara stood up. "Well, good-by for now, Barbara," he said, "and thanks for anything you can do. Drop by the house if you get a chance. Janet'd love to see you, and the kids would love it, too." He squeezed her hand. "Got to run before it pours," he said.

"Good-by, Billy," she said.

He walked hurriedly out of the room. She stood at the window and watched him as he ran down the front steps, across the driveway, to his station wagon. The sky grew even darker. There was a bright flash of lightning and then, a few seconds later, a deep rumble of thunder. She could hear the family now as they rose from the terrace and hurried into the house, carrying their cocktails in advance of the storm.

She turned and started out of the library. In the darkened hall, she met Barney. He stopped her with his hand. "They say you're going home tomorrow," he said. "Are you?"

"Yes, I must," she said.

"But you came up here to see me," he said. "You know you did."

She pulled away from him, suddenly angry. "That's not true!" she said. "Leave me alone, please! Can't you leave me alone?"

And his face, as he stepped back, looked all at once so hurt, that she said more softly, "Please, don't you see? Don't make things so hard for me. Everybody expects so much of me! And I'm simply not up to it."

"Barbara?" her mother called. "What did Billy want?"

"He just stopped by to say hello, Mother," she said. And she and Barney walked toward the living room where the rest of the family were gathering.

13

IN THE OLD DAYS THERE HAD BEEN MANY FAMILY PICNICS AT THE farm and it had been at one of these that Carson had first met Barbara's parents. He had gone home to Maryland for summer vacation, between his sophomore and junior year at Princeton, and in his pocket had been a letter from her, inviting him to come to Burketown for the second week end in June. He remembered it now, as he sat alone in his hotel room in London, just back from the movies.

It had turned out to be an American movie, and disappointing, but he had sat through it anyway, and afterward he had walked back along the streets in the late English twilight, encountering the bold London whores, some haggard and some beautiful, who approached him imperiously and shrugged when he turned his eyes away from them, who laughed and spoke loudly as he passed. He had walked past Hyde Park slowly, watching the late, slow strollers there, and turning north, had gotten lost briefly in a maze of little angular streets but had finally found his way to his hotel. Now it was nine o'clock, but the sky was still light, and from his open window he could hear the distant sound of trains as they steamed into the great glass vault of Paddington Station. Perhaps, he thought, it was the train sounds that reminded him of that other summer, the train ride south from Princeton with Barbara's letter in his pocket. Still, it seemed to him now that London trains had a different sound from the trains at home; London whistles were higher-pitched and their wheels sounded more fretful than lonesome. They had, he thought, a nervous, impatient sound, different from the steady, reassuring rhythm of the Pennsylvania Railroad heading south to Washington.

He remembered the summer vacation train, the vestibules crowded with suitcases, portable typewriters, tennis rackets and lacrosse sticks, and the heady noise in the club car where everyone gathered, jammed together, sweating, shouting above the noise of other shouting, and the way the atmosphere in the club car changed when the Bryn Mawr girls got on. You could tell, he had always said, a Bryn Mawr girl by her hair. Her hair was always smooth and shining, precisely parted on the left, so sleek and perfectly in place that she seemed to be wearing an invisible hair net. And her skin, too, was smooth, and her voice was smooth and expressionless as she talked of Gide, Bergson and Russian novels. But he had had no eye for the Bryn Mawr girls that summer because in his pocket there had been the letter from Barbara Woodcock. And he would be heading north to see her again in two weeks' time.

He had arrived at the farm on Saturday. Though Barbara had told him a great deal about the farm and had often described the house, he had been unprepared for what he saw. When the house first came into view around the corner of the bumpy road, it had reminded him, suddenly, of a Mississippi side-wheeler, painted white, set adrift among the rhododendrons, which were then in full bloom. A Mississippi side-wheeler, floating serenely among purple, white and scarlet-dotted waves; and yet, as more of it appeared, the house lost its resemblance to a boat. With jutting ells, its patchwork of styles and contours, it resembled absolutely nothing in the world that he had ever seen. Barbara had come running down the steps. "Welcome to the farm!" she had said.

That afternoon there had been a picnic. It was like no picnic he had ever been to. They had crossed the lake behind the house in boats, and on the opposite shore, in front of the guesthouse on a wide, flat stretch of grass, the picnic had been spread upon a large white tablecloth. They sat on canvas cushions in the grass and John, the Woodcocks' houseman, made cocktails and passed them on a silver tray. Carson had never been to a picnic where cocktails had been passed and where, presently, solid silver knives and forks were placed, wrapped in heavy linen napkins, beside china plates while a Negro chef in a white coat cooked steaks above an open charcoal fire. He remembered the huge, icy bowls of salads and the steaming loaves of herb bread and the yellow ears of corn pierced with silver skewers and the small silver pitchers of melted butter, and during the meal, there had been iced champagne in tall, crystal glasses with silver stems. "The champagne is in your honor," Barbara had whispered to him.

He remembered Barbara's mother most vividly from that afternoon. He had thought her a rather pretty woman, with a clear and youthful face and beautifully arranged white hair, and after the meal, when coffee was poured, she had beckoned him to come and have his coffee beside her. "Come talk to me, Mr. Greer," she had said, lifting her hand to him from where she sat and letting a tinkling cascade of thin silver bracelets run down her arm. He sat beside her, and as she talked, she lifted a palm fan from her lap and fanned herself, and he remembered the soft, pleasant fragrance of her perfume that stirred in the little breeze she created for them both.

"You're from Chevy Chase, Barbara tells me," she had said.

"Yes, ma'am."

"It's a lovely town. One of the loveliest suburbs, I think, of Washington. Tell me, was the weather warm when you left?"

"Yes, ma'am, quite warm," he said. "You know Washington."

"Oh, indeed I do!" Edith said. "But it's a beautiful city. Tell me, don't you think this is a pleasant spot for picnics — here, by the water? Pleasant, and lovely and cool?"

"Oh, I do, Mrs. Woodcock," he had said. "Very pleasant. Yes, a beautiful spot for picnics. And, I might add, a beautiful picnic, too."

"Why, thank you!" She gestured around her with a fan. "This side of the lake is quite different from the other side, where the house is, have you noticed? We've tried to keep it this way, nice and rustic. We've just let the trees go wild over here, and this strip of grass, where we're sitting now, is never mowed. We have it cut once or twice during the summer, just to keep the brush down around our picnic place, but otherwise this side of the lake is just as Mother Nature made it."

"Is there a road between here and the house?" he asked.

"Just an old wood road. Do you know our New England wood roads? The woods, all around here, are crisscrossed with wood roads. If you take a walk through these woods, you'll keep coming on them. They twist and wind around, through the woods. Woodcutters used them, years ago, and along all of them are the old stone walls. Sometimes I marvel at the stamina our New England ancestors must have had to build so many stone walls! They must have been extraordinary people, don't you think?"

"Yes, ma'am," he said. "Indeed they must have been."

"Some of the old roads we've cleared for bridle paths, for the horses. But not all. We always say that there are only two ways to get here, where we are now, from the house. And that's by boat or by horseback! Oh, of course they've driven in here with trucks and things, when we built this little guesthouse. But actually, the two best ways to get here are by boat or on horseback."

"It's a beautiful spot," he said.

"Thank you. We love it. Tell me, Mr. Greer," she said, smiling, "what are you studying at Princeton?"

"Well, I plan to major in history," Carson told her.

"History! Now isn't that interesting! I don't know whether Barbara told you or not, but my father was chairman of the History Department at Brown University."

"Yes, I believe Barbara mentioned it to me," he said.

"Yes. It's a pity my father is no longer living, because you would have enjoyed talking to him, I'm sure. He was a remarkable man, a true scholar. At his time, he was considered one of the best in his field."

"Is that so," Carson said.

"Yes." She smiled again. "But I'm afraid you'll find me rather poor at history. You see, I was brought up — in Providence — in, well, perhaps you'd call it the Old World way. My father thought that it was unnecessary for a woman to have a college education, though, of course, he considered it essential for a man. So history — except for a smattering of ancient history in boarding school — is a subject I've never really studied. Strange, isn't it? That a history professor's daughter should never have studied history? Well, all I can say is that I know you would have enjoyed my father."

"Yes, I'm sure I would have, ma'am," Carson said.

"Tell me," she said, "do you enjoy Princeton?"

"Yes, ma'am," he said. "Very much indeed. It's a fine school."

She laughed lightly. "I'm afraid you'll find the loyalties are split in this family, Mr. Greer," she said. "My loyalties are, of course, to Brown. But Barbara's father and most of his family are

Yale. However," she said, "we shall try not to be too unfair toward Princeton while you are here!"

"Thank you, ma'am," he said, smiling.

"Tell me," she said, "you roomed with our cousin Woody, didn't you?"

He felt his face redden slightly. "Yes," he said. "For one term."

"I thought that was what Barbara said."

"Things got —" he hesitated. "Things got sort of switched around. They — well, you know how a dean's office is. Changing things around. They switched us around, gave us new roommates."

"Oh yes," she said. "Well, to be perfectly frank, if I were designing a college, I'd design it so that no one had a roommate. I mean, I think it's difficult to share a room, and try to study, with another person, don't you? I think individual rooms would be far, far pleasanter. At the school I went to, for instance, there were individual rooms."

"Well," Carson said, "I think it all depends."

"Of course. It does depend." She raised her eyes and looked around at the others. "I was sorry Woody and his mother and father couldn't come to our little picnic today. Woody hasn't been feeling well."

"So — so I've heard," Carson said.

"But he's actually feeling much, much better. Did you meet Woody's mother and father, ever, at Princeton?"

"No, I never did," Carson said.

"They're both very dear people and we're terribly fond of them. Leighton deWinter, Woody's father, is a lawyer. He has an excellent legal mind. He does most of the legal work for our little company. And Mary-Adams, Woody's mother, is an absolute angel of a person. She was Mary-Adams Woodcock, my husband's cousin. Tell me," she said, turning to him with a bright smile, "does this family confuse you — so many cousins?"

He laughed politely. "Well, ma'am, you have more cousins than I do," he said.

"Well, it's really very simple. There were two brothers — my husband's father and another brother, William, who is no longer living. William had two children, Mary-Adams and William, Junior. William, Junior was killed, very sadly, in the last war, but you've met his wife, Victoria, today. My husband's father had only one son, my husband. So there it is! That's everyone! Simple isn't it?"

"Yes," he said. "Yes, I see now."

"Two members of the family whom you *haven't* met are my husband's parents, Barbara's grandparents. They live in town and they're both, I'm afraid, quite elderly, so they don't come on our little picnics any more. But you must meet them. Perhaps, if you have a chance tomorrow, Barbara will drive you in to town to meet them."

"Yes," he said, "I hope I'll have a chance to do that."

"Of course," she said, frowning, "they're difficult. I mean, they're quite old. They're both in their eighties, and old people are — well, difficult, sometimes, don't you think?"

"I suppose that's true," he said.

"Yes. And sometimes — I'm thinking of Barbara's grandfather particularly — they say things that — that they don't mean. Things that don't sound kind. But, I suppose we must forgive old people for that, don't you?"

"Yes, I do," he said.

She looked up. "Well, here's Barbara. I've bored you long enough, I'm sure, with talk of family."

"Not at all, Mrs. Woodcock!" he protested earnestly.

"You're very kind," she said. "Now run along, the two of you. Barbara, take Mr. Greer for a walk along the lake, along the old wood road. I've been telling him about the old wood roads that are all through here."

"I've certainly enjoyed talking to you, Mrs. Woodcock," Carson said, standing up. "And I can't thank you enough for asking me up this week end."

"We're delighted. Now run along, both of you, and have your walk. It will help you digest your lunch," she said.

He and Barbara walked side by side across the grass and when they reached the protective shelter of the trees he took her hand.

"Well?" she said eagerly, "Did you charm her off her pins?"

"I hope so," he said. "I tried."

"What did she talk to you about? What questions did she ask you? You were talking for hours!"

"Well, we talked about your family and how they fixed up the guesthouse, and —"

"But what questions? Didn't she give you the third degree?"

"No, not really," he said.

"Ah," she said. "That's good. That means the research was satisfactory."

"What research?"

"I think you've been looked into," she said. "By my grandfather. He likes to keep tabs on what all of us do. When he heard you were coming up here, he got to work. I'm sure he got a full report — on you, your family, everything about you."

He had been startled to hear this. "Is all that so important?" he asked her. "Would things like that really make any difference?"

She laughed. "Not with *you!*" she said. "Obviously, *you've* passed the test! He's put a little 'O.K.' next to your name! As long as that's happened, it's not important at all."

"What a funny thing," he said.

"You don't know my grandfather," she said.

"Your mother said we ought to try to see him tomorrow."

"Well, let's not *try*," she said. "If he calls us, of course we'll have to. But let's hope he won't. I'd like to spare you that ordeal."

"Is it such an ordeal?"

"He's the patriarch," she said. "In this family we indulge in ancestor-worship — especially the living ancestors, like him. He's the monster everyone's terrified of. He terrifies me, too. He makes all the rules."

"I see," he said.

"But I know he'll like you, so there's nothing to worry about. Mother liked you, and that's the first thing."

"Do you think she did, Barbara?" he asked her.

She laughed gaily, tossing her head. "Oh, I could tell!" she said. "I could tell she liked you. I could tell by the expression on her face!"

"Really?"

"Oh, of course! Of course. She adores you. She thinks you're the handsomest, most charming young man she ever met! And do you know why, Carson? Do you know why?"

"No. Tell me why?"

"Because you just kept nodding politely and smiling and letting her do all the talking! You idiot, didn't you know that's the only way in the world to charm a girl's mother?" With her hand still in his she circled his waist with her arm, drawing him closer, and for a moment he felt unsteady and almost deliriously happy, thinking he might very easily collapse on his knees to the ground. "You were wonderful!" she said, and they walked very slowly, kicking the dried leaves and twigs with their toes under the deep green shade of the trees, saying nothing, and he looked upward, into the branches above, feeling tears in his eyes.

And a few moments later he stopped her, turned her toward him, and kissed her. She looked at him wordlessly, her face grave and anxious, for a long time. Then they continued slowly, arm in arm, along the path through the trees, saying nothing.

Presently they came to a spot of open sunlight and she separated herself from him, ran across the grass, and lay down on her back, looking up and laughing. She reached for a long blade of grass and placed it between her teeth and the folds of her white cotton dress lay all along the contours of her body. "Do I look like the constant nymph?" she asked him.

"Better," he said.

"Better than Joan Fontaine? Really?"

"Much better," he said. He knelt beside her.

"That's nice to hear," she said. "Say it again."

"Much better," he said.

She put her head on one side. "I'm worried about my morals," she said.

"Why?" he asked.

"Don't you know why?"

"Well, perhaps."

"I do worry. It scares me. What are we going to do?"

"I don't know," he said huskily.

"I know right from wrong," she said.

"So do I."

"I know you do. But that doesn't help. Does it?"

"Not much," he said.

"We can't get married," she said. "We're too young."

"I know."

"No one would hear of it, would they? Your family or my family? It's quite impossible . . ."

"Yes."

"I think we're in love."

"Yes," he said. And, bending over her so that her face was in his shadow, he said huskily, "I adore you."

She looked up at him. "What a funny thing to say!"

"I adore you?"

"Yes."

"Why?"

"Because —" she shivered slightly. "Because — I don't know. If you had said, 'I love you,' I wouldn't have been surprised."

"But adoring," he said, "is more."

"I know," she said faintly. "And it's just what — just what I wanted you to say." And now there were tears in her eyes.

"Barbara —"

"We've got to get back," she said. Abruptly she stood up. "If we don't get back soon, they'll start looking for us."

He stood up also and they started back through the woods toward the picnic.

Just before they reached the edge of the clearing where the family was gathered, she stopped him with her hand. "Carson?" she said.

"Yes?"

"You *do* love me, don't you?"

"Yes."

"And it's mature love, isn't it? Grown-up love, not like children."

"Yes," he said.

She breathed deeply, "Yes. I think so, too." And then: "Carson —"

"Yes?"

She pointed. "The guesthouse. There's — there's a key to it."

He whispered, "Is there?"

"Yes. Tonight, we could go there."

"Yes," he said.

They were not looking at each other, and after a moment he said, "When?"

"When?"

"I mean, what time?"

"Whatever time," she said. "Whatever time — is best."

"You mean when people are —"

"Yes, when the house is quiet."

"All right," he said.

"Walk down to the lake and take one of the canoes."

"Yes," he said.

She looked at him doubtfully. "Unless —"

"No," he said, trying to make his voice sound casual. "No, let's do that."

"All right," she said.

Then, quickly, they started across the grass toward the others.

Late that afternoon he had gone to the pool alone for a swim. As he went down the stone steps he saw Peggy Woodcock. She sat on the tip of the diving board, trailing her feet in the blue water. At fourteen she had been thin and gangly, with legs and arms that seemed too long for the rest of her body. She was wearing, he remembered, a black two-piece bathing suit the top portion of which still appeared to be unnecessary; and her boyish face, shoulders and arms seemed to be composed of one continuous freckle. She had looked like a girl made of tortoise shell and her short dark hair stood out in damp, angry points all round her head. She was smoking a cigarette, dropping her ashes into the pool. "Hi," she said.

"Hi," Carson said.

With a stiff-fingered gesture she drew the cigarette to her lips, frowned, sucked in on it, and immediately exhaled a noisy stream of smoke. Another ash fell and disintegrated in the water.

"Been smoking long?" Carson asked her, smiling.

"Three years," she said, not looking at him but scowling at the surface of the pool. "It's a filthy habit."

He said nothing. After a moment, she said, "I know what you're wondering."

"Really? What?" he asked.

"You're wondering why my hair looks the way it does."

"I wasn't, really," he said. "But now that you mention it, why does it?"

"It's a butch haircut that's growing out," she said.

"Oh, I see."

"I gave myself a butch haircut. Mother had a conniption! My God!" she said, and laughed. "But there's nothing she can do now except wait for it to grow out."

He sat down at the edge of the pool. "That was a nice picnic today," he said.

"Oh?" she said. "Did you think so?"

"Yes. Very nice."

"Ha!" she said.

"Why? What was wrong with it?"

"Conspicuous consumption!" she said.

"Oh?"

"Yes. Haven't you read Thorstein Veblen for God's sake?"

"No," he said. "I can't say as I have."

"Ye gods!" she said. "Well, he's just about *God*, if you ask me. I mean, what about all that *champagne*, and all the *servants* and things? I mean, ye gods, how conspicuous consumption can you get at a picnic? The trouble with *this* family is," she said, "is that nobody feels any obligation to wealth. Now, in my opinion, wealth imposes a duty and an obligation on the wealthy, and if you're just going to waste it, and *fritter* it, then it ought to revert to the poor. And things like these picnics of Mother's, well, just how leisure-class-ish can you get?"

"I see," he said.

She flipped one leg over the diving board and settled herself facing him. "Where's Barbara?" she asked.

"In the house. Changing her clothes."

"Aha!" she said. "You see what I mean? There's an example? What's she changing her clothes for, for God's sake? What's wrong with the dress she had on? Do you see what I mean?"

"No," he said. "Not quite."

"Well," she said, "Barbara and I have completely incompatible ideologies."

"Oh," he said.

"But of course. Now *she* seems to feel that wealth is to be enjoyed, that's all. Whatever comes, she *accepts*. She's a very accepting sort of person. Talk about, 'she spins not, neither does she reap,' ye gods! That's Barbara all right. Now I, on the other hand, firmly believe that those of us who are born into this world more fortunate than others have a heightened obligation to our fellow man. I mean we should work, produce, *contribute* in order to deserve the luxuries we've got! Not just laze around all day and be fed like a fish. Ye gods!"

"In other words," Carson said, "the money should only go to those who work for it."

"Not *exactly*," she said. "My personal theory is that those who *have* the money have got to work to keep it. If they can't, then it should be distributed among those who can work. So I'm not a Communist. In fact I think my theory's far more advanced. I call myself a dynamic capitalist. Dynamic means active. I think that under our capitalistic system it should be worked out that only those who produce according to their means get to keep their means. If they produce, it means more employment and better living conditions for the working classes. But the thing we've got to get rid of is the sponges. Do you see what I mean?"

"Yes," he said. "I think so."

"What do you think of my theory?"

"Well, I'd have to give it some thought," he said.

"Yes. Of course it's highly revolutionary and unheard-of, but I'm planning to write a book on it and make it all very clear," she said. She took a final pull on her cigarette, spat out the smoke, and tossed the butt into the grass. "You're positively loony about Barbara, aren't you?"

He smiled. "Yes," he said. "I suppose I am."

Peggy shrugged. "It's not surprising," she said. "Most men are."

"Really?"

"Of course. Men turn to jelly over Barbara. It's easy to see why. It's because she's beautiful, is why it is. She's the pretty one and I'm not, why deny it? Personally, I'd rather be as I am. I think self-awareness is a very important quality in a person, don't you?"

"Yes, I do."

"Yes. Barbara's beautiful all right. But the trouble with Barbara is she's a sponge about that, too."

"What do you mean?"

"Sponge. Just sits there and soaks it up. Now my theory about wealth and advantages might be extended to physical beauty, too. Because beauty is a kind of wealth, too, isn't it? Beauty — and intellect — things like that, things some people have and others don't? Well, *my* theory is that beautiful people ought to deliver, too."

He laughed softly.

"I mean it," she said. "I mean I think people who are beautiful ought to work harder because of it! But not Barbara. No, she just sits back and accepts, and *accepts.*"

"You mean you think she's selfish?"

"No, not *selfish* actually. But lazy. Ye gods, she's the laziest girl in town, the laziest girl in the world. Ye gods, you've never *seen* a girl so lazy as my sister! And it's having looks and luxury that's made her that way, if you ask me. Now, I didn't always feel this way."

"Oh?"

"No. Up until about a year ago I used to absolutely worship Barbara. Oh, of course I still do. I think she's absolutely wonderful and kind and generous — generous *most* of the time — and I have the highest respect for her. But I used to worship her, literally, like she was some *goddess* or something! I mean I literally wanted to model my life on hers! But then I started reading some mythology, about goddesses and all, about the kind of person I thought Barbara was. And I suddenly realized that all those goddesses had to work to *stay* goddesses! They didn't just laze around on Olympus *all* the time. They went out and rescued some starving mariner, or *something!* Now of course Barbara thinks I'm loony and acts *hurt* when I say, ye gods, *do* something for your fellow man! She's definitely not the rescue-a-starving-mariner type. *She* wouldn't decide to give somebody the gift of fire. But, oh well," she shrugged. "Perhaps you'll be good for her. If you agree with my theories, perhaps you're just the sort of person Barbara needs. Have you got a coffin nail?"

He had come down to the pool wearing only his trunks. "I'm sorry, I didn't bring any with me," he said.

"Skip it," she said. "I only smoke Murads anyway, and nobody else ever does." She stood up abruptly, raised her arms above her head, sprang, and performed a neat little jacknife into the water. She came to the surface and swam to the side of the pool, next to where he was sitting, and rested her arms on the smooth concrete ledge. She looked up at him, her short-cropped hair plastered smooth against her skull. "You were Woody's roommate, weren't you?" she asked.

"That's right," he said.

"He didn't come to the picnic," she said. "Woody's having trouble coping."

"Is that so?" he asked.

"Yes," she said. "He was sick. Did you hear about that?"

"Yes," he said. "I did."

"Sick," she said, "or that's what they say. Actually, he tried to commit sewer-pipe with his bathrobe cord. Did you know that?"

"Yes," he said.

"But don't you ever dare mention those words around *this* family," she said. "It's supposed to be the deepest, darkest secret. Instead, we say, 'He was sick.' "

"I understand," he said.

"How did you and Woody get along?" she asked him.

"Oh, I always liked Woody," he said.

"*Did* you?"

"Yes. Of course."

"Hmm. Well, I like him all right I guess. Ye gods, he's my cousin so I suppose I've *got* to like him. But he bothers me. I mean I'm worried about him. Not Barbara, though. He and Barbara are the same age and they've always been thick as thieves. When they were little they used to play together *constantly*. But I mean constantly. And you should have seen what they played! Dolls, and dress-up, and house. Woody used to dress up in girls' clothes, what do you think of that? And then they'd have *secrets* — secrets all the time. Ye gods. Well, in my opinion what Woody has turned into is a morphodite."

"A what?"

"A morphodite. Don't you know what a morphodite is, for God's sake?"

"Well, I think I know what you mean. But where did you pick up that word?"

"In *Freud*, for God's sake. Haven't you ever read Freud?"

"Have you?" he asked her.

"Well," she said, "perhaps I haven't read *all* of Freud. But Daddy's got all the books right in our own library, and besides everybody at the school I go to knows about Freud. I'm really surprised you've never heard of him."

"Oh, I've heard of him," he said, amused. "Yes, I've heard of him all right."

"Well, the morphodite business is on every other page, practically. I mean it's all right there, in black and white. But of course!"

"I'll have to look it up," he said.

She sighed sadly. "Well, of course Woody's being analyzed. They're having him analyzed and *analyzed*. They've got a doctor that charges thirty dollars for every hour, just for talking to Woody. But *I* could analyze him," she said, "for a lot cheaper than that." She ducked her head under the water briefly and came up dripping, "Mother complex," she said. "That's Woody's trouble. Woody's got a mother who's an absolute creep, and I mean it. I mean she used to think it was *cute* when he dressed up in girls' clothes! Can you feature that? And after he did — you know — did what he tried to do, at Christmas time — after that Woody *cried* a lot. I mean he kept crying. So you know what Aunt Mary-Adams told my mother she did? Got into bed with him and *rocked* him, to comfort him! I mean, now really. How creepy can a grown woman get?"

He had said nothing because, once again, he had begun to feel very sad. And he remembered again the curious cobweb of feelings, tightly spun and taut as piano wires, and invisible, that had seemed to stretch everywhere within the walls of that room at college, and the tender treading between these wires, and the feeling of choking. He sighed and tried not to look at Peggy's small brown face that gazed intently at him from the water.

Suddenly Peggy reached out and grabbed his bare foot with her wet hand. "Come on in the water!" she said.

"No thanks. Not just yet —"

"Come on!" Bracing her feet against the wall of the pool she had begun to pull him and, for a skinny girl, she was remarkably strong.

"Hey!" he yelled.

But she laughed and cried, "Come on, you coward!" and pulled him into the pool.

"We'll have a race!" she said.

He had raced her for four laps of the pool then, and had won, but not by much. And when the race was over and he stood at the shallow end, panting, shaking his dripping hair out of his eyes, he had felt quite relieved to see Barbara coming down the path in her suit — to his rescue, as it were.

"Hey!" he called to her. "Come rescue a starving mariner!" and he glanced at Peggy, who looked glum.

Lying now on his bed in London in the darkening room, smoking a cigarette, with no lights on, he tried to remember and reconstruct the rest of that day so many years ago and miles away. Strangely enough, though they had met late at night at the guesthouse, the details surrounding that meeting had grown fuzzy with time. He could not, for example, remember whether he or she had got there first. And he could not remember taking one of the canoes across the lake, though of course he must have done so. He could not remember what, if anything, they had said to each other when they had met in the darkness, nor what she had worn. It seemed, now, trying to remember it, as though suddenly they had appeared together on the veranda from nowhere, and the only vivid moments that stood out now were disconnected ones, fragments of time, little flashes of the picture — as though he himself had been standing somewhere a short distance away and watching his image move with Barbara. He saw her, for instance, clearly, reaching for the key in the pocket of her skirt and pushing open the door of the guesthouse. And he saw them both enter. He remembered the damp, stale smell of unused rooms that had assailed them inside and he saw her go to a window and open it, letting in fresh air. They had turned on a light, he remembered, for he could see them both clearly, smoking cigarettes, sitting in chairs and talking, he was sure, about nothing at all. Their cigarettes, too, had been damp with summer and had burned slowly, and his thoughts had moved slowly with the weariness of anticipation. "So this is a rendezvous!" she had said. "I've always wanted to know!" And somehow the light had been extinguished and the cigarettes had been stubbed out, and he remembered her saying uncertainly, "Carson? We are sure, aren't we?" And he told her yes, that they were sure.

And a little later, in a small voice, she had said, "Carson? I don't know anything! Truly I don't. I'm a little frightened, I might as well tell you. I really don't know anything. So you won't — so you'll remember, won't you? That I don't know anything?"

And he had told her that there was nothing to be frightened of, although, indeed, he knew very little himself. And he had given her another cigarette then, and lighted it for her, struck blind by the sight of her face in the blaze of the match. And they both smoked that cigarette in silence, passing it like a cup of courage between them. Then the cigarette was gone.

And then, much later, she had said, "Oh, darling. Will it show? Will it show in my face? I've heard that it shows in your face? When I look at my mother now, will she know? Will it show?"

And he assured her that no, it would not show in her face.

And then he remembered waking, much later, and seeing her across the room. She stood looking out the window, a slender silhouette in the light that was the barest beginning of morning. He had called to her softly but she had turned to him and said, "We'd better go now, darling — it's getting light."

A few weeks later there had been a letter from her:

Dearest,

I am so happy and love you so much, and I do not regret anything, no, nothing — not one part of it, ever. Why should I? Do not ask me a question like that, Carson! I would do it again, now, tonight, and without the slightest, tiny doubt and this is because I love you, it must be. And do not worry because I am not p. I will not say that I wasn't frightened because I was. Awfully. I thought if something happens what will I do? Only run away, far away, as far as I can go because there is no one I could bear to tell about it here — no one, not Mother, Father, anyone. They expect me to be more than I am. Or maybe it is me who expects me to be more than I am. Remember I told you how I daydream? This is what I daydream about the most . . .

You see, my darling, I am such a coward. I have always been a coward, and I want you to know this about me since you said we will be married some day. And I know someday we will. I want you to know how cowardly I am and perhaps that is even why I love you. Because I am weak and you are strong, because I am a coward and you are brave. How simple!

All my love,
B.

They had not gone to her grandparents' house that week end in June. Grandfather Woodcock had been too ill to see them. That was the year that seasonal changes had begun to affect him, and each fluctuation of New England weather brought on new coughing spells and sent him to bed.

As it turned out, Carson did not meet Barbara's grandfather until several years later.

In between had come Barbara's year in Hawaii and his own two slow and uneventful years in the stateside Army. He had gone up to the farm on leave from his base in Louisiana — with the end of his Army career just two months away — and they had started making plans to announce their engagement. In fact, he had almost forgotten that he was supposed to meet Barbara's grandfather when Mrs. Zaretsky telephoned to say that the old gentleman expected him. He had gone to the old house on Prospect Avenue wearing his Second Lieutenant's uniform, with his brass and his shoes especially polished for the occasion.

Mrs. Zaretsky met him at the door and ushered him inside. "Speak up good and loud when you talk to *him*," she had warned him in the hall. "Don't worry about her, though. She's got ears like a fox."

Mr. and Mrs. Preston Woodcock, Senior, sat side by side in the turret-shaped bay window of the living room, bathed in the oleograph radiance of sunlight through stained glass. Their chairs were close together as though, from time to time, each one liked to reach out and touch the other. Of the two, Mr. Woodcock was clearly the more frail. His long face was cavernous and ruined, transversed with ridges and arroyos. His eyes, set in craters beneath jutting white eyebrows, were almost colorless. He wore pajamas, slippers and a heavy bathrobe. A crocheted afghan lay across his knees and an ancient yellow cat lay asleep on his lap. Still, enough remained of Mr. Woodcock to make Carson realize that he had once been an imposing man. This fact appeared, first of all, in his handshake; when Carson took his hand the old man's grip was firm. His voice, too, was surprisingly hard and clear. "How do you do, young man?" Mr. Woodcock said.

"How do you do, sir?"

He turned to Mrs. Woodcock. "Good morning, ma'am," he said.

She held out her hand. And, as Barbara had instructed him to do, he bowed slightly, took her hand, and raised it to his lips.

"Won't you sit down, Mr. Greer?" Mrs. Woodcock said.

He sat in the window seat, facing them. For several moments, there was silence. Periodically, Mr. Woodcock's hand moved to stroke the cat's back. The gold signet ring on his little finger caught the sun as he first ruffled, then smoothed, the cat's crackling yellow fur. The cat purred noisily. Carson looked around the room.

His first impression of the room was that it was very dirty. The winter sunlight, pouring in through filmed and rain-streaked colored panes, was cruel to it. It revealed the dust that covered everything. Dust hung from the fringed lampshades; it furred the dry petals of the straw flowers that sprouted, in a stiff arrangement, from a blackened silver vase; it rolled and gathered in kittens beneath the chairs and tables. Suspended in the stained glass window from rusty chains were planters which held two huge and drooping Boston ferns, and dust covered the leaves of these like a fine, October frost. The room smelled of dust and antiseptics, rubbing alcohol and medicines that stood in sticky bottles on a tray at Grandfather Woodcock's side. Housekeeping appeared to have been abandoned long ago, and now every effort was devoted to the preservation of the two relics who occupied the house.

Presently Mr. Woodcock spoke again. "Young man," he asked, "have you settled on a career for yourself?"

Barbara had warned him, "Don't let him talk you into going into the paper business!" So Carson mentioned several offers of jobs he had received and that he was considering. Among them

227

was the offer made by the Locustville Chemical Company.

Grandfather Woodcock looked up. "Locustville Chemical?" he said. "It's a good place. An excellent place, excellently managed. I know a great many of the men there, including Harvey Kendall."

Carson had said that, after all, he had several months during which to decide, and that he was weighing all his offers carefully.

"Don't put it off too long," the old man said. "They say man wants but little here below. That's horse manure. Man wants a damn lot, everything he can get his hands on."

"Yes, sir," Carson said.

"So don't put it off. If you put things off, someone will get there ahead of you. Of the offers you've got, Locustville Chemical is the best. Take it. That's my advice."

A few minutes later the interview ended. But Carson remembered it a week later when a letter arrived from Mr. Kendall, the president of Locustville Chemical. He had heard of Carson's interest in the company; he hoped Carson would give the company's offer his serious consideration; there were a number of other applicants for the position, so he hoped Carson would reach a decision soon. He mentioned, also, a slightly higher salary than had been discussed before.

It was really Barbara's grandfather, then, who had made him decide to take the job. He had never told Barbara this. At the time, he hadn't thought that it was important. Since then, he had not been so sure. It was Barbara's grandfather, actually, who had brought him last night to London, and who had separated them through so many other journeys. Often in the past, when she had complained of Locustville and the trips and the life they were leading, he had thought of telling her, but he never had. There was no point, really, in trying to blame her, or her family; it had been his own decision, he had made it. At the time, it had not been possible to look ahead. Of course it was never possible to look ahead.

He wondered what would have happened if it had been possible to look ahead, to see himself, years from the day Kendall's letter arrived, to see himself lying on this bed, in this hotel room, hearing these night sounds, thinking these night thoughts. "And here you are," he would say to the picture as he turned to it in the imaginary album. "This is London, summer, 1958. You have come to sell American paint to British automobile manufacturers. You look as though you've been through a lot, and you have. You've been through four promotions, three salary increases, a number of birthday parties, and two prescription changes for your reading glasses, your eyes having grown weak and unreliable from reading reports and memoranda and watching television. You will surely develop lung cancer if you don't switch to filter cigarettes. You have survived many dangers. You even had a brush with the law a while back when you were stopped for speeding on the Pennsylvania Turnpike, but — a true salesman — you talked yourself out of a ticket. Your forehead is wider than it once was, but the mind inside it is perhaps a little narrower, shrunk by habit and corseted by duty. Your gut sags somewhat, but the paraphernalia inside it still manages to churn lustily upon occasion. Once, when your wife's complaints about your job seemed more than you could take, you offered her a divorce, which she refused, which pleased you secretly. Since then, with the help of a few rules, things have not gone too badly with you both. Once, in a nightmare, you dreamed you read your own obituary. It was buried in the paper and the headline, in small type, said: 'Carson V. Greer Dies; Was Paint Salesman,' and when you woke you were not sure whether it was the announcement of your death, or the words that followed, that shocked you more . . . Your tennis serve is good, but it is doubtful whether you could still snap out a lateral pass. You have fathered two children and you own, free and clear, a pretty little house in Locustville. What do you think of yourself?" He wondered what his answer might have been.

But it was foolish to wonder. So many things had changed. Grandfather Woodcock had died, Barbara's family had changed. He and Barbara themselves had changed. There were no more family picnics at the farm. The farm had changed. No one used the little guesthouse any more.

They had used the guesthouse, though. They had gone there several times again that first summer, and the next one, and the summer after that. And they had gone to several other places as well. He couldn't remember them all any more, or their sequence, or the details of each. But he could remember that they had been very happy in all those places, and for a long time. It was strange to have forgotten so much of that long time because it was really not so long ago, though it seemed to be. It was because of the way time hurried on. It was funny, the way those days seemed to have flown away, and it was sad because he could not remember when they had begun to go or imagine where they had gone.

14

OH, PLEASE STAY!" EDITH WOODCOCK SAID. THEY HAD GATH-ered, the remnants of the family from the pool and the terrace, in the living room. The sky outside was growing darker and the wind was blowing in fierce gusts, punctuated by explosions of thunder. "Please," she said. "This storm will be over in a minute. We've had such a lovely family Sunday, with lunch and everything. Let's continue it through dinner, shall we? Please?"

But one after another, politely and regretfully — remembering convertible cars left open in driveways, open windows in their houses that irresponsible servants could not be counted upon to close — all the family insisted that they must, truly, hurry home before it rained. And there was a hurried, ill-organized search for the equipment — towels, bathing caps, sweaters, sandals and hand-bags — that they had brought with them, and then there were hurried, apologetic good-bys with special attention paid to Barbara whom, they all protested, they should see more often. Would she be coming to the farm again soon? They hoped so. And the next time she came, would she give them a few days' notice? They hoped she would because then they could plan a little dinner, or a little picnic, or a little luncheon, or a little group for cocktails, or a little something. And would she please give all their love to Carson? And bring him with her the next time? And the boys — Dobie and Michael? There were so many friends who asked about Barbara and Carson and the little boys, and who would love to see them. So, when they came next time, let it be for a real visit, they said.

And then they were all gone, dashing for their cars, as the wind blew leaves from the trees and stirred up whirlwinds of dust from the drive. Barbara, Edith and Barney stood at the window, watching them go. "Oh, I wish they had stayed!" Edith said plaintively. She turned to Barney. "Where's Peggy?" she asked.

"She went downtown," he said. "She had an errand to do."

"What sort of an errand would she have to do downtown on *Sunday?*"

"I think there was something she wanted to pick up," he said.

"*What,* for heaven's sake? Oh, dear! I just hope she's not out in the car in this storm."

"They say a car is the safest place to be in a thunderstorm," he said.

"But the *roads!*" Edith said. As they watched, the first heavy drops of rain fell. "Well," Edith said, "I just hope she has sense enough to pull off the road and let the storm pass." She turned into the living room and began turning on lamps. The sky broke, and with a sound that nearly drowned out the sound of thunder, rain lashed down against the windowpanes. The lawn outside was suddenly lit with a great flash of lightning.

231

Barney counted, "One . . . two . . . three . . ." And the clap of thunder came.

"What are you doing?" Barbara asked.

"Just a mile away," he said. "They say you can tell how far away the storm is — by the number of seconds between the lightning and the thunderclap.

"I've never heard that!" Barbara said.

Edith Woodcock sat down in a chair and reached for the enameled buzzer that rested on the table beside it. When John came, she said, "John, are you sure all the windows are closed?"

"Yes, ma'am."

"Then the lamps dimmed, flickered and came up again.

"Oh, don't tell me the power is going to go off!" Edith said. "At times like this, I wish we didn't live in the country."

Barbara crossed the room and sat down next to her mother; Barney still stood at the window, his hands deep in his trouser pockets, looking out. "Lord, look at it rain!" he said.

"What time is it?" Edith asked.

Barney withdrew one hand and glanced at his wrist watch. "Four-thirty," he said.

"It would have been so nice if they all could have stayed," Edith said to Barbara. "We could have had a little family supper. Do you remember, dear, the little family picnics we used to have across the lake? Weren't they fun?"

"Yes, they were, Mother," Barbara said.

Edith frowned, her chin resting on the curled finger of her hand. "I don't know *why* we don't have little picnics like that any more!" Then she smiled. "I guess we've just gotten out of the habit," she said cheerfully. "And anyway, today was a lovely, lovely day, wasn't it?"

"Yes. Lovely," Barbara said.

"Though I can't understand Billy running off like that — without even stopping to say hello to the rest of us. It's not like Billy to run off like that."

"I guess he had things to do," Barbara said.

"Yes, I suppose. Poor Billy. He does work so hard. I suppose we should all be very grateful to Billy."

"Yes," Barbara said.

"Barney, dear," Edith said. "Would you hand me one of my cigarettes from that little box there?"

Barney turned, went to the table and picked up the silver cigarette box. He opened it and carried it to her.

"Thank you, dear," Edith said.

Barney flipped his lighter and held the flame to her cigarette.

"Thank you, darling," she murmured again, through smoke. She raised one hand, and with a series of slow little waves, cut through the smoke with her fingers, dispersing it. "Now tell me," she said brightly. "What did we all think of Sally's young man?"

"Very nice," Barney said.

"Oh, Barney!" Mrs. Woodcock said gaily. "Really, you are the limit! You're so polite, dear — almost to a fault." She turned to Barbara. "Have you discovered how *polite* Barney is? Don't you think he's really polite to a fault? Honestly, I think that even if I introduced Barney to — to — well, to Nikita Khrushchev! — and asked him later what he thought of him, Barney would say, very politely, 'Very nice!'" She laughed, and Barbara and Barney both laughed softly with her. "Well," she said, "I did *not* think he was very nice. I mean, actually. I thought he was a little bit weird, wearing that funny little pointed beard!" She laughed again. "Goodness, I'm writing poetry — dear me! Weird, beard." Beyond the curtained windows a particularly brilliant flash of lightning outlined the trees and, simultaneously, the telephone jangled discordantly in the distance.

In the silence that followed, Edith said, "Well, children, what shall we do? Oh, I know! Let's play Towie . . . Barney, dear, get the cards, will you? In that little drawer there . . ."

Barney smiled. "You always forget, Mrs. Woodcock," he said, "that I don't know how to play Towie."

"Nonsense, I haven't forgotten," she said. "But this afternoon, Barbara and I are going to teach you. Goodness, we have to do something, don't we, to sit out the storm? And Towie is really the simplest game in the world. There's absolutely nothing to it. It's nothing but three-handed bridge, really, with a slightly different —"

Preston Woodcock appeared in the doorway and stood, one hand on the side of the door. Barbara looked up at him and Edith, too, looked up.

"— scoring," she finished.

"I thought," Preston said slowly, "that I heard the telephone ring."

"You did, darling," Edith said brightly. "Just lightning hitting the wires. It's forever happening, but it won't affect the service, I'm sure. Preston? We're just talking about playing Towie, but now that you're here why don't we make it bridge instead? Come, darling, and be our fourth. Peggy's out somewhere, and —"

He shook his head. "No," he said. "I'm still busy."

"But it's *Sunday*, dear!" Edith said. "You've been holed up in that study of yours most of the day! Come, now, and join us."

"In a little while," he said. "Not right now." He turned and walked back toward his study.

"Oh, dear!" Edith said. "He's been working so hard!" She stood up. "Excuse me a moment," she said. "I'm just going to see if he won't —" She left the sentence unfinished and went out of the room after him.

Barney walked back to the window and rested his palms on the sill, looking out. Barbara sat quietly in her chair and for several minutes only the sounds of the storm filled the room. Then Barney said softly, "It won't work."

"What won't work?" she asked him.

"She won't get him to come out."

"Really?"

234

"She'll be in there for quite a while, talking to him. But it won't be any use. He's too busy being alone."

She said nothing.

Still looking out the window, he said, "Are you angry with me?"

"No."

"You seem very quiet."

"I'm — thinking," she said.

"What are you thinking about?"

"Well," she said, "I'm a little confused."

He turned quickly and faced her, leaning back against the window sill. "Are you?" he asked. "Why?"

For several minutes she had been debating in her mind whether or not to tell him what Cousin Billy had said. She had thought first of speaking to Peggy or perhaps to her father, about it. And she had also thought that perhaps it would be better to speak to no one; tomorrow, she would be leaving, and perhaps it would be better to escape that way and leave the controversy behind. It was a controversy, she felt weakly, that she did not completely understand. She had never understood or cared about — as Peggy had said — the corporate intricacies of the paper business. Problems of the family, of course, concerned her, but not problems of the business. And yet the family was the business, as Billy had said, and she had begun to wonder whether Peggy and Barney were planning to betray them both. So she said, "I don't quite understand what you and Peggy are trying to do to the rest of us."

"Ah," he said. "Go on."

"Woody said something to me last night," she said. "And this morning Peggy said she wanted to buy my stock. Just now Cousin Billy said —"

He nodded slowly. "So that's what he wanted to see you about. He knows, then."

"It's a small business and a small family," she said. "It isn't easy to keep secrets."

"Of course," he said.

"What is it, exactly, that she wants to do?"

"It's very simple," he said. "I think you know all there is to know She wants to get a controlling interest in the company."

"But why?"

He shrugged. "She thinks she deserves to have it," he said. "And she thinks I could run the company better than it's being run now."

"Could you?"

"Possibly," he said. "I don't know."

"It doesn't seem from what Billy told me — to be a very practical thing to do."

"She'll have some trouble doing it, I admit," he said. "But don't underestimate Peggy. She's got all sorts of angles. I wouldn't be surprised, actually, if she brought it off."

"I'd be surprised," she said. "But most of all I'd be very upset if she did."

"Why?"

"Because she doesn't deserve it. She doesn't deserve to control the company. If anyone deserves it, Daddy does."

"Oh, I know," he said. "But I think Peggy has lost faith in your father."

"What do you mean?"

He raised his hands in an open gesture. "Just — just lost faith in him, that's all. As an administrator."

"I want you to ask her to stop it," Barbara said.

"Why? Why do you care?"

"I care," she said quickly, "because of Daddy. Peggy forgets. Maybe she was too young to remember what I remember. But I remember very well. It nearly killed Daddy when they took the control of the company away from him and gave it to Billy. He's really never been the same. What do you think would happen to him now if even more was taken away — and given to you? It's been bad enough for him, taking orders from a thirty-six-year-old man. Do you think he could work for a man who's still in his twenties?"

"I suppose you're right," he said simply.

"Then will you please tell Peggy not to go any further with this? I'll tell her, too, but I want you to help me."

"All right," he said. "But I don't know what good it will do."

"Barney," she said, "I'm confused about another thing. Where do you stand in all this?"

"What do you mean?"

"I mean — suddenly I don't know. This morning, when you met me at Nana's — and on the rock, was it all part of a scheme of yours and Peggy's? To get me to sell my stock?"

He came toward her. "Do you really think that?" He stood over her, his dark eyes gazing deeply at her. "Do you really mean that?" he asked her.

She looked away. "I don't know. I asked you," she said.

"Listen," he said, and his voice was a harsh whisper. "Don't ever say that. Do you want to know where I stand? I thought you knew where I stood. Remember me? I'm the family's pet Persian cat! I don't stand anywhere. This is Peggy's scheme, not mine. Of course she consulted me. No. Consulted is the wrong word. She told me, that's all, what she planned to do. A year ago, or even six months ago, I might have cared about what she wanted to do. But I don't now. I simply don't give a damn now. As far as I'm concerned she can try whatever she wants to try. I don't care, because it doesn't involve me any more. I'm going to leave her, Barbara. I've made up my mind. I'm not going to be engulfed in it — in the business, and the family — the way everyone else is. I'm going to escape, somehow — I don't know yet quite how. But I'm not going to let this family and this company — because they're the same thing, as everybody keeps saying — submerge me and destroy me the way they've destroyed everybody else. Do you understand what I'm saying, Barbara? Do you?"

"Oh, Barney—"

"Quiet. Listen to me," he said. "Listen! It's destroying you, too — it will, if you let it. It will destroy you, just the way it's destroyed your father, and destroyed Woody, and destroyed Peggy. You've got to escape, too. You asked me where I stood, and I'll tell you — there's only one thing I care about, Barbara. You know what it is. I want the two of us to go away together."

"But we can't."

"So you said this morning."

"Don't you believe it?"

"Not yet. Not quite," he said.

"How can two people run away from their responsibilities?" she asked, but the words which she had intended to sound sensible sounded foolish.

He smiled. "That's for the two people to discover," he said.

"We couldn't. Even if we wanted to."

"You mean you don't want to?" he asked her.

"I'm — well, I'm very flattered, of course, and —"

"Flattered? Is that all you feel? We're in love with each other."

"That's the point," she said quietly. "I don't think we are."

He looked momentarily stunned; his eyes closed. "But I love you," he said finally. "And you love me."

"No. I don't think I do."

"You told me you did."

"Did I?" she asked a little wildly. "I don't remember saying that, Barney, and if I did —"

"What about that night? That night in your room?"

"Did I say that then?"

"What else did it mean?" he asked her.

"Sit down," she said. "Please sit down."

He didn't move. Another of his small half-smiles crossed his face, then disappeared. "I want to stand up," he said. "I lost the argument on the rock this morning because I lay down. I let you gain the upper hand. This time, I want to keep my head higher than yours."

238

"You're such a funny boy!"

"Tell me what it meant," he said. "Please."

"Well," she said, "there were a number of things wrong with that night. Carson and I had had a quarrel for one thing. I was feeling sorry for myself. And I was younger then. It was only two years ago, but a person can grow up a great deal in two years. I've thought about that night often. I was immature then, I must have been. It was a very selfish thing for me to do, or think of doing. It was a very greedy thing. I thought you were attractive. I still do. I was playing a very silly little game. I flirted with you. I thought — how pretty to have this handsome young man like me! I thought, what fun! I thought, all right, why not? What difference does it make? I'll have an affair with him."

"An affair?" he said quietly. "Is that all it was going to be?"

"Sometimes I think I grew up too quickly," she said. "Other times I think I grew up much too late. Sometimes I think I'm a very unsatisfactory human being. Sometimes I think I should go off to a Himalayan mountaintop and contemplate the sunrise and find out what I am."

"An affair?" he repeated.

"Yes," she said. "Honestly, that was all I had in mind! A little affair we could both forget about afterward."

"What fun," he said. "How nice."

"I'm sorry."

"I don't believe you."

"I'm sorry, it's true."

"I don't believe it," he said, "because you're not the sort of girl who has affairs."

"I'm glad you think that," she said, "because, you see, we didn't have one."

He shook his head slowly back and forth. "You couldn't have thought that," he said.

"Anyway," she said, "what happened that night isn't important. Because nothing happened! We were very lucky. Saved — literally

239

— by the bell. The important thing for you to remember now is that I'm happily married. And you're happily married, too. Peggy is very dear to me, even though we're very different. She's my sister and I couldn't do anything to hurt her. I mean this, Barney."

"Peggy," he said slowly, "is a heartless and mercenary bitch, obsessed and consumed by the idea of money."

"You told me once that you respected money, too. You said you thought it was a perfectly decent thing to serve."

"That's true," he said. "I could serve money in a true way, not Peggy's way. You said yourself that what Peggy wants to do would kill your father. But did you know that Peggy knows this? And doesn't care? She doesn't care if it kills him because she thinks he's weak. And weak people deserve to be killed, according to Peggy."

"And I simply don't believe that!" she said.

"It's true. Of course she doesn't want him literally to die. Just — just spiritually. She wants to finish the job your dear old grandfather began."

"That's ridiculous," she said angrily.

"Is it? I don't think so. I think it's a family trait."

"Please, Barney!"

"No," he said. "You haven't seen it. You've seen the outside, the politeness, the family *love* as they call it. You haven't seen the way each one wants to gobble up the others. You see everything all so close and loving! You see the little dinners and the lunches at the pool. You see this room —" he started around the room, striking at objects with his hand as he went. "Curtains made in France, tables and chairs made in England, rugs from — I don't know — Persia, I suppose, and —"

"Don't be absurd," she said. "Rugs from Sloane's or Altman's. Barney, please stop this."

"What difference does it make where the rugs come from? The point is, that's all you see — lovely things, this lovely house, lovely people. I used to think I wanted everything the Woodcocks had, until I saw that it was all rotten." He picked up the cigarette box and slammed it down. "You're so loyal," he said. "It makes me sick to see you so loyal! Don't you know they'll never be loyal to you? The strong eat the weak in this house, Barbara, and they'll eat you because you happen to be good. And goodness is weakness in this scheme of things. Look at your father. Look at Woody —"

"What's wrong with Woody, for heaven's sake?"

"Haven't you seen him? Gone, defeated. Given up — just a little mechanical figure that hops along the ground!"

Suddenly there were tears in her eyes. "Be quiet!" she said. "You don't have any business talking this way! Just because you've never had a family that loved you, you have no business insulting ours!"

He came now and stood in front of her again.

"I think you're right!" she said. "You should leave Peggy! I think you should get out of this house and never come back. You never did belong here, and if you've hated this house and this family so, you had no business staying. You've lived as a guest in this house for two years. You should be grateful! We've done everything for you and if you can't be grateful, you should get out!" She started to stand up, but he quickly knelt beside her and seized her wrists.

"Barbara," he said softly. "Barbara. . . ."

"Let me go!"

"No, no. Wait. I'm sorry. You're right. Let me tell you something —"

"No, I don't want to hear any more!"

"Listen," he said. "Please listen to me. I'm sorry. You're right, Barbara, I am the villain. I'm the worst kind of person, Barbara. You said you wanted to find out what kind of person you were, but I know what kind of person I am. There's a dirty word for men like me. I married your sister under false pretenses. I didn't love her. Every word of my marriage vows was a lie. But do you know why, Barbara? Do you know why I've stayed here for two years?"

"No. Why?"

"It's a very simple reason. It's because, in this house, I'm as close to being with you as I can possibly be, without being with you. It's one of the advantages of being a family pet. I can go into your bedroom and I can open your closet doors and see a few dresses of yours that are hanging there, and your shoes, and I can open your dresser drawers and smell you inside there. I can go into the room that used to be your nursery, and see your toys and your old dolls and the books with your name scribbled inside them. I can look through the snapshot album on the piano and see your picture on most of the pages. I can see the photographs on your mother's dressing table. I can see the water-color in the dining room . . ."

"Please stop," she said.

"No," he said. "No — you asked me why. It's because I can walk along the path to the lake where we walked, sit on the pier where we sat — touch things you touched, see things you saw. I can do all this and nobody knows what I'm really doing — that I'm making love to you, seducing you! So you see! You see what kind of man I am? I'm not a very good pet, am I?"

"No," she said. "No . . ."

"Do you know where I was yesterday when you telephoned? I was all alone. I was in your room, doing what I always do there — touching your things. And when the phone rang, it was like a miracle! It was you. I'd been sitting there, remembering that night, the first time I met you on the terrace — the night you said you'd teach me how to swim. And the phone rang. And it was you."

Still holding her hand, he lowered his face and rested his forehead on the arm of her chair. "I didn't use to be like this," he said softly. "The thing is, I need you."

She sat quietly now, unable to speak or think. At last she said, "Do you mean that really?"

"Yes. You're the valuable thing. The only thing that will make me valuable."

"Such a strange thing," she said. "Such a strange thing to say. I don't think anyone has ever said a thing like that to me before."

"It's true."

Suddenly she bent and kissed his dark hair; immediately she felt awkward and ashamed that she had done it, but she had done it, and so she continued to hold him there, one hand seized in his, her face lowered to his head, a curious perching and suspended position which she tried to hold, thinking: It's true that no one has ever thought this of me, or loved me this much!

"I don't deserve it, Barney!" she said. "I don't deserve to be thought of that way, don't you see? I'm not that pure and good, I'm —"

Then there was a sound and she looked up. Nancy Rafferty stood at the doorway in a dripping raincoat. "Yoo-hoo!" Nancy said. "Anybody home? Oh, *there* you are!"

Barney rose quickly to his feet. Nancy came into the room. "Lord, what a storm!" she said. "I had a ghastly time at the station, trying to get a taxi to bring me out here, but at last I did. Oh, God, it's wonderful to be here, Barb!" She turned to Barney. "And you," she said. "You must be Barney."

Barbara was standing now, too. "Barney," she said, "this is my friend Nancy Rafferty. Nancy, this is Barney Callahan."

"I've heard so much about you!" Nancy said.

"How do you do?" Barney said. And then, "Excuse me, please." He turned and walked out of the room.

Nancy giggled and squeezed Barbara's hand. "Well!" she said. "I *do* apologize, Barb! I did *that* all wrong, didn't I? I should have coughed, or something, before barging in. It's a habit of mine, isn't it — barging in? Remember Schuyler? But he *is* attractive, isn't he?"

"Are your bags in the hall?" Barbara asked.

"Just one bag. I packed in an enormous hurry. But I had an hour between trains in New York so I dashed up to Saks and bought the most divine vamping dress. Let's go upstairs. I want to show it to you. If *this* doesn't wow Woody, darling, nothing will! Oh, Lord what a storm! I'm simply drenched," she said. Together, with Nancy holding her arm, they started toward the hall.

Preston sat at his desk and Edith sat behind him, on the sofa, smoking her cigarette. "I think the rain is stopping," she said.

He looked up absently. "Yes," he said.

"Won't you join us now, dear? The house is so quiet and lonely without you!"

"Not quite yet," he said.

She smiled rigidly at him. "Won't you tell me what you're doing?"

"It's just a little project, Edith. For the moment, it's a sort of" — he hesitated — "secret."

"I see," she said. She stood up and walked to the window. The window faced the terrace, and, beyond it, the sloping lawn. "I was remembering just a while ago, the little picnics we used to have across the lake. Remember, dear? They were fun, weren't they?"

"Yes," he said. "They were fun, Edith."

She turned to him. "Am I disturbing your concentration, Preston?" she asked him.

He put down his pen and smiled at her. "No," he said. He pushed his chair back and started to rise.

"Where are you going?" she asked him.

He smiled again, picking up his empty glass. "Just going to freshen this a bit," he said.

"Preston," she said, "you don't want any more to drink."

He laughed softly. "What is it about a woman," he said, "that makes her feel she knows exactly what a man wants and what he doesn't want?"

"Preston, dear."

"Will you have one with me, Edith?"

"Preston, that's not the point. You've had enough."

"And a woman is always sure she knows when a man has had enough."

"Sit down, dear," Edith said pleasantly.

His face, which up till then had been composed and cheerful, seemed to fall, and he stood there, swaying just slightly, looking haggard and bewildered. He raised his empty glass. "I — " he began. Then he sat down. "I've only had two," he said.

"I want to talk to you," she said.

"What about?"

"Something that's been preying on my mind."

"What is it?"

"I think," Edith said, "that when something preys on someone's mind, the person ought to speak about it, don't you? And not keep it — secret?"

"Yes, that's right," he said.

She lifted the fingers of her left hand and frowned at her rings. She let her hand fall quickly to her side. "Sometimes I think I tend to bottle things up in myself too much," she said. "When something worries me, or troubles me, I tend to bottle it up, not say anything, not express it. This time —"

"Yes, Edith?"

"This time it worries me too much. It's worried me for too long."

He said nothing.

"If I tell you what it is, will you promise not to be angry with me?"

"Yes," he said.

"Promise? Swear?"

"I promise," he said dully.

She drew in her breath and quickly said, "Preston, you're sick. Preston, you should see a doctor, a different doctor, a —"

"What are you talking about?"

"You're a drunkard, Preston. I know."

"I've only had two."

"You've had more than two."

"Now, don't call me a liar, Edith. I ought to know —"

"*Please*," she said. "Let's not have a scene."

He sat with his hands resting loosely on his knees, looking down at the square of green carpet beneath his feet. "Now look," he said after a moment. "This is pretty silly, isn't it? I mean, I —"

"You've been drinking all day," Edith said. "You're no longer sober, Preston."

"That's not true."

"It *is* true. I think we ought to talk about it. I think we ought to discuss it, bring it out in the open."

"Please leave me alone," he said.

"I think that's been part of the trouble, Preston. I've left you alone too much. Now it's gone too far. You can't be left alone."

"I'm not a child, Edith."

"No, darling," she said. "Of course you're not. I've revised my whole thinking about this, actually. You know the way I was brought up. Liquor was never served in our house. If my father ever touched a drop of liquor in his life, I never knew about it. We used to see the drunks on the streets in Providence and I was always told that they were horrid, dirty, sinful old men. Now of course I don't think that any more. I've become — oh, really quite modern about it, all things considered. I enjoy an evening cocktail as much as anyone, dear, you know that. But this is different."

"Is it?"

"Yes." She came and perched on the edge of the sofa again, facing him. She clasped her hands together in her lap, in an attitude of supplication, and leaned forward earnestly. "This," she said, "this thing with you is nothing to be ashamed of, Preston. It's a sickness, dear. It's like — well, it's like a disease, or a condition. I know this, Preston, because I asked Billy. Billy and I discussed it at some length. Billy says that a sickness, actually, is what it is. One of Billy's friends from Yale — that Stu Gates, remember? — went through the same sort of thing about two years ago, Billy said, the exact same thing. It was a sickness. And Billy says that the good thing about it being a sickness is that it can be cured, darling. But he says that the thing you must realize is that it *is* a sickness, and see a doctor. It isn't a sickness that requires hospitalization or anything like that, but there are definite cures that medicine has worked out for cases like yours. I don't know what they

246

are, but Billy assured me that in Stu Gates's case, it was simply incredible what happened to Stu. He's a changed man, now, literally, Billy says. And he'd been simply impossible before. And Billy says —"

He slammed the heel of his palm hard against the arm of his chair. "God damn it!" he said. "What the hell do I care about what Billy says? Shut up about what Billy says!"

"Preston!" She sat back.

"I mean it," he said. "What do I care what Billy says?"

"But Billy *knows*."

"What the hell does Billy know? And why the hell should you be talking to Billy about me?"

"I've had to, darling. I've had to."

"What do you mean you've had to? What else have you and Billy talked about besides this?"

"Lately, many things. More and more things, Preston. I didn't want to, Preston. But what else could I do? I had to seek advice from someone. I had to talk to someone."

"But why Billy?"

"Despite what you say about him, Billy has a logical mind."

"Don't I have a logical mind?"

"Not always. Not when you're the way you are sometimes. You can't see yourself the way you are sometimes. Billy has, though. And I have. So I finally spoke to him."

"And deserted me."

"What do you mean?"

"You've deserted me, too. Just the way Father did — deserted me for Billy."

"That's not true."

"It is. It is. Get out of here. Leave me alone."

She stood up, smoothing the front of her dress. "If you won't listen to reason, there's nothing more for me to say."

"I'll listen to reason. I won't listen to Billy."

"I'm sorry," she said. "But Billy knows. He knows you're a

247

drunken man. You're an alcoholic man. Everyone knows it. Everyone in the family, everyone in town. It's hardly a secret, whether you know it or not. It's humiliating! 'How is Mr. Woodcock feeling today?' they ask me — people in town, people I hardly know. People who wouldn't have dared speak to your father or mother on the street in this town now speak to me, accost me, feeling that they are privileged to speak to me because they've seen a bond of commonness in you! 'How is he feeling?' they ask me. 'Why, perfectly fine, thank you!' They smile at me. They think, who is she, so high and mighty? Who does she think she is? She's no better than Mrs. Pat O'Marra down on Railroad Street whose husband comes in reeling every night, too! 'Perfectly fine, thank you,' I say, and they smile at me and say, 'He was feeling no pain last night.' Where? Where was he last night? At the club. At what club? Oh, any one of a number of clubs — clubs that aren't really clubs at all, just taverns, dives and shacks — any place that has a bar. Places where you go after work, or where you go during work. Your secretary — at three o'clock in the afternoon, last week, when I called. 'Mr. Woodcock is out of the office. I don't expect him back today.' 'Where has he gone?' 'Oh, I really couldn't say, Mrs. Woodcock.' And last Thursday morning, a policeman. Yes, Preston, a *policeman!* A policeman on the corner of Main and Elm in Burketown. Suddenly, last Thursday, he stopped me, blew his whistle! Pulled me over to the side of the street. 'Mrs. Woodcock,' he said. 'Yes? Yes?' I said. 'Yes? What have I done, officer?' And he said, 'I'm Patrolman Olin, Mrs. Woodcock. My father is Frank Olin who's a cutter at the mill.' I don't know this man, Olin! But he knows you and he knows me! And I said, 'Yes, yes, what is it?' And he said, 'It's about Mr. Woodcock, ma'am. I really don't think he ought to be driving a car, the way he is sometimes.' "

"That's a lie," he said quietly.

"It's not a lie! Why should I lie? It's the truth. It's the truth! 'The way he is sometimes!' Don't you think I knew what he meant, Patrolman Olin? The way you are most of the time, he should have said! Oh, I'm so sick and ashamed of it, so sick and ashamed of it! Ashamed of pretending there's nothing the matter with you when all along — all along — everybody — oh!" From where she kept it tucked, beneath the belt of her dress, she tugged at her handkerchief, withdrew it, dabbed at her eyes and nose. "I'll leave you alone now," she said. She turned and went quickly out of the room.

He sat in his chair for a while, then stood up. He went to the cellarette and fixed his drink, carefully measuring it, just right, the way he wanted it. He swirled the liquid in the glass, admiring the pale glow. He carried his drink to the window and looked out. The rain had stopped and he looked out across the lawn, the trees, the acres of his domain. He lifted his glass and drank a toast to the acres so serene. Then, as if he had bidden it to, the sun came out instantly and brilliantly. In the immediate aftermath of the storm it etched every outline and detail of leaf and blade with such precision and sharpness that, for a moment, he felt almost overwhelmed, dizzied from the sudden clear beauty of it, and his chest filled with violent sunbursts of happiness. It was the way the grass lay, flattened by the rain, and the way the maple leaves hung limp and dripping, and the way all this green glittered as though God had sprinkled diamonds over everything.

Then, behind him, he heard Edith's voice again, at the door. "Preston, Nancy Rafferty has just arrived. Let's try, for Barbara's sake, to make it a happy evening, shall we?"

15

THEY HAD TRIED TO RECAPTURE IT, THAT SORT OF THING, IN their new house in Locustville. Perhaps, Carson thought, he himself had fallen in love with whatever it was, the spirit of grace and comfort that belonged to those summer family picnics at the

Woodcocks' farm. Together, after they were married, he and Barbara decided that the kind of life that Barbara's family led was the kind of life they would create for themselves. It was a little game, during that first year, before there were any children to think of, pretending that their house on Bayberry Lane was, or could be, a smaller version of Orchard Farm in Burketown. They had several carefully selected props, wedding presents, his silver cocktail shaker that his ushers had given him, the tall-stemmed glasses, the heavy table linen, Barbara's pretty dresses. Every evening they set the stage for themselves, changing for dinner, sipping their cocktails, eating by candlelight. Each night, ceremoniously, he sampled and approved the wine.

His own family had been different. He was an only child. Such cousins as he had were scattered about in other cities, in Virginia and the Carolinas. He had grown up as part of a threesome: his mother, his father and himself. His father had been a busy and successful banker, whose greatest wish, when he came home at night, had been for orderliness and quiet. His mother was a small, nervous, pretty woman with an obsession about cleanliness. Her greatest cares were the appearance of her house and garden. Though she had always had two colored girls who worked for her, she had never found a servant who would clean and polish and weed and prune with the devotion and meticulousness that she felt was proper. "There is only one way to have things as you want them," she often said. "And that is to do things yourself." During the day, she followed the maids through the house with a dampened scrubbing cloth, finishing their work, attacking whatever dirt and disorder the girls had overlooked. With her cloth she would lunge at a smudge on the woodwork or a speck of dust on the hearth. Grimly, with a polishing cloth, she would go over the just-polished silver. On her hands and knees she would search the crevices between the carpet's edge and the baseboards for signs of dirt, and, in the same attitude, she would grope through the soft humus of her spectacular perennial borders in search of weeds. In spring she grew perfect tulips, followed by iris, phlox, delphinium and roses, followed by chrysanthemums; in her garden, against all odds, eight perfect camellia trees flourished. Three or four times a year, she and her husband entertained at small dinner parties for six or eight guests — "The most I can handle." The guests were usually the same six or eight people, and three or four times a year these six or eight people had dinner parties for the Greers. Carson's mother's one activity outside her home occurred when, once a year, she served as co-directress of the Junior League show; for two or three months preceding this show, she devoted all her energies to it. His mother had a pretty singing voice and, each year in the show, the second act curtain rose on Lydia Greer, sitting alone in a latticed bower, while the two pianos played the introduction to "Love's Old Sweet Song."

Carson's relationship with his father had never been exactly an affectionate one; still, it had been respectful always and, at moments, warm. His father had been a reserved man, who was embarrassed by any display of emotion, particularly by displays of love or admiration.

Once, Carson remembered, when he was perhaps thirteen or fourteen, his father had asked him, "Young man, have you decided what you want to be in life?"

And Carson had answered quickly and — at the time — truthfully, "I want to be a banker, sir. Like you."

His father had smiled a shy and rather tender smile. "That's the one thing," he said, "that I shall not permit you to be."

Puzzled, Carson had asked, "Why not, sir?"

"Because," his father answered slowly, "you might someday have a son who would want to be just like you."

He had not understood that remark for a long time; it had stayed with him, recurring to him often, for many years. It was a strange remark, but now, long after his father's death, he thought he understood it. His father had understood the debt that any man owes to another who admires him — who admires him

251

enough to model his life on his. It was like many of the things his father said.

The summer before he had gone off to Princeton, his father had called him into his office and said, "Growing up is an easier matter than the psychologists would have you think. It is a question of deciding when you want to do it. You are going off to college in September. In my opinion, that would be an excellent time for you to decide to become a man. If you decide to put off becoming a man until later, then you must prepare yourself for a few more years of childhood."

"I think I would like to be a man now, sir," Carson had said.

His father had smiled the same brief smile. "Don't tell me your decision!" he said.

But Carson had decided to be a man then. There had seemed to be very little choice.

But perhaps it was because his own childhood and youth had been quieter and less spectacular, that the sort of life the Woodcocks appeared to have seemed significant and appealing. It appealed to him, or had in the beginning, not necessarily because of its richness, but more because of its completeness and, he had thought, its happiness. It had seemed to him that perhaps, indeed, the Woodcocks had achieved a kind of plateau or point of view from which every deed, every event, was not only orderly, but pleasant; not only cultivated, but meaningful. In any case, the illusion had been a naïve one, and short-lived. He saw it now, looking back, as merely a projection of his own point of view, the point of view of a young man who had fallen in love with the idea of being a happy young husband. The end of the feeling had come, as he remembered it, the day that the Woodcocks had first visited them in Locustville.

They had been in the house nearly a year. Edith Woodcock had wanted, for some time, to visit them and see the house, but Carson and Barbara had managed to put her off. Carson's family had visited them several times, but that was different. They wanted everything perfect, everything finished, before the Woodcocks came; they wanted the lawn to be flourishing, a few flowers to be sprouting in the garden, the painting and papering to be finished in the house, the furniture to be bought and arranged, and the flagstone terrace to be dressed with graceful iron furniture and planted with bright geraniums. When, at last, all these things were done it was late in May, and the Woodcocks were invited.

They arrived on a Saturday morning — Preston, Edith and Peggy, with John driving the car — and, Carson remembered, as they turned into the driveway the curve of the rear bumper on the Chrysler station wagon seized the branches of a small azalea he had planted, uprooted it, and dragged it up the drive. There had been profuse apologies and John had been put to work with a spade replanting the shrub. But the incident, in a curious way, symbolized the whole visit. The driveway, for some reason, had been too narrow for the Woodcocks' Chrysler, and in everything that happened afterward, there seemed to be difficulty with sizes; Barbara's family did not seem to fit into the house. The living room, with all of them in it, seemed too small; although there were plenty of chairs there seemed to be, for a panicky moment, doubts that everyone could be seated. The terrible physical disparity between the Woodcocks and other things kept creating fresh problems. Edith Woodcock, going into the bathroom to wash her hands, struck and bruised her arm on the doorknob, trying to close it and Preston Woodcock, in the living room, was shaking out dottle from the bowl of his pipe by striking it on a glass ash tray and struck the ash tray too sharply, breaking it in two even pieces. John, conscientiously, after putting the azalea back in the earth, sat in the kitchen, where he felt he belonged, and Carson, pushing open the kitchen door to fix drinks for his guests, tripped over John's feet. The day began to have a nightmare quality, a dream of giants in a dwarves' house and he and Barbara moved resolutely through the overcrowded house trying to fix lunch.

They moved out onto the terrace. Peggy Woodcock, down from

Wellesley for the week end, found the arms of the slim iron chairs too high for her elbows and settled for sitting on the flagstone. Preston, who insisted that the chairs were very comfortable, tipped back in his to show how comfortable it was and overturned a geranium pot. Edith Woodcock, to be helpful, looked for a broom which, for some reason, was nowhere to be found. The day grew very warm. The hot sun fell directly upon the terrace, blinding everyone. The chairs were then crowded into a tiny corner where there was shade. Edith tapped her brow with her handkerchief. Peggy said, "Oh, God, it's *hot!* Where do you go if you want to cool *off?* Isn't there any place to *swim?*"

They had planned a picnic, a copy in miniature they had thought, of the picnics at the farm. But there was a delay with something in the kitchen and Peggy stopped talking about the heat and switched the subject to her hunger. "Let's *eat!*" she said. "Ye gods, I'm *hungry,* Barb. Where's lunch?"

And the conversation disintegrated wholly into complaints, followed by apologies, followed by cheerful encouragements.

"Of course it's terribly small and we haven't done all the things we want to do with it," Barbara apologized.

"Oh, but I think it's really very sweet, I think it's lovely!" her mother encouraged.

"Will you put my Martini back into the shaker and chill it a little more, Carson?" Peggy said. "It's warm."

"Oh, we just wish you and Carson were *closer!*" Edith complained. "It's so lonely at the farm."

Lunch, of course, eventually came, but Carson by that time had already begun to discover the curious fact that the Woodcocks were not properly scaled for the house in Locustville. Indeed, their proportions seemed wrong for every place except the farm and Burketown. Perhaps, he thought, that was why they so seldom traveled anywhere else. Barbara's parents had been to Europe a couple of times, but in the last ten years they had not ventured much beyond their quarter of Connecticut. Perhaps they, too, had discovered that they fitted the farm and the farm fitted them, and that they were uniquely unsuited for any other habitations of the world. Like a chambered nautilus, they had constructed a dwelling place that fitted their contours; its dimensions were perfect for them; only within its convolutions were they comfortable and safe. Outside of it, on the sea floor, they might perish.

Carson lay on his back gazing at the ceiling. It was very dark now and only the small square of the window glowed palely. He looked at the radium dial of his watch; it was eleven-thirty. With the time change, it would be six-thirty in Locustville. He thought of Barbara there, and wondered what she was doing now.

The Woodcocks had gone back to Burketown that night as they had planned. (How could they have stayed? There were not enough rooms or beds in the house to sleep them.) In the big station wagon, they inched out the driveway. He and Barbara had watched them go, waved good-by to them as they returned to the infolding of their shell. And after they had left, he could tell that Barbara, too, was unhappy, dissatisfied with the way the day had turned out. They hadn't discussed it. But that night, before going to bed, he had heard her say for the first time the thing she had said so often since: "Of course, Carson, Locustville is only temporary." He had been struck with the thought of temporariness, and what it meant; with the realization that she regarded Locustville as only one stop on a long journey. The destination had been uncertain then; it was uncertain now. It was one of those seven cities where the company had sales offices: New York, Boston, Detroit, Chicago, Milwaukee, San Francisco or Los Angeles. (He was reminded of those mystically numbered seven cities every time he signed a letter, for they were emblazoned on the company's letterhead; how impressive they looked, embossed in blue on the white paper.)

And so, that day, they had begun a goal-less existence, or possibly an existence that had seven goals, which was too many. They never again tried to recapture the life at the farm, to recreate it in Locustville. Deprived of that old illusion, they tried to find a new one with plans, schemes, talk of what they would do some day.

So much time had been spent that way — six years. He had read once, somewhere, that every cell in the human body renewed itself over a six-year span; in other words, none of the cells that were in his body or Barbara's now had been there six years ago. They were different people, completely, the new cells living only with the memory of the old. He thought: I must be going to sleep; my thoughts are coming backward and upside down. He turned on his side, concentrating on keeping awake for a few moments longer. He was still wearing his shirt and trousers, which was foolish; he ought to hang up his pants. Pressing was always a problem on these trips and he planned to wear this suit in the morning.

It had been a quiet, lonely day, this Sunday. And yet, he thought, perhaps Sundays are not entirely lost days in selling. At least, on Sundays, a man had time to think, to go over his past and future, try to put his house in order. He thought, yes, there is some value in Sundays after all.

Suddenly he thought he would write Barbara a letter, right now, tonight, telling her — if he could — all the things he had been thinking. He rolled out of bed and stood up. But, standing up, he knew at once that he was too sleepy now to write a letter. So he pulled off his shirt and trousers, hung the trousers, as he had done at college, with the cuffs clamped in the top of the dresser drawer. In the darkness, too sleepy even to brush his teeth, he got back into bed, thinking that he would write her the letter tomorrow.

16

NANCY SPREAD THE YELLOW DRESS OUT ACROSS THE TOP OF the bed. "Isn't it divine, Barb?" she said. "Doesn't it look exactly like lemon chiffon pie?"

"It's very pretty," Barbara said quietly.

Nancy looked at her. "Barbara?" she said.

"What?"

"Are you mad at me?"

"Certainly not. Why should I be?"

"For bursting in like that right in the middle of your — ah — little scene? Honestly, Barb, I thought the room was empty!"

"I don't mind your bursting in," Barbara said coldly. "I'm just annoyed at the meaning you've attached to it."

Nancy opened her pale eyes wide. "Meaning? Oh, Barb! Now you and I have known each other a long, long time. Sweetie, I don't care what you do!"

Barbara sighed. "I know you don't," she said. "But it wasn't what you thought it was, anyway."

Nancy laughed. "Of course it wasn't!" she said. "He was frightened of the thunder and crawled up into your lap! What else would it be?"

"Oh, please be quiet," Barbara said.

"Barbara, I wish you wouldn't keep worrying about shocking me. Really. Goodness, nothing shocks me! I think it's perfectly fine — wonderful! I think you're terribly lucky, actually, because he *is* attractive. I don't blame you a bit. You know my philosophy, Barb — eat, drink and be merry for tomorrow ye may die! I'm the real, original, couldn't-care-less girl, and I'm *not* a little girl from the country any more, either. I'm a graduate *cum laude* of the school

257

of hard knocks, Barb. I'm a hardened old Jezebel, so please don't feel you've got to kid me."

"He said something very sweet, that was all."

"Of course. Why shouldn't he? Oh, Barb, you're so lucky! You've always had all the luck and I've had none of it. Last night, old Sidney Klein called me and wanted — oh, never mind. Anyway, I told him to go to hell. Now look at me — jobless, career-less, man-less. Why does everything happen to me? Oh, well," she said, "in the meantime, try Woody again will you? It's nearly six o'clock. He must be back by now."

Barbara lifted the telephone again and dialed. She waited with the receiver to her ear. "Still no answer," she said.

"Let it ring."

Barbara continued to hold the ringing phone to her ear.

"*Still?*" Nancy asked.

"No."

"Try dialing again."

Barbara replaced the receiver, waited, lifted it, and dialed again. Nancy waited, watching her. "He must still be out . . ." Barbara said finally.

"Oh, Barb!"

"I'm sorry," she said.

Nancy's face was petulant. "Now what will I do?" She turned to Barbara. "You might have called him earlier! You might have just *checked* to see — and told me. Before I got all the way up here."

"I'm sorry. Frankly, I forgot."

"How could you forget? Didn't he say anything to you about being away?"

Barbara sighed. "As I told you before, I saw him last night — he didn't mention anything."

Nancy shrugged. "Well, I might as well make the best of it. I'll put on my dress anyway. You can keep trying him, can't you? From time to time, during the evening?"

"Yes, I'll keep trying," Barbara said.

"Good. He's bound to come back sometime, isn't he?" She picked up the dress, and holding it up in front of her, she walked toward the mirror. "Isn't it the most dreamy dress, Barb? I had to have it. Ninety-five dollars — I could hardly afford it. But I thought after what I've been through, I deserve it." She swirled the chiffon skirts about her. "I think it's going to be a good-luck dress," she said. "I've got the funniest feeling something wonderful will happen when I put it on!"

Barbara stood up. "I'll let you get dressed," she said. "See you downstairs." She went out of Nancy's room and down the hall to her own.

Downstairs, the evening ritual of cocktails was beginning — indoors, tonight, because the terrace and the garden chairs were damp with rain. In the second of the strung-together living rooms, fresh flowers had been placed in bowls — white peonies and deep blue spears of bearded iris. The windows on both sides of the room had been opened, letting the warm breeze from the garden drift into the room and billow the heavy curtains, and the breeze carried with it summer smells, wild sweet-pea and Nicotiana, along with the clean after-rain smell, and the sounds were early evening sounds, peepers from the lake just beginning, lacewings in the trees, and cicadas. Though it was still light outside, John had lighted a few lamps in the room; each created a warm pool of light about it, and in one of these pools, the little table had been placed next to Preston Woodcock's armchair. Because Nancy was there, Edith Woodcock had put on a silver dinner dress and she moved in the room, arranging the iris and peonies in their vases. Then Preston came in, smelling of pine soap, wearing a wine-colored velvet jacket, black trousers, and black patent leather slippers. He sat in his accustomed chair and John appeared with the cocktail things on a silver tray.

Preston mixed Edith's drink carefully, then handed it to John, who placed it on a smaller tray, rested a napkin next to it, and carried it to Edith.

"Thank you, John," Edith murmured pleasantly.

Preston mixed his own drink from the little special pitcher. He raised his glass to Edith. "Well," he said. "Here's to another pleasant evening for all of us."

"Thank you, dear," Edith said. And then, after tasting her drink, she said, "I'm really beginning to be concerned about where Peggy is. She's been gone most of the afternoon."

"Oh, I'm sure she'll show up pretty soon," he said.

Barney came into the room wearing a light suit.

"Good evening, son," Preston said cheerfully.

Barney bowed slightly. "Good evening, sir," he said.

"Can I fix the usual for you?" Preston asked.

"Yes, please. The usual," Barney said.

"Still no sign of Peggy?" Edith asked.

"Not yet," he said.

"Where in the world could she be?" Edith said.

Preston interrupted her, speaking to Barney. "We're having a very lovely girl join us tonight, Barney," he said. "Did you know that? Barbara's friend, Nancy Rafferty, is here."

"Yes," Barney said. "I met Miss Rafferty a little while ago."

"She's a wonderful girl," Preston said. "Nancy's always been a great favorite of ours." He looked up. "Well, speak of an angel!" he said, standing up. Nancy, in floating yellow chiffon, stood at the door.

"Mr. Woodcock!" she cried. She ran, holding out her hands toward him, across the room. "You look wonderful, simply wonderful!" He took her outstretched hands and drew her to him, bending and kissing her on the cheek. "I can't tell you how wonderful it is to be here again!" she said. "It's just as though I'd never been away. Everything is so lovely! You're so sweet to let me come."

"What can I fix for you, Nancy?" he asked her.

"Oh — gin and tonic, I guess, please!" she said gaily. She turned to everyone in the room. "So wonderful!" she repeated.

"And it's wonderful to *have* you here," Preston said.

She hovered over him as he mixed her drink. "Do you remember?" she asked. "That you were the absolutely *first* person who ever got liquor to pass my lips? Well, you were! Remember — the night Barbara and I were going to Cynthia Burns's coming-out party, and I had the horrible hives and couldn't go? I was desolated! And you came into my room and said, 'What you need is a nice, stiff drink,' and then —"

"Oh, yes," he nodded, smiling. "Yes, yes, of course I remember . . ."

She stepped away from him, turning to the others, and pointed dramatically at Preston. "So it was *he* who started me down the garden path to ruin!"

Edith smiled. "What a pretty dress, Nancy!" she said. "Is it silk?"

Barbara stood in the doorway, watching them.

Presently her father looked up and saw her. "Well, well," he said. "Now we're all here except for Peggy."

Barbara sat down in one of the small chairs. "A light Scotch for you?" her father asked.

"Yes, please, Daddy," she said.

"Oh, this farm, this farm!" Nancy was saying. "To me, it's always seemed like one of the last, truly civilized places in the world. The last outpost of gracious living!"

"Well, we *do* have fun here, don't we?" Edith said.

When all of them had been served their drinks, Preston lifted his own glass once more and repeated the little toast. "Here's to another pleasant evening for all of us," he said. He smiled first at Nancy, then at Barbara.

It was the cocktail hour. Sitting in the little straightbacked chair and watching the familiar ritual, withdrawing herself, mentally, a little distance and observing it dispassionately, she thought that it possessed tonight a particular quality of artifice. All of them, she realized, had embarked together upon a little play; the lines came rapidly, unpunctuated by silences, as the actors one by one discarded reality and lifted pretty veils of illusion. For some reason, the pretensions seemed too elaborate. And as she watched, the performances seemed to grow more labored and the lines that were uttered seemed to come breathlessly, as though they had all run a great distance to this stage and could only maintain their characterizations by taking great secret gulps of air. She herself felt choked. The consistency of the evening seemed fragile and at any moment, clearly, it might shatter.

She felt fourteen. She was swept with the thought that she was a child-woman and that some essential element, some fiber, had been left out of her, depriving her of the possibility of human maturity. She was a little girl, shapable and powerless, ruled by abstract emotions and passions, governed by desires that were undefined. Hopelessly she saw herself even older, thickened and heavy, her hands veined, the flesh of her throat sagging, covered with a façade of age while still inside lurked the mind and spirit of an adolescent, a little girl who had run with her cousin Woody to the doll island, who had stripped off her sticky clothes with him, pretending.

She looked at Barney, and as if it were a signal, he looked at her. She looked quickly away and said something to the others, words she forgot as soon as she spoke them, words that were merely an assurance to the others that she was participating in the little play.

Her father put his glass on the table and crossed his dark-trousered knees. He was smiling. "Yes," he said, "a drink at twilight puts the chaos of the day in order. Sets things back in their place again."

"Well, I for one will have another!" Nancy said.

"What chaos?" Edith asked. "What things have been out of place?" She looked to the others for reassurance. "It seems to me that it's been a perfectly calm and ordinary day."

Nancy said, "Well, it hasn't been a calm and ordinary day for me. I know exactly what you mean, Mr. Woodcock."

"Poor Nancy," Edith said. "Barbara told me about your job."

"Yes. Suddenly I'm faced with the horrible prospect of carving myself a new niche in the world."

Preston Woodcock raised his glass and smiled at her. "And niche-carving is easier, isn't it, with one of these?"

"I agree absolutely!" Nancy said.

Edith cleared her throat. "Where in the world is Peggy!" she said. Her tone was peevish.

"Woody's disappeared, too, hasn't he?" Nancy said. She laughed lightly. "I wonder if they're together!"

Edith shook her head. "No. I talked to Woody after lunch. He said he was going — I've forgotten where he said he was going."

"Oh? You *talked* to Woody?" Nancy said eagerly.

"Yes. He — oh, he said something about going up to see a friend. In Lime Rock, I think. For a sports car rally, or something."

Nancy gave Barbara a brief, accusing look. "How far is Lime Rock?" she asked.

"I really don't know. It's not Woody I'm worried about. It's *Peggy.*"

Silence fell now, awkward and heavy. The cool breeze stirred the curtains; the sound of lacewings and cicadas filled the room again and the mood of the little group changed to one of waiting. New characters were needed to carry on the performance; they waited for them. Preston gazed at his glass. It was an ordinary cocktail glass and the liquid within it was transparent. His Martinis, Barbara knew, were made with very little ice, but the gin and vermouth of which they were composed were chilled ahead of time in the refrigerator. Next to the glass stood the little silver pitcher, frosted with chill, and watching her father, she suddenly knew that he too was waiting, not for a person, but for a certain period of time to pass. The liquid in his glass would soon be gone, and he was measuring the time that it would take to finish it, and he was also considering the time that must be allowed between emptying the glass and filling it again. The prospect of reaching for the pitcher, of making that specific move, seemed to absorb him completely. He seemed to be holding his breath, counting, suspensefully, agonizing seconds of time. Watching him she felt, as she had felt before, powerless. Now he lifted the glass to his lips and when he removed it the glass was empty. He uncrossed his knees. Then there was the sound of footsteps in the hall. Everyone turned. Peggy walked into the room.

"Hello, everybody," she said pleasantly. She was still wearing her white shorts and white cotton shirt with the tiny blue alligator embroidered on the pocket. She stood with her hands on her hips. Then she touched her shoulder. With one hand she pushed her short dark hair back. She smiled at them.

"Oh, Peggy," Edith said. "Thank goodness. I was beginning to worry, dear."

"I'm safe and sound," Peggy said.

"Peggy, you remember Nancy Rafferty?"

"Sure," Peggy said. "Hi, Nancy."

She went to one of the chairs and sat on the edge of it, stretching her brown legs out in front of her, her sandaled toes sticking straight up. She leaned forward, clapped her hands on her bare knees. "Fix me a drink, Daddy," she said.

"Did you get caught in the storm, dear?"

"No, Mother, I was safely indoors."

"Where *were* you, dear?"

"Give me a drink first," Peggy said. "I've had quite a day."

"Peggy —" Barney began.

She ignored him. When she had her drink she sipped it. "Ah!" she said. Then she turned to her father. "Yes, I've had quite a day."

"Where have you been, Peggy?"

With her red fingernail she stroked the side of her glass, etching a little pattern on its smooth side. She seemed to be smiling at her upturned toes; they waited, but she said nothing.

Preston cleared his throat. "Peg," he said, "just before you came in Nancy was saying that I was the person who first introduced her to the pleasures of drink. And that reminds me of a story that my father used to tell me when I —"

"Preston, dear," Edith said. "We want to hear where Peggy's been."

"No, Daddy, go on — tell your story," Peggy said.

Preston laughed softly. "Well, when I was a kid — fourteen or so I guess — my father used to tell me a little story. It seems there was this man who had a young son, like me, who was going off to school and college, and this man said, 'Son, I'll make a deal with you: If you'll promise not to drink or smoke until you're twenty-one, I'll give you a thousand dollars on your twenty-first birthday!' Well, naturally, the son promised his father not to drink or smoke until he was twenty one. He went off to school and then to college and, of course, pretty soon he started drinking and smoking and having a good time with the rest of the fellows. Had a fine old time, drinking, going to wild parties, all the rest. Well, pretty soon his twenty-first birthday rolled around. His father called him into the library and said, 'Son, tomorrow you'll be twenty-one. I wonder if you remember the promise you made me years ago when you promised not to smoke or drink till you were twenty-one.' Well, the son thought about this a minute — he remembered the promise all right — and he thought well, I guess perhaps I'd better tell the truth. So he said, 'Dad, I cannot tell a lie. I haven't kept that promise. I've drunk and I've smoked, and as a matter of fact, I've probably done too much of both.' Well, the father rose to his feet then and placed his hand on the son's shoulder. With a tear in his voice, he said, 'Son, I want to tell you I'm proud of you. You could have lied to me, but you didn't. You told the truth. You were honest. Son, you've got the markings of a man. And I want to tell

265

you this: Son, if I had a thousand dollars I'd give it to you!"

Everyone laughed.

Preston said, "Now of course in my own case, with my father —" He stopped suddenly and looked at his glass. It was a shy, puzzled look. "I mean —" he began.

"Yes, Daddy?" Peggy said. "What about your own case?"

"Well, I've kind of forgotten what my point was," he said. He lifted his glass to his lips and swallowed.

After a moment, Edith said, "Now. Peggy. Do tell us. Where were you?"

"Oh, I've had quite a day," Peggy said. "I've been investigating a crime."

Barney said, "Peggy —"

She smiled at him. "No," she said. "I know what I'm doing, Barn-Barn. This little crime concerns all of us, and I think I should tell all I know about it while the evidence is still clear in my mind." She looked straight at her father. "I've been down at the office, Daddy. Your office and Cousin Billy's office. Down at the mill. Going through things."

Edith said quickly, "Well, darling, suppose you take it up with Daddy later! After all, whatever it is it can hardly concern our guest, Nancy —"

"Nancy, you'll have to forgive me," Peggy said. "Perhaps it doesn't concern you, but it concerns everyone else in this room. And I'm going to get it off my chest."

"Peggy, please don't," Barney said softly.

"Shut up, Barn-Barn," she said.

He stood up and walked to the window and stood there, looking out, his knuckles resting on the sill. In the attitude of his shoulders, the shape of his back, Barbara saw the same defiance, the haughtiness, that she had noticed watching him standing against the lip of the pool. Helplessness again swept through her and choked her.

"It happens to be a crime," Peggy said, "that carries a prison sen-

266

tence. It's robbery. Grand larceny. And it's been perpetrated against us."

"Peggy, dear, can't it wait? Really, I think you should take it up with Daddy in private if it concerns the office," Edith said.

"No, it can't wait. You should be interested in this, too, Mother. We've been robbed, little by little, over a number of years, of a large sum of money. And some of that money is money you ought to have an interest in."

"Peggy, what on earth are you talking about?"

"I'm talking about our dear Cousin Billy. Our dear, loyal, devoted Cousin Billy who's worked so damned *hard* for all of us, and whom we all love and respect, and who's cheated and robbed us of damned near every red cent we own!"

"Peggy!" Edith cried.

"It's true. I've been at the office. Bill Adkins let me in. I had a lot of time there, undisturbed, checking and rechecking, looking over things. There were a number of things that Billy would have been smarter to have locked in a safe. But there they were, right in his desk and in the files. I guess he thought our dear Daddy was too dumb and too honest to snoop around! I looked through everything, and at first I was confused. I couldn't understand. How come Billy owned so much stock, I wondered? There must be some mistake. I looked, and pretty soon I began to see a pattern — it began to be clearer, how he's done it. It was simple, really — like taking candy from a baby. Little by little, he's been taking Nana's money! Getting her to give him money, then a little stock, then more money and more stock! He's got all of her stock now, and he's also got her house — every bit of property she owns. Nana! A poor, senile old lady — he's robbed her of every last cent, and so now, very generously, he pays her taxes and her light bill! He's robbed his own aunt, but she's Daddy's mother! That money and that stock were supposed to go to Daddy when she dies! That money is supposed to be ours. But Billy's got it all, he's got it all!"

In the silence that followed, Preston did not move but stared at his glass. At last, he said, "Peggy, what is it you want? Is it money? Because if it is, I'll try to work it out — to give you and Barney whatever you want, whatever you need —"

Peggy rose to her feet and strode toward him. She stood, leaning over him. Her voice was shrill. *"Don't you see?"* she screamed. "Don't you see what's been done to you? You've been robbed! Your mother's money! Your inheritance and mine —"

"Do you want money?" he repeated slowly. "Do you need money?"

"No! I don't want money! Don't you see, you idiot! All I've ever wanted is justice — justice, for what's been done to you by Grandfather and Billy! I want to get even! I've got a right to get even! I want revenge — that's what I want. I want to report this to the police. I want to have Billy put in prison!"

Preston shook his head slowly back and forth. "No, no, no," he said. "No, no —"

She seized his shoulders. "Don't sit there! Don't keep saying, 'No, no, no' to me —"

"No, Peggy, you don't understand," he said. "I know all about this. I've known all along. Billy told me what he was doing. He had my permission. He had to do it to keep things going."

"What do you mean?"

"To keep things going. The company, everything. My money is all in trust — so when the company needed funds, I couldn't help. Other things take a lot of money. He's paid for them. Somebody had to. It was either that or sell the company. He's loaned me money, too, Peggy, when the trust income wasn't enough. You mustn't talk about getting even with Billy, Peggy, because if it hadn't been for him and what he's done, we might not be here in this room . . ."

She stepped back. "That isn't true," she whispered.

"It is."

Then she advanced upon him. She struck him once, then again, then a third time with the flat of her palm and he rocked in his chair from side to side. His neatly combed and neatly parted gray hair fell awry and waved across his eyes and she screamed, "Oh! You drunken fool! Oh, you drunken bastard! Oh, you drunken dirty fool!" Then she fell to her knees. It was an awkward motion, graceless and unpleasant. Sobbing, screaming — as everyone ran toward her — she pounded her balled fists upon the floor. A cocktail glass overturned and shattered; its pieces, in the suddenly harshly lit living room, lay all around them in hard blue splinters as John and Emily, hearing the commotion, came running from the kitchen, crying, "Oh, sir! Oh, madam! Oh, sir!"

Dinners in New England are ceremonious occasions, conducted without ceremony; that is, there is ritual but little formality. Even when there are servants in attendance, it is not surprising to have the plates served family-style. Edith Woodcock's dinners were always served this way. The roast, the turkey, the leg of lamb — Emily was a substantial cook but not an inspired one and was happiest working with large cuts of meat — was placed in front of Preston on the silver carving platter with a tree design and a well to catch the juices, and Preston carved, standing. Each plate was passed along the table by the intervening guests to Edith, who waited, with a serving dish on each side of her, to serve the buttered peas and mashed potato. Sometimes the plates were returned to Preston to have him shape a crater in the mashed potatoes with a spoon and fill it with pan gravy. Edith, a New England woman, disliked showy menus. She preferred simple dishes, she detested sauces; her most ambitious dessert, one which she used often, was vanilla ice cream with green *crème de menthe* poured over it. The dining room was large, done in pale blue, with pale blue satin drapes at the tall windows, pale blue walls, chairs upholstered in a pale blue and white brocade; over the buffet, lighted, in identical frames, were pastel portraits of her daughters, and the artist had obligingly created a pale blue dress for each girl to match the color of the surrounding room. At the far end of the room was a portrait of Edith, painted when she was a girl in 1918; it was a sentimental-ized vision of her, her auburn hair caught in a crimson ribbon and a matching crimson rose resting on her lap. At the center of the table, suspended from the ceiling, was an antique chandelier of French crystal that was almost never lighted; its teardrop prisms caught the candlelight. Though the room would certainly have been called "formal," though Edith owned several sets of fine bone china and a quantity of excellent silver, it was commonest, on eve-nings when there was no one but the family at the table, for meals to be served on the inexpensive "rosebud" dishes — a set she had bought at Penrose's in Burketown — with the plated silver, with paper napkins. This Edith considered merely sensible. Tonight, of course, since there were guests, the good china was used, and the good silver, and the linen. The good crystal water goblets were on the table, along with wine glasses because, since there were guests, John had brought up a bottle of St. Emilion. Edith was very good at making dinner table conversation, at creating a little subject for discussion and drawing, one by one, all her guests into it. It was an art she had been taught by her mother in Providence.

Only the lightest subjects were considered fit for conversation at the dinner table: the weather; people they knew; a book Edith had read, or was thinking of reading; an amusing anecdote, perhaps, in-volving the whole family. Tonight, Edith talked about the strange and, she thought, quite ugly designs of the new automobiles, vul-gar and fat and chromey, with their enormous protruding fish-tails and their gaudy colors; she was grateful for their station wagon, which, though it was six years old, still looked the way an automo-bile ought to look. Did everyone agree with her, or was she being hopelessly old-fashioned? She was reminded of this because just this afternoon Tom Moriarty, who owned the Chrysler agency in Burketown, had telephoned asking if he could bring one of his new cars around to show her. Only once, that Barbara could re-member, had there been a quarrel at the dinner table. She had been a little girl and she could not remember now what the quarrel had been about, but she remembered her mother suddenly bursting into tears and dabbing at her eyes with the corner of her napkin. She had never seen her parents quarrel before; if they quarreled, they managed to keep it from the children. It frightened her, seeing her mother cry, looking at her father's face which was flushed and angry; frightened, she had looked at first one, then the other of her parents, wondering what to do. Desperate, thinking that she must do something, that something was required of her, that somehow only she could stop the quarrel and reunite them, she had stood up from the table, stepped a few paces away, and begun performing for them a little song she had learned in school.

> Oats, peas, beans and barley grow!
> Oats, peas, beans and barley grow!
> Do you or I or anyone know
> How oats, peas, beans and barley grow!

It had become, in fact, one of the amusing family anecdotes that her mother sometimes told at dinner.

17

AFTER DINNER SHE WENT TO HER ROOM AND CLOSED THE DOOR. A corner of her bed had been turned down in a neat triangle and she sat on one corner of it, impressed suddenly by the silence. From where she sat she caught by accident her reflection in the long mirror on her closet door. Her face, she thought, looked already old. She reached for the telephone and dialed "O."

"This is Buccaneer 3-7090," she said. "I want to make a long distance call, please, to London, England. I want to speak to Mr. Carson Greer, at the Dorchester Hotel."

She waited. Then she said, "Yes. I'm cognizant of the time change."

Darling? Darling, it's me, it's Barbara, she would say to him. Did I wake you up? It must be two or three o'clock there, I know. The operator just asked me if I was *cognizant* of the time change! I'm sorry, but I had to talk to you, Carson, I had to hear your voice. I suddenly miss you so much I don't know what to do. I suddenly don't know if I can stand the next few weeks. I'm at the farm. I came up yesterday, after you left, drove up. Flora's with the boys. Darling, I'm so unhappy. Today has been the strangest, most awful day! No, I don't want to tell you everything that's happened. It isn't important, really, except that coming up here was probably the worst mistake I've ever made in my life. I don't know what's happening to them, the family. Everybody seems to be disintegrating. I just want to get out of here as fast as I can. Darling, I'm sorry for so many things. I'm sorry I let Nancy ruin our last evening together. It was an idiotic thing for me to do. Darling, I want to get out of this place, but I don't want to go home to Locustville. You don't know how lonely that place is when you're away. Carson, will you let me do something? Will you let me get on a plane tomorrow and meet you in England? I have my passport, everything I need. It will be our little secret rendezvous! The company won't ever find out. I'll keep out of your way during the day when you're busy. I won't interfere with your schedule. Will you let me do it, darling? Will you, please? Because, honestly, if I don't — if you don't let me do this — then I just don't know what will happen . . .

Then she heard the operator's voice telling her that there was no Mr. Carson Greer registered at the Dorchester Hotel.

There was some mistake, of course, because she had his itinerary. His address was the Dorchester Hotel, through the third. He had checked in sometime late last night or early this morning, Mr. Carson Greer of the Locustville Chemical Company. The company had made the reservation and it had been confirmed. Would they please check again?

There was another very long delay. At last the operator told her that she had checked again. There was no Mr. Carson Greer registered. There was no Mr. Greer of any sort; she was sorry. Someone, one of the night clerks, thought he remembered a reservation, but it had evidently been canceled. Might he possibly be at a different hotel? She was very sorry.

"Thank you very much," Barbara said. She hung up the phone.

She sat quietly on the bed. Presently there was a light knock on her door and Nancy Rafferty opened it. "Oh, *here* you are!" Nancy said. She carried a gin-and-tonic in her hand. "Why don't you come down?" she asked. "Your father and I are having a little after-dinner drinkie."

"I'll be down in a minute," she said.

"I suppose it's too late to try to get Woody now, isn't it. It's after nine o'clock. Besides, look at my dress." She lifted the yellow skirt. "I caught it on the corner of the table. There was a little splinter sticking out. I didn't even notice it — during that little scene before dinner!" She laughed. "I suppose the less said about *that*, the better. But, goodness! I've never seen Peggy behave like that, have you? I really wonder whether she oughtn't to see somebody. For several minutes there, I really couldn't believe that I was here, at the farm, at all. What's the matter?"

"Nothing," Barbara said.

Nancy sat down beside her on the bed and put her arm around Barbara's shoulder. "Something *is*," she said. "Tell me. Tell old Aunt Nancy . . ."

"I just tried to call Carson," she said. "He was supposed to be at the Dorchester in London, but they say he's not there. They think he had a reservation there, but canceled it."

"Oh," Nancy said. "Well —"

"I'm worried. Where could he be?"

"Well," Nancy said, "I wouldn't *worry*, sweetie. He's just somewhere *else*, that's all!" She laughed again. "Carson deserves a good time, too, doesn't he? After all, he's only human. Now come on downstairs. Help me cheer up your father. Your mother's gone to bed with a headache and he's down there all alone. Come on. The poor guy deserves a little cheering-up tonight."

"I'll be down in a minute," she said.

"And cheer up yourself," Nancy said. "Here. Have a slug of my drink."

She accepted the glass that Nancy offered her and took a few swallows. It tasted strong and bitter and burning; gin-and-tonic was a drink she had never quite understood. She made a little face. "A cup of gall," she said, smiling.

"But oh so morale-boosting!" Nancy said. "Now come on!"

"You go down," she said. "Let me fix my face a little first."

"All right."

She rose and went to her dressing table as Nancy tiptoed out the door.

At the mirror she began, with lipstick, to perform a few perfunctory duties to her face, giving it, she thought drily, no more attention than it deserved. Then she stopped, stood up, and went to the closet where Emily had placed her empty suitcase. In one of the side pockets, in packing yesterday, she had tucked the typewritten sheet of paper. She snapped open the suitcase, found the paper, and unfolded it. She read the top line again.

Jun 26-Jul 3 Dorchester Hotel, Park La., London W.1, MAY-fair 8888. She put the sheet of paper back in the suitcase. She had just wanted to make sure.

She went out of her room and started down the stairs feeling oddly buoyant. She felt suspended, going down the stairs, like a ball on a slender rubber string. From the library she heard music playing — the record from *My Fair Lady* — and, above it, the sound of her father's voice and Nancy's bright, rather shrill laugh. She could hear ice cubes tinkling in glasses and it all sounded very gay, very partyish. She hesitated for a moment, then turned and walked toward the glass doors that led out onto the terrace.

The terrace was dark and still and wet from the rain. The storm had brought a few leaves down; she felt them underfoot as she

274

walked. She guided herself slowly between the damp metal chairs
and tables. Above the trees there was a moon, but below, where
she was, was a dark cave of heavy, dripping leaves. The air was
fragrant and clean, and from across the lake, the breeze carried a
smell of moist pine needles; the breeze stirred the branches above
and sent fresh drops of water down on her bare shoulders. She felt
detached, walking under the overhanging branches, feeling the
shapes of torn leaves through the thin soles of her shoes; she felt
detached and also, for some reason, able to view everything all at
once with detachment. Perhaps it was the clear, heady, night-
smelling air, or perhaps it was the short, stiff, bitter-tasting snort of
gin-and-tonic that Nancy had given her, but whatever it was she
now seemed to feel her mind working on all levels, taking everything in, absorbing it all and relating it all. It was as though for
years, literally, her mind had been blunted, her thoughts dulled
and blurred and made sloppy by her own self-sorrow — the sorrow
of living in Locustville, of having a husband who went away all
the time. Of wanting unattainable things. All that dispersed now,
like fog, and she saw everything with almost breathless clarity, saw
years of her life that had moved in a slow march in that mournful
cloud of self-pity, saw herself emerged from it in some bright and
shining place. She sat down quickly in one of the metal chairs,
never minding the wet that drenched her skirt, enjoying this new
sensation, this new, heightened sense of the way things were.

Absorbed, consumed by her own self-pity (self-pity, yes; self-
pity was what it was), she had thought of him only as a passenger
who arrived and departed again, who, ticketed and checked,
moved from place to place on his itinerary; she had never, on any
of his trips, supplied him with any sort of existence in her mind;
she had thought of him as shuttling from one place to another, like
a letter. But he was a human being, and he had an existence. A
complete life of waking, eating, sleeping, dreaming, planning
— everything — completely apart from her. How strange, she
thought, never to have realized this before! Perhaps he was now in

the arms of some pale, lovely English girl! It could be! He deserved, as Nancy had said, a good time, but that wasn't really the point. The point was simply that, whatever he was doing, it was something private and apart and special that concerned only him, that involved no sharing with her now or ever. She decided that she did not feel jealous. No. Instead, she felt rather relieved. She felt relieved because, like a signal, this realization pointed out something to her. She thought about this, thinking that she had passed some great frontier of knowledge.

Behind her, the faint music from the house stopped. *My Fair Lady* was over. She debated for a moment whether she wanted to go in, to join her father and Nancy in the library. She could hear their voices now, floating from the open window. She started to get up, then sat still. She heard her father say, "I must be boring you, Nancy. You've never had any children. You don't know what it's like."

"Oh, no! Go on. I'm fascinated, Mr. Woodcock," Nancy said.

"Well, you see," he said, and his voice sounded sonorous and sleepy, "the thing is, Mrs. Woodcock and I brought the girls up with the theory that everything in childhood should be fun. We wanted our daughters to be happy, at all costs. I suppose this was because my own childhood was unhappy. I was an only child, you see. There was another baby, but it died — only lived a few hours. For years, when I was a kid, I used to think about that other baby — I'd heard about it, you see. And I had it all figured out that the other baby was a little brother, named Bill." He laughed. "I don't know why I figured his name was Bill, except every boy in this family seems to be named Bill or Preston. Anyway, I decided that the other baby's name was Bill, and because everybody was so mysterious about what had happened to it — saying the baby had 'gone away,' or 'gone to Heaven' and so on, instead of saying it had died — I got the idea in my head that this brother Bill would come back some day, or that I'd find him some day — I had it all figured out what he looked like — and he'd be my friend. I planned all these things that we'd do together . . ."

His voice dropped suddenly and she could barely hear the words. "Loved —" she heard him say. ". . . So deeply . . ." Then, louder, he said, "When I was twelve years old my father took me out to the cemetery and showed me the little grave. Where the baby was buried. Its name was Cecilia." He laughed harshly.

"Oh, what a shame!" Nancy said.

"My father was a very strict man, very strict," he said. "I guess I got a little hysterical there, in the cemetery. I remember my father dragged me away. But that wasn't what I wanted to tell you. What was it I was starting to say? It was — Bill, then about —"

"About Barbara and Peggy, how you brought them up," Nancy said.

"Oh yes. Yes, we brought them up — Edith and I — wanting them to have nothing but happiness, absolutely nothing but happiness. We didn't want to have either of them ever know a single moment of disappointment, not a single moment. But maybe that was wrong, maybe that was a mistake. At the time we thought — life has troubles enough. Troubles enough, when you're older. Childhood should be full of happiness . . . yes . . ."

There was a long silence. Then he went on. "Nancy, we really did everything we could think of for the girls," he said. "When they were little, they were never — never — left alone! I mean — literally — Edith and I never left the house, for overnight, without the girls. Always with them. Had a German woman, of course, to help out with them. But there was never any time when we were not right in the house, too. It was so if one of them had a bad dream and wanted Edith, Edith was right there. If we went on trips, we took the girls and Fraulein with us. Europe. Bermuda . . . Florida. Up to the Cape. We wanted them to feel protected and loved every minute of the night and day . . ." The voice sounded low and rattling and distant.

"As they got older, we gave them everything they wanted. Tennis lessons. Dancing lessons. Riding lessons. Swimming lessons. Had their own horses. They had the pool here, they had music lessons — everything."

He laughed softly. "I remember — Peggy wanted to take wrestling lessons once. She was only ten. Terrific tomboy. Regular little — and she wanted to take wrestling lessons! I didn't say no. I showed her a picture of a wrestler in the paper, said maybe I'd get that fellow to teach her how to wrestle. Well, I guess Peggy thought he looked too brawny for her to tackle. Yes. Anyway . . . yes. I tried to give them everything. But when something happens, like tonight, I don't know. Were we right? I don't know. I don't understand it, Nancy, really I don't."

His voice rose. "What does Peggy *want?* Is it money? Look — Billy Woodcock's worked things out the way he has because — well, because he's had to! But he hasn't taken Peggy's and Barbara's inheritance away from them. There's a trust. When I die, it will go to them — all of it. They won't be millionaires, but they won't be in the poorhouse, either! Peggy and Barbara have always had plenty! Plenty! If Peggy needs more money, there are ways and means to get it! That's what I don't understand, Nancy, that's what I simply don't understand . . ."

His voice fell again. "Did you see her tonight, Nancy? Did you see her? See what she did? Hit me — slapped my face — my own daughter. As though I — somehow — I don't know. And then, down on the floor — the things she said. She's a grown woman, Nancy! She's a grown woman. How can a grown woman act like that, unless she's terribly unhappy?"

"I know," she heard Nancy say softly. "I know."

"Up in her room. Won't come down. Says she's never coming down again. Why? What have I done wrong? Do you know, Nancy? Do you?"

"No . . ."

"What she said . . . the way she said it. That hurt most. More than slapping. More hurting. I couldn't believe — couldn't believe. Barbara, too," he said.

"What about Barbara?"

"I don't know," he said. "You're Barbara's friend. Best friend. Maybe you know. Sometimes I look at her and wonder — is she happy? If she's not happy, how can it be? Tried so hard — nothing but happiness. And now Barbara. Sometimes I look at her and think: How can it be? If she's unhappy too, how can it be?"

She sat very still in the little wet chair in the darkness, her hands in her lap, hearing him say, "How can it be?" with a kind of childish wonder in his voice.

Then suddenly she felt something touch her arm. She turned sharply in terror — then saw Barney, his white shirt, dark face, standing above her. He knelt quickly beside her. "I'm sorry," he said. "I've looked for you everywhere — all over the house — in the garden —"

"Ssh!" she said.

"No," he whispered. "Don't listen to that. I heard it, too. It's only a ghost talking, the ghost of Harlow J. Lerner. It's this way every night. He haunts us."

"I'm going to him."

"No, don't. It won't do any good. Let sleeping dogs lie."

"Oh, Barney, I can't bear it!"

"Quiet," he said. "Quiet, darling. You've seen enough, haven't you? Heard enough, tonight, in this house, to know what I mean? You know why we've both got to escape, don't you?"

With a foretaste of experience, of knowing the new thing before it happened — the final stepping-across of the frontier to the unsampled continent, from the old self to the new — she said, "Yes, but how?"

"Where will you meet me?"

"In the guesthouse," she said. "Later. You know, the road through the woods . . ."

"I'll be there," he said.

He rose quickly and was gone.

For a while she sat there, still listening to the voices from the library.

"Poor Mr. Woodcock . . . poor Mr. Woodcock," she heard Nancy say. And then, "Shall we fix ourselves another tiny drink?"

There was a heavy silence. Then he said, "No . . . got to get to bed. Time. Another day. Win the world . . . another day, another dollar . . ."

Nancy said, "Barbara said she'd be down in a minute —"

Barbara stood up then and walked across the terrace toward the house.

As she came into the library, Nancy waved her glass gaily. "*Here* she comes!" she cried.

Preston sat hunched in his chair, staring straight ahead. "Get to bed . . . must get to bed . . ." he said.

"I think that's a good idea for all of us," Barbara said brightly. "Come," she said. She went to him, lifted his arm, and seeing his other hand struggle and reach for the arm of the chair, grasping for it to push himself upward, she helped lift him, feeling, for a moment, almost his full weight beneath her. "Come, Daddy dear . . . come, Daddy," she whispered.

18

ALONE, NANCY RAFFERTY LAY ON THE LIBRARY SOFA — HER feet in their yellow slippers up on the fat velvet cushions, her head back. Next to her, on the coffee table, her glass stood, and with one hand, she blindly reached for it. She found it and attempted, without lifting her head, to drink from it. But that was impossible from this position, and so for a while she contented herself with resting it moistly on her bosom; then she moved it, placing its damp coldness on her forehead. She closed her eyes.

After a while she turned on her side, and that way she could sip it easily. Also on the table was a low bowl of talisman roses. With one hand she fondled the flowers, then snapped off one bloom and dropped it, with a little laugh, into her glass where it floated prettily with the green wedge of lime that the glass already contained. She admired for a long time this bit of artistry. Then she heard footsteps in the hall and called softly, "Halt! Who goes there? Friend or foe?" Barney appeared in the door. "Oh, it's you," she said. "Come join me."

"What are you doing up?" he asked her.

"Having a party." She giggled. "All by myself. Looking for someone to party with — but no one will. Come sit with me." She straightened up, put her feet on the floor and patted the section of sofa next to her. "Waiting, waiting," she said. She lifted her glass and drank the little that remained, then set the glass down deliberately on the coffee table. "I'm a little tight. Will you forgive me?"

He came into the room but did not sit down next to her. He sat in one of the chairs opposite her and smiled. "How long have you been waiting?" he asked.

"Hours. Months. Years. It seems like that, anyway. I've been sitting here wrapped in thought." She waved at the bowl of roses. "I'm poor butterfly — by the blossoms waiting. For love to come to me by and by. But the love I thought was coming — hasn't come."

"Who is that?"

She laughed. "Mr. Right," she said. "Oh, I wasn't stood up — not that. He didn't know I'd be here. But I was hoping. A girl can hope, can't she, that suddenly, somehow, the impossible, wonderful thing will happen? That Mr. Magnificent — Prince Charming — whatever you want to call him — will come *swooping* down on his milk white charger, and *scoop* her up, and lift her lips to his! Ah, me . . . well, the trouble with me is, the impossible hasn't happened yet. All my hope has been" — she lifted the skirt of her yellow dress — "shredded! Like this dress. Look at what happened to my dress! But perhaps that's what hope is made of — silk chiffon!" She laughed again. "Am I deep?" she asked him.

"Very," he said. "Very deep."

"Ha! Well, now I'll tell you the ghastly secret. The Mr. Right I was waiting for — hoping for — wasn't even someone I was *sure* was Mr. Right. It was only Woody."

"Ah, I see," he said.

"Ah, I see," she repeated. "Why, whenever I mention Woody's name, do people say, 'Ah, I see'? What's wrong? Is Woody gay, Barney? Is that it?"

"I wouldn't know," he said.

"Hmmm. Well, I suppose I've shocked you. I'm sorry. I'm tight. *In vino* whatchamacallit. *Veritas*. However," she said, "let's not talk about me. Let's talk about you. How about *you?*"

"Am I gay, do you mean?"

"No, no! You — your life. Your dreams, your hopes, your aspirations — that sort of thing."

"I'm not very interesting," he said.

"Oh, but you *are!* You are! What about tonight, for instance? What did you think about that little scene tonight, before dinner?"

"I'm afraid I must apologize for Peggy."

"Oh, don't be an *ass!*" she said. "I mean, what did you *think?*"

"I'm sorry that —"

"To me," she interrupted, "to *me*, it was totally, utterly fascinating. I mean, really it was. Of course it was ghastly — family feuds always are. And I was embarrassed a little to be in on it. But I thought — how fascinating! An argument about money among the rich!"

"Yes, I suppose it was," he said.

"No, but seriously," she said. "To me, there is something fascinating about rich people. They look different, they talk differently. They even have a different *smell* — have you ever noticed that? The special smell very rich people have?"

"No, I can't say that I have," he said.

"I ask you," she said, "because I understand you're not rich. And neither am I. I've always been poor — poor as a tiny, little, itty-bitty, little —" She brought two fingertips close together and squinted through the tiny crack, "churchmouse. Poor as Poor Butterfly. Are you a conniver, Barney?"

"I'm sorry, I don't know what you mean."

She looked at him, surprised. "You *don't*? A conniver. After money. I ask, because in a way I'm one. *In vino veritas,* you see. Yes, I'll make no bones about it. Long ago, I decided — for my friends I wanted only rich people. Nice rich people. When I was in school, I spotted Barbara — by the way she looked and talked and smelled. And I thought: I want that girl for my friend!"

"I see," he said.

"I wonder," she said. "I wonder if you do see. Because what I mean is that in some ways I think you and I are very much alike."

"Really?" he asked. "In what ways?"

"Ways," she said. "Ways and ways. I mean it. We're both looking for something that will give our lives a little meaning. I am — and so are you. We're looking for doorways that will open to it — to the thing we want." She lifted her hand in a wide gesture. "Doorways," she whispered. "One of them is money. Or could be . . ."

"What do you mean by that?"

"It could be. One of the doorways. But then — something happens like tonight. And you see what happens to them — rich people."

"What happens to rich people?"

"Nothing much, I suppose. If they're like Barbara, they marry *other* nice people like Carson Greer and have children. Nothing special. That's the trouble. If they're like Barbara, they surrender to it. If they're like Peggy, they don't. But they still don't get anywhere!"

"Perhaps Barbara hasn't surrendered," he said.

"Oh, she has, she has. She surrendered long, long ago." Suddenly she pushed herself along the sofa, closer to his chair. "But we were talking about you!" she said brightly. "I want to talk about you! Why are you so quiet? Why don't you say more? Why don't you voice your thoughts?"

"My thoughts aren't worth much, I'm afraid."

She reached out and placed one hand gently on his knee. "Oh, but they are, darling boy, they are! Everyone's thoughts are worth — a great deal." She withdrew her hand. "Forgive me," she said. "I'm a little tight. But when I'm tight, I'm more perceptive. More ar-tic-u-late! Really. Do you want to know what I've perceived about you tonight?"

"Yes," he said. "What?"

"Well," she said, "for one thing, that you and I are more alike than you'll admit —"

"And what else?"

"And — well, I wonder. Are you in love with Barbara?"

"Why do you ask that?"

"Because I want to know. Are you in love with her? Or —"

"Or what?"

"Or is she just a doorway? Ah, poor Barney!"

"Why?"

"Because if you do love her — oh, it will be a mess. A mess," She laughed. "But then, life is a mess anyway, isn't it?"

"Not all of it," he said slowly. "Not quite all."

"Oh, Barbara is lucky. She's always been lucky," she sighed. "So, perhaps —"

"In some ways, I don't think she's been so lucky," he said.

"You don't? Oh, I do. Don't forget, I've known her a long time. She's very lucky. Not like you and me. Look at us! There are so many doorways, so many choices. Which one was right? Marriage? A job? Money . . . religion . . . love . . . service to something? Is it power and prestige? We try them all, looking for the right door!

But the trouble is —" she paused thoughtfully. "The trouble is, we're constitutionally unable. We're better equipped to stand outside doors. We're doormen! We don't have the needling power — the power to needle our poor souls, and drive ourselves! That's what we lack. So we expect, we hope. We dream of things, expect and hope that the right door will open to us — all by itself. Or that someone will ask us in. The thing we don't realize is that some of those doors need to be — to be blasted open! With dynamite! And forced open, forced until the doorknobs are bloody! And we don't have the dynamite or the blood or the — oh, God!" she said. "I don't know! Don't listen to me! I'm talking like a fool!" She sobbed suddenly and leaned forward, pressing her face in her hands. "You see?" she said. "Constitutionally unable. So I get drunk." She lifted her head and brushed the tears quickly away with the back of her wrist. "But you see, Barbara is different — she's never had to needle herself because everything's come to her. That's what I mean when I say she's lucky."

She reached for her empty glass and stared at it, at the rose and the wedge of lime that floated among the remaining ice cubes. "So many doors," she said softly. "I've tried them all — timidly, I admit. Pushed them open a tiny way — just enough to peek inside. But when opening them the rest of the way took strength and courage and muscle, I let them close again. I tried them, one by one. I don't have many choices left, but this," she said smiling at the glass, "is my current one. And it's empty. Barney, would it be too much to ask you to fix me another drink?"

"I don't think you should have another," he said.

"You're right. I shouldn't. But tonight I've decided to drink myself into a stupor. You don't understand, do you? But Mr. Woodcock does . . . he does. He knows there are times when the only answer is complete stupefaction. Drinking is a special kind of door. Will you fix me another or not?" she asked.

"I think you'd better go to bed," he said.

"Then I'll fix it myself," she said. She stood up and carried her glass toward the little bar. "It's a kind of suicide, isn't it? Drinking. I've heard that," she said to him as, with silver tongs, she dropped fresh ice cubes on top of the rose. "And so, I've heard, is immorality! Well, all I can say is, I've been immoral, and I'm still alive — or partly. Only part of me is dead from that — my poor, dear uterus! Don't cringe," she said, turning to him. "It's true." She returned to the heavy decanter of gin and lifted the glass stopper. "A partial hysterectomy, doctor? No, a total one, I'm afraid. You're the victim of a dirty knife, my dear. An infection. Whoever performed that operation — don't tell me who did it, I don't want to know! — used a dirty knife. Ah, well. It was a dirty operation — for such a little thing, a baby." She poured gin in her glass and set the decanter down. "I was unlucky, with that, too. Oh, you men! What you put us through, I wonder if you realize?" She began pouring quinine water into her glass. "All the devices, all the little things, all the dreadful little traps and poisons supposed to halt the sperm in its flight — I had them all. They lined my shelves! But I was unlucky. One chance out of ten thousand, but that was me — that one unlucky chance. I couldn't believe it. I thought — look at Barbara! How did she manage? Then I thought, of course. Barbara has always been lucky —" She turned to him, smiling, the drink in her hand.

"What the hell are you talking about?" he asked softly.

She lifted her glass. "Forgive me. *In vino,* you know. Forget it. Tell me — why do you love her, Barney?"

He looked at her evenly and calmly, but his voice was full of quiet anger. "It's because she's not like — like the people you're talking about," he said. "She's not like you. She's got the courage and the strength and the blood. And she also happens to have another quality you lack — decency. And cleanliness, and goodness and morality!"

"Oh, Barney!" Nancy said.

"What?"

"Oh, you *are* like me! Like I *was.* You *do* believe in pure things,

286

don't you? Pure love, pure money, pure God — but don't you see? Nothing is that way!"

"It can be."

"You don't mean that, do you? Those words? That's all they are — words. What you think about Barbara. Nobody's that way! Why — why, it's wonderful to think it, but so, so naïve, Barney dear! So innocent and childlike. Do you really have that much faith in her?"

"Of course I do," he said.

"Oh, Barney, forgive me. I love her, too, but you're making me laugh! She's my dearest friend, but I don't harbor such illusions about Barbara! People just aren't that way. No one is! Oh, some people have those qualities some of the time — but *always*? Oh, my dear boy, I don't know how old you are but you talk like a schoolboy! Love Barbara if you want to — I don't disapprove of that. After all, everyone has always loved Barbara. But love her with your eyes open! She's hardly a paragon, Barney. Hardly!"

He stood up. "I'm going to bed," he said. "I'm not going to listen to this."

"Listen. You're a babe in the wood. I've known Barbara for years. We spent that year in Hawaii together. Did she ever tell you about that year in Hawaii?"

"Certainly," he said.

"About — everything? Schuyler Osata, for instance?"

"Who is he?"

"Ah," she said. "You see? Well, take Schuyler Osata — take him for just one example."

"Who is Schuyler Osata?"

"A good question! Who was he? Who knew? He was just a boy — Schuyler Osata, the bronze boy! Barbara found him — on the beach. He came from Lanikai. He was born on the little island of Manana which does not, incidentally, mean 'tomorrow.' That's all we knew about him. A boy from Lanikai, born on Manana, a beach boy. Barbara brought him home, as proudly as a little girl who's found a beautiful sea shell. He was eighteen. Schuyler Osata. *He* was Mr. Magnificent. A primitive, a true primitive. He rode sea turtles from the reefs, across the combers! I don't think he could even read or write. But, my dear, there are certain fields of endeavor where the three R's are definitely not necessary! At these fields of endeavor he excelled . . ."

She suddenly turned her back to him, holding her glass with two hands, in front of her, and walked a few steps away.

"I said to Barbara — I know he's yours. You found him. But, please, let me play with him! Barbara is generous. She was brought up to share her toys. And Mr. Osata was generous, too, in bestowing his — shall we say — favors? And so we took turns, Barbara and I, in our apartment in Honolulu, on the hill. He loved us both — he said. But I knew differently. One day, by mistake, I came in when I shouldn't have — during Barbara's turn. It's a failing of mine . . . barging in when I'm not wanted. Like with the two of you, this afternoon. I saw — oh, only enough! Only enough to know that it was different. He loved Barbara best. They all did. But he was kind to me, too, that year. I suppose I was — just a change of pace!" And then, making no sound, she began to cry.

He stared at her, saying nothing, for a moment. Then he turned away.

She lifted her head. "And when she told me about you —"

He turned again and looked at her. "She told you about me?" he said.

"Yes, oh yes. A long time ago, one time in Locustville when Carson was away. And we were talking, reminiscing, and she said — oh, just mentioned that you and she —" She began to laugh. "Oh, I've forgotten all of it. It sort of slipped out, one night in Locustville, and she mentioned that once — in her room, here at the farm I think it was — you and she, just before you and Peggy were married —" She stopped abruptly, then slowly turned to him. There was a little smile on her face. "We always shared everything, Miss Woodcock and I."

288

He stood very still, looking at her.

"But she deceived us, you and me. She deceived us both," she whispered. "So perhaps we can comfort each other."

He came toward her.

"She deceived us both," she said.

"All right," he said. "Perhaps you're right."

With one hand he reached for the drink she held — the glass that floated whimsically a lime and a rose blossom — and she said a little laughing, "No!" But he seized the drink and set it down on the table. As she playfully reached for it again he grabbed her arm and turned her roughly toward him, pinning her arm back, bending her backward. She looked up at him. He pulled her, bent her body backward across the velvet cushions. Her knees bent and, with both hands now, he forced her down. She closed her eyes as she let herself fall into the sofa's depths. He pressed himself hard against her and she whispered, "Close the door!" And then, "No — never mind. They're all asleep . . ." He covered her mouth with his.

"There," she breathed. "There! Now you're acting like a big boy!"

19

THE TREES ABOVE HER ROSE IN ARCHES, THEIR BRANCHES IN ascending tiers. And though there was no moon now the pattern of sky that appeared between the leaves held a pale light and a few fuzzy shapes of stars. The road ran around the lake's edge, and in spaces where the screen of shrubbery fell and the trees opened, she could see the water, flat and leaden-looking and unmoving, with clumps of cattails rising from the shallow places along the shore. The sound of her footsteps in the gravel stilled the voices of peepers and croakers as she passed.

She had been walking with a rhythm; some sort of little quick march had been playing in her head. It was the rhythm, actually, of the little ball, bouncing up and down on the rubber string, and it made her walk faster than usual, with a kind of impatience, her hands deep in the pockets of her light trench coat. She had tied a bright yellow silk scarf around her throat, for confidence — confidence, because it was printed with bright French sayings: *Allo? Allons-y, Comment ça va? Ooh, la-la!* And she had put on a gay print cotton dress that tied at the middle with a belt composed of ceramic squares. For comfort, and confidence, too, she wore flat-heeled shoes. She walked as she might walk to a summer cocktail party, or barbecue, the kind that were given on back-yard terraces in Locustville, the kind where the host wore a chef's hat and apron that said, "Look Who's Cookin'," and though the trees and the darkness blotted her out, made her feel ectoplasmic, she knew she looked this way. Actually, a curious thing had happened to her mood in more than two hours since Barney had spoken to her in the garden. She no longer truly felt confident or sure or buoyant, convinced of anything. She had become less and less sure of herself, of her relationship to him, of what, if anything, she was going to do about it. She walked through the trees, exploring her feeling. They would have a little talk, perhaps, ("Now Barney, we must be sensible . . ."). Or perhaps she would let him kiss her a few times and see how she felt about it then. Or perhaps she would not let him kiss her, or even touch her hand. But really she was no longer certain of anything, of the kind of person he was, or — a more disquieting thought — of the kind of person she was. So in place of the confidence and knowledge she had had earlier was now nothing but the excitement of not knowing. It was this peculiar excitement, nothing more, that made her walk quickly along the dark road toward the guesthouse, the excitement of going to a party where you knew none of the people.

Suddenly she came out of the trees. Ahead of her was the wide stretch of grass and the dark shape of the house itself, with the screened porch running around it, just a few hundred feet away, and everything stopped. The march music stopped and the bouncing ball stopped and the night suddenly seemed enormous and she stepped back into the shadows, terrified. Something hot and unbearable welled and throbbed in her throat. She leaned back against the trunk of a tree, feeling dizzy. She thought: *Why have I come here?*

Why had she thought of the guesthouse? What curious chain of thought, what sequence of long-ago things had worked their way together so quickly in her mind to suggest, all at once, the guesthouse? Then she remembered the broken dollhouse and she thought how queerly the things that happen to children, one after another, reassemble themselves long afterward.

It was a huge, elaborate dollhouse, elaborately furnished. It had a front door that opened on real hinges and the windows had real glass in them. The green painted shutters could close, and inside — when the back of the house was swung open to reveal the little rooms — the windows had real curtains made of gauze and real roll-up shades. The bathroom even had a tub made of china for dolly's bath. She remembered once hearing Sylvia Sturgis ask her mother in a whisper, admiringly, "How much did it cost, Edith?" It was not a question that most people asked about things the Woodcocks owned, but Sylvia Sturgis was a straightforward woman and a good friend. She asked, "How much did it cost?" not to imply that the cost was the most interesting thing about the dollhouse, but in a businesslike way, as she might ask a sales clerk how much a thing cost. Edith, who understood the frank money-question, answered her frankly. "Ninety-eight dollars," she said. "Preston and I are trying to interest Peggy in more feminine toys. She's turning into such a tomboy!"

It had been a funny day, the day Peggy's dollhouse arrived, a summer day like today, warm and hazy and restless. Barbara was fourteen and Woody had come to the farm that day for his swimming lesson. After the lesson, she and Woody went into the house and she showed him the dollhouse. For a long time, in Peggy's room, they admired it, opening the little doors, rolling the little window shades up and down, arranging and rearranging the furniture. Then Peggy came in, ordered them imperiously to leave the doll house alone, and so they walked out onto the lawn, barefoot and bored, and presently they conceived their scheme of kidnaping Danny. In whispers, they plotted it.

Danny was beside the pool, stretched out on the walk on his stomach, asleep in the sun. He was a vain boy, and when his lesson-giving hour was over, he spent his time working on his tan, lying on first one side, then the other, rubbing himself periodically with a dark and unguinous liquid that he had prepared from Skol, coconut oil, and iodine. "It's what all the life guards use," he said airily. Already this ritual had had its desired cosmetic effect; it had turned his skin a dark, chestnut shade, the color of brandy, and with his dark hair and eyes, had given him a singularly Latin look. Barbara and Woody looked at him, rigidly asleep with tricklets of perspiration gleaming along the bronzed curve of his back. Then they went into the laundry yard, found two lengths of clothesline to tie him with and a linen handkerchief to use as a gag. Their plan was, as he slept, to bind his hands and feet securely — Barbara working at one end and Woody at the other — and then, when he was immobilized, to tie the gag around his mouth to silence the screams that would no doubt emerge. Beyond this stage, they had not planned. They didn't know, precisely, what they would do with him when they had him. But they would probably take him away somewhere and enslave him. He had angered them when, a week before, they had asked him to run away to New Haven with them, and he had said witheringly, "What? I wouldn't be caught dead in New Haven with you two creeps!" He had said the wrong thing. The time for sympathy was past. The time had come, as Woody said, for action. He would be sorry. They would make him grovel at their feet. They would make him call them "sir" and "madam," or perhaps, "master" and "mistress," or "your lordship" and "your ladyship." But, in any case, some day when he had suffered enough they would release him, and let him be their friend.

But their plan misfired. Woody was to tie his feet and Barbara his outstretched hands. Woody got his rope encircled about Danny's crossed ankles and got it knotted, but Barbara's job was harder, pulling the hands together from the distance at which they lay, three or four feet apart. In attempting this, she woke him. He sat up quickly. "Jesus Christ!" he yelled. "What do you think you're doing?" He jumped to his feet, hopped around crazily in his bonds, yelling and shouting, and toppled into the pool. He came up sputtering and screaming, "Mrs. *Wood*-cock! Mrs. Wood-cock! Help! Help!"

Barbara and Woody were convulsed with laughter. But when Edith Woodcock came running from the house to see what was the matter, and found Danny that way struggling and shouting in the water, they stopped. She helped Danny out of the pool and helped him undo the wet line that tied his ankles. "Jesus Christ, Mrs. Woodcock!" Danny said. "Look what those brats did! They tried to drown me, they pushed me in the pool!"

Edith was very angry. "Woody," she said, "go to the front steps of this house and sit there until your mother comes. I'm going to telephone her right now and tell her what you did, and have her come and get you. Barbara, go to your room and don't come down until I tell you to."

Angry and humiliated, she went upstairs. Peggy's room, as she passed, was empty, and in it stood the abandoned dollhouse. From the door she gazed at it. Then she stepped inside the room, went to the dollhouse, and leaned on it. It was simple and arbitrary at first, then systematic, as she smashed it. With the end of a wooden clothes hanger, she punched out each glass window. She shredded the curtains and crushed the furniture, shattered the little porcelain bathtub and wrenched the shutters from their hinges. Then she left the room.

293

She went out into the hall to the top of the stairs. She looked down at the hall below. It was empty. After a while, she heard Mary-Adams deWinter's car drive up for Woody, and, for another while, she heard fragments of talk as her mother told Woody's mother the story of Danny and the pool. Then Mary-Adams drove away. Her mother came into the house and disappeared in one of the rooms downstairs. Barbara felt disappointed then. She had wanted the tumultuous climactic scene now. Instead, her mother was going to make her wait for it. She went down the stairs slowly and out the front door.

A little breeze was blowing. The haze had lifted now and the sky was blue and clear and the thick maple leaves on the trees on the lawn were astonishingly green. The grass beneath her still bare feet was rough and dry and warm, and she walked slowly and thoughtfully across the graveled driveway, lifting her feet gingerly from the hot pebbles, across the lawn beyond the drive and under the trees. She walked to the stable and found Charlie Muir, the groom, sitting on the bench inside the door, in the sunlight, cleaning his fingernails with the blade of a jackknife. She smiled at him. "Mother says I may go for a ride," she said.

He folded the knife and stood up. "All right," he said and smiled at her. "Shall I go along with you?"

She considered this. "All right," she shrugged.

He saddled both horses.

They rode out. No one saw them go except Emily, who waved from the kitchen window. They took the back path, behind the garden, through the cluster of hemlocks, toward the road that led around the lake.

They said nothing. She had heard, a few weeks before, about the thing that Peggy and Charlie Muir sometimes did when they rode together; she thought of this now and began to wonder idly if Charlie would want to do the same thing with her, or if he was thinking about it. And when they reached the deep shade of the wood road and Charlie reined in his horse ahead of her and stopped, she came up beside him and stopped, too, curious to see what he would do next. He pulled a cigarette from his shirt pocket and lifted it. He said, "Want a drag, Bobbie?" He held the cigarette toward her, its end wet from his lips.

She shook her head. "No thanks."

"Your little sister likes a drag now and then," he said.

"It's very naughty of her to smoke," Barbara said primly. "She's just a child and smoking will stunt her growth. Daddy'd be very mad if he knew you let her."

"Aw," he said, "you wouldn't tell him, would you, Bobbie?"

"No," she said. "But still you shouldn't do it."

He chuckled softly and rested one hand on her horse's rump. She was riding the chestnut gelding who, because he had been a Christmas present, had been named Blitzen. Blitzen raised his head and shook his dark mane. For a while Charlie rested this way, smoking, and then she realized he was looking at her and she looked at him. His was a sly, somewhat questioning look and she looked quickly away, nonchalantly, through the trees. Then Charlie said, "Peggy and I've got a little game we play."

"Yes," Barbara said. "So I've heard."

He straightened up and looked hard at her. "She told you?"

"Yes."

"She tell anybody else?" he asked sharply. "Did *you* tell anybody, Bobbie?"

"No," Barbara said. "Why should I?"

His shoulders eased. "Just wondered," he said. And then, "Want to try it? What do you say, Bobbie?"

"No," she said.

"Why not, Bobbie?"

"Because I'm not a child," she said. "And it's a very childish game."

"Then how about a kiss, Bobbie?"

"No."

"What harm's a kiss?" he asked.

She considered this. "All right," she said.

He reached out then and, awkwardly, circled her waist with his arm and instead of offering her lips to him, she turned her face away and let him kiss her cheek, and for a moment or two, swaying slightly on the horses' impatient and quivering backs, they balanced, leaning together, and when she felt his other hand reaching for hers she pressed her heels gently into Blitzen's soft sides and pulled away from him, trotted a few yards ahead.

She remembered feeling an overpowering urge to laugh out loud, but they continued on, Barbara in the lead, under the sheltering trees, in silence. It was true, she decided, that only a child, only someone like Peggy, would find anything interesting, or even darkly fun, in what she did with Charlie. Only a child — or a man, like Charlie, because men, after all, were children too, weren't they?

So she had concluded at fourteen or so.

She felt superior to Charlie — superior in knowledge and understanding, and superior in position because he was, she reminded herself, a servant. Still, she knew that riding with him like this might be dangerous and it was reassuring to feel Blitzen's smooth, strong back beneath her. By simply digging her heels into Blitzen's sides she could break away from any danger, and escape.

Men, it seemed to her at fourteen, had so many curious, contradictory problems, so many crazy wishes and wants! They derived their intensest pleasures from the silliest things! And yet she did not regret having let him kiss her just now, that way, on the cheek. It had helped her discover some of the interesting facts she was discovering. And discovering facts was a part of growing up.

They came to the guesthouse.

"Let's go in there," Charlie said.

"No," she said.

"Aw, Bobbie, why not?"

"Because I don't want to."

"Why not?"

"Because."

"What do you mean, because?"

"Just because."

"Aw, come on, Bobbie. I've got the key."

She hesitated. "All right," she said. It was as though the simple fact that he had the key was enough to change her mind. She got off her horse and tied the reins about the trunk of a sapling. She waited, then, until Charlie had tied up his horse and unlocked the door. They went inside and Charlie closed the door behind her. The room was dark, its curtains drawn, and smelled damp and musty and unused. She stood in the center of the room and Charlie stood facing her, a few feet away. She studied him. Then, in his face, she saw again the crafty, questioning look.

"Well, here we are," he said. He stepped closer. "You won't tell your Ma," he said.

"No."

"Promise? Swear to God?"

"Swear to God."

"Swear to God that if you tell your Ma or your father or anyone the devil will come and throw a burning sword right through your stomach? Swear to God that if you ever tell a single, living creature . . ."

"What are you going to do?" She was suddenly wary, hearing the sound of her voice asking this uncertain question. She looked at him and his eyes were bright slits. A phrase, as they stood there facing each other, came to her head. It was a phrase — a term, an expression — that she and Woody had come across in a newspaper and had speculated about, wondering what it meant. The phrase was 'statutory rape,' and they knew, from the dictionary, what rape was, but what 'statutory' meant applied to it they couldn't imagine, unless, as Woody had decided, it meant rape that was committed from a standing position. It flew into her head now, and she asked him, "Are you going to do statutory rape to me?"

He drew back, his shoulders hunched, his eyes suddenly wide

and frightened. "What're you talking about?" he asked her. "What're you talking about? Listen to me — I never — look here, I never said —"

She turned and ran. She ran out the door, down the steps, untied her horse and jumped on the horse's back. She dug her bare heels into Blitzen's soft sides and rode off under the trees. She had discovered that all men were cowards, too.

She did not tell her mother. But it was not because she had sworn to God or feared the devil's sword. She had gone to the guesthouse for revenge against her mother; she felt that she had had her revenge now, for her mother punishing her, treating her like a child.

Her mother had punished her like a child because she had acted like a child. She had wanted to punish Peggy, too, for having the dollhouse. So, like a child, she had destroyed it. Like a child — but like a woman, too — she had gone to the guesthouse with Charlie; that way, she had punished them both. And of course later, when the broken dollhouse was discovered, she herself was punished again. What that punishment had been she couldn't remember now, and it hadn't mattered. Punishment, as it often seemed to her, was circular. It hadn't mattered because it simply completed the circle.

But was that why tonight — fourteen, fifteen, sixteen years later — she had suddenly thought of the guesthouse? She wondered whom she was punishing now. It had been all right then, long ago, with Charlie because she had been only a child; it had been only a part of growing up. But now she was thirty years old.

She stepped out of the dark shadows and walked slowly across the intervening space of grass, up the steps and unlocked the door. Immediately the remembered damp, closed, unused smell assailed her as she stood inside the doorway and groped for the light switch. Her hand found the switch and it was only then, all at once, that she remembered: she and Carson had come there, too!

298

How queer to have forgotten! How queer to have forgotten that she and Carson had come there too, so many times!

At one o'clock, Peggy awoke. She turned on her side and saw the empty bed next to hers. She had fallen asleep in her clothes, in the white shorts and shirt, and after looking at the dark and empty room for several minutes, hearing no sounds in the house, she decided to get up and look for him.

She tiptoed down the hall and down the darkened stairs. She turned on no lights. Downstairs, the house was dark also. She went out the door and into the garden.

She found him standing beside the pool, looking at the water, a solitary figure against the shadows of the shrubbery.

"Barney?" she called softly.

He turned quickly.

"It's me — Peggy," she said. She came toward him. "What are you doing here?" she asked him.

"I went for a walk," he said.

"What are you going for a walk for? It's after one o'clock . . ."

"I couldn't seem to sleep."

"Why don't you try? Why don't you come to bed?"

"I wasn't tired. I thought a walk would help."

"You're always going for walks!" she said. "You went for a walk last night, too."

"Yes," he said.

"Is something bothering you, Barn-Barn?"

"No," he said.

"You're always running off — trying to be alone."

"I'm sorry."

They were both silent. Then she said, "Come for a walk with me."

"No thanks," he said.

"Oh, please. Come on."

"No . . ."

"Why not? Please."

"No, I'm tired, now. Let's go in, Peggy."

"Please!"

He looked for a moment across the still water. Then he shrugged. "All right. Whatever you say . . ."

She linked her arm in his. "Where do you usually walk?" she asked.

"Just — anywhere," he said.

"Let's walk down to the lake."

He hesitated. "Well," he said, "no — let's walk out to the drive and back."

"The lake is so pretty at night," she said.

"No — it's too far to go."

"Oh, come on!" she said roguishly. "What's the matter? Scared of the dark?"

They started up the steps.

"I'm sorry about tonight," she said. "Really, I shouldn't have lost control like that."

"It's all right," he said.

"It isn't all right. I hate to lose control. But I've been thinking — I was wrong to insist that we stay here, at the farm. It was my mistake. I thought at the time it would be easier — to work at close quarters. But it was wrong. Do you know what I'd like us to do? Let's move out of here, Barney. Let's get a little apartment in Burketown, or — what do you think, Barney?"

"I don't care."

"Oh, I shouldn't have lost control tonight! If we hadn't been living here with them, it wouldn't have happened. I wouldn't have made a scene like that. I hate to lose control, you know that."

"Yes," he said.

"I still can't believe it, what Daddy said. If it's true — if it's really true — then it's one hell of an awful blow. All our plans. If it's true — well, I really don't know what we *will* do . . ."

"Yes," he said.

300

"Can you imagine it? What sort of — idiocy — could have made him agree to it! I really think we should have him declared an incompetent! I can't see any other course. He *is* an incompetent! *Non compos*, half the time, with drink! Everybody knows it. He should be put away."

"Yes."

"Do you agree?"

"I suppose so," he said.

When they reached the terrace, he stopped. "This is far enough," he said. "Let's go back."

"Let's go to the lake."

"I want to get to bed, Peggy."

"Oh, come on! Don't be such a sissy. It's just down the hill. It'll be pretty —"

"No," he said. "I don't want to go any farther."

"Please!"

"No."

She looked up at him. "Why not?" she asked. "Why don't you want to go down there?"

"I just don't want to."

"Why?"

"Because I'm tired, I want —"

"Barn-Barn," she said, "what's the matter? You're acting very funny. What's going on?"

"Nothing."

"Then come on. I want to talk. I've got things I want to get off my chest."

"Let's go upstairs and talk."

"I want to walk down to the lake," she said. "There's some reason you don't. What is it?"

He stood stiffly beside her, saying nothing. Then quietly he said, "All right. Let's go."

They walked across the terrace, her hand in his arm, toward the path that led past the clump of hemlocks to the curve of the hill.

They went down the path. She kept hold of his arm, walking toward the sloping lawn, toward the water, saying, "What do you think? Think we could ever *get* him committed? You're the business school graduate. Would that work?"

Then suddenly she gripped his arm and stopped him. "Barney!" she said.

"What?"

"Look!" she pointed. "There's a light in the guesthouse — see it?"

He didn't answer her.

"Who in the world?" she whispered. "Barney!"

He stood absolutely motionless beside her.

"See it? There's somebody there! Shall we call the police, or —" She let go of his arm. "Or — no. No," she breathed, and she turned to him slowly. "Is it Barbara? *Is it?* Oh, of course! *Of course!*" She drew back from him.

"What do you mean?"

"Of course it is! Why didn't I guess? Of course — the guesthouse — that's where she always takes them!"

"Who?"

"Her men. And last night, too — of course, that's where you're going. You met her there last night, too, didn't you? Oh, of course!"

He started quickly down the hill.

"Stop!" she commanded, and when he didn't stop she ran after him and seized his arm again. "It *is* Barbara, isn't it? It's been going on all along . . ."

He walked rapidly and she stayed beside him, holding his arm, trying to stop him. "It *is* Barbara! It is! Tell me!"

"Yes," he said.

"'Oh, God!" she said. "I should have known! That damn bitch! That bitch!"

He kept walking, faster now, down the hill.

"Stop," she said. "Listen to me. Listen to me!" But he continued, pulling her beside him. "Listen," she said savagely, "don't be a fool! Don't go to her! Don't be taken in by her! Listen. I know her. She's a rotten little bitch, a whore, she only wants you for one thing — listen to me —"

At the edge of the lake, he stopped. He looked across, then turned and stepped down to the sandy strip of beach. "Listen to me," she repeated. "Let me tell you what you're doing, listen —"

He jerked his arm away from her, but she ran after him. "Where are you going?" she demanded. "Wait. Listen to me —"

He walked to where the old canoe lay, the *Bobby-Boo*, its bottomside up, on the bank. He lifted it and turned it, and the paddle inside it rattled against its thwarts. He began pulling it toward the water.

"Are you going in that?" she asked. "Listen to me, Barney — please — for a minute. Be sensible. Look, maybe you and I are through — I'm willing to admit that. But don't do it for her! Don't be such a fool, Barney. Don't be more of a fool than you've already been!"

"I'm sorry, Peggy," he said.

She stopped and stood still, watching him. He pulled the canoe across the sand. Then she said quietly, "That canoe is full of leaks. You'll never make it."

"I'll make it," he said.

"You're an idiot. It will sink twenty feet out."

"It will take me farther than that."

"Listen to me, Barney," she said. "What are you trying to accomplish?"

"I don't know," he said simply.

"Don't be silly," she said, her flat voice seeming to grow flatter. "What good will it do you? Going to her. Do you love her? What good will that do you? Do you think she'll marry you? She won't. She's no fool. She has Carson and her children. They'll always come first with her, no matter what she tells you. She's really just not a very nice girl. It's that simple. And if you go to her now you'll lose both of us. And you'll be throwing over a damn good deal, my dear. Because you can marry one Woodcock girl. But not two."

In the darkness, he seemed to watch her thoughtfully, though his face was turned away. When he finally spoke, his voice was almost inaudible. "It's always the Woodcock girls, isn't it? It never changes. Well, Peggy, you may be right."

"Then come back to the house."

"I'm sorry," he said. He turned, seized the canoe and slid it into the water.

Peggy came two steps closer. She seemed to reach out for him, then lowered her hands. "Barney!" she cried.

"What?"

"I thought you were a leader!"

"No," he said, "I'm not a leader. I'm one of the led. I always have been. I let you lead me to this place, don't forget, to the farm. And I've let her lead me. I'm always being led." He stepped nimbly into the canoe, took the paddle and pushed off.

"Stop!" she commanded again. But he moved swiftly away, the shadows closing around him, and disappeared into the darkness. She could hear only the receding sound of his paddling.

She stood on the shore for several minutes, staring across the dark water. Far away, through the trees, was the little waiting light. Then she turned and started slowly up the path toward the house.

She was about halfway up the hill when she stopped and for several minutes more she stood very still, statuelike. She listened. She heard only night sounds, crickets and peepers from the marshy shore, and the faint, high sound of an airplane passing overhead, bound for New York.

She knew that the canoe would not make it across the lake. It could not. She had kicked her toe against it, many summers in the past; the bottom was like paper, full of wormholes and rot. From one shore to the other was more than five hundred yards, more than a quarter of a mile. The canoe would never make it, he could not swim, and the lake was deep. Very well.

She stood there. Her mind was filled with several images, which seemed to come all at once. In one, she heard herself screaming, running back to the house. In another, she saw water bubbling quickly through the bottom of the canoe, the lake rising swiftly about its sides, as he paddled. Then she saw Barney's body, white, long, like a piece of sunken sculpture, at the bottom of the lake, in the brown weeds under the clean water. She saw him lifted, ice-white, dead, his face bloated and horrible and disgusting. She turned now and faced the lake. She stood and watched, and waited, and listened. Very well.

The little light still glimmered through the trees — far, very far, away. She smiled at it.

She would hear his cries. As the canoe foundered, as he thrashed helplessly in the water, he would cry out for her and she would hear him. She waited for a long time, waiting for the cries, hearing only the crickets and the peepers, waiting and thinking: I'll decide then.

She waited, but there were no cries. Eventually — it was a little while later — she was struck with the thundering knowledge that he was dead, that he had sunk into the lake without uttering a single sound. And it was this, perhaps — the realization of this final, intolerable cheat, this ultimate robbery of her life — that he had gone like a thief, depriving her of even the sound of his cries — that started her screaming. She screamed until her throat hurt. Running, stumbling, screaming and sobbing wildly, she started up the hill again, crying, "Help! Help!"

In the guesthouse, things were as she remembered them. But the ruffled chintz curtains were limp with age and a thin, even film of dust lay over everything. She wandered through the rooms. In the bedroom, on the table beside the bed, she picked up a copy of the *Reader's Digest*. She turned its pages; they were brown and brittle, and she noticed that it was an issue dated February, 1946. She put it down. She opened the closet door. The closet was empty but, on the inside wall, someone — a child, evidently — had carefully written "Hello," in red crayon. She studied this strangely silent greeting for a moment, then closed the door. She turned off the bedroom light.

In the little, musty kitchen, neat rows of cups hung from hooks above stacks of plates and saucers behind the glass cupboard doors. She opened the refrigerator. In it were ice trays, thick with frost, a small can of tomato juice and a bottle, three quarters empty, of pre-pared Martini cocktails, left from some house party long ago. She removed the bottle, forced loose one of the ice trays and, in a little round glass pitcher from the cupboard, she fixed drinks.

She filled two glasses and carried them into the living room, where she placed them on the rustic cocktail table. She started to sip one, thinking it might give her courage, but then she put it down, knowing that it would do no good. Nothing would do any good. She sat back quickly and closed her eyes, her temples throb-bing. She sat for a long time in the dirty, stale-smelling little room.

She opened her eyes and then she began to laugh, a little hys-terically, at the absurd sight of two Martinis floating palely in the stemmed glasses on the dusty table, looking like two faded and foolish little flowers, and at the absurd sight of herself looking at them. She laughed until tears streamed down her face and then, wondering if she was truly going out of her mind, she stopped. She knew then that it was useless, that she would not and could not go through with it. And she felt suddenly much better, knowing this. She would go — run, just as she had run from Charlie Muir.

She stood up and started to go.

Then she heard distant sounds. She went quickly to the door and stepped outside. The sounds were cries and, far off, across the lake, where the house stood in shade behind the trees, she saw lights appear — first one light, then another, and presently the whole house was ablaze with lights, and there were more sounds, more cries. She grabbed her coat and ran down the steps, across the grass, down the road through the trees.

Everyone had gathered at the lake's edge — her mother, her father, Emily and John, Peggy and Nancy. She ran toward them.

"What is it? What's happened?"

Everyone was shouting.

"The canoe, in the canoe —"

"The *Bobby-Boo* —"

"Call the police —"

"Oh, no — not the police!"

"It's got to be the police!"

"What is it?" she cried. "What happened?"

"In the canoe — drowned —"

"Who? Who?"

Her mother suddenly seemed to notice her and turned to her. "What are you doing here?" she said. "Where have you been? What are you doing here? Get out of here — up to the house — into your room! Get out of here!"

20

CARSON'S APPOINTMENT WITH BILL BREWER WAS OVER AT eleven o'clock that Monday morning, and he left Brewer's office in Victoria Street with two hours to kill before his lunch date at one. The day was sunny and cool and he decided to walk. He felt much better than he had yesterday. It was mostly, he supposed, because it was good to be working again. The meeting with Brewer had gone well; he was pleased with himself. Whenever his spirits sagged, it was good to be reminded that he was, after all, a damned good salesman. He was a good salesman because he never had to sell very hard. People liked him right away and listened to what he had to say. He got along, he thought, particularly well with the English. They liked him because he was courteous and soft-spoken, with none of the braggishness and swagger that they resented in Americans. He had learned, with the English, never to boast of his product; in fact, he was carefully modest about it and they appreciated this. The company knew that he was good, too, and this was why they wanted him in the International Sales Division. He was a good ambassador.

He walked north, toward the park. As he approached Buckingham Palace he walked more slowly, as a sightseer now, looking up at the palace and down along the Mall, at the vivid red beds of geraniums that matched, almost exactly, the red coats of the guards' uniforms. In front of the gate, a little knot of tourists stood — all of them girls, college girls, Smith girls he would guess — combed and scrubbed and neat, sweatered and skirted with white raincoats and cameras slung across their shoulders. He imagined them all, on their first trip to Europe, traveling in a group of twenty or thirty with one or two chaperons, filing into the tour bus every morning with their cameras, stopping at Places of Interest, filing out of the bus, winding their cameras, taking pictures. Tomorrow they would do Stratford-on-Avon, where they would visit the Shakespeare Museum and Ann Hathaway's cottage. And the next day they would file into the bus again for a trip through typical English countryside to the Lake District with, perhaps, a side trip to an Abbey or Stately Home on the way. Carrying their cameras they would file, respectfully, through Wordsworth's Cottage, then into the bus again. He watched them from a short distance away. Their round, polished faces were intent upon what the guide was saying.

"The Palace," the guide said, "was built in 1793 as a mansion for the Duke of Buckingham. It was built on the site of a mulberry garden planted by King James the First for the support of the silk industry. The Palace still retains some of the atmosphere of a country house. The Palace has forty acres of grounds, including a five-acre lake, and enjoys a beautiful setting amid the trees and lawns of St. James's Park. The present façade, designed by Sir Anston Webb, was added in 1912 and completed in less than three months. The Palace is the London residence of the Queen, Prince Philip, Prince Charles and Princess Anne. When the Queen is in residence her flag flies from the top of that pole up there. There is no flag flying today because the Queen and Prince Philip are at the royal estate at Balmoral, in Scotland. . . ."

Carson skirted the little group and walked on toward Green Park. He decided to walk through the park. Then he would stop at the Dorchester and check on his mail.

❦   ❦   ❦

"But you sound so strange, Mrs. Greer!" Flora's voice said. "Not like yourself at all. Are you sure there's nothing wrong?"

"No," Barbara said. "Nothing's wrong."

"You're coming down with a cold then, a summer cold. My sister has one. She's all stuffed up with it, a summer cold. That's what you've got."

"No," Barbara said. "Actually, Flora, something has happened. There's been an accident here."

"An accident?"

"Yes. I ought to tell you this before you read it in the papers. My sister's husband was drowned last night."

There was a long pause. Then Flora's voice cried, "Oh my God, how awful!"

"So you see that's why I must stay a few days longer. The funeral is to be on Wednesday."

"Oh my God, how awful!" Flora said. "How awful!"

"Yes. You have enough food in the house, don't you? Enough until Wednesday? I'll be home Wednesday night. If you need anything you can phone —"

"How awful!"

"Lester's. Have them deliver —"

"He was a *young* man, wasn't he? A young man?"

"Yes."

"Oh," Flora sobbed. "My heart goes out —"

"It's all right, Flora — don't —"

"My heart goes out —"

"The boys are fine, aren't they?"

"Oh, they're fine, Mrs. Greer. Want me to put them on the line?"

"No," she said quickly, "don't bother, please —"

"Here's Dobie. Wants to talk to you."

"No, I —"

"Hello? Hello?"

"Yes —"

"Hello? Mommy?"

"Yes, Dobie. How are you, darling?"

"Are you coming home, Mommy?"

"Soon, Dobie. Now good-by. Now be a good boy. Good-by —"

Dobie said a few more words that she couldn't hear.

"Yes, yes."

She heard Flora's voice again saying, "Oh, God bless you, Mrs. Greer! And God bless your poor sister. Oh, what you must be going through, Mrs. Greer. Oh, such an awful, awful thing!"

"Yes. I'll see you Wednesday, Flora."

"Yes."

"Good-by. Good-by."

She put down the telephone and sat for a while in the morning sunshine.

❧ ❧ ❧

"My name is Elizabeth Gage," the woman said. "Liz Gage, from the Burketown *Evening Eagle*." She stepped into the garden where Nancy Rafferty was sitting having a drink — the first of the day. Miss Gage smiled at Nancy and held out her hand. She was a small, slim woman — thirty-five, perhaps, or a little older — and she wore a beige linen suit and beige shoes. She was hatless and wore her black hair pulled severely back from her face and tied at the nape of her neck with a black velvet ribbon. Her face was pale, smooth-skinned and oval, but not really pretty. Her deep black and closely spaced eyes were alert and questioning as she looked at Nancy. "You're not —? Oh, no. You're not Mrs. Callahan, are you. I can tell from the description you're not."

Nancy had not risen. "I'm just a friend of the family," she said. "Is there anything I can do for you?"

"I'm sorry to intrude," Miss Gage said. "My paper sent me, and I'm rather afraid I sneaked in."

"Really?" Nancy asked. "How did you manage that?"

"I saw the police car at the foot of the road — keeping people away. I knew the cop wouldn't let me in, press or no, so I parked my car about half a mile beyond and walked in cross-country. Look at my stockings." She put one leg forward to show Nancy.

Nancy looked at her coldly. "Now, I suggest that you leave the same way you came," Nancy said.

The woman gave her a brief, amused look. "Oh, are you going to be that way? That's too bad. I'm not asking your pardon. I know I'm guilty. But a job is a job. My paper sent me here to get a story, so I came." She smiled. "Someday — who knows? — you, too, may have a job."

"The newspapers have the obituary."

"I know. I'm here for a human interest story."

"There isn't any human interest here."

The woman smiled, very slightly, again. "Maybe not," she said. "But I had to try, didn't I?"

"Excuse me. I'm going to call Mr. Woodcock."

"Good. I'd like to meet him."

"I'm going to call him and have him order you away."

"Good. That'll give me a story!"

Nancy studied her. "What is it that you want?"

311

"First, I'd like to sit down. May I? I feel as if I've hiked up Mount Everest."

Nancy said nothing.

"Thanks." The woman seated herself on one of the garden chairs, crossed her knees and leaned forward. "Let's be friends," she said pleasantly. "Truly, I mean no harm. I'll ask a few brief questions, then I'll go."

"As I said, the newspapers have a full obituary," Nancy said.

"But there's always more, isn't there, to a person's life than what one can read in an obituary? Or don't you agree? I mean, suppose you read an obituary of someone you didn't know. How well would you *know* that person when you'd finished reading it? I don't mean to be mawkish, but there is, isn't there, always more?"

"Yes, I suppose there is."

"That's all I want," the woman said. "Just a few of those *more* things. The color of his hair, for instance. His eyes. A few words to describe this house, here, for instance, where he lived, and the grounds. And the Woodcock family."

"Why do you need to know so much about poor Barney?"

Liz Gage shrugged. "Frankly, it isn't so much him as whom he was married to. The Woodcocks are pretty important in this town. This is a Woodcock story."

"The Woodcocks deserve a little privacy."

"What's in that pitcher?"

"Lemonade."

"Might I have a glass, too? My throat is like leather."

"Actually," Nancy said, "it's Tom Collinses. I — well, I added a little gin to some lemonade."

"Is that what you're drinking?" Liz Gage smiled. "Well, you can't get outside of a whole pitcherful, can you? Give me just *half* a glass, then, would you?"

Nancy hesitated, then took a fresh glass from the tray and filled it, from the pitcher, exactly half full. She handed it to the other woman without a word.

Liz Gage sipped it. "I'll say it's got gin in it!" she said cheerfully. "Thanks. How well did you know Mr. Callahan?"

"Who? Oh, Barney. Hardly at all."

"Yet you call him by his first name."

"Only because I've always heard him referred to as Barney."

"I see," said Liz Gage. "How is his wife taking it?"

"Peggy is being very brave," Nancy said.

"Well, that's the only way to be, isn't it? Poor girl. They'd been married just a short time."

"Two years."

"Well, that's a short time. By the way, I don't believe you've told me your name."

"My name is —" Nancy hesitated. "Are you taking all this down?"

Liz Gage smiled. "I never take notes," she said. "A good reporter doesn't need to take notes."

"I don't want my name mentioned. I had nothing to do with any of this. I'm only a friend of Peggy's sister. I just happened to be here." Nancy reached for her glass and sipped from it.

"You're a bundle of nerves," Liz Gage said. "Your hand is trembling. Here, let me fill your glass for you."

"No thank you."

"They're really delicious Tom Collinses."

"I had a frightful headache. I had to have something. It's been awful, worse than you can possibly know." Nancy touched her forehead with her fingertips.

"Then have another. It'll buoy you up, Miss — did you tell me your name?"

"Rafferty. Nancy Rafferty."

Liz Gage rose and filled Nancy's glass.

"Thank you," Nancy said, and then, "I'm sorry to be like this."

"I understand perfectly. Were you here when he — ?"

"When they found him? Yes. I mean no. I was here, yes, but I hid. I couldn't bear, you know — to have to see."

313

"Of course. But it's fortunate, you know, that the body was found quickly. In some drowning cases, it's taken days . . ."

"Please. Don't talk about it."

Liz Gage was silent for a moment. Then she said, "I'm new in Burketown. I've been here only two months. Frankly, before I came here, I'd never heard of the Woodcock family. I mean, truthfully, they aren't a widely known family outside their own little sphere. Of course the minute I came here I was aware of the name — the paper company, the library, all the rest."

"They're a wonderful family," Nancy said.

"They must be. This morning I spent some time going through our clipping file, looking for material on them. Believe it or not, there was very little — only one or two rather small items. Considering all the Woodcocks have done for this town, the money they've donated and the things they've supported, that's surprising, isn't it?"

"They don't believe in making a splash."

"That's just what I was leading up to. In a way, it's typical of New England, isn't it? They do good deeds in secret, but the Lord rewards them openly, or however it goes."

"Yes."

"I ran across one item, though. Oh, it was a number of years ago, and there was a little stir involving the Woodcocks. Someone was fired from the mill — a Joseph B. Mount — and he accused Mrs. Callahan's grandfather of political discrimination or some such thing? Had you ever heard that story, Miss Rafferty?"

"Never. I'm sorry, but I don't know any of the family history."

"I wonder if some of the other things I've heard are true. I heard, for instance, that in the old days the Woodcocks really ruled this town like feudal lords. That they owned and operated all the schools and only taught trades connected with paper manufacturing. That they owned horrible little row houses where the workmen lived and rented the houses to the workmen on the condition that no alcohol be drunk on the premises? Had you heard that story? And that the Woodcocks paid the workmen to spy on each other and report any drinking that occurred? I've also heard that the Woodcocks used to run a company store where they kept all the workmen in their debt. This was all before the turn of the century of course."

"I don't know anything about that sort of thing," Nancy said.

"It was told to me as gospel," Liz Gage said. "But people do exaggerate."

"Yes."

"However, considering the prominence of the family in this town, there must have been a lot of opposition to the daughter Peggy's marriage."

"What do you mean?"

"Well, he's not, as we say, to the manner born." She paused. "I mean, *was* not."

"I don't know anything about his background."

"It doesn't matter. I've heard, actually, that there was opposition — considerable of it, but rather tastefully expressed — in the true New England manner. He was a Catholic, for instance, which must have been a bitter pill for the Woodcocks to swallow."

"Look," Nancy said, "I —"

"What was your impression of him? What was his single most memorable feature? Did he have a magnetic personality, as I've heard? For instance, from one of the secretaries at the mill, I hear that he had fantastic sex appeal."

Nancy put her glass down. "Look," she said. "Look here —"

"Sorry. I guess that wasn't very nice." Liz Gage smiled pleasantly. In a different tone she said, "Well, you've been very kind to talk to me. I don't suppose I could talk to Mrs. Callahan, could I?"

"No. Peggy's lying down. She's exhausted."

"Of course. She must be. I wonder —"

"What?"

"I wonder if any of the other members of the family would talk to me."

"I'm afraid everyone's too busy and upset."

"I see. You mentioned a sister, didn't you, who's your friend?"

"Yes, Mrs. Greer."

"Is she here?"

"Yes."

"And I couldn't possibly see her?"

"I'm afraid not, Miss Gage."

"Well, I get A for effort anyway, don't I?" Liz Gage laughed lightly. "Tell me about Mrs. Greer."

"What about her?"

"What's she like? Is she pretty?"

"Barbara is my oldest friend. My dearest friend."

"Is she older or younger than Mrs. Callahan?"

"A few years older than Peggy —"

"I see. Where is her home?"

"In Locustville, Pennsylvania."

"Oh, yes. Is she up here with her husband?"

"Her husband is in England on a business trip."

"Do they have children?"

"Two boys. Goodness, you ask a lot of questions."

Liz Gage laughed again. "Of course."

"It must be fun to be a reporter."

"It is."

"I wanted to be one once."

Liz Gage smiled at her intently. "You would have made a good one, dear."

"Why, thank you!" Nancy sipped her drink.

"To get back to Mrs. Greer — did she bring the children up here with her?"

"No, they're home."

"I wonder why she came?"

"What?"

"Why did she come up here all alone?"

"To visit her parents, of course. Why else?"

"But doesn't it seem strange —" Liz Gage looked across the terrace toward the house. "Well, it doesn't matter. I suppose she likes it up here."

"She does."

"Tell me," Liz Gage said slowly, "would you describe Mr. and Mrs. Callahan as having been a devoted couple?"

"I'm sure they were."

"Really? What outward signs were there — of their devotion? Of their love?"

"Really," Nancy said, "I wish you wouldn't ask me questions like that. I don't know how to answer them, and besides I think they're in rather bad taste."

"Sorry," Liz Gage said. Slowly she withdrew a package of cigarettes from her purse. She offered the pack to Nancy.

"No thank you."

She removed also a long, gold-stemmed cigarette holder. Deftly she screwed a cigarette into it, placed the holder between her teeth, and lighted the cigarette with a small gold lighter, "Tell me just a bit about last night?" she said.

"It was awful."

"Where were you when it happened?"

"In bed."

"Asleep?"

"Yes."

"What time did you go to bed?"

"I don't know — around midnight, I guess."

"And you heard cries which woke you?"

"Yes."

"Let's see — the time must have been around one-thirty."

"I guess so. About that."

"You heard cries and went down — running down, I suppose. Where was the rest of the family at the time?"

"Everyone was in bed," she said.

"I see. Then when you came running down, whom did you meet?"

"I don't remember, really. Everyone came —"

"Who? Who is everyone?"

"Myself, Mr. and Mrs. Woodcock, the servants — everyone."

"Well, now wait a minute," Liz Gage said. "I think, in the story she gave to the police, the widow — Mrs. Callahan — said she awoke in the night and found her husband gone. She dressed and went through the house, looking for him, and then she went outside. Then she heard him calling for help, from the lake, and she went running down. So *she* wasn't in the house."

"No, of course not."

"And the sister? Where was she?"

"She was in bed, too," Nancy said.

"So, then, all of you gathered at the side of the lake — there would have been, let's see, seven of you. You, Mr. and Mrs. Woodcock," she counted on her fingers, "the two servants, Mrs. Callahan and Mrs. Greer — all of you still in your nightclothes, I suppose, except for Mrs. Callahan, who was dressed."

"Yes . . ."

"And then what did you do?"

Nancy closed her eyes. "Please, I don't —"

"What did you do? Don't you remember?"

"Someone said we should call the police. We called the police."

"Who called?"

"Please — I don't remember!"

Liz Gage tapped the ash from her cigarette. "It really is too bizarre, isn't it?" she said.

"What do you mean?"

"I mean, really, the whole thing is crazy, isn't it? For one thing, what in the world was he doing in that canoe? It was full of holes, a mass of leaks, and he was no swimmer. And why, particularly, did he take it out at that ungodly hour of night? Really, the whole

318

thing makes no sense. If it was suicide — and there's nothing to indicate it was — he chose a damn queer way to do it. Why did he do it? Was he out of his head? What's your theory?"

"It was a hot night," Nancy said. "He was probably hot and couldn't sleep. He thought he'd cool off on the lake. In the dark, he couldn't see that the canoe had leaks."

Liz Gage stared at her a moment. "Level with me, sweetie," she said. "Do you really believe that?"

"Of course!"

Liz Gage shrugged. "For one thing, it wasn't a hot night. It was chilly. It *was* hot, but then it rained and cooled off. The temperature last night at midnight was sixty-four. That's not exactly torrid, is it?"

"It was hot here," Nancy said. "It was hot in the house. Now please —"

"Was it? *Hot?* Well, maybe, in an old house like this one. Holds the heat, I suppose — built like Fort Knox." She smiled. "By the way, did you know there was a story that this house was haunted?"

"No, I never heard any such nonsense. Now please — I've got a headache. You'd better go."

Liz Gage looked at her wrist watch. "You're right," she said. "I'd better or I'll miss my deadline." She stood up. "I don't know if I've got much of a story, but at least I tried." She smiled and extended her hand to Nancy. "Thanks. And thanks for the drink, too."

"I hope you won't use my name in your story," Nancy said.

"Why not? You're probably mentioned in the obit already — as one of the guests in the house when it happened."

"For Mr. and Mrs. Woodcock's sakes I'd rather you didn't quote me, or indicate that I've said anything."

"Well, I'll see," Liz Gage said.

"I let you stay here and talk to me. In return, I'd like you to promise me this."

Liz Gage squeezed Nancy's hand. "It's a deal," she said, smiling. "But I wish you could explain to me just one thing."

"What is that?" Nancy asked. They started across the terrace and Liz Gage took Nancy's elbow. Suddenly she stopped. "Oh-oh," she whispered. "Who is this? The widow?"

"It's Barbara — Mrs. Greer. Excuse me, I've got to —"

"Let me talk to her."

"No, I'm sorry."

"Oh, Mrs. Greer?" Liz Gage called. "Mrs. Greer? May I speak to you just one second?"

Barbara came across the terrace, a puzzled expression on her face.

"I'm Liz Gage," the woman said. "Liz Gage from the *Eagle*. I'm intruding, I know, but the fact is that your family has occupied such a prominent position in Burketown for so many years that this tragedy concerns every individual in the community. This is what my editor feels."

"I'm sorry," Barbara said. "We're all terribly busy and upset, and I'd rather —"

"Just a couple of quick questions. Please? How long had you known Mr. Callahan?"

"Since he and my sister were engaged. Now, I must —"

"Just one more thing. I'll ask you the question I was about to ask Miss Rafferty. I mean, really, the whole thing is a complete mystery, isn't it? Why would a young man who couldn't swim a stroke go for a ride in a leaky canoe? And why, *especially,* at that ungodly hour of night? One might think suicide if it weren't such a crazy way to commit suicide — though I must say I've heard of crazier. But this guy had everything in the world to live for. A beautiful wife — a rich wife . . ."

"Please, I've got to go."

"Just a sec. My point is, where was he going?" She paused and seemed to study Barbara's face a moment. "I came in here cross-country," she said. "Through the woods. I went past that little cot-

320

tage over there, across the lake, and I noticed that the door was standing open. I looked inside and, the funniest thing, there were two Martinis sitting on the coffee table inside. Two untouched Martinis, nice and warm of course. Now tell me, Mrs. Greer, what do you think of that? Doesn't it look as though *that* was where he was going last night, and as though someone was waiting for him there?"

Barbara sat down hard in one of the iron chairs and pressed her hands together in her lap.

"What's the matter, Mrs. Greer?"

"What do you want?" Barbara whispered. "*What do you want?*"

Liz Gage stepped forward. "I want the full story," she said. "No fibs."

Barbara bent sharply forward and clasped her hands to her face. "Oh, please!" she said. "Please . . . please! I've got two little children!" she sobbed. "I've got two little children!"

"I see," said Liz Gage.

❦ ❦ ❦

At the Dorchester, Carson waited while the mail clerk looked through a small pile of letters. "No, I'm sorry, Mr. Greer, there is nothing," the clerk said finally. "Thank you," Carson said. He turned away. Then the clerk called, "Oh — Mr. Greer?"

Carson turned back. "Yes?"

"Is it Mr. Carson Greer, sir?"

"That's right . . ."

"Are you stopping at the hotel, sir?"

"No," Carson said, "but my mail —"

"I see, sir. That explains it. Sir, I believe there was a telephone call for you quite early this morning. The operator tried to locate you, sir, but of course, since you were not registered . . ."

"I understand."

"I'm sorry, I don't know any of the particulars of the call, sir, but I believe it was an overseas call, from America."

"Thanks," Carson said. "It must have been my home. If there should be any other calls for me, I can be reached at Bayswater 0170."

"I'll make a note of it, sir."

Carson gave him a ten shilling note.

"Thank you, sir."

Outside the hotel, he looked at his watch. It was twelve-fifteen. There would not be time, between now and his lunch date, to go back to his hotel and make the call. He would do it first thing after lunch. He stepped to the curb and waved for a taxi. It couldn't be anything serious, he decided, or she would have followed the call with a cable.

🌷 🌷 🌷

Edith Woodcock tapped on Preston's study door. "Come in," he called.

She opened the door. "Preston," she said, "I'm afraid something rather dreadful has happened."

He turned in his chair. "Yes," he said dully. "What is it?"

She went to him and stood looking gravely down at him. "There's been some sort of awful woman here, a reporter, from the *Eagle* . . ."

"Yes," he said.

"Yes, and she managed to talk, darling, to Barbara."

"What did they talk about, Edith?"

"Darling, in some devious way — the way they all have — she got Barbara to say, or imply at least that it was because of Barbara that it happened."

"How could it have been because of Barbara?"

"Well, as I say, she managed to get Barbara to imply that she was across the lake, in the guesthouse, waiting for him. That he and Barbara had — some sort of meeting arranged there last night."

322

"I see," he said quietly.

"Nancy was there when the woman was talking to her, to Barbara. Nancy heard it. Poor Nancy is dreadfully upset, and Barbara is terribly upset, too. She's in her room, Preston, and — well, the only thing we must do is to keep anything of that sort from being printed in the paper . . ."

"Now wait a minute," he said. "Is it true?"

"Is what true?"

"Was she there last night?"

"Darling, I don't think that's what matters. What difference does it make whether she was or not? He's dead now. It's nobody's business whether —"

"They won't dare print anything that might not be true," he said.

"But they could *imply* things, suggest things —"

"The *Eagle* won't suggest anything that might be slanderous," he said.

She turned away from him, folding and unfolding her hands. "Well, my dearest," she said softly, "then — then I'm afraid we must assume that it is true. I, for one, am quite sure it's true. I haven't the slightest doubt that it's true. So, you see, we must do something."

He closed his eyes. "How can you think such a thing about your daughter?" he said.

She returned to him. "It's not what I think, Preston. It's what I know. I blame myself — I do. I saw it, I saw something happening, long ago. I should have done something then, at the time. I did — I tried. I talked to her, to Barbara. I thought my words had sunk in, but they hadn't. Yesterday morning I called Nana's house to see if she was still there. She wasn't. She'd met him there, Preston — they'd gone for a drive together. I'm afraid they've been seeing each other for a long, long time. Yesterday, I warned her again! But she didn't listen to me. So I blame myself."

323

"Why didn't you tell me?" he asked quietly.

"Oh, Preston! I tried, I tried yesterday. You were — your mind was somewhere else, Preston. You'd been drinking."

"Oh," he said. "Oh, I see . . ."

"Yes."

"So — perhaps we should blame ourselves."

"Perhaps."

He reached for her hand and took it, held it tightly pressed between his own two hands. "Well," he said finally. "Well, well. What shall we do, Edith?"

"Darling, I want you to call Billy, tell him. Tell him the whole thing. Ask him to call the *Eagle* and do whatever he can."

"No," he said, "no, no . . ."

"Why not?"

"We don't need to drag Billy in on this. No, I'll call the *Eagle*. I'll call Tom Daniels."

"Well —" she said. "I thought perhaps Billy, because, well, don't you think Billy might have more influence?"

He nodded slowly. "He might. Yes, but I'll do it, Edith. In fact I'll drive down and see Daniels in person right now." He stood up and reached for his jacket which lay across the back of his chair. "I'll do it," he said, "not Billy. She's not Billy's daughter. She's mine, you see, so I've got to do it."

"All right, Preston. All right. But hurry, dear."

❧ ❧ ❧

Back in his hotel room, after lunch, Carson picked up the telephone and gave the operator the Locustville number. There was a long delay, filled with mechanical crackling and distant dialogues between trunk operators. At last, he heard Flora's voice shrieking across the Atlantic, "Hello? Hello? Yes? Hello?"

"Hello?" he yelled. "Hello? Flora?"

"Yes!"

"It's Mr. Greer, Flora. Is Mrs. Greer there?"

"Why no," Flora said. "She went up to the farm, Mr. Greer. She went up on Saturday afternoon and planned to be back today but she'll be back now on Wednesday, Mr. Greer."

"Oh," he said. "Well, is everything all right, Flora?"

"Oh, everything's fine here, Mr. Greer. The boys are fine — everything's fine. Up at that farm of theirs, that family's farm of hers, things aren't so fine though, Mr. Greer."

"What do you mean?"

"Ah, Mr. Greer, there's been a terrible tragedy."

"What? What is it?"

"That sister of hers? Her husband."

"What about him?"

"Dead!"

"Dead? Barney?"

"Yes, sir. He drowned, Mrs. Greer said. In a boat. She called this morning. The funeral's Wednesday, see. That's why she's staying for longer. Oh, they're terribly upset, Mr. Greer."

"Yes," Carson said. "Yes, I'm sure they are. Well, that's — that's very sad news, Flora."

"It is, it is. I never met the man of course, but it does make me sad. Such a young man!"

"How in the world did it happen?"

"I don't know. That's all she said. Drowned in a boat."

"She apparently tried to call me last night to tell me and wasn't able to reach me."

"I'm sure, sir, that she wanted you to be notified first thing."

"Well, I'll call her, Flora. And I'd better give you my number here in case you need it."

"What number?"

"It's Bayswater 0170. Have you got that? That's where you can reach me in London."

"What was that number again."

"Bayswater 0170," Carson said.

"Let me get a pencil and some paper." Flora was gone for a

long time; when she returned, she said, "Now what was that number?"

He repeated it several more times before she had it. Then he said, "Thanks, Flora. Give my love to the boys."

"How's the weather over there?"

"Very nice."

"You sound so *close,* Mr. Greer! Like you were in the next room. I've never talked to London, England before."

"Well, good-by, Flora."

"Good-by, Mr. Greer!"

He sat for a moment, thinking about Barney. Drowned in a boat, Flora had said, whatever that meant. It was sad, shocking news, of course, but its effect on him was a strange one. He had never, for some reason, known Barney Callahan well. He had been with him often enough but now, having just heard of Barney Callahan's death, he couldn't remember ever having talked to Barney, or anything that Barney had ever said to him. They must have talked, of course, but what about? It was not that Carson had disliked Barney, really, nor had Carson really liked him, either. It almost seemed to him now as though he had, for several years, rather ignored Barney, and he wondered why this had been. Barbara seldom mentioned him. It was as if Barney had floated across a portion of their lives and, now, had floated out of it. The surface behind his path was smooth and unrippled. Drowned in a boat. How very strange because, now that he tried to picture Barney Callahan's face, he couldn't. What had he looked like? Even Carson's recollection of his face was blurred and watery — submerged. To Carson, Barney Callahan had seemed drowned for a long time.

It was nearly two hours before Preston's car drove into the drive-way again. Edith had been lying, stretched out, on the library sofa, waiting for him. Her head had begun aching horribly and Emily had brought her an ice pack. When she heard him drive in, she tossed the ice pack aside, jumped up and ran to the door to meet him. "Well?" she asked tensely. "Did you see Daniels? What did he say?"

He looked very tired. "I saw him," he said. "I talked to him. I think it's going to be all right, Edith."

"*Think?* Don't you know?"

"He didn't promise anything. He hadn't seen the woman's story yet. But he said he'd look it over very carefully, every detail."

"But he didn't give you any assurance?"

"I think he understood. I said — look, Tom, it's my daughter, and — well, never mind what I said. He was very nice. He told me I shouldn't worry."

"Shouldn't *worry!* That's easy for him to say!"

"Edith," he said, "I'm very tired. I want to lie down. I want to be alone for a while . . ."

"Oh, *Preston!*" she cried.

❦ ❦ ❦

And so, at five o'clock, when the evening paper was due to arrive, she was waiting for it. When at last it was delivered, she seized it, took it into the library, and began tearing open the pages, looking quickly at each. On the next-to-last page, there was a small, rather blurred photograph of Barney, and under it were the words:

BERNARD J. CALLAHAN, 28,
DROWNED IN BOATING ACCIDENT

Wife a Member of Noted
Burketown Family

And there followed a tasteful and brief obituary, and a note that the funeral services would be held on Wednesday.

There was nothing else.

Edith ran quickly with the newspaper to her husband's room. She knelt on the floor beside him. "Oh, my darling!" she said. "You're so wonderful . . . so wonderful." She wept. "I love you so!" she said.

A little later, Nancy Rafferty came down the stairs looking trim in her suit and gloves, carrying her bag.

"Oh, Mrs. Woodcock!" she said. She put her arms around Edith's shoulders and pressed her hair against Edith's cheek. "Oh, Mrs. Woodcock," she said, "I must go. I can get the eight-thirty train out of Penn Station. I thought for a while that if I stayed I might be some help — but I'm only in the way. It's the best thing for me to do, Mrs. Woodcock. Will you forgive me for running off like this? It's just that I'm no help, no help at all . . ."

"There, there, Nancy," Edith said comfortingly. "You've been an enormous help, my dear, an enormous help. And I'm terribly grateful."

"But I've got to go. I'd love to be able to stay — for the services and everything. But I'm simply not up to it!"

"Of course, of course," Edith said. "I understand perfectly. It's as you think best, Nancy, as you think best."

"You're always so kind and wonderful!"

"You're like our own daughter."

They kissed.

Then Nancy stepped back, opened her purse, and dabbed at her moist eyes with her handkerchief. She blew her nose. "I've got you all lipsticky," she said.

"And I you!" Edith smiled. They dabbed at each other. "Did you say good-by to Barbara?"

"Yes. Just now. Not to Peggy, though. I didn't want to disturb her."

"Of course. Will Barbara be coming down for some supper do you think?"

"Oh, I think she'd prefer to have it on a tray," Nancy said. "Though I don't think she'll feel like eating."

"Of course."

"And do say good-by to Peggy and to Mr. Woodcock for me — will you? And tell them how terribly sorry I am. And explain."

"Of course I will."

"And thank you — thank you for everything, Mrs. Woodcock."

"It's just a shame — just a shame that your visit couldn't have been a happier one," Edith said. "But you'll come again."

"Perhaps."

"I shall insist you do!"

"You're so wonderful . . . And I — I feel so helpless. So useless."

"There, there! Now, tell me, Nancy, what are you going to do?"

"You mean after I get back to Philadelphia?"

"Yes."

"Well," Nancy said, more brightly, "actually I've been thinking about it, just today. I'm no nurse — I've learned that. In fact, I don't know what I am! But I thought, I've got a little money saved up. I thought I might go to Europe — for six months, or maybe a year. I've never been, you know, and I thought for six months or a year I might just travel around, see the things I've always wanted to see, and learn things — new languages, new people, and sort of get things straight in my life again. Do you think that's a good idea?"

"Oh, I do, Nancy. I approve, most definitely!"

"Well, I may do it or I may not. Who knows? I may get married. There's a doctor, in Philadelphia — but who knows? The nice thing about life is it's unpredictable, isn't it? And you never can tell . . ." She started toward the door.

"Do you want John to drive you?"

"I've called a taxi. It'll be here any minute. Thank you, anyway. Oh, one thing before I forget. Barbara says she doesn't want to call Carson — doesn't want to talk to him. Right now, that is. But I

329

think she should — or someone should. Someone should tell him what's happened before he hears about it from somewhere else. Don't you think Barbara ought to let him know — in a letter, perhaps?" She hesitated. "A letter can be calmer — you can plan what you say."

"Yes," Edith said. "Yes, yes."

"Telling him — just about the accident. Not about the circumstances, you know —"

"Yes," Edith said quickly. "I agree."

"I think we understand each other," Nancy said easily.

"I suppose we do," Edith said. "It's funny. My problem has always been — forgetting that my children are grown up."

"We both love Barbara," Nancy said. "We both want her to be happy."

"Yes."

"Well, once again —" she opened the door. "Oh, here comes my taxi," she said. "Well, good-by, Mrs. Woodcock and thank you forever!"

"Good-by, Nancy, dear."

They brushed lips again, very quickly.

"Have a wonderful trip to Europe," Edith said.

"Oh, I will," Nancy said, "if I go! Don't ever worry about me. I always seem to survive. Good-by!"

"Good-by."

Nancy waved airily, blew a last kiss, turned and ran down the steps toward the taxi.

Edith felt relieved, somehow, as she walked back into the house and began turning on lamps. It was beginning to get dark. It had been a terrible day, the worst in her life, though perhaps the worst of it was over. She thought: Death always inflicts its severest blows upon the living. How unfair! And then she almost smiled, realizing that it was not yet her turn to know what blows death inflicted upon the dead. In the midst of life, she thought, we are in the midst of death. Each death around us brings us inexorably closer to our own. Thank goodness there was work to do. There were two days ahead to get through. If she could get through Wednesday, she would be all right. Just tomorrow and Wednesday, and after that she would see to it somehow that all of them got off to a fresh start. All of them would begin again, they would have family picnics again, the best part of the summer still lay ahead of them, and the best part of their lives. Oh, yes.

No day could ever be as bad as today. There was comfort in that. She turned on more lamps in the library and stripped off, with her fingers, a few dying heads of roses in the vase. Then she went upstairs to see how many of her family she could gather for supper.

But on Tuesday, Liz Gage had the last word. Her story never appeared in the *Eagle*, but, with journalistic ingenuity, she had managed to peddle it elsewhere. One of the New York morning tabloids picked it up. It was not on the front page, nor on the second, nor on the third. But it was there, and prominent enough, with the headline:

WHICH HEIRESS WAS HE AFTER?

Was Ex-Milkman Paddling for Midnight Martini with Millionaire's Married Daughter?

Tom Daniels saw it and fired her.

Woody saw it very early in the morning when, weary and a day late, he got back to his apartment from Lime Rock. He immediately went downstairs, got in his car, and drove to the farm.

His idea had been to break it to them gently — as gently as possible. But when he got there, the news had already reached them.

21

PEGGY SAID, "THE CALLAHANS ARE HERE. CAN YOU COME DOWN?"
"Do they want to see me?" Barbara asked.

Peggy stepped into the room and pulled the door gently closed behind her. "They haven't asked to see you, no," she said. "But I thought it would be a good idea. And it would be a tremendous help to me, Barb."

"All right," she said. She sat up. "Just give me a few minutes."

She went to her dressing table and sat down at the little bench. Before her stood bottles, jars and tubes, extravagantly designed and colored, sensuously named, creating — even though they were capped and stoppered — a faint, persistent fragrance in the air. She reached for her brush.

Peggy came and stood beside her. On the glass top of the dressing table there was a little pile of bobby pins, and, slowly, with her fingertips, Peggy began arranging these. First she placed the pins in the little marching row, like soldiers, then she destroyed this pattern and began arranging the pins in a series of little box shapes, small square O's. She concentrated on this. Then she said, "I was premature. I was an idiot to think that I could do anything to shape up the company at this point. It's just too early. I still think we can do it some day, though — we're going to have to. You and I will have to do it. We'll have to wait until the trust comes to us and then see what we can do. My mistake was being impatient. And I think I was wrong to hang my hopes on Barney. He was the wrong kind of person. His heart wasn't in it. I should have known."

Barbara said nothing. She continued brushing her hair.

"We'll form a sort of partnership," Peggy said. "You and I — some day. That's the best thing. You and I understand each other,

332

after all." She finished the final square with the pins. Then she put her hand on Barbara's shoulder. "Barb," she said, "May I tell you one thing?"

"Yes," Barbara said. "What is it?"

"Barbara — I want you to know — whatever is said, whatever this stupid gossip is, I don't believe it."

Barbara sat motionless, her brush in her hand, staring at her reflection in the mirror.

"I couldn't believe it," Peggy said. "I could never believe it. Do you understand? If there's an explanation — even if there is an explanation — I really don't care what it is, because I know that it's a perfectly good, perfectly sensible explanation. I'd never, not for a single moment, think that there could have been anything between you and Barney. Because there couldn't have been. I knew him too well, and I know you too well, to think that any such thing could be possible. And — well, that's the only thing. That's all I want you to know." Then Peggy paused and placed one polished fingertip in the exact center of one of her O's. "Of course," she said, "there must have been someone there, in the guesthouse. But who that person was," she added, "is something we'll never know, isn't it?"

After a moment, Barbara said, "Peggy — I —"

"No," Peggy said. "No, I don't want to hear anything. The subject is closed. We'll never discuss it again." She reached for a tube of lipstick and handed it to Barbara. "Here — put some of this on." She smiled. "Now, I want us both to go down and talk to the Callahans together. We'll show them a united front, the good old Woodcock united front! Put on lipstick and we'll go down." She dropped the tube in Barbara's outstretched hand.

Barbara put the lipstick on, then closed the tube and stood up. She followed Peggy to the door. In the hall, Peggy squeezed her arm. "You're a damn good sport!" Peggy said.

Barbara said, "Peggy — what are you going to do?"

Peggy stopped and turned to her with a puzzled look. "What do you mean?" she asked. Her face cleared. "Oh, you mean now that he's dead, what will I do? Well, for one thing, I'm not going to be a widowy widow. And then — well, I suppose I'll marry again. Yes, I'm pretty sure that's what I'll do — marry again and then perhaps I'll astonish the world with the number of children I'll have!" She linked her arm in Barbara's and they went down the stairs.

Mr. and Mrs. Callahan sat side by side on the brown velvet sofa in the library. They both wore black and Barbara was startled to see how old they both looked. They sat somewhat stiffly, in almost identical poses, their hands folded in their laps, and they looked fragile and ill. Their faces were pale and blank.

"I'd like to present my sister, Mrs. Greer," Peggy said. "Barbara, these are Barney's parents, Mr. and Mrs. Callahan."

Mr. Callahan quickly stood up and held out his hand, then withdrew it nervously. He extended his hand again, then, as Barbara held out her own. "How do you do, Mrs. Greer," he said, and their hands met. His voice was soft and tremulous.

"How do you do," Barbara said. "I'm so —"

"Yes . . . yes . . ." he said.

"Do sit down," Peggy said.

They all sat, and, for a moment, there was a painful silence. Then Mr. Callahan said softly, "We stopped by, on the way, to see him. He looks — they've done a beautiful job — he looks — just as though he's fast asleep."

"Yes," Peggy said.

Mrs. Callahan reached for her handkerchief and touched her eyelids quickly and perfunctorily, though no tears showed there.

Outside, on the drive, a car drove up and stopped. Distantly, the front doorbell rang and distantly John's slippered feet moved across the house to answer it. In the library, they listened, waited, heard the front door open. They heard a few softly murmured words and they waited as though the caller might be bringing some portentous and long-awaited news. Then the door closed and John tip-toed past the library door bearing a long, slender, green cardboard box.

"Flowers," Mr. Callahan said, and his soft voice was full of awe. "More flowers! This is three bunches, now, that have come just since we've been sitting here. He must have had a lot of friends in this town, a lot of friends."

Then there was another long silence. Barbara felt the afternoon passing slowly and sleepily somewhere beyond them all as they sat, with grave faces, in the sunny library where rainbow refractions of light streamed from the teardrop prisms of the sconces on the mantel and fell in gay little shifting patterns on the rug; they sat, bewildered, hunting for some single significance or symbol that would lift from absurdity the whole business of life. Sounds of toil, as they searched, seemed to fill the room. Words and sentences tumbled in her head and vaporized and she continued to sit absolutely still, inarticulate, numb and anchored to her chair. Peggy lighted a cigarette and waved out the match. Barney's mother slowly twisted the rings on her left hand.

John arrived with things on a tray. There was tea and there was sherry. No one wanted sherry. Peggy poured perfectly. Barbara held her cup and stirred it.

Barney's father was talking in a low, soft voice that was filled with a kind of spellbound wonder. He was talking to no one in particular and as he spoke his eyes traveled all around the room, stopping to rest on no one thing. "Yes . . ." he said. "Yes, he was a fine boy. He was in the Army. He never told me too much about the Army or who his buddies were. He didn't like to talk about it. He was in Korea thirteen months . . ." Then he turned to Peggy, eagerly. "He got a — they call it a Letter of Commendation! Did he ever tell you that? From his commanding officer — from a colonel! Did he ever tell you that?"

Peggy sipped her tea. "No, I don't believe so . . ." she said.

"It was for helping establish a Supply Depot. And it said he —"

He fumbled in his jacket pocket and withdrew a folded piece of paper. "I found it when I was looking through his things. It was there — right there with his discharge papers all along. But he never told us about it. It says — well, perhaps you'd like to read it yourself." He unfolded the letter carefully, rose and handed it to Peggy.

Peggy read it. "Very — very wonderful," she said at last. And then, "May I keep it, please?"

Barney's mother spoke for the first time. Her voice was expressionless. "That's what he brought it for," she said.

"Thank you so much."

"Reflects credit on the armed services as a whole!" Mr. Callahan said. "That's what it says. And from a colonel."

"So nice . . ."

"Yes. Even then he was headed for success. They knew it then — even in the Army."

Peggy cleared her throat. To Mrs. Callahan she said, "Will any of your other children be able to come down?"

Mr. Callahan answered for her. "No, just Mrs. Callahan and myself. That's all. The others live too far away."

"His brother — Jerry. Barney used to mention him so often. He was so fond —"

"Yes, but Jerry's in the Army now, you know. He's in Germany. Yes, they were very close, he and Jerry. We had the Red Cross send Jerry the telegram yesterday. But Jerry won't be able to get home."

"That's too bad."

"Jerry's doing all right in the Army, too," he said. "A corporal already — and only in six months. But he'll never be the soldier his brother was . . . no, no. No, he was the best soldier and — and a fine boy." He stared at his untouched teacup. Mrs. Callahan gazed at Peggy, then at Barbara, her pale face composed and quiet.

"Yes," he went on. "He was headed for great things, for success. He could have been — anything he wanted to be. We always knew that, didn't we, Annie?" He turned anxiously to his wife for

336

confirmation. She nodded. "I mean," he said, "I mean even in school. Remember, Annie? Remember when he was — oh, when he was first starting school, in the first grade. He got the best marks! Gold stars the sisters put on his work — gold stars on everything! Spelling . . . arithmetic. He was the first one to learn to read, remember? He was the smartest one in his class. Oh, we knew even then that he was headed for success. He won that spelling bee, remember? And popular, too. Not snooty about being so smart. President of his class in the eighth grade, and a good little athlete. A good little football player, a good little tackle, but always too light for the team . . ."

"He was too thin," Mrs. Callahan said quietly.

"Yes, but he ate like a horse, remember? When he was fourteen, fifteen — but he was all skin and bones, you're right. It all went to height. He was taller than me. Healthy, though — always healthy, like my own father, never sick. Oh, he had the usual things — measles, mumps, whooping cough — things like that. Things all kids get. But he was never really sick. And he was a good kid, too — obedient, willing to work. Always had some odd job or other — selling *Saturday Evening Posts,* peddling papers. He worked in my store two summers, running errands. He was always willing. Everybody always loved him because he was so willing and helpful and co-operative. I remember — when I was working in the store — before I got sick — people would call up for something, and they'd say, 'Send little Bernard over with it, will you, Mr. Callahan? He's always so cheerful!' He picked up more darned tips than anybody!" He shook his head slowly back and forth, admiringly. "And he was smart about money. Never wasted it. He saved it, started his own savings account — all by himself. Came home one night with the little pass book and said, 'I've put my money in the bank.' Just announced it, just like that. He was — oh, maybe eleven then."

"Nine," Mrs. Callahan said. "Only nine."

"Yes, only nine. Yes, he was starred for success, bound to succeed."

"Yes . . ." Peggy said. "Yes."

"Remember, Annie?" he said. "Remember how he started that savings account, what he said?" He chuckled softly. "He went into the bank, big as life — nine years old — and said, 'I want to see the manager.' Well, the manager came out, and Barney said — oh, very politely, he was always a polite kid — he said, 'How much are your assets, sir?' And when the bank manager said so-and-so many million dollars, he said, 'Well, that sounds pretty good. I'll start an account here,' and he made a deposit of seven dollars! Seven dollars!" He removed his glasses, breathed on the lenses and slowly polished them with a corner of his dark jacket. Then he replaced them. "Seven dollars!" he repeated. "But do you know how much money he had saved up in that bank by the time he started high school? Two hundred and fifty dollars! That shows you how he was."

"It's still there," Mrs. Callahan said.

"That's right. He worked his way through college — odd jobs, everything. And Harvard Business School, the same way. But he never touched that savings account. That money's still there — more, now, with the interest. I found the pass book with his things." He reached in his jacket pocket again. "That balance is still there. It's yours," he said, and he held out the small frayed and faded envelope to Peggy.

"Oh, no — no, you keep it, please!" Peggy said.

"No, it belongs to you."

"Oh, I can't — no, really —"

"It's yours," he repeated.

She took it and held it awkwardly in her hand, staring at it, a curious expression on her face.

Then Mrs. Callahan said, "Of course it probably doesn't seem like very much money to you."

Peggy looked up quickly. "No, I meant — I meant perhaps Jerry could use it, or —"

"No," Barney's mother said. "It belongs to you. Morally — and legally."

"He always planned to send money home. I know he did," Peggy said.

Mrs. Callahan's eyes grew wider. "Did he? What for? We never needed money."

"He was headed for success," his father said quietly and proudly. "Like this . . ." He nodded about the room, at the books, at the tall windows, at the winking crystal drops on the mantel sconces. "A house like this, and a job like the one he had here, with you people. That was what he was always cut out for — right from the beginning."

Mrs. Callahan said, "He must be buried in Holy Ground."

"I beg your pardon?" Peggy asked.

"He must be buried in Holy Ground," she said. "That's the only thing."

"You mean —"

"Yes. That's the only thing we ask, Mr. Callahan and I. That's why we came down here as quickly as we could, because it must be arranged. Bernard has not been a good Catholic, I know, for several years. He had a — a misunderstanding once that involved the Church. But that was all it was — a misunderstanding. That was why he was married out of the Church. He may have told you that he lost his faith, but that isn't true. He couldn't have. In his heart, in his soul, he still had his faith. I knew my son, you see. His faith could not have gone. It was there. He must be absolved. He must have a Catholic burial. That is all my husband and I ask of you people. My son must have that. You must not deny him that. It may be difficult — because of the last few years, but we must arrange it. I have tried, through our priest, at home. But he is opposed. So you must help us arrange it here, in this town. You must help us arrange it here, in this town. You must help us do whatever we can do. That's what we came for."

"I see," Peggy said. And then, slowly, "Yes — I think we can arrange it."

"Good."

"We — our family — have always supported all the churches here in Burketown, and quite generously. We always make gifts to Saint Mary's, along with all the other churches. It was one of my grandfather's particular concerns, since — well, since our people at the mill are of all faiths. I'll call Father McGowan at Saint Mary's and see what can be done."

"Thank you," Mrs. Callahan said, and the first glimmer of tenderness appeared in her pale eyes. "Thank you. You're very understanding, my dear."

Barbara said, "Mrs. Callahan — I think you're making a mistake."

"*What?*" Mrs. Callahan asked sharply. "What did you say?"

"I don't think you should do this," Barbara said quietly. "Really I don't. He wouldn't have wanted it. I know he wouldn't have wanted it."

Mrs. Callahan leaned forward. Her voice was shrill. *"You!"* she screamed. "What have *you* got to do with my son? You're the one who killed him! You're the one who —"

"Annie! Annie!" Mr. Callahan said.

"She is! She killed him! Everybody's read about it! Murderess! She killed him!"

Barbara sat rigidly in her chair. Peggy stood up and walked to where Mrs. Callahan sat. In a low, even voice, she said, "How dare you speak to my sister that way? *How dare you?*"

"She did!" The teacup trembled in the older woman's hand as she set it down. Then she sobbed. She leaned sharply across the back of the sofa crying, "Oh, my little boy . . . oh . . . oh . . ." Her voice was childlike and despairing. "Oh, my angel son! She killed him. She killed him!"

Barbara stood up.

"Quiet! Be quiet!" Peggy said harshly.

340

Slowly Barbara turned and walked out of the room. She heard Peggy saying, "That's a damned lie. Now be quiet. Stop this. If you'll just be quiet, I'll telephone Father McGowan . . ."

Barbara went up the stairs.

In the upstairs hall, she met her mother. Edith was tugging at the belt of her blue Shantung dress. "Darling, will you zip me up?" Edith said. She turned her back to Barbara. Barbara reached for the zipper. "Did you meet them?" Edith asked as Barbara raised the zipper and then fastened the two little hooks at the collar. "Were they too ghastly for words? Really, I don't know how much more of this I can bear!" She turned to Barbara again. Then she seized Barbara's elbows and drew her toward her. "Oh, isn't this hell! Isn't this utter, utter hell!" she said. There were tears in her eyes.

"You'd better wait a minute before going down," Barbara said. "They're very upset . . ."

"*They're* upset! How do they think *I* feel? Oh, my poor little girl — why did you have to get mixed up in it? It isn't fair. It just isn't fair."

"It was all my fault."

Edith Woodcock's eyes brightened with anger. "No!" she said. "Don't you ever say that! Don't ever let me hear you say such a thing! Don't ever think it. It was *not* your fault. It was *his!* He had no business coming here to begin with. I saw, I knew, right from the beginning that the auspices were all wrong. He had no right to even look at either one of you. Cheap little milkman! I should have known this would happen, I should have thrown him out —"

"Oh, Mother! Mother!"

"Hush. Don't ever think it was your fault. The blame was all his." She squeezed Barbara tight against her. "My beautiful little girl! He poisoned you! That's what he did — poisoned you. But thank God it's over and done with, thank God we're through with him!" They stood for a moment, swaying slightly, in the hall with Edith's arms bound around her in a violent grip. Then Edith released her. "Well," she said, "I'm going down now, to see them. I shall try to be courteous." She went toward the stairs and Barbara returned to her room. On her dressing table was the neat row of small, square O's that Peggy had fashioned with her bobby pins.

The study was filled with sunlight and the door was locked. Preston was writing in his journal.

> This is no longer a biography of Father. That was a foolish venture. I can't remember now why I began it and perhaps that is just as well.
>
> Perhaps I should write this as a diary.
>
> Very well. Today, I am fifty-seven and one hundred and fourteen days old, keeping pace with the century, just a few weeks behind it. Today is sunny and warm, comfortable but not hot. Some of the fields look shaggy. It is probably time they got a second cutting for the summer, but I don't know. I have never been a farmer, though I live on a farm.
>
> I have not had a drink since Saturday night, which I calculate to mean that I have not had a drink in slightly more than forty-one hours. I am not sure whether I feel any the better for this. Will I stop? I don't know. I am approaching the most difficult time of the day, late afternoon, when the habit begins clutching for me with its fingers. A drink has always helped me get through a crisis, and so in the present crisis I feel the need for one particularly strongly. A drink at this moment would be understandable, surely, as therapy. I think Dr. McDonald would agree.
>
> But this is only rationalization. Excuse-groping now,

at this hour, as I feel the fingers. I used to make a number of excuses, such as thinking that a drink brought me closer to myself. But Edith says that I have spent too much time too close to myself. So this notion was malarkey. Or perhaps it wasn't, I do not know.

But at least I am sure of a few things — my age, and my general state of disrepair. And that the day is warm. And that the fields look shaggy.

It is interesting to speculate about what father would have said about this last terrible business. But perhaps, if he were alive, it wouldn't have happened. He might have prevented it. It is equally interesting to speculate about what might have happened if I had done as Edith wanted — asked Billy to call Tom Daniels. Billy probably has more influence. But I couldn't ask him, for reasons that seem more than obvious to me. Tom Daniels is a sweet fellow. Called me this A.M. Terribly sorry, etc. Gage woman fired. Suggested I sue. He ought to know that there are some damages that cannot be recovered in a lawsuit, but he is a sweet fellow all the same, and I appreciate his calling. His voice was like something from the tomb.

This morning, when it first happened, I thought: This is the end, the final disintegration of Father's great dream. In three generations, we have struck mud. We have come all the way down. Poor Barbara. Sometimes I see so many of past events as a series of catastrophes, each small, but each one leading us one step further toward degradation. This is ironic, because most of the money's still there. Company is in trouble at the moment, but the personal money is still there. Trust account re-valued at $521,000; sales of West Hill

343

properties, part of the trust, should bring increase next year, plus other odds and ends. Pay back some of money borrowed from Billy — future bright in that respect. There is no doubt that Billy saved my money by doing what he did with Mother's. Barbara and Peggy are the only heirs, after Edith. They will be rich women some day, ironically enough.

But my mind keeps changing. I am thinking now that what I first thought was wrong. This last thing, with Barbara, is not the final step toward any degradation of the family. The final step was taken years ago, by Father. This is just another part of the punishment. Like running the gamut, Barbara was merely unlucky enough to be standing next in line. Father committed the original sin in this family. Barbara, myself, the rest of us, are merely the victims of it, innocent victims. Like a curse, a mummy's curse. This is a very funny thought and if I were a humorist I might try to write a humorous story about a mummy's curse, with the family in it, but I am not much of a humorist, and won't try it. Not here, in any case.

Father's dream. That was the curse. See, I am mixed up in my metaphors already! But Barbara, anyway, is innocent. And that is so comforting to me. Some day when things are quieter for her I will try to explain it to her, though the explanation will take more strength and skill than I fear I possess. It is not 'bad seed,' not like a disease, like syphilis, hemophilia, passed from generation. It is more like a supernatural thing — a curse! Not a physical thing, I mean, but the opposite of physical — the word that I want escapes me. I fall into hokum, like closet-skeletons, mummies and other trash. Anyway, I think I have an

344

idea here, and that some day I could comfort Barbara with it.

Some day . . .

What we might have been . . .

Still, I am terrified of the future! In the future why do I keep seeing a great fire? I used to think I could save the family if there was a fire, get them out of the house, to safety. Now I see us all consumed in it! I am terrified mostly of myself. Am I truly an innocent victim, like Barbara? It seems like an easy excuse. I hope I am.

All diaries must be burned before writer dies, but how to know? One of Shaw's plays, I think, said don't worry about the future. It is enough that there is a future, or something like this. Cold comfort, surely.

> SCHEDULE FOR EVERY DAY
> Before lunch, 1 Martini
> Before dinner, 2   "
> 1 wine with dinner
> 1 brandy after   "

Schedules always help.
No they don't. Burn this now.

At the farm, it was four o'clock. In London, it was nine. Carson snapped on the light and reached for the ringing phone by his bed. "Hello?" he said.

"Mr. Carson Greer?"

"Yes."

"One moment, please."

There was a long delay and presently he heard a faraway man's voice saying, "Carson? Is that you?"

"Yes," he said. "Who's this?"

"It's Woody — Woody deWinter."

He swung his legs over the side of the bed. "Oh. Hi, Woody."

"Where *are* you?" Woody said. "The operator's been trying every hotel in London."

"I moved," Carson said, "Where are *you?*"

"I'm here — at the farm."

"I heard about Barney," Carson said. "That's terrible news, Woody. How did it happen?"

"Oh — you heard? How did you hear?"

"Yesterday. I talked to Flora, the girl who works for us in Locustville. Flora said he'd been drowned — while he was in a boat. Is that it?"

"Yes. Yes, that's about it. Canoe tipped. Carson?"

"Yes, Woody?"

"Carson — can you come home?"

"For the funeral, you mean?"

"No, not that. No, there's something else, Carson."

"What do you mean?"

"Carson, there's a reason why you should come home — as soon as you can."

"What reason? What's the matter, Woody?"

"I can't tell you — except that you've got to come home and see Barbara."

"Where is she? Is she —"

"She's here. She's perfectly —"

"Let me speak to her."

"No, she doesn't know I'm calling you, Carson. That's the only thing. She didn't want me to call you, but —"

"Is she sick?"

"No. No, I told you she's perfectly well, Carson. She's fine. We're all fine. But you should come home, Carson, please take my word for it."

"Will you please tell me what the reason is?"

"I can't. It's something that Barbara will tell you when you see

346

her. All I can tell you is that it's important, terribly important that you come."

Carson's voice was cross. "Look here, Woody, if something's the matter — if there's some kind of trouble — tell me what it is. I'm here on business. I just got here and I've got work to do. I can't come flying home for some damned silly reason of yours. Especially if you won't tell me what the reason is."

"I'm sorry," Woody said. "I can't tell you anything except to come."

"Then I'm sorry, too."

"Carson — it's something that involves only you and Barbara. I shouldn't even be in on it, I suppose. But I swear to you, Carson, it's important for you to come home."

"Look," Carson said, "hang up. I'm going to call Barbara back and find out what the trouble is."

"You can't do that," Woody said.

"Why the hell not?"

"Because it's too important, Carson. It's too important for a phone call. You've got to see her in person."

A cold wave of fear filled Carson's chest. "Look," he whispered. "She's sick, isn't she? She's been hurt, or —"

"Carson, believe me, she's fine. So are the children. Damn it, Carson, why are you so dense? Can't you imagine that there might be other reasons, other than health? I tell you it's urgent that you come home. She's going back to Locustville tomorrow, after the funeral. If you can get a plane tonight or early tomorrow morning, you could be there tomorrow night —"

"Woody, you've got to tell me why."

"I can't."

"Does it have something to do with Barney's — death?"

"It's worse, Carson. By that I mean it's harder to solve."

"If she's in trouble of some kind, tell me what it is."

Woody's voice was faint. "Carson, I'm begging you. I'm imploring you."

"Tell me."

"You've got to believe — believe that I wouldn't ask you, if it weren't necessary."

"I won't unless you tell me."

"Carson," Woody said, "listen to me, Carson, please. I owe you something — you know what I mean, from the old days, from Princeton . . ." Woody's faint voice wavered. "Remember? I remember. And I owe you something — a debt, for that. That's why I'm willing to — to demean myself, to beg you, Carson, to come home. It isn't easy to beg you, but it's my duty — my debt. Because you must come home. You see, I've got a little honor, Carson, a little honor. I can try to repay my debt to you by this — by telling you that you must come home. And don't forget, Carson, we both hurt each other. You hurt me, too — before. Maybe you owe me a little something, too. If you do — if you think you do — then you can repay a little debt to me by — well, by just *coming*, Carson. Will you come?"

Carson was silent a moment. Then he said, "She'll be in Locustville tomorrow?"

"Yes. Go there."

"All right," Carson said.

"Thank you, Carson."

There was a distant click as he hung up. Carson replaced the receiver in its cradle and sat for several minutes on the bed. Then he picked up the telephone again to call the airline.

Later that afternoon Barbara walked alone out across the terrace, down the series of garden steps to the pool. She was going no specific place, for no clear reason, merely for a walk.

When she got to the pool she saw that Woody was there, in the water, swimming face down with his face mask, fins and snorkel. He did this often, swimming slowly, looking down through the clear water. People often asked him what he expected to see or find. "Nothing," Woody said. In Woody's ocean, no bright fish flashed. There were no terrors in his deeps. Perhaps this was why he did it; the very absence of anything to see but blue and filtered water was, perhaps, consoling to him. From time to time he would descend, drop to the bottom, as if to inspect a tiny flaw or crack in the tile, or the operation of a drain. Then he would rise and blow air noisily from his snorkel and then continue, face down, swimming slowly.

She walked around the pool's perimeter and Woody, seeing her shadow, raised his head and looked up at her through his mask. He lifted one hand above the water and waved to her, a high salute. Then he went back to what he had been doing, swimming slowly up and down. Barbara sat in a chair and watched him, listening to the harsh rhythm of his breathing through the snorkel.

After a while he raised his head again and swam to the edge of the pool where she was sitting. He pushed his face mask back and pulled the snorkel from his mouth. He looked at her, his elbows resting on the pool's coping. Then, expertly, he lifted himself out of the water and stood up beside her. In the course of the summer he had become darkly and evenly tanned, and his pale shock of yellow hair had been bleached almost pure white by the sun. He stood beside her now, looking down, his slim brown body looking almost frail, with the brief, triangular wisp of white silk that served him as bathing trunks looking not at all like a polite bow to convention, but more like an arrogant defiance of it. His blue eyes were deep and grave. Barbara lifted her head and looked at him. He stooped, bending his dripping head and shoulders over her, and kissed her.

Then, for a while, he sat in the chair beside her, his legs stretched out straight in front of him, and they said nothing.

Then he said, "I hear there's been a change of plans. Services at Saint Mary's now."

"Yes."

"Well, I suppose it's just as well. I've always thought the Catholic religion must have a lot to it. I mean, if you're going to be religious, that's the most religious religion there is."

She nodded, and they were silent again.

"Life is funny, isn't it?" he said. "Were you in love with him, Barbara?"

"I don't know," she said. "That's the funniest thing about it, I suppose. I really don't know."

"Poor old Barney," he said. "Poor little guy. He didn't know what he was in for, did he?"

"I think he knew — finally," Barbara said.

"But then it was too late, you mean."

"Yes."

"Poor little guy," he repeated. "He had all the right ambitions. But he just didn't know what to do."

Slowly he began to pull the flat rubber fins from his feet.

"I wonder," he said, "if I'd been here Sunday night, if it would have been different? The evening might have gone differently. I talked to your mother on the phone that day, you know. She asked me to come for dinner. But she let it drop that your Nancy Rafferty was coming, so I let out one yelp and fled."

"Oh," Barbara said. "I wondered where you were. I tried to call you, too."

He smiled faintly. "Did you? Ah, you should have known — you, of all people. But poor Edith was shocked. Poor Edith never quite understands. But still, if I'd been there, maybe it wouldn't have happened."

"Woody, it's silly to think that," she said.

"Still, I keep wondering —"

"It would have happened — anyway. It was me."

"I called Carson," he said.

"What?"

"I called Carson, a little while ago, in London."

"Oh, Woody," she said. "You *didn't*, Woody."

"Yes, I did," he said simply.

"Where did you find him?"

"Tried the big hotels. He'd left a number at the Dorchester."

"What did you say to him?"

"He knew. He knew already."

"Oh," she said softly.

"Only about — only that Barney was dead. That's all. He'd called Flora and she'd told him that, yesterday."

"Oh," she said. "I wonder why he called Flora?"

"I suppose he was simply looking for you," he said.

"Yes," she said. "Yes, I suppose so. Well, I suppose I should thank you, Woody, for calling him. He had to find out and the only thing was — well, I didn't feel up to calling him myself. I didn't know, I wasn't sure, what I might end up saying."

"Sure," Woody said. "I understand that."

"He — he hasn't heard anything about what the papers said?"

"No," he said. "You can tell him about that tomorrow night."

"Tomorrow night? What do you mean?"

"I told him to come home."

"And is he?"

"Yes. He's going to try to be in Locustville tomorrow night. And that, of course, is where you'll be tomorrow night."

"No," she said quietly. "Under those circumstances, I won't be there. I'm not ready to see him, Woody."

"Yes you are."

"I'm not." She turned to him. "You shouldn't have done this."

He sat facing straight ahead. "It's too late," he said. "I've already done it."

"Why? Why did you?"

"Because you love him, and he loves you, my dear. And because your home is in Locustville, Pennsylvania, and that's where you both ought to be when you talk about this."

"You're being a little presumptuous, aren't you? Is it really up to you to decide whether Carson and I love each other?"

"Go on," he said. "Go on, I can take it."

She was silent. Then she said, "Woody, it isn't fair. I need time, time to plan what I'm going to say to him and plan what I'm going to do. I don't want to see him tomorrow night. I can't see him because my plans aren't definite yet."

"What do you mean by your plans?"

"I have a lot of plans, Woody. They're all different. But they all involve going away somewhere, permanently, with the children. Leaving Locustville, and leaving Carson."

"Leaving him permanently also?"

"Yes."

"You shouldn't talk that way. This is why you've got to see him."

"No. That's why it's useless to see him. Besides, it's no business of yours!"

"It is, actually," he said, and his hard brown hand closed around hers. "I know a little about love," he said and his eyes shone. "I know a lot about love, my dear — both sacred and profane."

"Oh, Woody, you've got me into a terrible mess."

"On the contrary. I'm helping you escape. You do love him, don't you?"

"Do you honestly think he'd want to go on, after this?"

"That's for him to decide, not you. Let him decide that. But it's up to me to make sure that you see him. I'm responsible for both of you. I introduced you, don't forget. If it hadn't been for me, you would never have met."

"Oh, Woody," she sobbed. "Leave me alone. Why don't people leave me alone?"

"Lilias," he said softly, swinging her hand in his. "Lilias de Falange. Where's your old fire, where's your old spirit? Show your grit, woman! The kind of grit you showed when we tried to kidnap Danny Vogeler right beside this pool! Where's your fight, where's your courage? Lilias de Falange had the eyes of a dove but the heart of a falcon . . ."

"Woody, Woody . . ."

"Remember who you are," he said.

She looked toward the house. "You must have made it sound urgent. He wouldn't fly all the way back unless he thought it was urgent."

"It *is* urgent."

"But didn't he ask? Didn't he want to know what was wrong?"

"Of course. But I didn't tell him."

"And still he agreed to come. How strange."

Woody said, "I told him you wanted to see him, and so he said he'd come. Is that strange? He loves you, in other words."

"But when he finds out," she said, "when he hears the whole thing, hears the scandal, he won't. He won't, Woody. He won't."

"Never mind that now."

"Last night I thought: Where can I go? Suddenly there didn't seem to be any place. I can't stay here. I can't stay in Locustville — I've always hated that. Where can I go, what can I do? I thought: I've got to go somewhere, though, and do something and take Dobie and Michael with me. Last night I thought I might go to San Francisco, get a little house on the Peninsula or in Marin County, and try to get a job. A nurse for the children — and a job, some sort of job. At least, I thought, San Francisco is far away and a good place to start."

"To start what?"

"To start seeing if I am — if I can be — a decent human being."

"Ah —"

She turned, suddenly, and gripped his shoulders with both her hands and pressed the side of her face hard against his bare, smooth and still wet chest. "Woody!" she cried. "I'm so damned scared!"

For a moment he circled her with his arms and held her tightly to him. He stroked her hair. "Ah, poor little Lilias, poor little lost Lilias! There are certain advantages, I guess, to being like me — trapped in my environment, imprisoned forever in my gloomy tower."

"Don't you see what's happened to me? There's nothing for me now. I've discovered how truly worthless I am! I don't deserve my children any more, nor my husband, nor my home — nothing. I've done this to myself and now I've got to live with it. I don't deserve anything else . . ." Tears streamed down her face.

"Hush," he said. "Hush, hush, hush!" His voice was low, musical and theatrical. "You shall have towers," he said. "Towers and minarets and spires and palace gates, forests, shores and islands, gems and pearls and scepters and all the Emperor's diamonds, and every brilliant in King Oberon's bright diadem! This I swear to you on the grave of Fraulein Ungewitter — that you shall have temples and mosques and fountains, rings on your fingers and bells on your toes, fountains and waterfalls and tapestries and flowers and thornless roses, and —"

"Oh, Woody!" she sobbed. "Woody, please!"

"But it's true!" he said earnestly. Suddenly he pulled her to her feet. "You shall! You can!"

22

LEAVING THE FARM WAS VERY SIMPLE. AT TWO O'CLOCK THEY returned from the cemetery, and for a while afterward, the house was full of people, family and friends, most of whom had attended the services but some of whom had not; and they wandered in chattering and affectionate little groups through the rooms that were burdened with bouquets of summer flowers, out

354

onto the terrace and into the garden — men in dark suits and women in black dresses, hats and veils, who contrasted sharply with the brilliant day and the vivid colors of zinnias, petunias and sweet alyssum. The talk was polite and cheerful, in the mood — intimate and almost gay — that it becomes every mourner's duty to create after a funeral. They squeezed each other's hands and kissed each other warmly, the old and dear friends and members of the family. Some had traveled considerable distances to be here, and some had not seen others for several years. Some were old, like Barbara's grandmother, who drowsed in her wheel chair, with Binky Zaretsky, who wore an ornate black-fringed dress, standing beside her; and some were young, like Cousin Billy's children. But all of them shared a bond of love and sympathy with Edith and Preston Woodcock, with Peggy and Barbara, and their farm and their sorrow.

A few accepted drinks which John passed, but most of them held glasses of ice-water or cups of coffee. They moved, bowing and smiling, taking special care to greet and say a few words to the Callahans, to say that the services had been lovely, that the church had looked lovely, that the house looked lovely and Barney — so peaceful. The pallbearers were graver than most and grave also were some of the people who knew the Woodcocks less well, certain of the older employees at the mill who had never been inside the Woodcocks' house before. They stood in a little respectful group, apart from the family, and left early. Talking, Mary-Adams deWinter overturned her cup and spilled coffee across the front of her dress. As several gentlemen rushed to her assistance with their handkerchiefs she assured them that it didn't matter. "Please," she said, "Please — it doesn't matter," flushed and embarrassed at having caused the attention of the gathering to turn, even so briefly, to herself. At one point, Emily appeared and handed Barbara a letter.

She withdrew a little distance from the others to read it. "*Sweetie* —" it began:

355

How too ghastly what you must be going through. I read it in the paper and feel responsible — for not having shooed that impossible woman off. I'm so sorry! Darling, I don't know what you're going to do or what your plans are, if any, but I can offer you one if it appeals to you . . . let's take a trip somewhere together, go to Europe! Remember that wonderful year we had in Hawaii? Let's do something like that again — even go to Hawaii again if you like. Remember, we said we measured out our lives in coffee spoons? Let's do that again and forget all this other mess! Will you let me know?

> *Love always*
> *Nancy*

Barbara folded the letter, thinking that *that*, at least, was one thing she would not do.

As people began to leave, she prepared to leave also. As she spoke to her mother and father, her grandmother, Peggy and the others, she realized that they were all too busy and distracted with the business of greetings and leave-takings to really notice, or care, that she was doing anything different from the others who were ready to leave. It seemed only incidental that John was carrying her suitcase down the stairs to her car. And when she had, in fact, left, and had joined the slowly moving line of cars that was making its way out the long drive, she realized that she had not, in so many words, ever said good-by.

She made one stop. She had not planned to, but when she reached the road she turned left instead of right and drove to the cemetery again. It was on a hill, on the east side of town, an old and crowded cemetery from which the original handsome cedars had long since been cut, and Barney had been given one of the few places that remained available, in one of the less desirable corners, though a small copper beech tree grew nearby. The grave was covered with massed flowers that were melting sweetly in the sun. She had brought no offering. Indeed, there seemed to be a surfeit of offerings already. She stood among the clutter of marble crosses and weeping angels, looking at the flowers.

It was a silly custom, a sentimental custom, bringing flowers to the dead, who could no longer see them and no longer knew. Perhaps it was even a morbid custom, bringing as it did the past so sharply into focus again, sheerly for the sake of recollection or for the sake of tears. Or as an excuse for tears. But then, of course, maybe they did know, maybe they even saw. She didn't know. She had never had a concrete theology and she could not speculate. Still, she thought, if perhaps in the moment before death came there was the feeling and the assurance that someone would see a spray of white carnations and think: I'll put them there, with you — then it would be a comfort, to have that sort of knowledge just before. She supposed she hoped someone would put flowers on her grave. But you see, she reminded herself, this is what you mean by being sentimental.

The thought that struck her most, standing there, was how little she had really known him, and how different his life had been from her own. He had always seemed such a sad young man — sad and impatient and intense — and she supposed he had never known, or imagined, any of the places that she had known or known what it had been like to be young in such places.

There were certain places that had shaped her life, but not his. And if it meant anything, it meant only that they had both been misshapen. They had both been crippled, but by different places. She started back toward the car.

The town looked very pretty from up here — the mills, the river, the buildings scattered below almost at her feet — and, beyond, the highways stretching to Hartford, Boston and the north, and in the other direction toward New York. Yes, there was a better view from up here than there was from West Hill, or from Prospect Avenue, or from any of the garden patios she had ever stood upon, and it would have been better, she thought, to have developed this as a residential section rather than as a cemetery. She stopped and tried to picture this hill built up with houses and New England tugged suddenly at her heart, here with its dead — its alien and separate Catholic dead — outlined against its living. There was really very little difference. Both had a sense of quiet and repose. In that respect alone, she and Barney were alike. She went on down the hill to her car.

It was dusk when she reached Locustville. The sun was setting behind Sunrise Heights. She turned into Bayberry Lane and the little reflector signs — "Sage . . . Bryson . . . Bishop . . . Hodgson . . . Greer" — sparkled in its last glimmers. She turned into their driveway and the sun gilded the rigid rooster weather vane.

The boys greeted her wildly, hugging her knees and tugging at her skirt.

"They've had their supper," Flora said. "I let them stay up a little later so they could see you."

At her desk, she wrote out a check for Flora.

"Mr. Greer called Monday morning," Flora said.

"Yes, so I've heard."

"It was — oh, no more than an hour after you called me. He called from London, England. My, that was a real experience for me — talking on the telephone to London, England."

"Yes."

"I told him about the tragedy, about Mr. Callahan." She lowered her voice. "I didn't breathe a word to the children, though. I thought I'd let you tell them in your own way."

"Thank you, Flora."

"Gone on a trip, that's what I'd say if they were my children. I'd just tell them that their uncle had gone on a long, long trip."

"Yes."

"And you can be sure I didn't mention to them, or Mr. Greer, or anybody else about that story in the paper."

358

"Oh," Barbara said. "Then you heard about that."

"Hear about it? Goodness me, it's been the talk of Locustville if you ask me!" She stopped abruptly. "I'm sorry, Mrs. Greer, honest I am. What a terrible thing! And what a terrible story to print in the paper."

"Yes," Barbara said.

"Of course I've got a theory," Flora said. "I've got a theory about why they write such things in the papers — not that I think a single word of it is true! Want to know what my theory is?"

"Yes, Flora, what is your theory?" Barbara asked.

"It's Communists. They're the ones to blame. They're the ones that print those sort of things about decent people like yourself, Mrs. Greer. They're against our American capitalistic system, so they try to print things like that — just anything they can think of — to make folks think there's something bad about wealthy folks like yourself, Mrs. Greer. Now I know for a fact that there's Communists in this town, more Communists than you could shake a stick at, and they're out to get the decent people. I could name you names, but I won't. They're the ones Mr. J. Edgar Hoover should be out to get, Mrs. Greer. He should get them and string them up by their toes. They're trying to get us all turned over to Soviet Russia, that's what they want — so they're printing dirty stories in the papers like the one about you, and they're doing all the talk that's going on in this town. That's my theory, and I said the same thing to my sister on the phone . . ."

"Yes," Barbara said. "Well, thank you, Flora." She handed her the check.

Then, after Flora left, she played with Dobie and Michael for a while. Then she got them into their pajamas and read to them the story of *The Little Engine That Could.*

"When's Daddy coming home?" Dobie asked her as she tucked the covers around him.

"Soon," she said. "Perhaps tonight."

"Can I stay up?"

359

"No. But if it's not too late, perhaps I'll wake you up . . ."
She kissed them good night.

Then, alone, she went into the living room and lighted the lamps. She still wore the black dress she had worn to the funeral, but she was too tired to change. She realized that she had had nothing to eat since breakfast that morning, but she didn't feel hungry. She sat on the white sofa. The room looked comfortable and clean, as it always looked. Indeed, it was hard to believe that she had ever really left it. Nothing was changed. Behind the fireplace screen she could see the white scraps of paper among the ashes where she had tossed them, angrily, on Saturday after tearing up the note about the garbage cans. She waited and wondered if he would come.

Later — it was nearly ten o'clock — she heard a car drive in and knew that it was Carson's taxi, and that he had come. She waited. She heard him open the front door with his key, step inside and set his suitcase down in the hall. He came and stood in the doorway. He looked haggard and tired, in need of a shave. "Well," he said. "Well, here I am."

"Hello, Carson," she said.

He came and sat down in the chair opposite her. "Two times across the Atlantic inside of a week," he said. "A miracle of the air age."

"I understand you phoned here on Monday."

"Yes. Someone had been trying to call me Sunday night. I thought it might have been you."

"It was me. I called the Dorchester, but you weren't there."

"No," he said. "I was at another place, nowhere near as fancy."

"But the Dorchester was on your itinerary."

He smiled. "Yes," he said. "That's the system. You find the cheapest place. It's one of the tricks of the trade, I'm afraid. I'm sorry — if I'd known you might call I'd have left the number with them, but I didn't think of that till later."

"You never told me about this system."

"No. It's just one of the ugly facts I wanted to keep from you. There were so many things you hated about Locustville."

"Oh," she said, "I see."

"Did you think I was off in some boudoir in the West End?" he asked her.

"Well, I wondered."

"I'm sorry," he said again.

"Woody called you then?"

"Yes. That's why I came."

There was a silence. "Can I fix you a drink?" she asked. "Something like that?"

"No thanks," he said. "I just had one, actually."

"Oh?"

"Yes. I would have been here earlier, but I stopped by the office — to explain why I was back. Jesse Talbot was there and — well, Jesse insisted on taking me out to a bar and buying me a drink. I didn't want to go, but he sort of insisted."

"Oh," she said. "Jesse Talbot . . ."

"Yes. So I sort of know the story . . ."

"Oh," she said.

"Yes. It's — well, it's too bad, Barbara."

"What did Jesse say?"

He stared at his open hands. "Well," he said, "Jesse was very nice. Jesse is a nice guy — I really like him a lot. Jesse is a gentleman. And Jesse told me, Jesse said — well, first he told me the story which I hadn't heard, though Jesse thought perhaps I had — and he told me that he didn't believe it. That nobody who really knew you, and knew me, really believes it, but, as Jesse said, that wasn't the point. The point was that Locustville is a small town and that the company plays an important part in the life of the town, and that — because of this and things like that, community relations and all that business — I would be doing a disservice to the company by staying. And he gave me the opportunity to resign."

"Oh, Carson."

"Yes. That's about it."

"I'm sorry!"

"Yes. Well, I'm sorry, too, of course — but you don't need to be. It isn't really your fault, Barbara, because the point is — nobody believes the story, nobody who knows us, and I don't believe it either."

"Carson," she said, "the point is that the story is true."

He looked at her.

"Yes," she said, "that makes a difference, doesn't it? Especially for me — and for you. The story is true, every word of it, every word the paper said. I —" she said. "No — don't interrupt. I've been listening, all day, every day — since it happened — to all of them, at home, saying it isn't true, it couldn't be true, it's a terrible lie — saying it wasn't my fault, making excuses for me, blaming it on someone else, on themselves! And I'm sick of it, I can't bear it. I'm sick of all the excuses and the blaming it on others — leaping in, trying to save me and my poor reputation. Because it's true, Carson, the story is true. I'm responsible for what happened. *I killed him.*"

"You mean you had an affair with him?"

"Going to — I was going to. I made the date with him, to meet me at the guesthouse. Oh, at the last moment, yes — I changed my mind. When I got there, I changed my mind. It was too late then to change my mind. I might as well have done it then, because I'd really done it long before — committed adultery — because I'd been unfaithful to you, in my mind, considering it, making all the plans. Why was I going to do it? I don't know — there's no excuse. Oh, I had dozens of excuses — I made all the excuses. I told myself that it was because Peggy was being such a bitch to him, and driving him, and destroying him — and I told myself I didn't want to see him *hurt.* And I told myself that it was because I was lonely, and bored, and because you were away all the time, and because I hated Locustville so much. And I told myself it was because of the way everything has become at the farm — all of them tearing at each other's throats, like wolves, and because my father's turning into a drunkard and my mother is a shrew and Billy is a fool, and because I told myself that I might just as well go along with them as I always have, and be just as predatory and awful as they are! And I told myself the opposite, too — that I was a wonderful, beautiful, true, honest woman and that any man would be the better for my having offered my beautiful body to him. And, oh, yes. Yes, I had one more excuse. Jealousy. I called you, you see — and you weren't there. And I thought, if he's out somewhere having fun, then why can't I? But I'll tell you something else — something more important. This wasn't something recent, something that just happened. It didn't begin this past week end. It began two years ago, when I first met him — and it would have happened then, as long ago as that — it almost happened, would have happened, one night before they were married when he and I were alone in the house one evening and you were off at Cousin Billy's house for the bachelor party, watching Billy's sex movies! It would have happened then — he was there in my room and I was all ready for it — but we were interrupted. Somebody came home! And ever since, all the time in between, we'd both been plotting, planning ways to do it, and I'd been thinking up all the excuses I had for doing it. But the thing was, there wasn't any excuse, or any reason. I wanted it just because I wanted it — the way a child wants something. The way Dobie wants something of Michael's and takes it, that's the way I wanted it. So now you see the kind of woman I am."

He sat there, staring at her. Then he said, "Well — I'm glad you told me, Barbara."

"Yes." She stood up and walked to the window and looked out. "Yes, I'm glad I told you, too. You can't believe what it's been like — listening to them, Mother, Father, even Peggy — saying that they'd never believe it as long as they lived. Saying that their sweet, darling, beautiful little girl could never, not possibly, do such a thing. Saying it — but suspecting, I suppose, all along that it probably *was* true. Why *was* the guesthouse all lighted up, with cocktails poured, and ready for a rendezvous at midnight? But never mind, they said — it couldn't be true, it was all someone else's fault. Thank God I've told you. And don't tell me you don't believe it."

"You know," he said softly, "it's funny, really. Do you know that I really don't remember much about him? If you asked me to describe him now, I couldn't do it. Tall, yes, and rather dark — but that's about all. When Flora told me he was dead, I thought — Barney. What does he look like? I didn't know. I guess he never made much of an impression on me. I remember him being around, there, at the wedding — all that. But I guess I never really noticed him too much. I don't believe I ever exchanged more than two or three words with him."

"Tell me you believe it."

"Yes," he said. "I believe it."

"Good!" She pressed her palms against the wide glass. "It was just — just that I wanted him, the way a child wants a toy. And I'll tell you more — even more. I've always been like that. True, I've never, actually, physically been unfaithful to you. That much I *can* say. 'Not since we were married,' as the expression goes. But that isn't because I've had any *moral* feeling about it. No — you've just been lucky. Because I've always been this way. That year I was away, for instance — that year Nancy and I spent in Hawaii — you and I were practically engaged at that point, weren't we? And you were in the Army. That year there were several. There were two Navy boys, Charlie and Charlie — the gold-dust twins as Nancy and I used to say. And there was a terrible delinquent boy who hung out on Waikiki Beach, and stole and slept with rich women for a living. And I wrote you such sweet and lovely letters to Camp Polk! And then my beach boy rang the bell and I let him in, and sent him home later with carfare and a little extra! So you see!" She turned and faced him fiercely. "You see what I am! I'm

364

no different from Nancy! I'm an immoral woman! What are you going to do with me?"

Very quietly, he said, "If you sit down, I'll tell you."

She went to the sofa again and sat down. For a moment or two she faced him, her eyes bright and defiant. Then she put her hands to her face. "Oh, Carson. Please — please don't be kind to me."

He stood up, went to the sofa, and sat down beside her. "I'm going to be kind to you," he said, "because you're my wife and I love you very much. Now tell me something . . ."

"What? What is it?"

"Do you still love me?"

"I don't know. I think I do, but I don't know." She looked up at him again. "Do you know what terrifies me?" she asked. "I'm terrified that I'm not even the kind of woman who just has affairs — but the kind of woman who has to have affairs to be happy, who always has to have someone else besides her husband, a secret one somewhere. There are women like that, aren't there? And if I'm like that, Carson, it means that Barney really helped keep you and me together for the last two years — and not the rules. It means that having him there, in Burketown, to think about was something I needed in some crazy way to sustain my end of our marriage. And if that's the kind of person I am, what is there to hold you and me together now that he's dead?"

"Nothing, unless you still love me," he said.

"But I don't know if I do."

"But you think you do . . ."

"Yes. Oh, yes . . ."

"That's all I wanted to know," he said, and his voice shook slightly. "Now listen — please listen to me."

"Yes."

"Tonight, after talking to Jesse, coming here in the taxi, I had one idea."

"What is it?"

"I don't know if it would work. Or if it would be possible. But I thought I might talk to your father, or to your cousin Billy, or whoever's in charge up there."

She straightened up. "What about?"

"A job."

"A job? What sort of a job?"

"A job with the paper company."

"Oh, no!" she said. "You're not serious."

"Yes I am," he said.

"But why?"

"I've got to get some sort of job. Perhaps they can use me. Besides, I think we ought to go to Burketown."

"I'll never go back there. I couldn't."

"But I think that's what we should do," he repeated.

"Why? Why do you think we should?"

"Maybe they don't need another salesman. But if they do, it will be a job —"

"There are hundreds of other jobs."

"Yes, but there are other reasons."

"What? What reasons are there?"

"Well, one is that if they hired me perhaps I could do something for the company. At least I'd be in a position to try. From what I gather, it's been pretty badly managed. They're up to their necks in mortgages. I owe it to your family at least to try."

"Why? What do you owe them? You owe them nothing!"

"I do, as a matter of fact," he said. "I've never told you this, but it was your grandfather who helped me get this job — here, in Locustville."

"What?"

"Yes. He helped a great deal. It was through his influence."

"Why didn't you ever tell me that?"

"I suppose it was because I was ashamed of it," he said. "Still, it's the truth."

"Well, what difference does that make? He's dead."

366

"And there's another, even more important reason — the main reason."

"What is that?"

"I think we should go back there for your sake," he said. "That's why I'd be willing to take almost any job they offered me, even if it wasn't a selling job. For instance, I was thinking — they might even let me have Barney's job."

Very softly she said, "Why do you say it's for my sake? I hate it there."

"Of course," he said. "It's not something that I want to do, either. I dread it, too, just as much as you do. It probably won't be pleasant or fun or anything like that. But after this — after what's happened — with this scandal and with it involving you — I think the worst thing in the world that you could do would be to run away somewhere and try to hide from it. The best thing would be to go back, and face it, and live with it — and show everybody that you can live with it. And I'll be there helping you show them. And it's more than just what effect it would have on what other people think. It's mostly the effect that it would have on you, and what you eventually come to think of yourself."

"No," she shook her head. "No. I don't understand you. And I don't care. Because I'll never go back there, and that's all there is to it."

"But you've got to," he said. "It's what will give you your maturity."

"My maturity. Don't you see — there's something wrong with me. Something was left out of me. Maybe it's the ability to mature. I should have matured, but I didn't. And it's their fault — they kept me from growing up. I know that now — something I never knew before. That's why I'm never going back."

"I used to think that marriage was a very simple thing," he said. "I used to think that being married would mean that everything got simpler, and all the problems got smaller and easier. But that isn't true. The opposite is true. Things get harder, and it's doing the biggest and the hardest things, being able to do them, forcing yourself to do them, that makes it work out in the end . . ."

"No, no. I can't, that's all. Look," she said, "I own a few shares of paper company stock and Peggy would like nothing better than to get her hands on them. I can sell my stock to her, Carson, and it would give us a little money to go on. We could move somewhere, far away, and start over again."

"No," he said. "That's the thing we can't do."

"And, with that money, there'd be enough so you wouldn't have to work for a while — you wouldn't have to take the first job that comes along."

"No," he said again.

She stood up quickly and walked across the room. "Then you'll have to go alone," she said. "I won't go with you."

"Of course there's no assurance it would work. I can't promise you it would work. But the thing we'd have to do is try. And I don't mean we'd have to stay in Burketown forever, either. Perhaps a year, perhaps two years. As long as it takes."

She stood with her back to him. "Didn't you hear what I said?" she asked him quietly. "I said you'll have to go alone. I won't go back there with you."

"Barbara —"

"What?"

"Don't you understand why we must do this?"

"I'm sorry." She turned and walked toward the kitchen door. She hesitated, then turned and pushed open the screened door that led out onto the little terrace. The air was chilly as she stepped out, and she shivered. He rose and followed her.

He stood behind her in the doorway. "Barbara," he said, "do you want to hear my philosophy of life?"

She looked at the night and the trees and the neat little garden. "All right," she said.

"I was thinking — on the plane, coming back. It's funny, but riding on a plane always makes me think philosophical thoughts,

368

about life and what life is all about because — well, to me at least, a plane trip is always like courting death. I think each time I take off that I'll never land alive and I always thank God when I do. That may sound silly and cowardly, but that's the way I am. And perhaps it's a good thing if it makes a person stop and think," he said. "Do you understand what I mean?"

"Yes," she said. "Yes, go on . . ."

"And I was thinking today, on the plane, about God, and how God made the heavens and the earth and the fishes and the beasts — and He made Man, shaped him and molded him. But then I thought, God is a crazy potter. Look at the strange shapes He's turned out on His wheel. But in His own mad way, He managed to make a bit of sense from it all. He was mad, certainly, to create such a thing as love. Because it's love that makes the pottery crack the worst — like homemade clay left out in the sun too long. But then I thought: He also gave love the power to patch up the cracks — not perfectly, not good as new perhaps, but patched nevertheless. And then I thought about myself, what I am. Like any madman, God turns out certain masterpieces now and then. But I'm not one of them. I'll never write a bit of poetry or paint a picture, or leave much of a footprint in the sands of time. I'm a salesman. Does the world need salesmen? You could argue about that, I suppose, but anyway that's what I am. I'm not one of God's masterpieces. But I can offer you something, Barbara. I can offer you a place, a plateau, from which to view the world if you are looking for such a place. And I can offer you my love. What you've said — what you told me about Barney, about the boy in Hawaii — that doesn't matter so much to me, Barbara, because, to me, those are only little cracks and perhaps I can help you patch them. With my love, I mean. And if you will come with me to the place I have in mind, all I'll be doing will be selling paper, selling napkins, selling whatever there is to be sold. That will be your husband — from nine to five, anyway. But the rest of the time I'll be loving you, Barbara — in this place. There'll be no more rules," he said softly, "except this one. And this isn't a rule at all, but a promise. Does anything I've said make any sense to you?"

His words sounded very simple, even innocent. And yet they affected her in a queer way, moved her in one of those rare — increasingly rare as we grow older — floods of longing, happiness and love. She turned and looked at his face. It was a simple, unspectacular face with no surprises in it. But it was his dear face, the face she had loved so dearly back at Princeton, the face she had watched from the darkened seat next to her in dozens of movie theaters, the face on the pillow in the morning, drunk with sleep, the face he turned to her when suddenly a pleasant thought for them both occurred to him ("Let's go out to dinner. Let's take a drive in the new car."). It was the face that she had grown so used to seeing, whose expressions and moods and depths and smiles she knew so well — her husband's face. She let this feeling hover over her, as it seemed to, with small, silently beating wings. His face now was troubled and anxious, waiting for her answer. In his hand he held a cigarette, rolling it this way and that, nervously, between his long, well-knuckled fingers.

"Barbara," he said quietly, "it doesn't make any difference where we live, does it? As long as we love one another?"

She had been about to speak when he added — spoiling, though only slightly, the effect his words had just had upon her — "Besides, it's only temporary."

After all, he would be always Carson.

"All right," she said. "I'll go home with you."

She turned quickly away and stood on the little terrace, her back to the house, looking out at the tiny strip of view, at the broad, dark valley, at the silhouettes of the prim brick houses on the street, and, beyond the houses, to the hollow in the hill where all of the lights of Locustville swam before her eyes. Locustville had always seemed most beautiful at night, like Italy! And she thought: Yes, it's all right; I never knew where home was.

She suddenly discovered that Dobie was standing just beside

her. Their talk had awakened him and he stood in his pajamas, rubbing his eyes, but, half-asleep, he hadn't seen his father standing in the shadows. She saw Dobie's face looking up at her. She knelt, placing her hands beneath his armpits, and lifted him into her arms. He was getting so heavy that she almost lost her balance and stepped back quickly to regain it. She held him tightly.

"*Where* are we going, Mommy?" he asked her.

"To grandmother's house, Dobie," she said. "Over the hill to grandmother's house." She carried him toward the door. "Won't that be fun, Dobie?" she said. "Won't that be fun?"